AN EDINBURGH SUICIDE:

THE DEATH OF HUGH MILLER

'Although formally, in many parts, fictitious,' says Mr. Gilfillan, in speaking of his work in a few introductory sentences, 'the quality by which I hope it will be found peculiarly distinguished is fearless truthfulness.' And of this general truthfulness, the reader is, we think, given unequivocal evidence. Mere fiction is always flimsier in its texture than most of the stuff of which this work is woven, and does not so fill the grasp. But the fictitious form of the narrative is, in many parts, positively provoking; the reader has frequently no means of knowing whether he is acquainting himself with the particulars of a real incident, or with merely the circumstances of an ingenious invention; and, notwithstanding all the amusement which the book in its present form furnishes, and the instruction which it conveys, there are few who would not prefer a faithful autobiography of its original-minded author, that would not only be essentially true in its leading features, but faithful also to the lesser realities of occurrence and event.' *Review of The History of a Man,* edited by George Gilfillan. London: Virtue & Co. *The Witness*, June 28, 1856.

'For the future, Edinburgh bids fair to take its place among the greater provincial towns of the empire; and it seems but natural to look upon her departing glory with a sigh, and to luxuriate in recollection over the times when she stood highest on the intellectual scale.' Hugh Miller, '*Edinburgh An Age Ago*' *The Witness*, 12 July, 1856.

AN EDINBURGH SUICIDE:

THE DEATH OF HUGH MILLER

A FICTIONAL HISTORY IN THREE PARTS:

THE WITNESS

Brian McLaughlin

Brian McLaughlin

Visit my website at: fabricatedfictions.com

Formatted by Simon Hough (www.wordhook.com)

Printed in the United Kingdom

First Printing September 2022

ISBN: 9798835627455

Because of and for Rhona

Part 3

THE WITNESS

Contents

The Suicide Letters

Things We Find in the Sea

'It's singing!' Maggie McTaggart cried, as she held the shell to her ear. Her three companions paid no attention, too caught up in their own discoveries. Emily Ramsay, the intrepid farmer's daughter, was talking to the starfish she had tipped into a grey milking pail, marvelling as its languid fingers searched for a corner in the round tub. 'You'll come home with me, and I will look after you.' Emily was always rescuing small animals and wee beasties, and stoical about their stubborn refusal to survive her care. She was distracted by a scream: her wee sister Molly, shouting that a crab was chasing her. 'It's blowing bubbles oot o' its mooth!' And indeed, she could see an enormous brown partan scuttling down over the rocks, making for the pool next to Molly.

Emily laughed then peered at Maggie, who had a look of intense concentration as she listened and listened for the hoped-for song from the shell pressed against her right ear. Maggie was always listening for the music in the trees as they trembled with the wind, for the song of the sighing grass. She once whispered to Emily that she could hear the blood roaring in her head. Such a strange lassie. Her mother needed to pay more heed to her and not just farm her off on Emily's mother. At least that was what Emily thought.

Plop. She turned around in time to see May Watson tipping a smooth round stone into her pail.

'You will hurt my starfish,' she shouted. But May just stood, staring down into the bucket, as if seeing a world in that stone. Emily could never understand someone like May who seemed to prefer stones and dead twigs to plants and animals. Maybe it was because she lived in the city, in Edinburgh, that grey sooty carbuncle over there across the Forth from Burntisland.

She put on her sternest voice, relying on the authority her few years' seniority gave her over her companions. 'Come on now, lassies. Mr Curtis will be coming down on the farm cart to fetch us soon.'

They paid not a whit of attention.

'And he will let us sit in the back!'

A few glances.

'With the sheepdogs and a poke of barley sugar!'

This did the trick and the three of them straggled up over the wide strand with her towards the dunes next to the track leading to the Jawbane Road and Ramsay's Farm. Wee Molly needed to be coaxed along as she was feart of more crabs popping out from under the boulders scattered on the wide seashore. Low tide in Burntisland exposed a huge expanse of rippled wet sand and gave access to all sorts of treasures, depending on your quest. We all find something when we go down to the sea.

And indeed, in the middle of the nineteenth century it seemed that the whole scientific world was searching for treasure on a beach. Darwin in the Galapagos, Owen on the Devon Coast, tugging at stones or laying out the strange creatures recently dredged from the waters. Thousands of amateur geologists, palaeontologists, and botanists, all bent on discovering new species or on trying to measure the age of the earth and Nature from the rocks, plants and fishes thrown up by the teeming oceans. They could feel the ages moving under their feet, could glimpse Creation winking at them from the silver plankton on the rolling waves.

'Look at those funny men in galoshes, and suits like daddy wears to the office!' May said, pointing down over the bay to the group of seven or eight young men hauling in a skiff from the waters then crowding round it as if welcoming some sailor home from a long expedition. One was carrying a banner in the shape of a triangle!

Another was laying out a large tarpaulin on the sand. When the boat was dragged up almost out of reach of the waves, the men began carting up buckets and sacks, stones and seaweed and depositing them on the canvas sheet. One man remained standing at the prow, his long hair rippling in the breeze like some Eastern potentate or the tenant of a royal barge on a state visit to Windsor. The girls stared at him, wondering what he was waiting for. 'He's like that Canute king in reverse,' Emily nearly said, biting her tongue so she didn't have to explain to the others who that was.

She was stirred from her musings by a scattering of sand kicked up by the rough boot of a giant striding down the dune towards the boat. He was the ugliest man she had ever seen! A nose as long as her uncle Willie's collie's, sunken eyes that seemed to swivel, and the same long hair as the fellow in the boat, though more unkept and greasier.

'Forbes! I have come all the way from Ainster on an awfully bad horse. Forgive my tardiness. Welcome to the Kingdom of Fife!'

'Ahoy, Goodsir!' yelled the man on the boat. 'It is the very *Spratman,* come here like a reformed *Spartan* to welcome we Athenians. Behold the treasures we spread out in homage to you in the spirit of the Oernomathic Brotherhood. Come hither my good fellow!'

As he finished his declamation, the other went splashing into the water, his body flapping awkwardly like an overanxious spaniel relieved to find his master returned home safe. He held up his arm and the regal figure disembarked. A red ribbon hanging from his neck glinted in the sun. Walking up towards the outstretched tarpaulin together, both men, with the swagger of those in their early thirties who can taste the thrill of their years of labour and study bearing fruit, suddenly seemed like reflections. Reflections in a dented mirror, with Goodsir a strange parody of the handsome Forbes. Both were tall, with long, flowing hair and prominent chins. Forbes' chin complemented his bold features, Goodsir's seemed a make-shift appendage.

Six or seven other men in galoshes and dark suits huddled round the two as they began to examine the specimens laid out on the tarpaulin. Two of them, damper than their fellows, stood back from the other more senior men, passing the banner to-and-fro, and shifting ground to point it in the direction of the moving throng. Their feet were cold. Young Maxwell said to the other, '*Spratman?* What does Professor Forbes mean by that? Is it just another of their coded nicknames?'

'No,' Johnson replied. 'Professor Goodsir was asked by Professor Forbes to go to the Justiciary Court in Edinburgh last January to explain the difference between a sprat and a herring in a fisheries' case. The judge maintained the first grew into the second. Goodsir dissected one of each in front of his lordship and counted out their different number of vertebrae. It was a very fishy business!'

Their cackles were interrupted by a call from Forbes, his deep nasal Manx voice rising into the air like a siren.

'Johnson, Maxwell. You have mislabelled the *Pelonaia corrugate*, the worm species first identified by Professor Goodsir and my humble self. Have you chaps listened to a word of my lectures? Roll up that banner and sort things out here.'

Edward Forbes was a talented botanist, zoologist, palaeontologist, and natural historian. Thanks to his wide curiosity and need for professional employment, he would move between all these fields, becoming an acknowledged expert in each. Just under six months ago he had returned from a dredging expedition in the Aegean Sea and was preparing a talk to the British Association later in that month of May 1843, expounding a theory he hoped would make his name.

'Do you remember good old *Clausilia*, the snail from Arthur's Seat you showed me back when we started to lodge together, John? My introduction to molluscs. I remember the wonder of your dissection, how you made Nature translucent. You uncovered structure from the mess of organs. I knew then you were an artist, dear boy. And that this art was the key to understanding life. And a pioneer. Hardly anyone thought of dissecting live creatures then.'

As ever, Goodsir's mind flashed back to the flat in Lothian Street he had shared with his two brothers and Forbes, George E. Day and two lads who worked in the University and served them as grooms. They shared the space with a menagerie of God's creatures, from 'Jacko' the monkey, 'Coco' the tortoise, 'Caesar' the dog, 'Doodle' the cat, and occasionally guinea-pigs and urchins, all with the freedom to run around the establishment; the birds were caged, and a great eagle stood Prometheus-like on his Caucasus; whilst shut up in the attics, or claiming part of the cook's precincts and in improvised aquaria or vivaria, were frogs, fishes, molluscs, echinoderms, and various odds and ends of invertebrata.

The apartment had served as home, laboratory, seat of the Brotherhood and meeting-place for those the young men admired, and who admired them. Knox had visited regularly, and they had even once had a visit from the great Agassiz!

Forbes recognised the gleam in his friend's eye. Neither of them had ever really left that apartment.

He held up a small snail of the *Clausilia* species. 'I collect these whenever I come to Edinburgh. This one is from near the shore. You can see it has a different colouring and more valves in its shell. It's the variation in altitude that makes the difference. These snails from the same altitude all over the world are identical. And John,' he paused as if to gain dramatic effect. 'It is so neath the seas too. Animals and plant life change in scale and number as we descend into the depths. The bed of the Aegean is almost bare. I have calculated that beyond a depth of 300 metres, life cannot exist. It is below as it is above on the highest mountain peaks. Animal life and species depends on their terrain. They are adaptations, but of the same species. We have no record of any new species being produced. Dogs cannot mate with camels and an oyster species is but a variant on the original. Will you come to see me explain this to the British Association?'

Goodsir nodded, to suggest the idea was worth pondering. Though diffident and shy, he had a high opinion of his own intellectual worth and felt himself a colleague and not a disciple of his learned friend. Others might cringe as they saw him at Forbes' heels, but he knew that he was the one Edward depended upon for confirmation of half-formed ideas, for the fleshing-out of theories on zoology and anatomy. He was Edward's best hope for landing a professorship back in his beloved Edinburgh. If only old Jameson would die or the trustees fund a new chair! No doubt too his collaboration would be needed in finishing Forbes' paper for the Association. He smiled, then frowned, cautioned by the knowledge he would have to be careful lest he upset he University authorities. He had clambered up the ladder via curating the Surgeons' Hall Museum and then the University's own Natural History collection. He had published and been widely applauded. But now, in 1843, any move away from scientific convention or the views of the established church could have him sent home to his fishing village on the East Neuk of Fife to practice general medicine on farmers and fisherfolk. He shivered at the thought. The attacks on orthodoxy were being responded to harshly by the Kirk. And the Kirk controlled the University.

He forgot all these forebodings as he watched Forbes charm the assembled group. He called them his 'Red Lions'. He declared himself 'The MAN from the Isle of Man' and pointed out with exquisite detail all the elements of the specimens spread out before them. 'Note the hierarchy in Nature, gentlemen. No Reform Bill there! Our duty is to see' he went on. 'To see, to properly observe, in a way that no one has ever done before. Our life, our civilisation depends on it.'

And as he talked, he drew, throwing off lifelike cartoons of those present and handing them out like a certificate of their worth in his eyes. Suddenly, he looked up at the young waifs on the dune. 'They are silkies waiting for us to be off so they can slip back into the sea in their mermaid form,' he cried as he produced a sketch of half girls, half fishy creatures.

'Look at that creature squatting by the shoreline! He is more rock than man. Perhaps Hutton mistook the order of creation. Perhaps we do not just return to dust, but to stone!'

And he dashed off a portrait of the petrified soul.

'Let us be off back to Edinburgh. John, we shall take a ferry boat to Granton. The other fellows can sail back. You and I have much to talk about.'

With that, they sauntered off and up past the girls. Forbes handed Emily his sketch of them. She kept it till the end of her life, on the wall next to her dresser, a memory of her days of innocence.

A few hundred yards away the petrified figure stirred. The time for reflection was over. The disruption was upon them all.

Words Like Stones

It had all started with a letter. Years of writing poems then historical sketches and local tales had carried him not to literary renown but to a job in the Commercial Bank in Cromarty. At least that had enabled him to marry Lydia. But oh, the fame he had dreamt of as Scotland's Bard had passed him by. Then he had written an *Open Letter from One of the Scotch People*, to Lord Brougham, the Scots-born former Lord Chancellor and brilliant polemicist, in 1839, protesting about the plan to override the local congregations of the Kirk's right to choose their own minister in favour of the English custom of granting that privilege to the local landowner. Hugh had spoken as one of the people, a simple Scotsman. He had expressed himself as an uneducated person, but in an Augustan style. It had worked. Overnight he became *Hugh Miller, the stonemason*, a plain workingman. He had not wielded a hammer in ten years but surely the cause justified the pose.

A few months later he had been called by Candlish to Edinburgh to edit the newspaper which was to champion the cause of the anti-patronage churchmen against the more pliable Moderates. He could see them round the table now: Chalmers, Cunningham, Candlish, Abercrombie and all the other grey, serious men.

'The literati are in the camp of the Moderates. We need a powerful, articulate voice against the intrusion of the State into Church affairs,' Candlish had insisted. Hugh had hesitated. What did he know of newspaper publication? He had contributed articles to *The Inverness Courier*, but this new publication would appear every Wednesday and Saturday.

He had insisted on writing a prospectus for the committee's approval. He composed it as he lay beside Lydia in their wind-wracked hotel off the High Street, wondering if he should just flee Edinburgh as he had as a young man 15 years ago. But he thought of Willie Ross and how proud he would have been of him. And Lydia was happy here. He stayed.

They had guaranteed him three years' salary, whatever happened, and agreed that it should be a real newspaper dealing with politics and general intelligence with no allegiance to a particular party, but which would maintain the spiritual independence of the Kirk. His first disappointment had come when the committee had rejected his choice of its name: 'The Old Whig,' neither aligned with the pro-patronage Tory Government, nor the new Whigs who had brought in the electoral Reform Act. Scalded, he had decided to maintain as much distance as possible from the committee. Candlish had insisted that such compromises were necessary.

'You are new to the Capital, Mr. Miller. And we must build bridges to Parliament, not alienate both sides.'

In the next four years Hugh had built *The Witness* into the second most popular newspaper in Scotland, beaten only by *The Scotsman*. He had done so by insisting on its role as a social organ, by including general news and politics. The very first issues had featured articles about Darwin among the natives and their piety in the South Seas, about Geology, and others lambasting the Chartists and Socialism. Lambasting. He had heard that some called him the 'Great Lambaster.' Well, so be it. They were generally men in power, such as that arch Tory and enemy, Lord Aberdeen. Did they not see he meant none of it personally? It was the sin, not the man he was chastising.

The need to provide so much copy, much of it by his own hand, had meant including articles on diverse economic and scientific questions. In some of the first numbers, in 1840, he had inserted essays on the geological composition of Cromarty. These had become his first successful book, *The Old Red Sandstone,* and its evidence that these formations did indeed contain fossils won him praise from scientists and popularity among the public. '*Hugh Miller, the stonemason*,' became '*Hugh Miller the geologist*,' another role he had not sought while he wandered erratically down the byways of literary production. Now it all seemed almost automatic as he turned the pages of his recent life in his head. But it had been such arduous work. He hardly saw his wife and children.

He would be 40 in October. Was that why he had crossed the Forth and come to this beach at low tide? Perhaps. Perhaps he needed to look across the Firth, as so often he had done in Cromarty, and think, 'They are on the other side. I must get to them. I must traverse this border. Conquer them.' This was Edinburgh, however, and not a small village on the opposite shore in his boyhood.

He shook himself, sending sand and mites flying. He was not accustomed to keeping still. Even when writing he composed while striding up and down in his drawing-room, reciting lines to Lydia, asking her if 'that were well-put?' And on Wednesday and Saturday afternoons after the publication of the newspaper, he walked miles into the country, into East Lothian or to the coal deposits in West Lothian. But today he had felt the need to be still. To think. To contemplate. To be alone.

Out in the bay, gannets were plummeting into the waters, puncturing the smooth sea with their stiletto bills. White daggers of the sky, he thought. Or no, white rapiers. Daggers, rapiers, blades, which one was the most apt? That was the problem with being a professional writer, you took on the burden of words. You became what he now was, a witness. Observing, noting things down, looking for evidence to back up your claims. Thinking how to appeal to your audience, over there in the smoke-shrouded capital. '*Hugh Miller, wordmason*.'

He shook himself again but resisted the urge to stand up and walk. He could feel the damp stone he was perched upon digging into his knee. He must find a name. The name for the new church he expected to be born at the Assembly in a few days' time, one that would respect its national character. Avoid words like 'Reformed' 'Independent,' anything that suggested comparison to the myriad of evangelical sects or Methodist chapels but claimed the same rights for the disestablished church as the established. A name which spoke of the new church's unshackled right to speak to the State in the name of its congregation, in the name of Scotland. There had been several unfruitful committee meetings at Chalmers' house, where they could not even coincide on the principles. Committees and compromise were strangling him.

He could hear peals of laughter skipping across the strand. He twisted his neck and espied a group of University men being addressed by a tall long-haired fellow. Their professor, no doubt. But who was that other fellow at his side? He believed he recognised him. They seemed to be examining specimens dredged up by that boat. Perhaps he should go over and have a look. No, he would shun social intercourse today. And what had he to say to university men? He had refused to go to university, and he would not court their favour nor risk their condescension.

Their privileged lives would go on whatever happened in the Assembly. But what would happen to a minister who abandoned the Kirk? How would he live? How would he support his family? Hugh thought of his own minister and friend in Cromarty, John Stewart. He would have to preach in the streets! And was it honest to write encouraging articles to his fellow non-intrusionists when he himself was safe? Indeed, the tension of the last few years had been tremendously exciting for him and had increased sales of *The Witness*. No doubt the coming turmoil would do the same.

He stirred, brushing off the sand that insinuates itself into you if you sit on the beach for long. Some of the University men were putting the boat to sail. They seemed like refugees, abandoned yet looking for a distant Ithaca. 'The Pioneer Church?' Too pagan.

They had all gone by the time he approached the dunes, the boat a distant fleck in the blue sea and the two professors only visible by their bobbing heads as they walked round towards the promontory from where the ferry boats departed. A clump of figures was perched upon a dune, as if stranded.

'Are you alright, young ladies,' he asked, looking at the oldest one. 'Where are your parents or your governess?' The eldest girl laughed. Hugh had a way of talking to children that made them feel important. They liked him and he enjoyed that. In Cromarty some of the local youngsters used to follow him about, for his stories, for how he talked to them.

'I am Emily,' she said and introduced the others. 'We dinnae hae a governess, Mister. We are a free and easy bunch, and everybody kens my father in Burntisland. Mr Curtis from the farm was supposed to fetch us in his cart.' Emily was interrupted by Molly 'I am free,'

'No, Molly, THREE' corrected Maggie.

'with a poke of barley sugar.' Molly continued unabashed.

'And his dogs, I like the black one,' Maggie added. Only May remained silent.

Hugh bent down then perched her on his shoulders. She did not seem surprised or scared as he hoiked her up.

'Now see if you can spot the cart. Can you see that thing moving yonder, up by the churchyard?'

May peered with intense concentration.

'I see it now. Emily, I have found Mr. Curtis.'

'So you have, lassie. You have saved the day.'

Emily smiled at Hugh's words, but May just nodded her head. There was something strange about this wee lassie, Hugh thought.

He waited till the cart approached, keeping the girls entertained by admiring the contents of the pail. He understood the childish wonder at fragments of nature. He felt it himself.

Mr Curtis looked at him defensively, as if expecting a scolding for his lateness. But Hugh's smile and the girls' laughter put him at ease.

'I am awfie sorry to be late. I got stopped by the engineers doing the surveying back there.'

'The engineers?'

'Aye sir, they are prospecting the path of the railway to Perth. No carts needed then!'

Hugh's face darkened like the sea when the sun is obscured by a rain cloud.

'The railway! That engine of spiritual annihilation! Good day ladies, Good day, sir.'

And he marched off as the girls clambered up into the back of the cart.

'You are a fool, talking about spiritual annihilation to a farmhand and a bunch of lassies. And losing your temper at nothing.' He turned around to wave goodbye and smiled when they waved back.

Suddenly he became aware of a weight in his pocket. He introduced his hand and discovered a smooth round black stone!

'Free!' he laughed. He had argued for 'The Free Church of Scotland' for months now in *The Witness*. Out of the mouth of babes!

We Are All Lions

He had slipped into the snug bar at Mathieson's, next to their brewery on Leven Street between Tollcross and Bruntsfield. The bar was tucked in just past the crossroads and the snug offered privacy for people, women mostly, who preferred not to be seen in a tavern. His employers didn't like their workers to be drinkers and promoted all sorts of activities and classes to keep their eighty staff out of the pubs. He had managed to avoid the unspoken requirement to attend the Kirk but thought it better to frequent taverns on the other side of town from Waterloo Place. These Scots temperance men! In Barcelona and Paris he had taken part in *tertulias*, in open discussions over a ballon du vin or a beer in a bar or café. Everyone had heard about the cultural discussions in Edinburgh but it seemed they were largely for the well-to-do or the churchgoers. Protestantism was a dry faith, in every sense, he told himself.

He placed his dram on the table and added some water with one hand while he extricated his sketch pad from his coat pocket, his long fine fingers then producing a pencil as if from nowhere. He flicked through the drawings of machine parts till he found the one he was working on and was engrossed in that till another man squeezed his way through the door and into the tiny room.

'Room for one more?' He nodded and moved further up the table. The man looked to be in his fifties, with his white hair severely side-combed, perhaps to conceal baldness. He had an air of an usher at court, or a porter at hospital, someone used to dignified service.

He too ordered whisky, but two glasses.

'Have a nip, your one is almost done, and I dinnae like drinking alone. No, dinna protest, it's only a whisky, son.

It'll no be laing noo,' he went on.

Silence

'The days are fair getting longer…

Are you not from here, son? That's what we say here to start a conversation. All you need to do is repeat that it'll no be laing noo, and aff we go. My name is John Arthur. How do you do?'

At last the other put down his sketchbook and looked at Arthur, as if sizing him up.

'My name is Enric, but you can call me Harry, or Eck or any of the other versions I get here.'

'Oh, dear,' John Arthur thought, 'this was what you got for talking to strangers. A foreigner and not even an English one!'

And now this fellow produced an egg from nowhere and handed it to Arthur! He then raised his glass and toasted to the health of 'the universal workingman.' 'Because, sir, though I may have been born far from here and in different circumstances, you and I are equals, brothers even, through our membership of the working classes.'

Arthur was accustomed to meeting all sorts of strange characters at the University; he had always supposed it was just part of the territory, that so much learning cut you off from real life and made you eccentric. Some of the professors thought he was strange just because he was so normal! Now here he was sitting in a bar with a foreigner, with a hardboiled egg in his hand! He gingerly placed the egg on the table.

'Well first of all, laddie, I do not consider myself as part of the working classes. I am a professional technician, something like your good self from the look of those drawings. And even the working classes are different, depending on their nationality and race.'

The other man winced. 'Is this your British sense of superiority and class snobbism?'

'No, I am Scottish through and through. And it has nothing to do with snobbism and everything to do with zoology and anatomy.'

What do you know of these things?

'I assist Dr. Knox.'

Enric's attention was caught. The famous Knox!

'Do you really know Dr. Knox? The client of Burke and Hare?'

'Oh, dinna give me all that guff again. That was years ago when you couldn't get corpses for love nor money. Only the bodies of hanged convicts were legal. Something had to happen, someone had to get caught. Even now we have to make it quick when the police arrive. But we have our means. It takes them a long time to get into the room. Knox is a brilliant man and my boss idolises him. We all do. But what about you, laddie? Tell me about yourself, Mr. Magician.'

While they talked, the whiskies appeared steadily. He must be a regular here, Enric thought to himself. People came in and slipped out of the snug clutching sweating bottles of Matheson's stout. The darkness was falling and Enric felt as if he were in the cabin of a ship rocking its way through the swelling tide.

'And where do you work?'

'In a printers, in Waterloo Place.'

'Chambers'. As far from here as the University is! And what do you do there? How come they had to hire a foreigner?'

'I have much experience in steam printing and they needed someone to help Mr Gunn who had constructed the prototype steam printer they built in their place on Rose Street Lane.'

'The one all the neighbours protested about because of the noise?'

'Yes, and now there are ten machines in Roxburgh Close and the editing is in Waterloo Place. I liaise between the two and help maintain the machines. As they were built for us you can't buy parts off the shelf. I make drawings of the pieces, suggest improvements and look for spares.'

'Why a steam printer? Edinburgh is full of good printing shops.'

'Our ten steam printers are in constant activity and produce 900 sheets each an hour and the machine doesn't get drunk or take time off. The *Journal* alone sells 80,000 copies a week. It has to, to keep the price to a level ordinary people can afford.'

'Why the drawings of the sails, though?'

'That I will tell you on another occasion, if we coincide again.'

As he rose to go, he felt a hand on his arm.

'If you would like to see Dr. Knox, he will be through from Glasgow on Thursday, to give a demonstration of aesthetic anatomy. 10 am sharp.'

'Aesthetic anatomy? What on earth is that?'

'It's what I was telling you about. Come along.'

John Arthur handed him a white ticket. 'This is an observer's pass. You will be able to watch but not participate nor ask questions. '

'I will accept this in the spirit of class solidarity, John Arthur.' He pushed the heavy door open and stepped out into the night before the other could reply.

Two days later, John Arthur let a smile escape when he looked up and spied the lad from Mathieson's in the Anatomy room. Enric had arrived late, having first gone to the College of Surgeons and been sent with a sarcastic sneer by the doorman, 'Next door, to Mr. Barclay's hoose. No 10. This is the University sir.'

Enric remembered John Arthur telling him that more private professors of anatomy and surgery taught in such extra-mural establishments than in the University itself, where the aged Professor Monro Tertius exasperated rather than instructed his students with his bumbling, antiquated style. Knox's lectures were attended by hundreds of students and though he had had to move to Glasgow after yet another of the scandals that followed him, the room was full. It was one of the most amazing sights Enric had witnessed.

Though John Arthur looked different in his white coat, and beside him stood an exceedingly ungainly fellow with long hair, Knox transfixed Enric. He had read that he had been disfigured by childhood smallpox and indeed, his face was heavily marked. It had caused him to lose his left eye and the socket where the eye should have been made Enric shiver. But it was the way that he commanded the room that most impressed. He strode about, uttering phrases in different languages, pointing at students and laughing, even jeering at some. He seemed like a wind-up mechanical soldier, marching in short bursts round the room sending people scattering to get out of his way.

His speech was a fantastic babble of declamation, learned discourse and dissertations on everything from anatomy to zoology with history and politics in between. Enric could not follow it all nor understand the medical terminology, so he decided to make sketches of the scene. Just as he was focussing on Knox and wishing he would stand still for a moment, the man pointed straight at him.

'There you see a specimen of Homo Latinus, gentlemen. A creature suited to hot dry climates. I hope you survive Scotland, sir!' The crowd roared with laughter.

'Don't laugh so quickly lads. His race produced the Roman Empire. We Anglo-Saxons have so far managed to conquer only inferior races and our gifts are not those of genius: we invent nothing, have no musical ear, and are so low and boorish that we do not know what is meant by 'fine art.' However, we are thoughtful, plodding, industrious beyond all other races, and lovers of labour for labour's sake. We are of course held back by the Celtic blood that infects many of us.

Now you are shocked! Don't be. It is merely applied zoology. We are simply different races. The Highlander is suited to the misty glens, to surviving on nothing and to avoiding initiative. You or I would die in the mountains. They struggle to survive in our cities as you can see in the slums of Glasgow or Edinburgh.'

Many in the audience nodded their heads in acquiescence. Enric felt uncomfortable.

'But there is not just *division* in nature. Anatomy also shows us the essential harmony of creation. From studies of the embryo we can find that all life is there. In some species, aspects are developed, in others they are discarded or unused. Some deformations in embryonic developments produce what may seem like freaks of Nature, but if the external conditions are propitious, they can not only survive but produce a leap in evolution. Distinct species of animals, indeed of man, may have been extinguished in the past. But man is a genus, a category above species. To understand this we have to read Goethe' (here he began declaiming in what Enric recognised as German).

Now he began to speak in Greek, quoting Plato apparently.

'There are transcendental archetypes in the living world. Unfortunately, it takes genius to perceive them. And that perception is an aesthetic one which can find the archetype immanent in the totality of the species, although present in none of them save by hints, by echoes. There is a general unity of composition and connection in nature, gentlemen. As I will now demonstrate.'

Enric scribbled notes which he hoped John Arthur could help him with later. But did John Arthur understand what Knox was saying? Did anyone? Did Knox?

Just when it seemed like the apex of speculations had been reached, Knox clapped his hands and John Arthur and the long-haired Professor, Goodsir it seemed his name was, prepared to pull back a sheet covering a corpse.

On John Arthur's table lay the cadaver of a middle-aged man on his back, his arms spread out on the wide table. With a shock, Enric saw that the long bone, (the humerus, he later discovered) running from the shoulder to the elbow, was stripped open. Knox was pointing excitedly to what he called a supracondyloid foramen on each arm, which seemed to be a bird-like spur protruding from the bone. This was a vestige found on cats to protect an artery, he explained.

Other anatomists would have produced a skinned cat to show the existence of this bone in the mammal. Knox snapped his fingers and Goodsir swept back his sheet to uncover the corpse of a most magnificent jaguar! Its yellow-and-tan fur and the skin on its legs had been stripped to the bone and Knox indicated the spur then insistently invited all those present to pass from one cadaver to the other and compare.

'Men are lions and lions are men, gentlemen. Think about that. I bid you Gooday.'

Everyone cheered. It was more like a religious revival meeting than a scientific lecture, Enric felt. Then he remembered that these were days of great fervour in anatomy and what were becoming known as the natural sciences: zoology, natural history, anatomy and even geology. He had heard that Edinburgh was at the centre of the debate. Perhaps he was the one who was out of step.

John Arthur whispered to him to meet him outside on a bench in the central garden in Surgeons' Square 'once he had had time to clear the corpses away.' Enric was too dazed to do more than nod in acquiescence.

He had so many questions. Confused images were running around his brain, meaningless words teasing him. He had to understand. If he had followed Knox, Man was a genus that included the different human species. And different races were adapted to different terrains and would not prosper in others. He had heard these opinions before, but not dressed up in scientific language. And all of life is contained in the embryo. So if we understood how the embryo developed we could understand how the person would? This seemed to make some sense. But Aesthetic Anatomy, what could that mean?

'Enric Serra i *Maristany*' he repeated to himself over and over till someone coughed and he looked up to see John Arthur standing before him. The older man was smiling, triumphant, even.

'Did you enjoy the lecture?'

'I didn't understand it all. And some of it appears to be just a sophisticated excuse for racism.'

'But Dr. Knox is one of the fiercest opponents of such prejudice! He was sent back from service in South Africa because of his criticism of how the Dutch settlers treated the poor hottentots. He even believes that when the industrial age is over, the savages will overcome us and rule because they are better fitted to the struggle.'

Enric raised an eyebrow. 'Science is being used by the upper classes to divide the working classes. And what does Aesthetic Anatomy mean?'

'Do you mind that egg you magicked up the other night?'

'Yes, I can't help doing tricks sometimes, I know it is silly.'

'That's not the point. And if you could see your raised eyebrow just now. The same oval shape. There is an aesthetic connection between everything. That is the real proof of creation and a Creator. If we can find similar structures or forms in different plants, animals and man, like the one the Professor showed us today, we can see a unity in creation. Not one of cause and effect, not one which is plainly visible, but which shows sign of a design. That is Aesthetic anatomy or zoology.

Why don't you come to my rooms in Dumbiedkyes, overlooking Arthur's Seat and I will explain it at greater length. And no, dinna smile like that. The name of the hill and my own is a coincidence — not everything is transcendental, laddie!'

St Paul and the Two Holy Candlesticks

Hugh disembarked at Granton like St Paul arriving in Ephesus: the prophet whom people expected to interpret happenings and point the way they should go. Or so he felt. He strode up the jetty, past the impatient throng waiting to sail back to Fife and headed up to the High Street about four miles away. A cabbie pulled up his horse, but Hugh waved him on. He needed to think, to compose.

First, he would go home to see Lydia and kiss little Harriet and the bairn goodnight, like a soldier off to the campaign. Then consult with Chalmers and Candlish about Monday's Assembly. Should they go for a vote on accepting or rejecting the latest decision of the Court of Session to enforce the right of the laird and therefore of the State to appoint a minister? Or was it more astute for their leaders just to walk out and hope that everyone would follow? If the second, they would have to organise a place for a new Assembly. He would stop off at Canonmills on the way up.

He passed several churches on his way. Soon many would be emptied of congregation and minister if the Disruption took place. The rows of factories and houses that had sprung up in the different waves of speculation in the last twenty years were like grey soot-stained fingers clutching at the remnants of green-covered soil that ran down to the sea. He passed Cannonmills Loch and stopped off at the Tanfield Hall to confirm it was vacant and readied. Then up the steep slope of Dundas Street to Princes St, snail-like in his grey cloak. Above him crouched the sleeping lion of the castle. He scaled the Mound, called in on *The Witness* office on the High Street then up and over the Meadows to his home in Sylvan Place.

He remembered when they had first moved in. Lydia had come down from Cromarty to join him in his lodgings in St Patrick Square. He still recalled her outrage when she met the wheedling widow and dissolute offspring he boarded with. 'This is not respectable' she had almost shrieked when they were first alone in his tiny room. 'You are no longer a stonemason, Hugh!'

She had swiftly found them a home at a new development of three houses at No 5, Sylvan Place, across the Meadows from George Square with a fine, uninterrupted view to Arthur's Seat to the East. The first days had been hectic, Hugh still making his way at the newspaper, trying to find his place in Edinburgh society. Poor Lydia had discovered that in the Capital tenants had to supply their own fittings, coal grates, lamps, window blinds etc. She had spent time in the city as a young woman fifteen years ago, under the care of Mrs. Grant of Laggan, but had no idea where one bought these things. 'It was my Edinburgh Enlightenment!' she had joked. But that was afterwards, once they had settled and the bairn had been fetched from Cromarty.

The Meadows were still being drained in those days and geese swam in the surviving small pools. You could still imagine the series of lochs that had once dotted Edinburgh, from Duddingston, to the Burgh Loch in the Meadows, over to the Nor'loch where now stood Princes Street Gardens, then down to Canonmills Loch, up to Blackford and over to Costorphine. As a local wag once remarked, had many of them not been drained, Edinburgh would have resembled the Venice of the North more than Athens.

As he crossed the Meadows, he stopped to make sure he was not being followed, squinting, to reassure himself no one was hiding behind a tree, ready to jump out at him. He caressed the gun he kept tucked beneath his waistcoat. When he had been left in sole charge of the bank in Cromarty while his superior was on holiday, he had taken to carrying a firearm lest he be attacked by the tinkers who lived in the woods. He had scared a couple of them off simply by patting his pocket, pretending he was carrying a weapon. Hugh was aware that he had made enemies by his attacks on the Kirk's adversaries. He would be ready for them!

At last he was safely back in Sylvan Place. A patch of railed ground guarded the entrance to the house. It was bordered on each side by a pleasant market-garden and a small, white-washed dairy glimmered through the trees at the farther end of the lane. Beyond, lanes and fields led up to the gentle slopes of the Braid Hills, where Hugh would often go walking, when not called by the shore and the raised beach at Leith.

'Ha-Ha!' he cried as he stepped into the house and young Harriet ran into his arms, her waist-length blonde tresses flying behind her. Ha-Ha was a name she had invented herself and would not reply to any other. She gave names to everything and composed poems and little songs which she sang in her true, sweet tone. She lived for the moments of her father's return, when he would pick her up and she would bury her head in his shoulder, surrounded by his warmth and his strength. Not even her mother could enjoy that all-enveloping privilege. She was only four years old and like many children of her age, a seeker of treats. In two seconds she had discovered something in his pocket. She reached in and pulled out the little black stone.

'Papa has brought me a present from the sea!'

Just then Lydia appeared, carrying their six-month old son, William, in her arms, followed by James Mackenzie, a theological student who worshipped only the true church and Hugh. He waved to his leader and made to take Harriet from him, that he might embrace his wife.

But Hugh seemed on edge and just gestured to Lydia, standing with his back to the window in the sparsely furnished room, empty, except for some chairs and the books piled up around the walls and Hugh's desk at the end. He handed Ha-Ha over instead to young Harriet Ross, the daughter of a Cromarty friend, who had been brought down to lend them a hand. His life was full of Harriets, he once joked: it was his mother's name, his daughter's and now this young lady's who was of so much service to them. The little girl protested as Harriet led her from the room.

'*Daddie has come home, and he's brocht me a wee round stone!*' the wee lassie sang, holding out her treasure to show Harriet.

They all smiled, except Hugh, who began to walk up and down, his nervous defence. He could not add domestic concerns to his already overburdened mind.

'*Daddie has left me alone*

With only a wee round stone.'

Lydia called Harriet back and handed over baby William to her. Then she stepped forward, distancing herself from the young man and approached her husband.

'At last, Hugh. Where have you been? Candlish has sent a man to inquire after you two times today. He is impatient to see you tonight about his sermon.'

'I am off there right now,' he said, running his hands through her silk-soft hair. I just wanted to wish you and the bairns goodnight as I fear I may not be back till past midnight. The time is coming, Lydia.'

'You must eat something. You look tired.'

He smiled, easier now that he was on his way again.

'Don´t be concerned for me, wife. I may find a bite to eat at Candlish's but leave the usual herring and ale out for when I get back. I have never felt more alive in all my days, Lydia.'

And with that, he kissed her, picked up his cloak and swept out the door and down to the New Town again, to Randolph Crescent in the West End. The afternoon was dissolving into evening and the birds on the Meadows were seeking shelter in the trees, their wings whirring above his head as he cut across the grass to gain time. He thought of St. Paul again, voyager, ceaseless haranguer for the Gospel and for the essentials of Christian belief. The apostles were important not just as witnesses to the living Christ, not just because they attested to his existence on this earth, as Paul had never met the Lord in the flesh. They were important because their lives and sacrifice were living testimony to the truth of the Bible and of the Gospels. They embodied the truth. They held Jesus, the Dear Redeemer, in themselves. Could he do that?

Such thoughts meant he scarcely perceived the crowd in Tollcross. He did notice a tall, foreign-looking man making sketches of the new buildings under construction there. A Galilean? he thought laughingly to himself. Were these the days of signs? He thought of Paul again and how he ordained presbyters in the churches of Lystra, Iconium, and Antioch. Paul simply presented the bishop or presbyter to the Church, and the whole congregation testified their acceptance by uplifted hands. Paul did not choose the priest nor did the Roman authorities.

He arrived at the large townhouse in Randolph Crescent where Candlish lived. Or rather, 'resided,' Hugh thought to himself. He wished he felt more comfortable with the great preacher and defender of the Kirk's independence. After all, he owed his appointment as *The Witness* editor to him. Perhaps that explained it. Hugh was never comfortable with indebtedness and avoided it whenever he could. But you couldn't always, he admitted to himself, cleaning his boots on the scraper beside the door. Scraps of mud dropped onto the marble porch. Like little continents, Hugh thought. He was examining his new world when the door opened.

It was Candlish himself!

'Come in, Miller, come in. We have been awaiting you.'

Hugh followed the smaller man through a lighted corridor, past the drawing room and into his large study. Candlish parted his hair in the middle, his broad bare forehead gleaming in the candlelight and his locks as if attached by long side-whiskers. 'A peacock,' no. 'A spaniel,' Hugh thought. He checked himself. Why these irreverent thoughts? And at this serious moment?

'Dr Chalmers is here, unaccompanied. I have dismissed the servants for the evening. We must debate our next steps in the strictest confidence. We are in Gethsemane.'

If Candlish had been his sponsor, the white-haired eminence

who stood up to greet him was his mentor, his pole star, his hero. His protector. Hugh had tried to see Chalmers on his first visit to Edinburgh all those years ago and had corresponded with him as an earnest young man in search of a literary future. He had shared in his soul the minister's emphasis on the role of the Church in raising the poor out of indigence, of educating its people. Of the power of charity and Christian love and the refusal to be usurped by the state or workingmen's combinations. To Chalmers, the Church was the people, and the people were the Church, whether they realised it or not. Candlish only saw the Church and its duty to itself.

'Well, Hugh. We are here at last.' Chalmers always began his conversations and even his sermons softly, so you had to strain to hear him. Once he had you, once he had captured you with his large round eyes, his douce tones, his learning, he would increase the volume and the pace till you felt like you were on a train of inspiration where the destination was preordained and inevitable.

His host waved a sheaf of papers at him. 'I have just been rehearsing my sermon at St George's on the eve of the Assembly.' Candlish had made the most influential and richest church in Edinburgh his fief, regularly filling the place and adored by his congregation. 'I am going to prepare them for the Disruption as an ineluctable fact. Listen, '*tomorrow's sun will behold its goodly structure rent in twain; that before the setting of tomorrow's sun, scenes will be enacted, which will find the Establishment of the country as the company of two armies; and to prevent this, I believe that nothing short of a miracle would be sufficient.*'

'Sufficiently muscular for you, Hugh?' Chalmers asked. Hugh laughed. At last, they were a fighting church!

'And I want to bring in the colonies, Europe and our American supporters. This is a global conflict. We must claim the universal.'

Hugh's face darkened slightly. Since he had been granted a D.D. by Princeton College in 1841, Candlish always tended to claim his role on the world stage.

'Pray, do let me see what you have written.'

Candlish handed him a sheet. There were no corrections, no gaps.

'*How do men of other nations look upon us? I do not say in England. England has her faithful ones; but alas! over her there is come a cloud of awful delusion and heresy. But cross the Channel, or cross the Atlantic, and how do men there look upon us? I speak of the serious, the thoughtful, the religious men of other lands. Brethren, they know the value of these principles for which we contend, and they see that, though not in deed too dearly bought, yet we are willing to sacrifice to them our earthly all; and they look on with intense interest to see what will be the end of this momentous struggle.*'

Hugh had to admit that Candlish's strident, even aggressive tone chimed better with his own than Chalmers' reasoned suggestions. He saw the clashing armies, he had visions of Bannockburn, of the Covenanters racing across some wild heath. This was his time. He went through the text, emphasising contrasts, underlining that this was a national movement. They were not the deserters; the Moderates were.

From the sermon he surmised that there was to be no call for a motion to reject the Court's latest injunction to admit ministers selected by the authorities or their representative.

'We have been in command of the Assembly for ten years now,' Chalmers whispered. 'I have gone to London, I have preached forbearance, but the Moderates insist. And Lord Aberdeen's compromises are traps. You cannot compromise on truth. The time has come for action. Let us demonstrate our force.'

Aberdeen! A Scots Tory minister who had fought against the Kirk's independence under the guise of common sense, fairness and all the other sleight of hands of the deceiver.

'What happens if the elders of the parish refuse a man because he has red hair!' he was said to have exclaimed.

Hugh had attacked him without quarter and how his readers had loved it. Righteous anger is a mighty weapon!

Once he had finished with his revision there was a silence. There had been little that required emendation. He began to suspect that the sermon had been just a pretext.

Chalmers coughed. Coming from him Hugh couldn't tell if it was a cough or a sigh.

'Hugh, while we commend ourselves to action and the Holy Spirit, to walking out of the Assembly and trusting that God will give many the fortitude to follow us, we cannot depend on deeds alone.'

Hugh nodded and waited for instruction.

'Now we really do need you as our witness. In the coming days you must arm public opinion, emphasising the justness of our cause and its importance for the future of Scotland. And at the Assembly and in the later deliberations in the Hall, you must take down all that is said in an official record of the new church. For that is what national churches and not mere sects do. Your place will be at the front of the Hall. Men will speak to you, and you will speak to the nation for them. Do not falter, do not fail us, Hugh.'

Hugh simply nodded. As he picked up his cloak and headed for the door, he glanced behind at the two anointed ones, like the holy candlesticks standing beside each other. The time of fury and disruption had come. May his God keep him strong!

Against Obituaries

He imagined what they would write.

'By the early 1840s Robert Chambers was one of the most prolific authors in Britain, with over thirty books and the larger part of the weekly *Chambers' Journal* to his credit. His brother William took charge of the industrial processes and most of the commercial efforts while he produced a vast range of articles and books, many unsigned. Two penniless brothers from Peebles seemed to themselves and to others the paradigm of the resourceful Scot, pulling themselves up by each other's bootstraps. If Robert's skill as a popular writer and friendship with Sir Walter Scott was the fuel of their progress, then William's hard-nosed business sense and organisational skills did the rest. They had come a long way from the second-hand manual printing-press they had bought in 1820, to the four-storey state of the art plant in Waterloo Place. People queued to wonder at it. Edinburgh was a force in international publishing, with companies such as Chambers, Nelson, and Constable. They all had to contend with the distance of Edinburgh from the mass market. Some printed in London, some, like Chambers, concentrated on reducing costs and increasing the scale of their editions.

The possibilities of production on this scale first became apparent when they began to publish Combe's *The Constitution of Man Considered in Relation to External Objects* from 1835. This became the most widely read of all the reflective treatises in the Reform era and the single most important work for debates about natural law and progress in Britain and the United States. Chambers' extremely cheap editions made the *Constitution* a popular phenomenon.'

Good Lord! That was the sort of twaddle they would probably scribble about him, in *The Scotsman* or *The Times* when he had gone. Did you struggle all your life, fight, love, worship and work just so you can be reduced to some patronising lines in an encyclopaedia? He smiled, despite himself. How many lives had he summed up in neat formulae in his publications?

And the facts were broadly true. But there was a gap between facts and the truth that this coldly mechanical age refused to recognise. It seemed to him as he looked back on the last twenty years since the heart had been burned out of old Edinburgh, that everything had accelerated till he felt literally dizzy. The world was out of balance because, as phrenology had taught him, we had disobeyed the laws of our bodily constitution. He had done so through constant and intense mental action.

And so that morning in Spring of 1843, he had waited till the meeting with the managers had finished and tugged William's sleeve, their signal since boyhood for an urgent private consultation.

William had remained standing till Robert's stubborn silence persuaded him to sit down across the polished gleam of the table and say, 'Well, Robbie, what are you unhappy about now?'

'My mind needs reorganising, William. And this factory too, but not in the way you were proposing to the staff this morning. It is not all about expansion!'

'We have worked hard, Robbie, and need to run to stand still. Not just for the financial but for the social rewards.'

'I cannot hear you for the damn thump thump thumping of the presses. Can you not understand, the industry is killing me!'

'Industry is what gives you those fine houses in Edinburgh and St Andrews. The printers are what prints your money for your jaunts down to hobnob with the intellectuals in London. '

Robert just sat there with his head bowed. Silent.

William stood up and came around to the other side of the table.

Pulling up a chair he sat by his brother.

'Robbie, you have lost two children, two wee lassies, one of them only a bairn, in the last year. And mother's recent passing, though expected, has affected us all. Now is the time to work more, not less, brother.'

'What is it with this age that so glorifies hard work! It is defined as a curse in Genesis! Ach, here I go again. William, I don't mean to cause trouble. I know you work as hard, even harder than I do. But I can't keep churning out articles for the masses. I am dry. There is no ink left inside me.'

'What do you propose, Robbie?'

'Well, we need to become mainly publishers instead of authors. We cannot depend so much on my productions. Perhaps you should carry on independently, or the *Journal* should close.'

Now it was William who bowed his head. He had seen this coming for the last year but had put off facing the crisis, hoping it would blow over. Then Robert's wife, Anne, had come crying to him a fortnight ago about how irritable and unpredictable her husband had become.

'He doesn't know where he is going or where he wants to go, and we are suffering at home, William. You will have to talk to him. This crisis is caused by his professional pressures and must be resolved in the business.'

Instead of seeking out his brother, this confession had only made William avoid him, cancelling appointments and inventing commitments. For he had no solution. There comes a time when we have to admit we cannot solve our brother's problems without sinking ourselves.

He had in fact been keeping his distance from Robert for a while now. This was made easier by his brother spending so much time at his house in St. Andrews. William had no idea what he did there but had hoped the quiet of the countryside and the comforts of the large house would soothe his strained nerves.

Writers were prone to stress. William, above all others, knew that. They were a queer bunch: proud, arrogantly foisting their views on others, yet as desperate for recognition and praise as his little red setter. And Robert was one of a curious group, those who enjoyed great public success, except among the intellectuals, the experts, just the people he most craved acceptance from. William gauged success by circulation numbers, by subscriptions. He was also clear that their public was the self-educating working-classes and professionals, not so much interested in knowing *about* things but in knowing *how* to do things. The elite could go hang themselves!

They had started their business just around the corner at the top of Leith Walk. Robert's researches into antiquities and legends of old Edinburgh along with the usual editions of Burns had given them a foothold in the market. But it was only when they had realised the huge thirst for practical knowledge, for technical pamphlets for the thousands of courses in engineering and production that they had found their path. William had seen the opportunity. As always. What recognition did he get for that?

How often had he told his brother that if they had started by writing about the past, success now was based on writing about the future! The old Edinburgh was gone. The new Edinburgh looked to the empire, to London and to the confident generations marching forward into prosperity. Work, yes work, was what made this generation different. Work allied with scientific progress would save them all from the doubters, the nay-sayers, the Chartists, and the defeatists.

Work, and respectability. He had learned that the glue that held everything together was increasingly conformity to a strict moral code, one that the new middle classes were imposing on the others. It was their badge of authority and gave them power which otherwise they would have had to purchase like their betters, or plead for, like the working classes. Fortunately, Robert seemed to agree with him there, at least in paying lip service to social demands. He was registered at two churches, so that if one congregation commented on his absence, he could allege attendance at the other. And he always passed his writings to William, the gatekeeper of morality and conformity. So far it had worked. William hoped that at 41, Robert was just passing through the same kind of wobble he had experienced at the same age, two years ago. It had surely been made worse by the recent deaths, but he would grow out of it, just as William had done.

Though as he looked at his brother, he began to have doubts.

'Why don't you take a trip to America, Robert? You could see our clients there and the change would do you good, refresh your spirits. I can manage the business while you are gone.'

'You think you can manage everything, William. Life will show you otherwise, eventually. I shall not go to America, but don't expect me here as much as in the past. You will need to find another reservoir of opinion and elucidation for the *Journal*. And hang the consequences!'

With that his brother picked up his hat from the stand and strode out of the room down to the front hall with scarcely a gesture to those he passed.

He was too like his father, William reflected. And look how that had ended!

On the way out, Robert dropped in at the library he had insisted they set up for the staff. At first, William had rejected the idea because of the cost, but when Robert had argued that they were in the business of sharing information and that the library would stand as a commercial symbol of their mission and be good for their standing, he agreed. It had been a remarkable success and a good advert for them. This was during working hours, so he expected it to be empty. In the far corner, he spied a dark-haired man bent over a table, engrossed in a book.

The librarian told him in a resounding whisper that it was their foreign printing expert.

'If his meetings with Mr Turner are delayed, he comes in here. He doesnae waste a minute, that one.'

His whispering made the man sit up and look round. In doing so, he knocked his satchel off the table, its contents spilling on to the floor in a concertina of books and papers. Feeling responsible and embarrassed, Robert hurried over to help in the retrieval of the documents. He stopped short when he realised he was holding a copy of Goethe in his hand. In German!

'Do you speak German, sir?'

'Yes, sir. And French and Spanish and Catalan.'

Robert had not heard of the last.

'And English, sir.'

'Yes, you speak that excellently, if with a mixture of accents. My name is Robert Chambers.' He held out his hand.

'Enric Serra.'

Robert sat down and invited Enric to do the same. He asked about the Goethe and was told about Professor Knox's lecture and the aesthetic principle.

'I am trying to understand it.' Enric talked plainly and directly, without the subservience of the other staff. Robert liked that. There was something in this man he could use. But what?

Their conversation was interrupted by Enric's boss, John Turner, who was now ready for the meeting. Robert could see that the young man did not know who to obey, so he waved him on to the meeting, with a 'won't keep you' remark.

Robert waited a few moments, reflecting, then left the room. He felt elated by the conversation and a sense of release at standing up to his older brother coursed through his veins. The day suddenly looked brighter. A pathetic fallacy, he laughed. He walked along Waterloo Place to Princes Street. In front of him, at the East End of Princes Street Gardens, loomed the imposing tower of the monument to Sir Walter Scott.

It was set to reach almost 200 feet in its final elevation, making it the biggest monument to a writer ever built. John Steell had been working for almost four years on the massive statue of Scott which was to occupy its central plinth. Gangs of masons laboured in a huge shed near the base, and on windy days dust escaped in yellow spirals along the thoroughfare. People complained, but few worried about the effect of the dust on the workers' lungs. No one questioned the economic cost either, and it had certainly given work, not only to the masons, but to the myriad of sculptors who were carving out more than half a hundred figures from Scott's novels and other Scottish historical worthies. The preponderance of the former perhaps testified to the scarcity of the latter, Robert mused.

He had known Scott, the man who created a nation! Now there were Abbotsfords not only up and down Scotland, but around the world. Scott would have approved of the competition to design his monument being won by a man who called himself 'John Morvo,' after the designer of Melrose Abbey. He might not have been so happy to discover the architect's real identity as a young man of low class, George Meikle Kemp, a joiner and self-taught architect. Robert thought the building looked like an emaciated cathedral built by a child. Soon Scott's statue would be installed in the plinth and that is what he would look like and be for future generations. Locked inside his stone obituary.

And now people had themselves immortalised in photographic images. A picture of Hugh Miller holding a mallet flashed into his mind. He had seen a recent calotype by Hill and Adamson and had thought it ridiculous at the time. A writer posing as a working man, when as far as Robert knew, Hugh had not worked in a quarry for more than a decade and lived comfortably in a smart section of the city. True, no one could describe him as a gentleman. He was a strange creature, an intellectual among the radicals in the Kirk, a Whig with Tory beliefs, a Highlander who had no Gaelic and a fiercely independent Scot who wrote in the style of Addison and Steele. He was a contradiction as a man too: bad-tempered but gentle, proud, yet almost self-effacing at times, at least in the intercourse Robert had had with him. They were not friends, he thought, but Hugh had consulted him from Cromarty about the direction his writings should take. 'Avoid being a merely local writer,' Robert had answered, even though the pieces he had published in the *Journal,* were mainly slices of local colour and Caithness legends.

After he was gone, the image of the rustic stonemason would eclipse the geologist, journalist and writer. Robert could almost pity him.

There he was again, criticising others when the same darts could as easily directed be at himself, a man from a humble background who had won success in the city, a gentle creature who had forged a business empire through unbending ambition, someone who craved respectability yet disdained the prejudices and superstition of the public. And locked in the embrace of his brother and their joint enterprise.

Miller would no doubt go down in history as the stonemason writer and he as the faithful brother who composed the Journal of his times. We all become our obituaries, they said. Well, he would see what he could do to escape his!

Letter 11

For the Sake of an Argument

There are just so many arguments a man can have. Even a Scotsman. Some greasy fellow had whispered to him that we are granted only so many ejaculations of our seed. Perhaps it was the same with arguments. Because they wore you out. They left you trembling, whether you won or lost. They left you wanting more.

'That fellow would argue with his own shadow' so the saying went. Did they not realise that is what he did all the time, so as to be ready when the real opponent presented himself? Every tuft of grass became an adversary, every knock at the door a challenge to a dispute. That quick riposte had been prepared in advance by imagining just what each person he came upon could possibly find fault with him for. Sometimes the knockout blow did not come. Then he had to rely on his fists, as a boy, or his intimidating glare as an adult. Stand up straight, look right into their eyes. Make it clear it is not just their ideas you object to but the fact they hold them. It is they themselves who are so offensive.

Of course, you might argue, (there he was, rehearsing again), that such aggression is only justified if the cause is right, if you cannot be in error. Perhaps that was why he had at last come to defend the true Christian faith in its most combative version. He was a fighter for his faith. They could not condemn him for that, surely. Damn them if they did!

He was lucky to be a Scot, a nation who had made argument an art form, whether in the flytings or in the argumentations of Hume and the Common-Sense philosophers who rebutted him. They showed what could not be true or relied on self-evident 'facts.' Only the radicals and the new scientists put forward positive arguments now. And Edinburgh had exiled those like Carlyle who had championed systematic German thought.

He was self-educated and ill-equipped to share a ring with university men, lawyers and the learned. But he had a prodigious memory and could recite whole poems, essays and speeches in defence of his positions. What if his memory went?

What? You object to the opening statement because it only speaks of men? I expected nothing else from you.

"Hugh Miller"

The Gifts We Give

Harry was coming and John Goodsir had to finish the sketch he had been working on for two hours, looking at the specimen through the microscope and then lifting his eyes up and drawing. At least the light was good. The sun served for something. He was tired. He heard a rustling and looked up. No, not Harry hanging up his coat, but the eagle stirring. The predator he and Forbes had captured on the Orkney expedition seven years ago was studying him. Goodsir shivered. It was savage nature in essence. He remembered the wonder he felt when he had caged it in Anstruther. As dead meat or carrion failed to preserve the beauty and grandeur of its plumage, the villagers would happily bring live animals in order to watch the eagle being fed. When a cat was thrown into the cage, no matter how wild it was, it was at once cowed. The eagle perched in regal dignity, first cast a glance at its prey, then suddenly pounced upon the cat, striking its back with the talons of one foot, and paralysing the body before the stroke, and as the head of the feline was raised, it was at once enclosed within the talons of the other foot and crushed, causing immediate death.

With the mastery of his victim came forth the display of his own excited nature, in the elevated head, the feathers of the neck stiff and erect, the wings flickering and spread to make the victory complete; then the epigastric section by its beak with quick despatch of thoracic contents, the disembowelling and carrying the strings of the intestines to its mouth with a rapidity worthy of the hungry Neapolitan swallowing macaroni, and finally the tearing off the muscular parts and leaving but skin and skeleton as vestiges of the feast. What a study of animal life within the Anstruther cage! The eagle in royal ease, the cat appalled, the descent from the perch, the clutch and death-stroke; the nobility of triumph evidenced in eyes of light, coloured radiance, and high feather; the evisceration, the feasting amidst hot blood, and the steamy vapours of vitality and quivering muscles mocking life in death, constituted a picture as generic as it was grandly exciting and picturesque to behold. The eagle's love for things of the flesh would have caused the death of a child incautiously brought by its mother too near the cage, the wooden paling of which gave way under the impetuous dash of the ravenous bird, had not Harry Goodsir come to the rescue. Yes, the eagle was no pet. It was nature in all its cruel glory. John had mastered it and he would master Nature just as Western civilisation was doing. It was the Christian mission given to Adam in the Garden.

'Where shall we go?' Was he talking to the eagle or to himself? Sooner or later, he would have to move from 21 Lothian Street, which some of the Brotherhood referred to as the 'barracks' though John preferred the 'Palace.' Once he had secured promotion. George Square, perhaps, to be near the University and the Infirmary. Or the New Town? Social order perhaps demanded that. He had no ambitions for wealth or for social gaiety, but it was important that the prestige of a professorship was reflected in his abode. He felt he was leaving youth behind, though he was only thirty-one.

There were some things he would not abandon, however, chief among them his friendship with Forbes. He had promised to do all in his power to win Edward a chair at Edinburgh and he worked tirelessly to promote his reputation and keep his name fresh, referring to his recent publications and expeditions in his own lectures and social encounters. He knew some called him, Forbes' poodle, but he didn't care.

He laughed as he remembered the satirical magazine they had published as students, *The Maga,* modelled on the famous *Noctes*

Ambrosianae edited by their hero, Professor John Wilson, 'Christopher North.' They used to follow him at a distance as he walked home, too awed to approach. They not only shared his satirical turn but his Toryism. Forbes would also later copy his effusive oratory when lecturing, gaining him the same reputation as 'a turn,' a popular lecturer.

John fingered the ribbon holding the silver triangle he, like Forbes, always wore as members of the highest order of the Oineromaths, a Brotherhood at the service of truth, for the glory of God and the good of all. He smiled when he thought of the ignorant who asked how the triangle came to be chosen as their symbol. Some associated it with the pyramids or esoteric totems. Goodsir had never said but he knew it came from Forbes' fascination with trilogies and the number three and from the symbol of his native Isle of Man. The Order was founded on the ninth day of the third month, its symbol was the triangle, its motto a triad, its ceremonial officers nine, the hour of meeting three minutes past nine. Schoolboy whimsy perhaps, perhaps not. He was beginning to feel there was a structure, as Goethe said, uniting creation. But not simply a poetic one.

He rose at 5am every morning to get work done before going to the University. Sometimes his days seemed to pass in a half-waking dream, punctuated by moments of exuberant precision. He must concentrate, as Harry would be here soon, and they had to talk about the Collection. John had decided to give up his role as Conservator of the Surgeons' Hall Museum and he was anxious that his brother should succeed him. He smiled at the irony, given his criticism of the Professor of Anatomy, Monro 'Tertius,' for being the third of his family to inherit the post of Professor of Anatomy. But Monro called himself 'Junior,' for heaven's sake!

Just then the door sprung open and Harry entered, a bolt of energy, a ripple of clear water in a muddy stream.

'Hello, old man.'

John winced. Five years difference had been significant as boys, but surely not now.

'Have you tried these delicious cranberry tarts? They are Spring in a titbit!' Harry half-mumbled, as he waltzed around the room, stepping nimbly over specimens, his mouth occupied with the pastry. And have you looked outside at the sky? That clear blue, so unusual in our smoky metropolis. What do you think of this jacket? I think it's braw and makes me look quite the dazzler. Oh, and here are the proofs!'

He said this as he plucked a sheaf of papers from his jacket pocket and plumped them down on the table, somehow missing John's sketch.

John waited for the eruption to subside. Harry always made an entrance. As a boy he would steal the others' toys or pull on the maid's apron strings as he came into the room, anything to gain attention. Once calmed, however, he had the same steady concentration as all the Goodsirs and was as meticulous as his older brother.

On the first page, in Harry's hand appeared a new title, *Anatomical and Pathological Observations.*

'I thought this read better than '*Unpublished Lectures, 1841-1842,*' Harry explained.

'It brings into focus your power of perception, of seeing what others don't.'

John nodded. He wished he also had the power, like Harry, of seeing things as others saw them.

'But, Harry, I don't see your name on the title page beside mine. The whole point of this enterprise is to make both our marks, myself as a claim to succeed Monro as Anatomy Professor and to give my recommendation of you to Surgeons' Hall the proper weight.'

'I appreciate that, old boy, but they are your lectures.'

'But many are based on our joint expeditions in Fife.'

'And more are results of your work with Forbsie.'

Did John detect a note of jealousy there?

'That is different. The focus here is entirely yours and mine. Edward has moved on from anatomy to zoology and will move on again if the fancy and academic employment beckon. And you are here with me and still share my passion. Besides, your influence is patent throughout, in the changes to the style and the labelling of the graphs. So your name goes on, and we will add, 'with some zoological, anatomical, and pathological observations,' by Henry Duncan Spens Goodsir.'

'You are saying this because you are my big brother and I love you for it. I love you so much that I have brought you a cranberry tart. And another for me as you could not possibly eat alone! I will make tea.'

As they sat bathed in the translucent Spring sunshine, they talked, of the family in Fife, of whether they should respect the local pronunciation of their name as Gutcher, reflecting their German origin, of how glad John had been to leave dentistry behind. Of how Harry wanted to discover the world and how his brother insisted in vain that that could be done through a microscope.

'What about Edward's expedition to the Aegean? It made his name, and he became positively Hellenic!' Harry replied.

'He almost died of fever and is still not the man he was when he embarked.'

'I will not be the man I am and want to be if I do not see the world, John.'

'Well, we first have to make sure you see the inside of the Museum. That collection is important to me. It is organised according to the principles I imbibed from Dr. Knox and its integrity is vital. A collection is a dialogue with the intelligent visitor and with your help we can maintain that intercourse.'

'Bye the bye, did you hear what Junior Monro said about the Kirk?' Harry thought it opportune to change the subject. His brother became tense when friends or family talked about leaving Edinburgh. He still talked about Forbes' departure as a loss, though his friend was a born nomad and always on the move.

'He has said nothing to me but do go on.'

'Well, you might as well discuss the political significance of those entrails you are drawing, but he issued a stern warning that the University would resist any moves by what he termed the 'more disruptive elements' in the upcoming General Assembly to make science follow doctrine.'

John sipped his tea and nodded. 'It's true that the Church is in ferment. We will see what happens at the Assembly. As Edward says, once you have given people a taste for reform, they demand it in everything. That is why 1832 was such a bad step. Now this craze has reached the Church. We must guard against it in the University.'

'*The Witness* talks in terms of revolution. Of the need for a spiritual rearmament of Scotland.'

'Oh, that is just the spoutings of that frightful man, Hugh Miller.'

'Have you read his articles on geology? He has a naturalist's eye and writes clear, steady prose.'

'Not bad for an unschooled workingman. But with such a narrow scope. And such aggressivity in the name of religion! He is too learned for the brickyard and too uncouth for society. And like all these sectarians, obsessed with the Book of Genesis. One would think the Bible stopped there.'

And so they talked on, the light spilling into the room and throwing longer shadows as the day declined. John even decided to miss a meeting of the Aesthetic Club at the Royal Society.

He would remember that afternoon for the rest of his life. He did publish the *Observations* as he had promised. The work not only gained him fame, it cemented Harry's reputation and secured the post at the Museum. It also procured Harry the appointment as one of the crew of Sir John Franklin's expedition to the Northwest Passage in 1845. He was listed as a medical officer, but his role was as a naturalist. The public were still not ready to pay for a pure scientist, Forbes remarked.

The two ships disappeared in the Arctic wastes. Despite several searches, including two involving his younger brother, Robert, only skeletons were found. One had what is described as remnants of a silk vest and a gold filling of the type implanted by John Naismith, the dentist John had worked under. A voyager in the frozen wastes does not need a silk vestment. Unless he is a member of the Brotherhood.

John would think of his published lectures. Of the fame they had given him. Of the death warrant their joint attribution became for his beloved brother. Oh, save us from the gifts we give!

The Great Disruption

Shortly after noon, on Monday, May 18th, 1843, the multitude had followed the procession led by the Lord High Commissioner, the Marquis of Bute, from the reception at a crowded Holyrood Palace, up by the Calton Hill and the North Bridge to the High Church of St Giles, to hear Dr Welsh, the retiring Moderator, preach. Many had been disappointed not to spot more royals on the turrets of the old Palace but consoled themselves with the spectacle of horse and guards making their way with firm step past the thousands of spectators.

'Let every man be fully persuaded in his own mind' was the keynote text and Welsh preached with his customary thoroughness, delighting the more intellectually minded, though perhaps exasperating those in search of something more rousing. None of the Moderates attended, guarding their time anxiously in the site of the Assembly at St Andrew's in George Street.

The public benches in that church had been full since the doors were opened a few hours earlier. Many were standing to allow more to squeeze in. The doorkeepers had rejected bribes on the night before from people wanting to occupy a pew overnight and they had locked the doors with padlocks in case some had made copies of the keys. People had come not only from all over Scotland, but from England and the colonies. Dr. Stewart of Erskine claimed to have made an uninterrupted journey from a health spa in Constantinople just to attend!

About half-past two o'clock, Dr Welsh entered and took the

chair. Soon after, the measured tramp of the soldiery could be heard outside, then the swell of martial music, with the sound of the Queen's Anthem announcing the approach of the Commissioner. The Marquis entered and swiftly moved to occupy the throne. Welsh presented himself formally, then offered a prayer in a voice unusually clear and firm for him and which could be heard in the farthest reaches of the hushed church.

In normal times, Welsh would have embarked upon the proceedings of the Assembly. As everyone knew, these were not normal times. Many of those present had tears in their eyes, either of elation at what they knew was coming, or in distress. Candlish's sermon had made it clear there was to be no backing down, no avoidance of the rift, of the disruption in the Church. Welsh produced a paper, 'the Protest,' he called it and announced that business could not proceed as usual given the government's unwarranted attacks on the independence of the Church and on men's conscience.

When the reading had concluded Welsh placed the Protest on the table, lifted his hat, bowed respectfully to the Commissioner, and moved towards the door. Chalmers then Gordon moved to accompany him. Many on the orthodox side, Hugh Miller among them, held their breaths. The destiny not only of their church, but of Scotland was hanging in balance. How many would follow Chalmers and Welsh? It is one thing to make promises over a cup of tea in your warm Manse, another to walk out of Church, house and home on a fresh spring day in Edinburgh. Dr. Cook and the Moderates waited nervously too, like men praying that a dam will not burst, that only a trickle of water will overflow.

One by one the benches emptied, without hurry or confusion. A loud cheer rang out from the gallery and was immediately hushed by those on both sides, conscious of the solemnity of what was happening. When Chalmers and Welsh appeared on the street leading their fellows, an electric shock ran through the crowd. People parted to permit the ministers to walk four abreast along the road. Many cheered. Some cried with emotion either at the rupture of Scotland- for the Kirk was the nation and the nation the Kirk, or at the sight of these modern Covenanters raising the standard once more in the name of proud independence and liberty of conscience.

Meanwhile, in the half-empty church the Commissioner looked about, unsure what to do. People on the Moderates' benches were mainly too distressed to look at him, though some maintained a haughty confidence that the rebels would be back.

'They will soon tire of preaching to the poor in the fields. That is if the Lairds even let them use the fields. My Lord, the Duke of Buccleuch has taken my advice and will not. 'Roundheads' he calls them.'

The speaker was a fine-featured white-haired man in his late fifties or early sixties. His coat was well cut and his bag of good leather.

When his neighbour introduced himself as Smith of Dundee, he replied, 'Hardie, once of Inveresk, now curate to his Grace the Duke of Buccleuch.'

'Curate?' Smith queried. 'Are you an Episcopalian?'

'Of course not, my good fellow. However, my Lordship is, and though supportive of the established Church's prerogatives in Scotland, such cosmetic concessions have no effect on my vocation while smoothing the intercourse between us. It is a lesson that not only the rebels, but my fellow clergymen might do well to learn.'

The Reverend Smith excused himself. He really had to talk to Mr. Johnston of a neighbouring parish.

• • •

Outside, the head of the procession was coming to the corner of Hanover Street while its tail had still not fully exited the church.

'The incubus of Moderatism and secularity has been shaken off,' a flushed young minister whispered to his companion.'

'Aye,' replied the other, 'Truly, it has been the Exodus from Egypt.'

Many men in the crowd removed their hats and bowed their heads as the train of ministers passed. A young girl ran into the procession and kissed the hand of an aged minister then disappeared back into the multitude. Everyone there understood the importance of the event. These men were leaving everything behind, they had no homes now, no civil station. Was it the end of something or only the beginning?

Hugh had no doubt that it was the start of a Scottish religious renaissance, freed from the compromises with the British State and an opportunity to re-establish the purity of Knox's Calvinism. He was already waiting in the courtyard of a packed Tanfield Hall, reached by passing between two turrets, lending it a more imposing air than other places for civic meetings. When would Chalmers arrive?

Candlish had insisted on continuing with the business of the General Assembly to show that *they* had not left the Church, that *they* were indeed the Church of Scotland. Chalmers was more wary of outright defiance and would probably insist on a different though parallel Assembly. Hugh had already taken notes on the day's events, but as a journalist. Now he was to be the scribe of the new assembly, if it took place.

Lydia had insisted he wore his plaid over his shoulder that day. 'If you appear in a photograph, or in a sketch, let it be as my fine lad from Cromarty,' she said, smiling as she held their daughter up for him to embrace. He had worn the plaid when he first came down to Edinburgh in 1824, striding fruitlessly up and down in front of Sir Walter Scott's residence in Castle Street. Now it had almost become his uniform, though he was no shepherd nor a Highlander. But the costume becomes the man, he thought to himself, and he felt distinguished today among all the black-hatted crowd.

He walked to the gateway and could see the beginning of the long black train snaking its way towards him. He sent a boy to alert those inside and he went up to greet Chalmers and to join the march.

Chalmers gave Hugh his hand and held it for a moment then they all poured into the yard and through the open doors, onto seats and benches already laid out. Welsh uttered a solemn prayer. There was a pause.

'We must choose a new Moderator, I move...,'

As he said these words Welsh looked over to Chalmers. Everyone did and the whole Assembly rose and broke forth in enthusiastic applause.

Chalmers accepted the position of Moderator, but of what? The successor of Welsh would have been the new Moderator of the Church of Scotland. Chalmers seemed to be the Moderator of the new Church of Scotland. There was an overlapping, which some saw as deliberate. In his articles Hugh would claim that the authentic church, the church of John Knox and of the Covenanters was what, at his proposal, was called the *Free Church of Scotland*. That name was only fixed on after a few days and a variety of titles were employed by the different divines, such as *The Protesting Church of Scotland* and the *Free Protesting Church of Scotland*.

They remained in session until six pm. Hugh took note of everything and prepared his articles. There were about three thousand people in the Hall and in the surrounding courtyards, all attentive to the smallest rumour, to a hint of what those left in George Street would do, to what the Queen would say, to how the country would respond. They remained in session for over a week. On the Sabbath the preacher had to be hoisted above the shoulders of the packed crowd to the makeshift pulpit at the head of the hall. The four hundred and seventy-one protesting ministers imagined themselves thus, once they got back to their parishes.

'Man, it makes you feel like one of the Apostles, preaching the Good News in the fields to their flock,' Macpherson of Airdrie wrote to his wife. Mrs Macpherson was feeling like one of the homeless she used to pass on her way to the Parish Board. She would never forgive her mother, who had pushed her into this marriage with a steady, settled fellow. Settled!

On the second day of the Assembly, Candlish had recovered the Protest and lain it out on a table in front of Chalmers.

'Let whoever wills, sign,' he commanded.

No doubt he was thinking he was in Philadelphia at the start of the American Revolution, Chalmers thought, though he kept silence.

Hugh was there from start to finish, indefatigable in his effort not only to stand as a witness, but to be seen to do so. He accepted the primacy of Chalmers, Candlish and the rest, but where would Christianity have been without the compilers of the gospels, Mathew, Mark, Luke and John?

He would stop off at the office on his way home. Luckily, he had prepared a string of articles and essays in advance, so there was no interruption to the publication. He would arrive home around 8.30, worn out from his labours. Then around ten he would revive and sit with some porter and fish at his desk and compose. He had caught the habit of night-time composition in Cromarty and he never lost it, even when, like now, he had to be up and away from home early. He hardly saw Harriet or the baby. Mackenzie reassured him that she was well, he had taken her out for walks in the lanes. Hugh was grateful. Lydia made fun of the young man, because of what she called his 'feminine cast of affection.'

'Sometimes I believe you love him more than me!' she teased.

'He does love me, and for that I am grateful,' Hugh replied. 'Love between men is a Christian virtue, think of the Apostles and of our Saviour and the beloved John.

However, I love no one more than you, Lydia, and you are cruel to suggest otherwise, even in jest. And you spend hours in gossip with the lad when he is no spiering me about the latest movements in the Assembly and making fun of the 'American Senator' Candlish.'

But these were isolated sparks of intimacy in a round of comings and goings, of handshakes and arm-slapping in the corners of the Hall, of people raising their hats to him in the streets. Hugh was in his glory. Consulted by all, hearing his words in the mouth of respected clergymen. He discovered with surprise he was famous. And not just for his religious writings but for his scientific essays, for his geology. People from all over Scotland kept inviting him to visit 'a particularly interesting rock formation' in their part of the country. Whigs and Tories alike seemed to respect him and vindicated his insistence on keeping the newspaper free from party ties.

He glowed in the open warmth of Chalmers' appreciation. Was he wrong in detecting a certain coldness from Candlish and Cunningham? Candlish seemed concerned at the lack of attendees from positions of government or the aristocracy.

'It is all very well to count on the support of the coming men, but we need the stalwart sustenance of established forces,' Hugh overheard him muttering.

The Assembly decided that they should replicate the institutions of the Kirk they had left: its churches, schools, training centres and committees. They were boosted by the adhesion of all the Church of Scotland missionaries abroad, from the Holy Land to Africa and China. Most current theology students had adhered to their cause too, a delegation arriving, Saltire in front, the banner of both their faith and their country.

On the last evening of the Assembly Hugh had walked home. Edinburgh seemed different. From how many of its churches and civil institutions was he now barred? He shivered, then thought of John Knox and how he had turned rejection into triumph. He would do the same.

And that night, lying beside Lydia, he had flown again. The whole country was beneath him as he soared in a cloudless sky. He could see the top of Arthur's Seat as he passed over it and wasn't that Mackenzie and Willie Ross, hand in hand waving to him? Fife rolled below him and now he was over the North Sea, the waves roiling and heaving, fishing boats casting their nets and the men looking up as if he were an omen of heavy hauls. Then Cromarty and the East Church with the Reverend Stewart piling his earthly goods onto a wagon, not in a desperate, forlorn way, but with the air of Moses about to enter the Holy Land. On he flew, to the Western Isles and then down over the smoking chimneystacks of Glasgow. 'The Free Church will set the workingman free,' he yelled down at the hunched figures in the alleys.

He was free, they were all free. He was just heading back towards Edinburgh, skirting Stirling Castle and Bannockburn on his left when he felt the tugging on his trousers. He turned his head around and saw the witch, her one-toothed grin making him stare at her open maw and feeling he was being sucked into it.

He was not able to leave the house for the next three days.

'You have been working too hard again, Hugh. You must rest. You will be yourself again soon' Lydia had said.

Perhaps that was what he feared, he thought to himself. He collapsed back onto the firm mattress but could find no rest, no comfort. Finally, he sat up and felt below. There it was: the small round stone!

The Pavement Artist

Though Enric started to meet up with John Arthur once a week in the tavern, he learned no more from him about his science than he had in that first visit to his flat in Dumbiedykes. Then, as on the following occasions, the elder man had talked only of practice, of how bodies were procured, stored and dissected. Of how odd many of the students and teachers were.

'Tak Dr. Knox, a very firecracker of a man, and a genius sir, but a genius let down by his temperament. And Professor Goodsir. A very ugly man, but meticulous and an artist with a scalpel.'

He explained that Goodsir had been the first to introduce the routine use of microscopes, revealing a new world to the students and to John Arthur himself, although he preferred the snap of bone and the slicing of tissue.

'And he is a quiet body, but a Fifer, a bit sleekit. As we say here, 'it tak's a lang spoon tae sup wi' a Fifer.' They are always looking out for the best advantage for them and their ilk. He is a good man, but extremely ambitious, though most folk can't see beyond his enormous nose and a face that would stop a clock. They don't know how hard he works. He never takes holidays, and his idea of entertainment is to spend his trips to other cities in their museums! The lad will kill himself with overwork, you mark my words. But if he disnae, he will take Professor Jameson's job, or even Monro's, though that auld devil has outseen more rivals than Napoleon Bonaparte!

When Enric had tried to ask about the Aesthetic Theory of Anatomy, he quickly realised that John Arthur's grasp of it and other abstract concepts was limited. He was like the librarian in the Bibliotheque National he had visited in Paris, who identified the location of all the books and could list many of their contents but who had read few of them and understood none. However, John Arthur knew the names of other anatomists and naturalists and their theories. Lamarck, Cuvier, Lyell, and a former Edinburgh student and it seemed a very brilliant man, Charles Darwin. He hadn't published much, but Knox had a high opinion of him, it seemed. Each time, Enric left John Arthur with more questions than answers and little idea of where to find them.

How often had he been in the same predicament since he had abandoned his native Catalonia? After first wandering in the South of France he had decided against bohemia and had travelled to Germany via Vienna, spending time in Berlin. Then on to Paris where he had honed his printing skills and learned of the latest technical advances. They told him he was good at imagining how things could work and his drawing abilities meant he could often sketch a solution. His knack for mechanics was only equalled by his facility in learning foreign languages. After a few months in a place, he adopted the local tone, if not always the accent. He attributed his linguistic skills to the fact he had been brought up speaking both Catalan and Spanish, though the latter he only used in Barcelona and not at home in nearby Masnou. El Masnou, 'the new house,' he supposed that translated into in English. But there was no real translation for 'la masia,' even into Spanish, as it represented not just a house, but a unique vision of society, with its grand fireplace with seats arching out from it where grandparents, adults and children would sit, all in order. He looked around him now at the crumbling tenements in the High Street, stuffed full of compartments more than apartments, where humans lived like rabbits, no, like vermin. What vision of society was that? He had travelled enough to know that there were slums everywhere. But was not Edinburgh the seat of the Enlightenment? Had he not read of its glories in the translations of Scott he had devoured on board schooners? Now he preferred fact and pored over any journals and scientific texts he could lay his hands on. Working for a printer's gave him access few workingmen had. Besides, Chambers provided a library for their staff in their premises on Waterloo Place and it was almost his second home. He had read in a report by a Dr. Tait that 50% of the children in the Old Town died, compared with an infant mortality rate of 8% in the New Town, just ten minutes' walk away. Here, in the capital city of Scotland, part of the United Kingdom which was conquering the world in the name of a superior civilisation! He had come here, attracted by the fact Britain had been the first to abolish slavery, and to Scotland, because, like Catalonia, it was a nation without a state, on a journey of expiation and discovery. So far, very little of either.

He was so engrossed in these thoughts that at first he remained deaf to the protestations of a fellow sitting on the pavement, his back to the wall on North Bridge.

'You are scuffing my paintings! You have cut off Bonnie Prince Charlie's nose, man!'

Enric swung around to face a panting, red-faced young man, who was shaking in rage and pointing at him then swinging his arms about as if appealing to the passing multitude or some invisible deity for justice.

'That's worth threepence, no fivepence, if it's worth a penny!' he was remonstrating now and pointing down at the pavement.

Enric followed his finger and could make out five garish portraits sketched in a rainbow of colours under a sign that said, 'drawn from real life.' He spied Queen Victoria, Thomas Chalmers, William Wallace, Sir Walter Scott, and apparently, a defaced Bonnie Prince Charlie.

He must have scuffed it when he skipped sideways to let a man laden with coals pass. It was the public pavement, after all, and not his fault. He was about to pass on when he looked at the young man and caught the desperation in his eye, like that of a shipwrecked sailor. He stopped.

'Are you alright?'

The man staggered back against the wall and then sank down on his knees as if felled by a blow.

Enric hunkered down till their eyes were at the same level.

'Please don't worry about the drawing, I will pay you for the damage. But what is wrong with you, my friend?'

'I am hungry. I am hungry. Nothing to eat. Nothing to take home.'

Enric took a piece of cold sausage from his pocket. The man gobbled it down. He seemed not to care that people were looking at them, pointing at him.

'Where do you live, brother?'

'I bide in the West Port, but I canna gae hame. My wife is waiting for me to bring food or money and I havnae one nor th'ither.'

'Here, take my arm. We can stop for food on the way down.'

'Why are you doing this?'

'Because you are my brother.' Seeing the man hesitate, Enric added, 'And I like your drawings. We should all support art.'

The man nodded and allowed himself to be helped up. He leaned on Enric's arm, and they set off up towards the West Port on the far side of the Grassmarket. Enric was surprised when the fellow turned his back on his precious portraits and stumbled off without a glance back. Hunger does that to you, whether it be hunger for food, or drink, or love, he thought.

The High Street and its closes had been completely deserted by anyone who could live elsewhere. Only the church, the Council, lawyers and the army had premises there, but its fulltime denizens were the poor and the destitute. Ever smaller apartments were rented out furnished with the barest minimum or unfurnished; some were divided into dormitories occupied by different families with the sexes and ages mixed in together. Dirt reigned everywhere.

Once they had purchased some bread and eggs, they clambered up the stairway to the West Port apartment. As was normal, the steps to the first floors were made of stone and those above of wood. The homeless spent their nights on these higher ones. The artist was still leaning on Enric and their progress upstairs was slow. He nodded and opened a black door, revealing a dirty room containing a bed, a small table, a chair that had lost its back, and an upturned box. A candle stuck against the wall threw a sickly light around and streaked the wall with smoke and soot. A young girl was sitting on the box, her head in her hands, a picture of dishevelled dejection.

'George!' she wailed as they walked in, her eyes going straight to the bag of provisions in Enric's arm. 'I thought you would never come back. I thought you had abandoned me again.'

She looked up at Enric, as if she had just noticed him.

'I'll no dae nothin, no matter how hungry,' she hissed.

'No, Jane, it's not like that. This man has bought a painting and as I was a bit weak, came to help me home. We bought some food with my takings, didn't we, er...'

'My name is Enric and your husband is right. I paid for one of his paintings and as he did not seem to be well, accompanied him back here. But I will be going and leave you two alone.'

'No, no, sit down,' the artist said, pointing to the backless chair.

Enric did so and watched as the two of them tore open the parcel with the bread and the eggs. They fried four in some grease and spread them on the dry loaf in almost complete silence. He felt in the way and made moves to leave but the artist would not hear of it.

'You are my patron now. Please sit and we can talk.' George had rediscovered his voice. Even Jane nodded for him to stay. He decided he would. He wanted to learn how people lived here.

'We have been having a bad run of luck. It has been raining almost every day for the last week and my other job mending pans has not been worth it since the spinning factory at Dalkeith closed and men came to do any work at any price. At first, I didna worry as two weeks ago I earned the tidy sum of twelve shillings at my post on Lothian Road. The polis roughed me up when they moved me on and I haven't dared to go back there. My life is a hunger and a burst, some days I earn good money but then there are times when I can't find a penny. And Jane can't go out in case her family find her and take her away from me.'

Jane flushed and seemed pleased by the mention of her name.

'They didna want me to get married. But I love George, for all that he is a wayward lad. And things will get better, if we can just have a run of good luck, wont they, George?'

'Have you always been a painter?' Enric asked, surprised to see no sign of art in the dwelling.

'Ach, no. I do whatever brings money in. And the sketching is fine as long as it doesnae rain, or the polis leave you alane, or it's not winter. I can work a few days and then have time off. Be a free man.'

'George says being free is the most important thing. What do you think, sir?'

'Enric, not sir, please.'

'Was this type of liberty just freedom from responsibility?' he found himself thinking before he silently reproofed what he had learned in Paris to call his 'bourgeois morality.'

'How do other people get by here?' he asked. 'How do they live?'

'Like we all do' Jane went on. 'Struggling to pay out four shillings a week rent. If the man has steady work that is not impossible but look at Mr McFadden downstairs. He got sick and the parish would not give the family relief because of our address.'

'Your address? I am sorry I don't understand.'

'Maggie McFadden went to see the Parochial board with her three bairns. They refused to help because this building has an evil repute, and they cannot be seen to give relief to persons whom they suspect of leading an immoral life. They suggested she move to a respectable locality. But to do so she would have to pay the new landlord a month's rent in advance and if she canna pay the rent right now they are asking the impossible.'

'So how do they live?'

'Well, she goes out hawking, or charing. And does bucket-ranging. Looking for scraps in the buckets, though there is little of worth in them. She rises early in the morning and makes a raid on the ash-buckets. She can sell things she finds there for twopence or threepence. She keeps the cinders for her own fire and if she is lucky will find pieces of bread and meat to feed her family.'

'Ach, Jane, going on about it willna change anything. And Eck here doesnae want to hear your litany of troubles.'

'Oh but I do. I want to know how people live,' insisted Enric.

'What happens if someone can't pay the rent?'

'That depends on the landlord. The landlady here will be patient, but finally there is eviction. She comes in and takes away the bedclothes so people are cold in the night. They leave.'

'The exploitation of the poor. We all have a right to a dwelling.' Enric burst out.

'Are you rich that you don't know these things? You have a posh voice, well different anyway. I suppose that's posh,' Jane replied. George remained silent but seemed to be staring at Enric as if examining his clothes. Should he fear for his safety, alone in this building of ill-repute? He was comforted with the thought that he could hold both of them off with one hand.

George broke the tension.

'Wherever you are from, Eck, you saved us today and I thank you for it. But where *are* you from and what do you do?'

As he related his story once again, they all relaxed. He tried to explain that though there were differences of languages and culture, those were mostly among the middle and upper classes of each country. The working classes were basically the same, united by their exploitation. They stared at him when he used words like exploitation. Abstractions don't work in Scotland, he was learning.

'You are a Chartist, then?' George suddenly asked.

Perhaps he had been wrong.

'No, we will never get justice by asking our exploiters nicely for it. But we must organise like the Chartists, in factories and in housing like this.'

He couldn't help himself. He began to talk about his political ideas. To preach, even, he reflected afterwards. As the evening drew on, he gave Jane money to buy some more food, which they shared together.

As he was about to leave, he had an idea. Perhaps he could get George a place at the printers, even if only menial work. He knew he was liked there and had never asked a favour. George was delighted with the idea and they agreed to meet at Roxburgh Close the next morning.

Perhaps practical help to a comrade was as important as the revolution, he reflected as he climbed into bed. As he looked around at his comfortable room he thought how lucky he was. He would help George and see if he could do something for Jane.

He waited for fifteen minutes at the head of the Close the next morning. George did not appear. After work he went to the lodging on the West Port. It had been vacated. Mrs McFadden told him she had seen them both leave as she was bringing back the cinders. They hadn't said where they were going to.

Blindsided

Do we become the characters we read or write about? Hugh asked himself this as he walked the half mile or so back down to his house. Several years ago, the wealthy with homes in the New Town had taken to building country residences away from the bustling city centre on the nearby hills close to Bruntsfield and down to Canaan Lane and beyond. Unlike the New Town or even the developments in Stockbridge or in Marchmont, there was no planning, each new house built according to the whims of its rich owner. The fashion had been started by the mansion he had just visited on the crest of the hill, East Morningside House, owned by the Ferrier family. Their townhouse was in Northumberland Street, the smartest address in the city. Mr Ferrier, writer to the Signet, one of the principal clerks of the Court of Session and legal advisor to the Duke of Argyll, had cemented the family fortune at the beginning of the century. Friends and those who read any of the portraits inspired by him in his daughter's novels felt they were in the presence of a Scotsman of old, a pawky eccentric figure who was the living example of many of his friend Scott's couthiest characters. Hugh had not met him as he died in 1829, cared for by his youngest daughter, Susan. She had given up a literary career and possible husband to care for her father. Her first novel, *Marriage*, had been her most successful. Like the others it had been published anonymously, though all of Edinburgh society knew the secret. She had been feared and admired as a wit and was an assiduous attendant at the social dinners and events of the first twenty years of the century where she was courted by Sir Walter Scott and even invited to Abbotsford. Her novels were full of sharp observation and bad plotting, extremely amusing at times and sentimental at others. Many recognised the jokes and their real-life inspirations. People noted how she would withdraw from the conversation at the dinner table, dreaming of her book, observing and recording character. A critic said she recalled but did not create.

Hugh knew all this because he had done his research when Chalmers had issued his invitation to visit her with him. He couldn't help noticing how she, like him, converted people into types, then attacked them, often in three-part sentences. His style was not so original after all, he realised with a grimace.

He had been surprised by Chalmers' insistence that he accompany him on his visit to the house.

'She has joined us in abandoning the Church. Few intellectuals or people of letters have. In this lies her importance, Hugh.'

'But why do you need me to accompany you?'

Chalmers had answered that Hugh had a special way with the ladies. This was true, he admitted to himself. He conversed freely with bairns and with women. He was regularly invited to give talks to ladies' groups in many comfortable houses in Edinburgh and he felt at ease there. He had a feminine side to him, Lydia said, and that helped him win over women. He did not have as much luck with men. If they adhered to the Church of Scotland, he was seen as a renegade. The intellectuals shunned him as a zealot, not forward-thinking enough, some had told him. If they were enthusiastic Free Kirkers, his science and his lack of sectarian passion made them suspect him.

He perhaps had had some success with the women's study groups, but Miss Ferrier was an educated, polished member of the upper class. Hugh was so anxious to avoid being patronised by his social betters that he tended to exaggerate his rustic airs or fall into deep silences. They thought him a boor, a square peg. Surely, she would feel the same.

He had felt his disquiet grow when he passed between the gate pillars, entered the extensive grounds and espied the white house at the far end of the large garden, peeking through laburnum groves and bowers of honeysuckle and roses. He felt as if he was stepping back into the last century. This was not his world!

When he was admitted by the housemaid, Chalmers had not yet arrived. Hugh proposed to wait in the hall for him. The smartly-clad maid would not countenance it. 'She thinks I am going to steal the silver,' he found himself thinking as he followed her through flower-bedecked hallways into an enormous salon, full of hunting paintings and dusty portraits of landed ancestors. There were a few candles fighting the afternoon gloom and losing. Seated at the end of the salon near some French windows leading out to the garden, he saw a figure in white.

As he was led up to her his astonishment grew. Before him was a small old lady, almost completely blind, just like a character in *Marriage*, written almost thirty years ago, a Mrs. Lennox, struck sightless by grief!

He found himself wishing her a good day and following it with all the usual social pleasantries, but in a volume more appropriate to a crowded kirk than a salon. He suddenly saw himself in all the previous introductions in Edinburgh, standing tall, bowing with proudful condescension, holding his strong hand forward, and felt ridiculous. Moreover, none of this was of use in a meeting with an almost sightless person. And how blind was she? Perhaps those half-lidded eyes saw more than she seemed to acknowledge.

'Good afternoon,' she said in a voice that sounded like a violin being tuned.

He was reassured that she had heard him and was acknowledging him.

'Is Dr. Chalmers not with you?'

He felt the shadows lurking in the salon reaching up to drag him to the floor. Put in his place by 'his betters,' once again.

He was rescued from his discomfiture by the sound of plodding steps. Miss Ferrier exclaimed,

'Chalmers! Why sir, you will be late for heaven!'

'We all arrive late to heaven, my dear lady! Those of us the Lord chooses to invite are granted entry only after years of toil. But there are pleasant moments on the way, such as these visits to your beautiful house. I trust your health is not causing you too much distress, my gentle friend.'

And so they were off, the two of them. Chalmers rested his hand on Hugh's shoulder as if to include him in the conversation, as if he were just speaking for them both. Or was it to keep him from leaving?

At last the duet between Chalmers' soft clarinet and Miss Ferrier's squeaky violin seemed to be reaching its coda.

'I invited Mr Miller to accompany me as he is a man of letters, an author and a keen observer of life like your good self, madame.'

'My health and blindness make even the revision of my old writings a task that may be beyond my powers. Literature is a toy for bored youth or idle folk. Only salvation occupies my mind now.'

'Hugh is editor of *The Witness*, the organ of the Free Church.'

'Yes, and my friends Lord Aberdeen and the Duke of Buccleuch are most put out by some of that organ's diatribes against them.'

Now it was Chalmers' turn to feel uneasy. Would Hugh believe he had been brought here to be humiliated?

'But you have joined our church, madame, and must understand Hugh is defending us from attacks by the powerful. Sometimes he may be over-strident, but he is an ardent man and fearless in the defence of the truth.'

'No doubt these qualities were useful and appropriate among his fellow workingmen.'

Chalmers bowed his head and pressed his hand on Hugh's shoulder once more. They must not flee. They must not lose Miss Ferrier.

Hugh could take it no longer and was about to rise and leave when the lady began to laugh, in a sound like cutlery falling on the floor.

'Aye, forgive me, gentlemen. I am being uncharitable. It comes from sitting here on my own all day. And I have just had a visit from my sister's father-in-law, John Wilson, who filled my head with spleen about some of what he calls your Whig excesses. No doubt I will preach on the virtues of dissension to the next poor fellow to visit me. Years of listening to and regurgitating others' conversations has quite emptied me of independent thought.'

Chalmers laughed, a little too heartily, Hugh thought.

'And I meant no offense to you, Mr. Miller. Your rise from the ranks of the workingmen is worthy of admiration. I am not however, comfortable with people from outwith my class. I fear I may encounter some furibund Chartist or even worse, bore them.'

Hugh is an enemy of the Chartists and of all who do not acknowledge their betters,' Chalmers interjected.

'Well, he does not seem too comfortable with their enemies either,' she sniffed.

'I do write on other matters.' Hugh decided to make a last attempt to placate this genteel harridan.

He pulled out a piece of grey silicate from his pocket.

Chalmers started with alarm. Surely Hugh was not going to try and show a fossil to this half-blind old dame!

However, Hugh remained silent, and just slipped the wafer into her hand. She reacted to its coldness and looked at him in puzzlement when he said. 'What can you feel, madame?'

'I feel a smooth stone, well smooth except for some ridges, some irregularities.

'Imagine a scarab beetle, madame and run your fingers over it once more, please.'

She slowly did so and began to smile. At last he could see the imaginative person inside her as she turned the stone over and over in her hands as if seeking some trick entry for the beetle. She turned to stare at Hugh.

'I refuse to be treated like a blind person. But even with sight, this wonder is better perceived through touch,' she marvelled.

'What am I feeling?'

'Well, it is the fossil of a *Holoptychius* I excavated up in Cromarty. It would have come from the seabed.'

He felt the pressure of Chalmers' hand on his shoulders when he said this. He shrugged. The ladies in his lecture groups always responded with enthusiasm to his fossils and the uncomplicated way he explained them and their provenance.

'But you are really feeling *time*, Miss Ferrier. Great aeons of time.'

Now both his companions looked startled.

'This may be several million years old. You are feeling time in your hands.'

With a gesture of disgust, she thrust it back at him.

'Dr. Chalmers! Really! You have introduced one of these evolutionists into my house. This is unforgivable. The Bible, sir, the Bible!'

'We all believe in Genesis,' Chalmers replied, shaking his head at Hugh.

'We do, madame. But it is a poetic description, describing the ideal state and a day is not always twenty-four hours.'

She made as if to call her servant. Chalmers took her hand.

'This is not relativism, my lady. I too have had to wrestle with the interpretation of Genesis. I differ in some parts with Mr Miller, here, but not in his determination to face down the natural philosophers who assault belief with their atheistic science.'

'God made us scientists and we must have confidence in Him, my lady,' Hugh protested softly. 'I trust in Him and have no fear we will defeat the worst of the unbelievers and convince the others. The missionary work of the Church will be in this field as much as in the tropical jungles and far-off deserts. Geology is the battleground of the day. And fear not, my lady, we will win!'

He looked up at Chalmers and received an unconvinced 'Amen.'

Miss Ferrier put her head back and closed her eyes. She seemed to be looking in her thoughts for something.

'No doubt you are a brave man, Mr. Miller. Evidently you are a fighter. But this talk is all so strident, so full of echoes of warfare and strife. Just like the Disruption. Just like the Chartists. I miss the days of my youth when battles were for soldiers far away on the Continent. I long for the days of good old Scots society, when people respected one another and when it was not all about overcoming the next fellow in a pitiless fight.'

She struggled to her feet. Chalmers gave her his arm, waving at Hugh to stand back.

'I have some matters concerning my pew at the Kirk to discuss with Dr. Chalmers. It is not necessary to trouble you with such trifles, Mr. Miller, so allow me to wish you a good evening. Sarah will show you out.'

Hugh looked at Chalmers, but he had already turned his back and was leading Miss Ferrier towards a door in the corner.

'Good afternoon, madame. And God bless.'

Sarah was waiting to escort him out and back onto the street. She sniffed as if to say, 'We won't be seeing your like again round here.'

He walked slowly home, reflecting on the meeting and deciding that he would never again kow-tow to his 'betters.' He would simply avoid them. At least Chalmers would desist from further introductions. He would never make mention of this afternoon's meeting, except to Lydia, who, as a budding novelist, had been delighted to hear of his invitation and had conjectured all sorts of interesting meetings with the lady writer. She would be crestfallen. She had accused him before of alienating people with his pride, with his humility, with his politics, with his lack of political partisanship, with his, with his...'

He stopped and leant against a tree. He was being unfair to ascribe to his wife failings that really were his own. Just yesterday he had felt like a colossus standing on the top of Arthur's Seat, master of all he surveyed. Now he felt friendless, alone and misunderstood. He was happy enough with his own company and he had young Mackenzie as a devoted companion. When he wanted him. However, he understood that he needed allies, even now, at the height of his influence. But if the intellectuals snubbed him, if he could not manoeuvre the ins and outs of Edinburgh society and Church politics, where would he find an influential friend?

It was just then that he thought of Robert Chambers. It had been a while since they had dined together. He must go and see him!

Annals of the Disruption

Every revolution has its summer, its time of sweet sacrifice and heroic acts, its giddy moments of solidarity, often in unexpected places. We all remember the sunny days of our youth, the exhilaration of making our own way, a time when even the obstacles seemed welcome as they confirmed us in the firmness of our resolve. The Disruption was no different.

Hugh bound together those scattered days of striving in *The Witness* like a farmer does the wheatsheaves in a golden harvest. He wrote reports of his friend John Swanson preaching to his flock from a boat after being expelled from his Manse. He described in inspiring detail the open-air services in fields dotted all over Scotland, from the smooth undulating Borders to the bruised purple mountains of the North. They were the Covenanters again and all Scotland was with them. So he told them, and they were comforted.

He met with Candlish and Chalmers several times a week. The old man seemed to hold out hope that the Government would relent and also exert pressure on the Church to take back its rebels. The Tories were the party of order and tradition, he said, they could not let Scotland be fractured.

Candlish proposed an alliance with the Whigs and urged Hugh to be friendlier to them in the Paper.

'After all, their name comes from Scottish cattle drovers and the Covenanters. They are our natural allies. And you yourself have always professed to be a Whig, you even wanted the Paper to be called *The Old Whig*, if I remember correctly. Why this squeamishness now to use the power of our newspaper to call them to our side? We need help, man!'

'Yes, I am a Whig but mainly because I cannot bear to ally myself with Aberdeen and his secular politics. We must remain above party. If we appeal to the Tories, the Whigs will attack us and if we court their favours the Tories will react.'

Such plain-speaking happened only once, late at night at Candlish's residence but the same battle was fought out in more subtle terms again and again. It wore away the gleam on the bright sword of Calvinism, Hugh said to Lydia.

'Our party is Scotland; we cannot align ourselves with factions.'

He maintained this stance in article after article. The Free Kirk belonged to no party. It was the National Church and not just another Voluntary Sect like the Baptists or the Methodists. Once again, he spoke not just as a man of the people, but *as* the people.

And his arguments, his vigorous exhortations seemed to work. The circulation of *The Witness* soared. 'If Hugh Miller says so, it must be right,' was a phrase often overheard throughout the land.

Lydia was worried that this renewed burst of energy would take its usual toll on Hugh and steeled herself for the coming bout of black despair. However, it didn't happen. Hugh was flying, carried high in zephyrs of rhetoric, passion, and fervour.

'I have never seen Hugh so much himself' young James Mackenzie reassured her when she confessed her worries to him one evening while she waited for her husband to come home, worried that he would not have eaten since breakfast and was wearing himself out.

'He is so full of manly righteousness,' he added.

But what if all this passion and energy was for nothing? What if the established Church or the government strangled the new body?

The confirmation that all the students in divinity colleges had adhered to the Free Kirk as well as all the members of the Church of Scotland missions around the world, cheered them.

Hugh's next battle was against Voluntarism, and the self-support expected of the myriad of evangelical sects.

'Look at the Glassites. They broke away from The Church of Scotland and they number but a few hundred now, continually splitting into smaller and smaller sects. I believe they have even recently expelled the great Sir Michael Faraday. We cannot become an inward-looking band of fanatics. We must retain the principles of reason aided by Revelation, not purely one or the other.'

The proposal to replicate all the parish churches and schools was swiftly put into practice. Chalmers was adamant that the contributions from wealthier parishes should be spread out to avoid a church of rich and poor officers. All ministers were to receive the same stipend; all church buildings to have similar budgets.

'We must seek, wherever possible, to build the new kirks and schools in the same vicinity as the former buildings. We will not abandon our flock; *we* are the historical Kirk of Scotland!' In articles and in speeches, Hugh demanded the same rights for the new Church as the old, portraying the Church of the Moderates as the usurper of the rightful privileges of the Free Kirk.

Those who had not abandoned the established church were at first at a loss about how to react. As usual in such cases, this meant they voted to establish a committee to examine *The Protest* and to decide what to do. No report was ever issued.

'We must be steadfast, gentlemen, in the defence of our faith and the social order. These rebels will melt away like summer blooms when winter sets in.'

Hardie had called an informal meeting of ministers from the mostly rural parishes situated in the lands of the leading proprietors of Scotland, all of whom opposed the Free Church. He came with news from the nation's biggest landowner, the Duke of Buccleuch, he said.

To fill the sudden vacancies in the parishes the Church had been forced to promote many inexperienced probationers to the post of licenced ministers. A few occupied important parishes, such as young Archie Mcintosh from Bute, who had been promoted to Minister much to his own surprise. He tottered from boldness to timidity in an effort to find his place with what was left of his congregation, sometimes borrowing from the Old Testament prophets for his fierier sermons, then the following week donning the cloak of New Testament forgiveness and redemption. Last Sunday he had been Jeremiah. Now he coughed and stood up to speak.

'We cannot persecute these people. Many of them are our friends. Besides, they are well-loved by the community. And I am distantly related to John McPhail, whose parish I have assumed.'

He blushed as he finished, impressed by the cold steely glare of some of the older ministers crowded round the fireplace. He had rehearsed this intervention several times and his wife had told him she loved him when he was gentle, 'her lamb, her dove.' He blushed again at the thought of her affection.

Hardie sighed, as if pained by so much misguided feebleness, then stood up, looked round the room and in cool measured tones, addressed them all.

'We have crushed Chartism, just one of the deformed spawn of the Reform Bill. The Free Kirk is but the latest manifestation of the modern scourge of reform, of the revolt against authority, though this time on behalf of the middle-classes. Where the authority of the established Church is challenged, the State and the Monarchy are put in jeopardy. I had the honour of participating in a meeting between the Duke and Her Royal Majesty, the Queen Victoria, and I can tell you, gentlemen, she is most unhappy, most unhappy about these schismatics. They have caused her almost as much disgust as the perpetually revolting Irish!'

Sympathetic murmurings coursed round the room. He had them!

'We should try them for treason!' young McIntosh found himself exclaiming, becoming a lion at the mention of his poor slighted Queen and wondering if he could meet her too.

But the group by the fireplace still just glared.

'Well, vigorous Christianity is all very well and justly employed against the heathen,' Hardie replied. He paused, shuffling some papers while he attempted to gauge the mood of the room. Some stirrings from the older ministers seated near the fireside suggested he should still proceed with caution. He looked at his notes and at the annotations beside each man's name indicating whether they had been known to take part in any dissent against their betters. A blank sheet, except for Thomson of Balgonie, who had called off his attendance, alleging a case of the shingles.

'These men are not heathens. They are something worse. They have led true Christians away from the right path, blinded by their arrogance and the false democratisation of the age, despite all efforts by the authorities and the Church to compromise. As the prophet Jeremiah says, "Woe to the shepherds who destroy and scatter the sheep of my pasture!" declares the Lord.'

'Amens' and 'Verilys' were exchanged around the room like silver coins at an auction when men want to show they have a right to be there and are as sound as their fellows. They were all tired of being left behind, of ceding protagonism to the rebels.

Hardie paused, then emitted a mournful sigh.

'But of course, we cannot send in the troops nor try them for treason. We must be Christian and turn the other cheek.'

Silence in the room. First confuse them, then lead them way you want to. The Duke had taught him that.

Young Mcintosh did not know whether to be the dove or the lion. Others felt the same. They waited for guidance.

'We must simply maintain the status quo. The Manse is occupied by the established minister, not by a usurper. The laird is also free to decide to whom he rents his properties and to express his wish, discreetly, that no rebel be granted a home in the parish. But this must be done without fuss or remonstration. When a petition is received to use a hall for one of their services, we must not refuse it. We should simply not reply. My Lord has at least three rebel congregations literally cooling their heels while the impertinent fools wait for his answer.

When the refusal finally comes it will be winter.'

He paused and saw that several of them were scribbling down his remarks. At last he was in the position he had dreamed of for years! Respected, feared, not liked perhaps, but he cared not a whit for that. He had left behind the need for affection and human warmth years ago. Or rather it had been taken from him by his runaway wife. Oh, if she could see him now! See the man he had become!

They talked on, making up lists of ministers expelled from their homes and their current situation. How many of them could be enticed back? How many congregations could be evicted from temporary halls of worship? What social pressures could be applied? The price of rebellion must be made evident.

The cost of the Disruption was made very clear to many and Hugh shook with rage whenever he was told about it, in letters to the Paper or often through gossip passed on in a morning walk with Mackenzie.

'Did you hear about the Rev. Thomas Davidson of Dalmallie in Abertaff?'

Hugh waited, as it was unnecessary to ask James anything in order to receive an answer.

'The only accommodation he could obtain was a hut twelve feet square and six feet high and so open he had to keep the wind and the rain out by means of blankets and bedcovers. The man woke up drookit on most mornings! His wife's health could not resist, and she is not long for this world.'

'Such cruelty! Though Knox himself suffered thus and it forged the Kirk's triumph, God spare them and me from such trials.'

'And it is bad in Arbroath and other airts where the lands are in the hands of a hostile proprietor like Lord Panmure. He has chased all our ministers away. Dr. Wilson in Carmylie was obliged to reside about seven miles from his charges. He had to walk twice that distance every day just to visit the sick and attend to his flock, sometimes more on the Sabbath. His faith keeps him strong he says, but what will he do in winter?'

'Yes,' Hugh assented. 'It's all very well to attend the Sabbath services outside while the weather is good but what will happen when the cold draws in? How will the congregations stand it?'

At the anti-Disruption meeting, after they had drawn up the plans which resulted in these hardships for the ministers and their families, there was a call from the back of the room: The Reverend Atkinson of Auchterarder. A tall, splenetic-looking fellow whose gait reminded one of a lame chicken, one step forward, then a half-step. 'What about the press? It is scandalous how even *The Scotsman* has made these braggarts out to be modern-day saints. Can we not do something to discourage such misguided hagiography?'

'*The Scotsman* is a lost cause. The Ritchie family are too, how shall I say it, well, rich!' Hardie answered. They all chortled. No-one had laughed at his jokes before.

'*The Witness* was a Church paper, and it is the chief spouter of Free Kirk propaganda. Can we not do something there?'

'It is an independent newspaper and well-funded thanks to the sales from Miller's tirades against his betters.'

'Something must be done!'

'Have faith and patience, gentlemen. We will attack the false prophets, the preachers of error in the pulpit and in the press. To quote Jeremiah once again,

'*Thus saith the LORD of hosts, Hearken not unto the words of the prophets that prophesy unto you: they make you vain: they speak a vision of their own heart, and not out of the mouth of the LORD.*

Behold, I will feed them with wormwood, and make them drink the water of gall."

'Amen!'

Letter 12

Charles Darwin Among the Natives

Charles Darwin was seven years younger than Hugh, but a fellow geologist whose clear descriptions of rocks, fossils and plants no doubt sparked a feeling of proud kinship in the breast of the Cromarty man. Both were becoming known in the early 1840s to those interested in geology and natural history, though after his five-year voyage on the Beagle, Darwin had won wider applause from the scientific community. Unlike Hugh, he did not have to support his scientific work by flogging his thoughts on everything from political affairs to the price of bread in newsprint, as his father's investments allowed him to live independently.

Hugh published an article in the very first number of The Witness on Charles Darwin Among the Natives in the South Seas, noting their piety and the scientist's tender affection for them. For whatever their class or race, surely the closer men are to Nature, the closer they are to God. He imagined the toothy dusky natives abandoning their wattle huts and sitting adoringly in front of the foreign sage, offering him gifts, listening to his teachings passed on through the words of a local interpreter.

He was also inspired by the Englishman's vast collection of specimens of fossils and flora and fauna. Hugh was assembling his own, showing the God-given order of Nature and one day it would form the basis of the National collection.

Darwin's relationship to Edinburgh was less simple. He had studied medicine at the University but abandoned that degree, complaining of the dullness of the lectures. Uncharitable voices gossiped that the real reason was his distress at the surgery classes and described him flinching at the bloody dissections in the anatomy rooms. He had been similarly critical of Jameson's natural history course. It seemed the only teacher he had respect for was John Edmonstone, an assistant in the labs whom he hired for over 40 private classes in taxidermy and in the flora and fauna of his native Guiana and Latin America. Yes, John was black, the freed slave of Charles Edmonstone, who had brought him back with him to his native Scotland! He had been taught taxidermy by that man's son-in-law, the naturalist, Charles Waterton. He lived in Lothian Street just along from Goodsir and Forbes. In his classes with Darwin, the black man enthused about the tropical rain forests in South America, and it may be that inspired Darwin to explore these regions. There was something disturbing about the thought of a civilised man taking classes at the hands of a native of the colonies, even if people said Edmonstone was well-mannered and had an open deference about him which no doubt helped to explain the success of the taxidermy shop he ran on Princes Street and South St David Street for many years.

In any case, Charles Darwin abandoned Edinburgh for the lofty cosmopolitan spires of Cambridge, just as later James Clerk Maxwell did, perhaps tired of life among the natives!

"Hugh Miller"

The Shape of Things

How many times do we walk down the same road, even if it is in different cities? Skimpy little Thomas De Quincey was asking himself that question as he hurried to keep up with John Wilson. As it seemed he had been doing for decades. 'As I *have* been doing for decades,' he grimaced. 'I suppose it is a sign that we are old, asking such questions.' He wished Wilson's gait was more in consonance with a man almost sixty years old than with that of a young pony! They were literally almost at the end of the road, he realised, though many would have bet on his early demise since before he had even run away from his debtors up to Edinburgh almost twenty years ago now. And debt had also brought Professor Wilson here to take shelter in his mother's house.

With Lockhart they had written *Blackwood's Magazine*, the *Maga*, as everyone called it, and become famous on both sides of the Atlantic, Wilson under the nom de plume of Christopher North. By sheer volume of work, if nothing else, they had both become men of stature, even if De Quincey had never escaped the whiff of scandal and the pursuit of creditors which made him continually flit from one elegant secret residence to another. They had changed less than Edinburgh, though; once a convivial Georgian city below a medieval redoubt, now a grey metropolis powered by steam and finance, its centre surrounded by increasingly sooty industrial tenements and slums.

Both had lost their wives a few years ago. Wilson had retreated to his estate in Elleray in the Lake District and mainly came to Edinburgh for his philosophy lectures. He still missed Jane.

Did *he* miss Margaret? 'I suppose I do,' De Quincey thought. Although the loss of two of his sons had probably affected him more. At least he still had his daughters to look after him.

The commissions from *Blackwood's* had dried up after he had published in the rival *Tait's Magazine*. The publishing world was so parochial, so territorial! And though Tait was anything but a Tory, De Quincey felt grateful to him. He had commissioned a series of essays on his erstwhile friends, the Romantic Poets. Ah, the Romantic Poets! Nearly all gone now, or senile. Only old unforgiving Wordsworth lingering on, desperate to have the last word. But De Quincey was determined to have that. As Wordsworth would find out when he read the essay.

'Are you sure we are on the right path? Thomas, Thomas, stop daydreaming! Where are we?'

They had gone down towards Stockbridge and not up and along to Waterloo Place. It was easy to get lost in the empty New Town streets, devoid of shops and with one street mirroring the next. An eighteenth-century vision of perfection, perhaps, but as blankly impersonal as dry rationalism is apt to be.

'I thought *you* knew the way,' the small man protested. De Quincey was so used to running to escape creditors that he scarcely ever looked around himself or caught anyone's eye. He had been out of debt for almost a week and had relaxed, perhaps too much. He had only come down to this part of the New Town on his private submissions though not for several years now. His wallet could not afford it, his soul could not either. Yet suddenly he felt the dangerous sting of desire. He looked desperately at Wilson.

'I do know, but I was thinking about geometry.' Wilson gave this reply as if it were the most perfectly reasonable response. Coming from him and addressing De Quincey, it was!

'Let's sit down and take our bearings, John. Ah yes, India Street.' An intellectual conversation would calm him, slow the whirring in his brain.

'Ovals, ellipses! That's where that young chap lives. The one who is writing a paper for the Royal Society on them. He is so young a professor will have to read it for him! Geometry is the coming thing, down with the lies of algebra! You and your German philosophers no doubt agree, Thomas.'

'Yes, algebra is an abstraction, translating geometry onto another plane. It is therefore one more step away from reality.'

Wilson nodded. Encouraged, De Quincey went on,

'A line is not just a point, only in algebra does it not have breadth too. But here is the magic. Look at those neatly cut slabs on the front of this house. The line between them only exists when they are joined, yet when separate they occupy the same amount of space.'

He could tell from the older man's quizzical look that he had lost him. Better to stick to the concrete. Why would Wilson insist on talking about things he was incapable of understanding! So he just added, 'Young Maxwell's paper is based on David Ramsay Hay's work. A man good for decorating your salon but with dashed little of the philosopher in him!'

'This is the age of forms, of imposing contours on things. Some say that our ancestors had a different shape from us!' Wilson had stood up, as if lecturing to a hall. 'Instead of seeing to the heart of things we construct models. I had dinner at the Anatomy Club the other night. At least twenty of the younger fellows brought microscopes with them. It seems they can't see anything until they have reduced it to its tiniest detail. When you and I preached that the truth was in the unseen, we were talking about hope, love and liberty, not the common gut!'

'He sounds like Wordsworth, the poor chap,' De Quincey thought to himself. But he just nodded back with his practised subservience.

'What was the talk about?'

'Oh, I have to admit it was interesting. Though it was given by the ugliest fellow you ever saw in your life! And to make matters worse he asked to be introduced to me, declaring that as a student he had edited a sort of pseudo-*Maga* and that I had been a hero to he and his fellows!'

'You always end up a hero in your stories,' De Quincey thought, in silent reproof.

'What was the talk about?'

'Well, this Goodsir chap says the basis of all plant, animal and human life is the oval! The cell, he called it. He can show you these ovals with a microscope, but I am not sure that is not just a trick of the lens or that we see what we are expecting to find. Wouldn't God be a bit of a bore to make everything out of the same pattern?'

'The problem with all this design is that it robs us of individuality. We become just like pages churned out,'

'By Chambers' steam-presses!' Wilson interjected 'Come on, man, we are late. This is the age of punctuality. We must run!'

Thus it was that fifteen minutes later a tall stout man and an emaciated stick of a person collapsed on the benches in the reception room at Waterloo Place. As they attempted to catch their breath, they kept having to pull their feet in or sit back to let the flurry of comers-and-goers pass. Wilson thought back to the happy chaos of the old Blackwood's offices not one hundred yards away and almost shed a tear.

It was five minutes before Mr. Johnson appeared.

'Mr Chambers will receive you now. Pray follow me, gentlemen.'

They followed him up stairs and down corridors to a large bright room, with a leather-topped table and some low armchairs next to the window.

Chambers was nowhere to be seen! They were invited to sit down and just as they were doing so a door at the far end of the room clicked open and in walked the imposing figure of the publisher. He was studying some papers and frowning, though a smile seemed to magically appear when he peered over at them.

Both men realised they were in a different world. The world of business, of bells rung and orders carried out. Of numbers and efficiency. People had told them that Waterloo Place was the future, a business based on communicating, on putting people together and on finding and sharing information. What did philosophy and literature have to do with such commerce?

Without knowing how, they found themselves sitting side by side across the table from Chambers. He regretted that they had been held up, as it meant he did not have much time for them. But little matter, Edinburgh was small, and they had all coincided at many meetings and events.

They talked, or rather Chambers led them through several subjects: the young Queen and the influence of her German consort, the changes in paper duty and its effect on publishing, a passing reference to the troubles in the Church of Scotland, which though all Episcopalians, did not leave them untouched. Wilson wondered what he was doing there. Of course, there was much 'Professor Wilson,' or 'My thoughts exactly, Professor!,' but the conversation steered increasingly to his friend and especially to his knowledge of the German language and philosophy. Translation. His library. Could Mr De Quincey advise Mr Chambers on the current cultural scene in German lands?' 'He could!' 'Wonderful, Mr Chambers would be most grateful.'

Once Mr Johnson had magically appeared again and shown them down to the lobby, they found themselves on the street in an instant and having to step aside to let others enter.

'I feel, well, I feel…' Wilson stammered,

'Displaced!' De Quincey said.

As they walked back along good old Princes Street, they realised it had changed. Edinburgh had left them.

By now Chambers was in another meeting, one of the many he held in different rooms, sometimes simultaneously. Before him sat his Catalan employee.

'Thank you for coming to see me.' This time there was no hurry, no pushing the conversation along.

Enric waited. He knew they both understood he could not have refused his employer.

'My pleasure,' he answered.

Chambers glanced at a page of his papers then placed them on the table and rested his hands on them. He looked straight at Enric.

'I am pleased to meet you, Mr. Enric Serra i Maristany.'

Enric started. He had only used his first surname here. How did this man know about the second? He was about to deny the family name when Chambers went on.

'How long were you with that travelling circus?'

He looked at his papers again and then answered his own question.

'Two years, it seems, before you went on into Germany and then finally to Paris before coming here.'

'May I ask what makes you say all this?'

'It is all here in the report. And much more besides.'

Enric made to stand up and head for the door.

'One moment please, sir. There is nothing untoward about this and you have nothing to fear from me, though it would be well if my brother remained ignorant of this report and its contents.'

Enric sat still.

'You see? I have already entrusted you with a confidence regarding William. I would like to entrust you with more of greater import. Which is why I have to be sure of you and why I commissioned this report.'

'Is it normal in Scotland for employers to commission secret reports on their employees?'

'Well, laddie, I am sure you will have observed that we are a very advanced company. We look after our workers and offer them a range of benefits and freedoms most uncommon nowadays. We also have to be correspondingly vigilant. And more of our fellow business enterprises will follow our path.'

Enric remained silent. This information had only been presented to him in that interrogation which had impelled him to leave France. 'Keep quiet and plan your next move,' he told himself.

'Are you a Chartist, sir? An Owenite? A socialist who scorns his betters? This is what the French authorities think of you.'

This was too much!

'If I were, your remarkable report would no doubt have told you. I am a member of no organisation. I do believe that men are equal all over the world, although some have the advantage of superior education. I believe in education, that knowledge will set us all free. And I believe in seeing things for myself. That is why I am here. You can have no complaints about my work. Your presses would not be running were it not for me, sir.'

Now it was Chambers' turn to be silent. Had Enric gone too far? Was there a policeman outside waiting to arrest and deport him?

'It is true your workmates cannot recall any conspiration by you. You even seem to keep yourself apart from them. Though not because you are not a social man, as you do enjoy visits to taverns across town.'

'I am from a different culture, sir. And I enjoy my work. Perhaps I am just an observer of people. I like to know what makes people, erm...'

'Act? Do you ever think the key to understanding Man and Society may lie in something beyond them?'

'I am not religious, Sir.'

'And neither am I. There is a second confidence already. And Mr. Maristany,'

'Mr Serra, if you please.'

'Very well, Mr Serra, if you give me your word to be a loyal worker to the company and to work for me with total confidentiality, I will correspondingly keep this report to myself. If you feel unable to continue in our employ, I shall not hand it over to the authorities till three months after you leave us, so you may have time to quit the country.'

Both men drew breath and waited. From beyond the windowpanes the hum of horses and carts and street sellers insinuated itself into the deathly silence of the room.

They talked on for two or three hours. Chambers was passed a note by Johnson with a list of those waiting to see him. 'Cancel,' he wrote.

Enric was a good listener. He felt he was hearing several different people: the self-made man, proud of his achievements, the author, equally proud and ashamed of his journeyman skills, the young man come to Edinburgh and the grieving father, the philosopher and the hard-nosed businessman. But weren't we all several people? We didn't speak as such, however. Chambers changed his expression according to the role. However, beneath all the guises Enric sensed a strong, wilful personality.

'He must have broken many people to get where he is now,' he told himself.

'May I ask what you require of me, Sir?' Enric finally asked. 'And of what interest, as an outsider, I may be of to you?'

'Your condition as an outsider to my country, my class and even my culture, aligned with your obvious intelligence (the German files lay special emphasis on your 'intellektuellen Fähigkeiten') and your linguistic skills, make you exactly what I need.'

'I am not an intellectual, Sir. If you are planning some sort of European encyclopaedia, I am not your man.'

'I had a meeting this afternoon with two of the last-remaining literary savants of old Edinburgh. Windbags, the pair of them! I have consorted and curried favour with their like for decades. They do not believe me capable of a single original thought. I will continue to associate with people like De Quincey and Wilson, to invite them to expensive dinners, cultural soirees, and ask for their opinions, their recommendations. Any ideas that I may publish will be done so anonymously. People will not identify my writings, as their ideas will differ completely from the ones these Edinburgh intellectuals will boast of serving up to me.'

'I don't understand, sir.'

'You will be my source and my Mercury, Maristany. I have already amassed much literature, but my project will need some revision and continual amendment. Scottish science is mere technology. I need insights from the Continent. I can read some French and German.

You will help me with particular passages. You will search for articles for me. Articles paid for at my expense of course.'

'Why do you think I am capable of understanding such technical material.'

'Because, Captain Enric Serra i Maristany, you were the best young navigator produced by the Iberian Peninsula in the last twenty years! Your reports of your voyages included a panoply of natural, zoological and anthropological observations. At least according to the report from the Spanish authorities. And you are moved by ideas, like I am.'

'I need to think about this, Sir.'

'Very well, if you accept, come to my house in St Andrews on Saturday. Johnson will arrange your trip. If not, I will regretfully have to ask you to hand in your notice and leave the country shortly. I realise this must sound brutal, but my project and my life depend on it. Good day, Mr. Maristany.'

As Chambers swept out of the room with the report in his hand, Enric caught a glimpse of its cover. It was emblazoned with a sketch of an eye with below it a name in capitals: JAMES PINKERTON, DETECTIVE.

He thought he recognised the style of drawing.

Three Revelations

What Ho, Brother John! How goes the toil in the vineyard of learning? I trust you are at least earning enough to keep you in warmth and comfort in these months of approaching winter. For all its dark days, Edinburgh remains my sun, my beacon, thanks to my studies with you, the friends who dwell in that beautiful city and the work I still hope to do there.

I am still an invalid, and this is my third day out of bed. I fancy, during my recent visit to Ireland I caught the potato- disease, for I am sorely afflicted in the kidneys. It knocks me up for good work, and as I am in bad humour with the imperfection and delay of all I do, or rather attempt, I am not in the best condition for getting well speedily. You and I are both creatures born to endless labour and yet not to complain. Indeed, when I am staggering like the donkey I am under the publication of my notes on the Aegean trip, my contributions to the Annals of the Geological Society, my lectures and my conference speeches, my only solace and inspiration is that you are doing more, dear John.

I must publish, I must make contacts with the high and influential if I am ever to succeed Jameson.

'Succeed Jameson?' I hear you laugh. I don't know which is more pitiful: that the same man has *occupied the Chair of Natural History at Edinburgh since 1804 or that every time he gets a cough my heart wavers between concern for a decent fellow and wild dreams of succession. It is wearing to be always awaiting news of his demise. His good health is ruining my constitution! I have turned down offers of Professorships in Botany and Zoology so as not to harm my chances of the Edinburgh post. I am like a sailor whose ship has gone down, and who is floating about the sea with a frail hold on a rough plank, but dares not give it up, lest he go to the bottom.*

And now I would not only have to overcome the prejudice towards a Southerner taking the post, even though I am a Manxman and of Highland forbears, but the rivalry with the Free Church, who will no doubt want to install one of their own in the chair.

I am due to meet with Robert Chambers tomorrow. He is down to London on one of his regular jaunts. He seems to find Edinburgh provincial, even stifling, he called it. It is true that many Edinburgh men are excellent fellows out of Edinburgh, but sad masses of prejudice when at home. Chambers wants to talk to me about getting Sir David Brewster's help for a professorship at St Andrews. But you and I tried our best to snaffle one there five years or so ago and I think another go would suffer an equal fate. Yet Chambers rarely proposes something beyond his powers to achieve.

Should this succeed, I would need your good offices and delicacy to let it be discreetly known in Edinburgh that St Andrews for me would represent

a step towards, and not away from, Edinburgh.
Your friend and fellow and Brother,
Ever yours E Δ F

Goodsir had received this letter three days ago and reread it at 5 00 am every morning as he started work. He could not get the triangle out of his mind: friend, fellow, brother. Which one formed the apex? Did it matter?

He realised with a groan that it did. Forbes had many friends, they appeared at his footsteps like forest mushrooms after rain. All the members of the Society were brothers. He rejoiced in that filial feeling, but it was not enough.

And fellow? As in 'a jolly good'? Or as in my equal, my peer, my companion? Yes, he hoped that was the one.

If only Jameson would die, if only he could get the chair for Forbes, they could be real fellows, work together, teach together, publish, and live together as they had in this very flat in Lothian Street. Here he was, publishing too, taking over the Anatomy Collection, making sure he would be Monro's successor. But for what? He was admired, his family respected him. Was he loved? He looked over at the dead coals from last night's grate and thought, they are like me: burnt out, no longer needed. And he laughed at such mawkish sentimentality.

He tried to focus on his work but was distracted by the noise of the streetcleaners complaining about another wet day, by the cries of the fisherwomen come early from Newhaven, by the sounds of traffic reverberating up to the high flat. At about 8.30, he stirred and after a breakfast made up of last night's dinner, he washed and headed out onto the street. His route took him through what local folk called *The Society* after the old brewery of the same name, onto Brown Square. It had lost any claim to be a quadrangle when the George IV Bridge sliced off its western part, but its pan-tiled roofs reminded him of the East Neuk and he enjoyed walking there. He was wandering. What would he say if he met someone, a student, a colleague? They would think it strange to find him strolling about to no purpose. Perhaps he should turn back.

He tried to think of Forbes' letter without thinking of the man. Its mention of the Free Church worried him. For if even he, from a traditional Church of Scotland family had been required to stress his orthodoxy in the face of those who believed anatomic dissection was a sin, if even he had now to convince the triumphant Calvinists of his probity, what chance did a brilliant, dancing creature like Edward have?

He heard someone distantly calling his name and realised with a shock he was crying. He couldn't be seen like this! He put his head down and strode across the road leaving the Square behind him. In front stood Greyfriars Kirk. He would seek succour there. He raised an arm as if to wave goodbye to his pursuer and for the first time in months, entered the grounds. People claimed that graveyards were just specimen-farms for anatomists. What did people know about men such as he?

He walked round to the back of the church and saw the turrets of George Heriot's school glistening in the slanting sun after the morning rain. He dried his eyes, shocked at his own weakness. 'This will not do, John. This will not do.' He almost wept anew when he realised he was repeating a scolding phrase from his late father.

After ten minutes walking round the kirkyard he felt calmer, almost himself again. His friends were right when they told him he worked too hard. Some even warned him he was killing himself with overwork, that he should take a holiday from time to time. He had taken one a few months ago in Paris and had spent every day in the anatomical museum. His friends had scolded him for that, even Forbes, who had sent him a satirical sketch of a man secreting specimens in his clothes and shielding himself from the sun with technical papers while unnoticed lilies vainly attempted to attract his attention. He had torn that drawing up. What did they expect him to do: waste precious study time on sightseeing? Socialise? He already found it difficult to participate in the *The Red Lions* dinners where normally dry-as-dust scientists sang after-dinner silly songs and recited doggerel verse.

He had enjoyed this sort of thing in the student flat but noticed that at every one of these reunions he seemed to be seated farther away from Edward.

John was standing behind the church when he had the revelation. He looked up at the rather drab windows. As the first kirk to open after the Reformation, there was limited decoration and perhaps this is what made him focus on the shape of the windows. They were a standard narrow arch on a flat base. It was only when he stood back that he saw the quivering reflection of one in a puddle. It was literally fluid, breaking up at times into fragments. His eyes struggled to organise the images, to follow them properly and keep in mind the stone and glass original. And then he saw it. An image of the window with its reflection in reverse, as if joined at the base, the two apices forming its north and south. An oval, but with an internal structure, like the cell.

He closed his eyes to retain the image in his brain. Yes, he had wondered about the inner structure of the cell and about the role of its supports. Did they just hold it together or did they also serve as communicating links to other cells? Did electric life pulse through them? He must make haste back to his apartment to note this down, to think on it before his morning lecture erased the vivid image from his mind.

He was winded when he reached home after almost running up the stairs, brushing past one of the serving-boys and hurrying into his study. They knew better than to follow him there. He tried to sketch his vision of the window doubled on itself. He was a good, accurate drawer, in those days a prerequisite for a naturalist, though he normally drew from life or with the specimen under the microscope. Here he was sketching the almost invisible. 'Concentrate on the form, and not on the decorative details,' he told himself. He tried drawing an elongated oval and adjusting the shape. 'No, that was not it.' Then he started with a rhombus. Better, but no inner structures. So, no, that was not it either. He cleared more space on his desk. He placed the letter in a drawer where he kept his private papers. And then he had his second revelation. Edward's signature! Of course!

E Δ F

If you inverted the triangle and joined the two, you produced a shape which approximated his vision. The angles might need to be adjusted, but

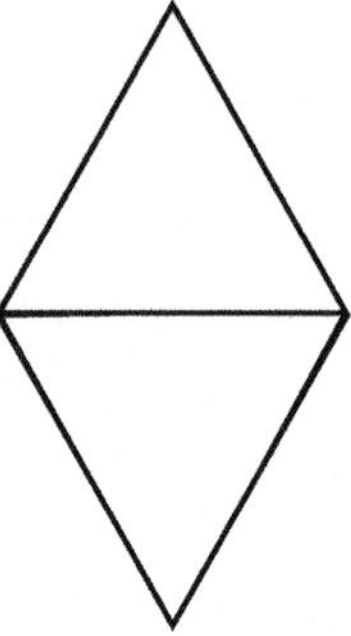

what if the cell was a type of double triangle, instead of an oval or a rhombus? One had to be cautious in interpreting the limited images provided by the microscope. He also knew that Nature repeats itself. Were there more triangles than ovals in the world around him?

A knock on his door awakened him from his dreamy speculations.

'You will be late for the lecture, sir. Ye maun run.'

He picked up a sheaf of papers and made for the door, refusing the cup of tea Mrs Maxwell was holding out to him.

He was giving a series of classes in substitution for another professor who was off sick. The man had offered him his notes, but Goodsir had characteristically made up his own course from scratch. So far it had gone well, and the student numbers had actually increased. His matter was better than his manner, he knew, and even if he could spy a few wags up at the back laughing at his long, dry declarations he could tell the class appreciated his introduction of a version of the English tutorial system, allowing them to interrupt and question him. Other professors disapproved of this as unpatriotic and requiring too much specialisation on behalf of the students and teachers alike.

'Lazy buffoons!' he called them.

As he hurried down the wet, narrow street, pushing past the

dawdlers he thought of his revelations, of his discovery. Had he found the fundamental structure of life? He must be careful; he must not make a fool of himself. But it seemed that revelation was not just for the religious zealots taking over Edinburgh. When would his next revelation come?

As he prepared to step over a large puddle on the South Bridge, he glanced down and saw a vision of his own face, revealing in a magnified form his dreadful, shameful, defining ugliness.

The Last Natural Philosopher

Enric had been to the Kingdom, and he didn't know what to do. Johnson had sent a boy to accompany him to the ferry at Newhaven. When it arrived at Pettycur the other passengers had warned him to take heed of his baggage as the place was full of vagrants. He had been pointed to a carriage which trundled along the toll road through Cupar all the way to St Andrews. When they stopped off to pick up two more passengers in the long thin seaside town of Kirkcaldy with its flax mills, he had admired the shopfronts in the High Street and been excited to spy the sailcloth manufacturers at the end of the town with the sailing boats dotting the bay sending a keening nostalgia for home into his heart.

It had taken most of the day to reach St Andrews where another carriage waited to take him to Abby Park, an imposing two-storied country villa flanked by hay fields and a market garden with some tree-lined avenues behind it leading to the University and the shore.

He was greeted by a servant who led him to his bedroom on the second floor of the imposing building. The first test passed, he thought. Not treated as an employee, but as a gentleman guest. And who would he meet here? Robert Chambers his employer, or the country squire?

'I will come back in a wee while, and take you downstairs,' the girl said, in a soft, country accent. He realised it was the first time he had been in such a large bedroom since, well, was it Cuba? A knock on the door interrupted his musings.

When he had followed the servant down the marble stairs, she led him into a room leading onto a garden terrace. Two people were waiting, Chambers and his secretary, he surmised.

'Good afternoon. I trust your journey was not too onerous. May I introduce you to my wife, Mrs. Anne Chambers.'

Could this be the mother of a dozen or so children? At the press, the lads made fun of the fecundity of Chambers, and his capacity to 'publish' children annually. And before him was the mother, no earth goddess, but a pretty, slender woman with a pale complexion and dark, smouldering eyes. She greeted him without undue warmth and announced she would go to the kitchen to order the evening meal. Was he wrong, or did she shrug her shoulders as she left them? She seemed irritated by something.

'My wife complains that I don't know how to rest. I tell her that if even the Divinity only took one day of repose, how can I do more?' As Chambers laughed, so did Enric.

Chambers stopped laughing almost as quickly as he had started and Enric could hear the harsh cry of the magpies in the trees.

'Did you come alone? Are you sure you were not followed?'

'The only time I have been followed in Scotland, I believe it was under your commission,' Enric replied. There were limits to his subservience.

'Hmmph. Very well, shall we get to work? Have you read the texts I sent to you?'

'I am already acquainted with the work of Comte and of Saint-Simone, who, I think, is the real originator of these ideas. In fact, he was one of the reasons I went to Paris.'

'What interested you in his work?'

Enric felt as if he was suddenly transported back to Paris and the smoky conversations in mirrored cafes. He had hoped to find that life in Edinburgh but had been disappointed. Now he came alive with intellectual excitement and the pleasure of being listened to.

'Well, as a boy in Spain and then travelling to the tropics I could see, no, *feel*, what Comte calls the Theological Age, and Fetishism where people rely on supernatural or religious explanations of human behaviour, And in France the Revolution and Napoleon with their focus on abstract ideals took us into the Metaphysical. We are now in the Positive, or Scientific stage where sociology will govern.'

'If you don't mind me saying so, you continentals have a dangerous predilection for abstract terms and labels. Carlyle has become quite unintelligible; by reading so much German he writes in Teutonic! Mill seems to be able to stick to plain English and I beg you to try to do the same.'

'Well, remember I am a European and English is my poorest language. But let us just say as examples that the Christian looked to the cross as the Indian his Voodoo doll in the first stage. In the second, God or Gods are replaced by abstract ideals, like liberty or justice, and in the current and final phase, science, empirical laws and rational thought must be our guidelines.'

'Can you underline the texts in French where these points are made? I can read enough of that language to grasp only their general import. Mr. Maristany, I beg your pardon, Mr Serra, do you think society is ready for science to reveal the essential laws governing us? Are we really in the third stage? If not, how can we usher in its arrival?'

They had talked on for two hours or more, ignoring repeated calls then supplications from Mrs. Chambers to desist and have their supper.

The next day the maid came to wake him early, saying that the Master wished to breakfast alone with him. Once Enric dressed he found Chambers walking up and down in front of the empty fireplace. He gestured for Enric to take a seat and they both attacked the food in silence.

'What more can he want of me?' Enric asked himself.

'I have ordered a carriage to take you to Largo. There is a ferry from there to Newhaven and it will save you miles on bumpy roads. No one must know you have been here. If they ask where you were on Saturday just tell them you had to collect some parts.'

'So you want me never to retrace my steps when I come here. Very well. You seem to have experience with spy craft. Is that what I am, your scientific spy?'

Chambers blushed and waved his arm as if to sweep the accusation away. Enric went on,

'Excuse me, why all the mystery? Our discussion last night might bore or baffle people, but I see nothing scandalous in it.'

'I am afraid this is not Paris, sir. I have made my fortune by appealing to the desire for social promotion and respectability of the new educated classes. Respectability is the keyword, the fetish, as you might term it. The recent events in Scotland, with the rise of the radical Calvinists has made matters worse.'

'We have the same problem with the Catholic Church in much of Europe.'

'Ah, no. Fortunately it has not come to that here. Of course, many of them would return to the days of banishing music and destroying images, but they are not the real problem. The threat is from the well-intentioned, even politically wise, in my view at least, sir. They are taking control of the universities, town councils and public institutions like ivy slowly strangling the tree that gives it sustenance.'

'I have noticed a certain lack of interest in the arts here, but it is unfair to compare everything to Paris.'

'I am old enough to remember a different Scotland, a different Edinburgh, one more open to ideas. I was an ardent phrenologist as a young man, and I still retain respect for Combe and for much of his teachings. He could put forward his ideas and still be received in polite society by those who disagreed with him. We were open to Europe and to new perspectives. These new men are turning towards America where an idea is only discovered every decade or so while they are looking for gold!'

Enric sensed more than frustration in Chamber's speech. He was getting something off his chest, he thought they called it.

'To make matters worse, the Free Church of Scotland is a democratic organisation, even more so than the established church and that may increase the problem.'

Now it was Chambers' turn to pause, alerted by the frown on Enric's face.

'No, sir. Don't worry, I am not attacking your political beliefs. The problem of the democratic nature of the Kirk, especially this new, energetic version, is that they all have the same rights to speak, to be listened to. They elect the leader every year and now the Free Kirk has given power to local parishes. Chalmers may be able to sway them thanks to his considerable moral and intellectual authority, but he will not be with us much longer. What the minister in Bute says, may be contradicted by the Reverend from Auchtermuchty. And this chaos is being dealt with by a rush towards ever-more radicalism.'

'Are you sure you have not read Comte? In any case, I can tell you that government by the Holy See is not a solution that foments ideas, and it produces a similarly stifling control of thought.'

'I am a member of the Episcopalian Church, which seems a good compromise to me, but I fear its social censure too. And an even greater danger than blind rejection is the subversion of new ideas into a palatable, but false form. We are about to face the greatest debate since Galileo, sir. And I fear the ignorant less than the academics and gentlemen *scientists,* as they have taken to call themselves. We are no longer natural philosophers, it seems. We no longer have to concern ourselves with nature as a whole, only tiny bits of her. Perhaps I am the last natural philosopher!'

'Well, perhaps as our knowledge increases, things become more complicated and we need to focus our energy on what we can take in or understand.'

'No doubt Comte and his like would agree with you. I think it is a dangerous wager: we may give up more than we win. One day these scientists will live locked up in their laboratories and forget nature and any ideas that cannot be weighed and measured. A new high priesthood who dress their defence of their privileges by attacks on any minor flaw in an argument. They control the journals and the magazines. I have some experience in the field, so take my word for it.'

A bitter smile cut across his face as he said this. He stood up and went over to a bookcase in the corner of the room. It was replete with his own publications and a section on Geology. He picked up a slim, red-covered volume and placed it on the table in front of Enric.

Enric picked it up. *The Old Red Sandstone.* He looked up at Chambers.

'Here is the front line in the battle that is about to engulf us. Geology, sir. If I may say so, a field where the United Kingdom, and particularly Scotland, leaves Europe, with the exception of Agassiz, trailing. This book was written by a good man, a pioneer in many ways, an amateur in the best sense. But its argument is retrograde and its success amongst the public will make my endeavours more difficult.'

'Are you proposing some kind of censorship, proposing an attack?'

'Not at all. I am a democrat of the republic of letters, Enric. I have profound respect for the life and efforts of the author, a Mr. Hugh Miller, whose path in life has mirrored my own in many ways. I published him and will publish him in the future, no doubt. If I am to overcome such arguments, it will be thanks to my own merits and not to any of the underhand strategies I accuse others of employing. But you can see why I am seeking your help in rounding out my arguments, in seeking out evidence in other publications.'

'You are proposing some collaboration in writing a book?'

'No, sir. I have already done most of the work. I do not even require that you read it. Indeed, I would rather it was a secret even from you. Your role will be other. Yes, I suppose you can be my scientific spy. Without opening my book, perhaps you can serve me better by protecting the secret and sheltering me from persecution. If our conversation last night has persuaded you of the rectitude of my motives and that I am worthy of protection.'

'I know what it is to be persecuted for my thoughts.'

'Because you sympathise with the Socialists?'

'No, not for their content, not for the thoughts, but the thinking. In Spain, thinking is almost a capital offence.'

'You told me you believe in knowledge. I do too. What protected me from despair as a boy were six volumes of the *Encyclopaedia Britannica* I found in a box. I have always believed in the saving power of knowledge. It helped me overcome my, my debility.'

As he said this, Chambers held out his hand with a nod for Enric to examine it. He noticed that there was a scar beside one of the fingers.

'Have you not remarked the strangeness of my walk, my irregular gait?'

Enric realised that he had. But many men hobbled a little. He had given it no importance. What else had he missed?

'My brother William and I were both born with six fingers on each hand and six toes on each foot. My parents decided to spare us shame by having the extra digits extirpated. William's operations were completely successful, mine left traces. And not just on my body. I used to feel as if I were not a wholly developed human; other times that mankind was lagging behind me in its development. Both ideas are of course ridiculous, but they stir in me still from time to time. Comte says the scientific age is one of observation. You need to open your eyes my young fellow and not just to read books or make drawings of machines.'

When Enric frowned, Chambers reached across and patted his arm. 'Excuse me, Sir, I forget I am talking to a naval officer, sometimes. I did not mean to offend you. I could not sleep last night thinking about our conversation. It has decided me to test whether, as Comte says, we are in the Age of Science. I am going to publish a scientific book explaining the laws behind the Universe and all Life. What do you think of that?'

'I think you are a brave man, if what you have told me about respectable society is true.'

'Well, I have decided to publish it anonymously. I am brave up to a point, sir.'

Suddenly Enric felt Chambers grip his arm.

'Can I trust you, sir? In the name of science, of knowledge and the laws, can I trust you?'

'Trust me to do what?'

'To translate, to discuss, to deliver documents for me and above all, to go to your grave with the secret.'

'To go to my grave. Is the enterprise a military one, sir?'

'Not at all, but this secret must not be told till I am cold and in the ground. The hardest thing in life is to keep a secret for more than a few years. Believe me, I know this to my cost.'

'I will have to think about this, Mr. Chambers. And if I refuse?'

'Oh, your papers are safe with me. We have gone beyond such petty blackmail I trust. Should you refuse, I will ask you to leave my service in six months or so, and I will pay your passage over to the Continent and supply you with references. But science, Enric. Science!'

And with that they had said goodbye. Chambers had handed Enric several banknotes and some papers to peruse during the journey. And the book. But as he travelled home through the winding lanes of the East Neuk of Fife, he could not concentrate. What was he being asked to bind himself to? Some type of conspiracy?

He had forgotten these concerns when the ferry took him out into the wide Forth estuary and he could watch the birds swoop and wheel and feel the swell of the waters below him. Perhaps the sea was where he belonged. If he belonged anywhere.

By the time he arrived at his lodgings he was tired and ready for a nap, a 'migdiada,' as they called it at home. At home? Did he have a home? He had left the Kingdom in more ways than one.

He was awakened by a rapping at his door.

'Will you be coming doon for your tea?'

He smiled. Maggie was a little pest, but it was good to be welcomed back to a normal life of rough bread and boiled bacon. He would eat and then read.

Runaway Trains

Candlish had proposed to visit him, but Chalmers decided it was more advisable to meet at the Reverend's abode. That way he was in control of how long the meeting lasted. An old trick perhaps, but often necessary with that irascible man. Yes, Candlish was intelligent, indefatigable and a powerful preacher with a strong intellect. Why did Chalmers find him so irritating, even unpleasant? He thought about this as the carriage plodded on up the High Street through the morning traffic, the coachman hurling most unchristian insults at all around him. He really must talk to young Tam, remind him that even as a distant relative from Fife he had to remain within the limits of respectable comportment. God save us from relations in need. So why did he feel uncomfortable with such an impressive man as Candlish, someone no doubt who would take over his leadership? No, no, there was no jealousy there. What, then?

The coach wheeled round and onto the North Bridge at a dangerous pace. More shouts. Chalmers shuddered then looked down to the East and spied the tall chimney stacks between him and the sea belching out smoke, proclaiming their power and reminding everyone where the wealth of Edinburgh increasingly came from. They reminded him of Candlish. Perhaps it was just the suggestion of candle in his name! He laughed, despite himself. Most unchristian of him, most unchristian. However, these stacks and their factories made him uneasy in the same way that his colleague did. And now he realised what it was: modernity! Candlish made him feel like a relic of a more gentlemanly time, a depository of old, outdated knowledge.

What did he know of America? How much of modern commerce did he really understand? Candlish moved in the modern world. He was the man of the decade, a hustling, bustling time of newspapers and parliamentary influence.

The carriage jerked to a halt and Chalmers clambered out before the coachman could get down. He rushed up the stairs to ring the doorbell himself, hoping to escape the clumsy attentions of the Fife ploughboy. Tam was not to be outdone, however. His auntie Nessie had told him aye to tak tent of the Reverend Chalmers. He jumped down and picked up the black hat rolling on the pavement. 'Reverend!'

Chalmers turned around just as the door swung open, presenting his back to the maid and glaring at Tam. He grabbed his bonnet, about-faced, then hurried into the dark entrance, almost pushing the maid out of the way.

'I will wait for you, Reverend.'

Tam was good at saying unnecessary things.

The maid glared at him at first and indicated the post further down the street for stationing the horses. Tam bowed. She laughed and shook her head.

'You're a bonnie lassie!' he cried after her. Was he wrong, or had the door paused in its closing?

Such frivolity rarely passed the porch of Candlish's residence. Chalmers walked down the dark corridor, past the open Bible on the table and entered the salon. Light streamed into the dark wood-lined room, an optimistic reminder of the banished day. He sat down. No doubt the maid would announce his arrival to her master.

Candlish was upstairs deciding on his attire for a dinner that evening. Tonight, there would be a mix of academia and lawyers. So, sober, professional, academic even. However, his message was success, so his best-tailored outfit. He looked through the wardrobe and laid a new suit on the bed. That would do.

He heard Chalmers come into the hall. That swish of his coat, the cough that generally accompanied him these days. He would take his time. He would make Chalmers wait, he told himself. An old trick perhaps, but it did help increase his authority and show who was in charge of the meeting. When the breathless maid knocked at his door, he said, 'Five minutes, Mary' and sat down on the bed again. He fingered his suit, glorying in the fine cloth. Was that a sin? Sin was everywhere, he reminded himself. Sin and greed and insanity. How could he make Chalmers see that, see what needed to be done?

He descended the stairs, letting his deliberate step echo softly. 'Keep calm,' he whispered to himself. 'Do not be extreme. Be reasonable.'

He touched the open Bible and kissed his fingers before entering the salon.

Was the old man sleeping? He was hunched in his chair and did not react when Candlish entered the room.

'Good morning, sir.'

No reaction.

'Trains, sir. The trains will topple our new project.' The old man looked up at him with large empty eyes. In a flash the real Chalmers appeared. Attentive, wary, incisive.

'I am sorry, I tend to doze off sometimes. When I am comfortable.'

He stood up and extended his hand to Candlish.

'Was he really asleep?' Candlish asked himself.

'I received your note last night and have come as soon as my duties permitted. I may not be able to stay long, however.'

That old ruse again!

'I trust this meeting will not take long, Dr. Chalmers. Things have become so serious that clarity has imposed itself.'

He walked over to his desk and picked up a file of newspaper cuttings and handed them to Chalmers, who looked at him with his wide, round eyes.'

'These are from *The Witness*. I have read them before. What is their importance?'

'They are testimony to a dangerous obsession.'

'An obsession with what, exactly?'

'Railway carriages. Railway carriages, sir. The railways. And progress. And commerce. And good sense. The man has gone mad!'

'Please explain yourself. And try to keep calm, my good friend.'

'I will demonstrate that what might be seen as an understandable defence of the holiness of the Sabbath is really nothing of the sort, but an irrational prejudice against modern life that is but one example of the blind fanatism which has taken over our newspaper and threatens our sacred cause.'

'Well, Miller can be a bit strident in his tone, but his arguments are our cause.'

'I can be fairly abrasive myself, Dr. Chalmers. Enthusiasm for the Lord can make us all lose measure occasionally. But I have the discipline of my ministry, the care of my flock, to chasten and guide me. This man has only his own pride to tell him what is right.'

'Please moderate your language, sir. We have all experienced the warmth of Mr. Miller's ire. But you promoted him several years ago in part for his enthusiasm.'

'Yes, yes. And of course, I am not going to attempt to portray him as a hopeless case. Nevertheless, he must submit to control. Though I fear his temperament is beyond curbing, as I want to show you today.'

'Proceed with your case.'

'Here is one of the first numbers of *The Witness*, congratulating a west of Scotland railway for not running on Sunday. He describes the railway as a 'tool of unbelief.'

'Inasmuch as the railway facilitates the non-observance of the Sabbath, he has a point.'

'A point, yes. But he returns to it time and again, and his diatribe of a few months ago, just when we were about to break from the Established Church, borders on delirium and makes us look like Luddites. It is an apocalyptic nightmare vision of the country once trains are allowed to run on Sundays. He speaks of Edinburgh as a desert, and '*of the shouts of maddened multitudes engaged in frightful warfare; of the cries of famishing women and children; of streets and lanes flooded with blood; of raging flames enwrapping whole villages in terrible ruin; of the flashing of arms, and the roaring of artillery.* Even the prophet Jeremiah is more restrained than this!

And it increases in delirium. Listen to this passage, typical of it all.'

'*There was an open space in front, where the shattered fragments of the engine lay scattered; and here the rails had been torn up by violence, and there stretched across, breast-high, a rudely piled rampart of stone. A human skeleton lay atop, whitened by the winds; there was a broken pike beside it; and, stuck fast in the naked skull, which had rolled to the bottom of the rampart, the rusty fragment of a sword.*'

And here,'

But Chalmers stopped him before he could go on.

'I have already talked to him about this piece. I pointed out that it was exactly the wrong moment to attack the railways when we were in such dire need of their financial support. He promised to restrain himself and I have not encountered any real objections among the public.'

'From the public, perhaps not. But I have intelligence from a more dangerous quarter.'

Candlish picked up a yellow sheet of paper embossed with a coat of arms. He passed it to Chalmers, who mouthed the words as he read it, like a sergeant receiving orders from a general.

'So the Duke of Buccleuch says we are not only at war with him over theology, but also over politics, the rights to property and the respect for commerce.'

'Yes, and he is not alone. Here is a veritable tirade from the legal representative of the Duke of Sutherland about Miller's latest piece of rabble-rousing on what he calls the Clearances: *Sutherland As It Was And Is, Or How A Country May Be Ruined.* He quotes several pieces from *The Witness* article, all of which he declares are defamatory and alleges that Miller's spleen is directed at the Duke because of his refusal to allow the construction of new kirks. And he notes that there have been no other publications in any other journal about the agricultural reforms his Lordship has had to carry out. Another example of the *The Witness* newspaper's and the Free Kirk's vindictiveness, he says.'

'This presumes that the great landowners are against us out of a feeling of hurt at our vulgar criticisms, rather than accept they are in the pocket of the Moderates. And Miller's controversies attract new readers who may become converts to our cause.' Chalmers looked away when he said this as if clinging to already rehearsed phrases rather than elucidating an opinion.

'He is making *The Witness* a byword for fanaticism and for outrageous attacks on the great and the good.'

'At least he attacks politicians on all sides.'

'And therefore offends them all. What good does that do us? Lord Aberdeen is still smarting from his satire and half the Whigs too. He will smash us on the rocks of his uncontrolled righteousness.'

Chalmers could not help himself. He stood up as if to make for the door. Yet for once he was not irritated with Candlish but with the situation and with his own role. He had been excited by the thought of harnessing the brute force of Hugh's intellect to the Kirk's cause. And Miller had been loyal to him. He suspected Candlish of promoting his own schemes, his own causes. Perhaps Miller had refused to cooperate. However, it was undeniable that the man's invective had angered, indeed hurt, many decent people. Chalmers thought suddenly of the bull terrier he had had while teaching at St Andrews. Loyal, fearless, so fearless and aggressive that he had had to have it put down. He would strive not to do the same with Miller. But what were they to do with him? He sat down once more.

'So you are proposing we terminate his contract, release him from his responsibilities as editor of *The Witness*?'

Candlish surprised him with his answer. 'No, we cannot do that. A schism in the Free Kirk of such dimensions would only give succour to our opponents who see us as just another fractious sect.'

Chalmers nodded.

'And' Candlish went on, 'he could do us more harm outside than in.'

'He also owns shares in the business now. It might be a difficult business to remove him from his post.'

Candlish stood up and stretched like an athlete getting ready for a race.

'What if we just promote him?'

'Would that not make matters worse?'

'Not if we put him in charge of a team of dependable men who can take some of the work off his already tired shoulders. Men we can trust. And you and I can offer to write some editorial comments, as guests.'

'I doubt he would accept that, but we may try.'

'We might also consider a closer alliance with our Glasgow publication, *The Guardian*. It has a more restrained tone and quite as big a circulation.'

'You are a west-coast man, Dr. Candlish. I am from the East. Edinburgh is the Capital, and it would see the takeover as an affront.'

'Unless it were from London. But let us not squabble over such trifles. He might accept if we appointed him joint editor of the two publications.'

'If he does, I would hate to be in the other editor's shoes.'

'I have talked to the man about it and assured him of our support in any dispute.'

There was silence in the room, broken only by the clattering of hooves on the street. Candlish went on.

'We might go a step further and unite all our Presbyterian publications by including *The Northern Warder*. Its editor, McCosh, is a very forceful man. He has indicated his willingness to come to Edinburgh and to work in conjunction with Miller.'

'One more forceful man! Is the multitude of strong, independent characters not the source of our problems here? Whatever happened to Christian meekness? This is a matter for the committee. It is also one that needs careful consideration. Hugh is a powder keg; we must take care not to cause an explosion.'

Chalmers made again as if to rise, but he felt weary. He remained slumped in his chair. Candlish was draining the energy from him and seemed electric in his vigour as he stood up and opened his arms.

'I agree. But we must do something to mollify their Lordships, or the government will harass us with new legislation. May I at least indicate to them in confidence that their calls have been heeded?'

'What are you up to?' Chalmers thought, as he pulled his jacket about him and almost spat at his companion.

'One thing is to be politic; another is to be a politician. As long as you remain the former, Candlish, I agree to vouchsafe such contacts. And now I really must be going. Talk to our fellow elders in private and we shall discuss this further. Do you have someone in mind to form part of an enlarged staff in Edinburgh?'

'No, sir. I would not dream of going so far before talking with you. Let me escort you to your carriage.'

Candlish walked to the door and saw the maid standing by the front window in the hall.

'Mary, alert the coachman. Dr. Chalmers is about to depart.'

When the girl opened the door, they heard a sound like a concertina falling, a mixture of neighing and wheels rattling. They hurried out onto the street in time to see Tam chasing the carriage down the road, uttering all manner of oaths and imprecations. He had spent the whole time trying to get a keek of Mary through the window and had but loosely attached the horses to the post. A passing stray dog had done the rest.

'You may take my carriage, though it is a simple affair. Mary, call David.'

Chalmers accepted with good grace, though realised he would have to invent a scheduled appointment for the new driver. He insisted on not occupying the good Dr. Candlish's time further.

Unleashed, Candlish almost skipped upstairs to a study he used for personal affairs. It took him only a few minutes to finish the missive and hand it to a boy he used for such messages.

There was no sign of Chalmers or his carriage when he descended.

'Peter, please take this note to the Reverend Hardie's residence at this address. Confirm to me that he has received it. Now, make haste, laddie.'

Letter 13

The Herring

We changed the shape of your country. You follow us from our early spawning grounds in the Hebrides, over to Shetland, down the east coast as far as East Anglia like pirates in search of hidden treasure. Your King James VI thought to make use of our displacements to civilise some of the wilder parts of his kingdom and encouraged Fife fisherfolk to establish a colony on the Isle of Lewis. But the Islanders would have none of that and Jamie abandoned the project, perhaps distracted by the prospect of his move to England. Better luck was met by a similar attempt in Cromarty, as can be gauged by the Lowland surnames there and the strict lack of Gaelic, as well as the Whig allegiance of the area contrasting with the traditional Tory tendencies of its Highland neighbours.

I am sure such historical sweep is not something you expect from a fish. I am surprised myself and until this moment, I didn't know I possessed such a gift. I am normally just swept along by the tide. I suppose we all know things in a collective way that we don't know as individuals and that is especially true of fish. So just take these remarks as coming from the school of herring.

You first transported us to Ireland and the West Indian plantations to maintain the dependent and enslaved creatures alive, but later we became a prized delicacy in Germany, Eastern Europe and Russia. The British government gave bounties on herring sold abroad and once the railroad network was extended, we could be sold around Britain easily. Thanks to us the Scottish fishing industry became the biggest in the world, with around 30,000 vessels.

Because we are so rich in fat, once caught, we need to be used or cured and packed quickly, otherwise we rot in just a day.

Teams of lassies gut and sort us into baskets or small barrels. Many teams travelled all around the British coast and many a lassie never returned to her old home. We were not the only harvest! Each team consists of three women, two gutters and one packer. The packer is in charge and a curer engages a team for each boat. Packing in salt is the only way to preserve us for our long journeys. I have only heard of this from some escapees, but it seems the lassies gut the fish in one stroke of the knife, often able to clean out one per second. There is no one like the 19th century Scot for evisceration. You emptied the small farms in the Lowlands and then in the Highlands surgically removed your own people. Why should I be surprised you did it to us?

It seems we are more vulnerable at night and that is when the killing boats hunted us as we rose to the surface to catch a glimpse of the yellow moon. The ships would return to port, their timbers groaning with their catch at around 5am. The crew would sell their catch, get their money and go to the pub. In Wick there were around 40 licenced establishments and more than 800 gallons of nearly 70% proof whisky- roughly 5,000 bottles, were consumed every week. Perhaps they have consciences after all.

Some thought it was just brutishness brought on by the life of a fisherman, spending all day sleeping then gathering bait and cleaning his tackle. Starting up with his own gear at 17 and married by 20 to a younger woman, with no education and no routine labour in the off seasons. And during their hunt for us the men spend only two nights a week in beds and the rest perched on the ships' benches, sleeping 'neath a sodden sail and jumping up at short intervals at the sound of a buoy popping or a cry from a nearby ship. The Highlanders among them would sing laments for their abandoned lands which the evening breeze wafted over the rolling waters.

And how we made those waters roll and churn as we rose

in our millions, leaping a few inches into the air, then sinking with a hollow plumping noise, the twinkling of our skins making the water seem like a blue robe sprinkled with silver. When the heavens were glowing with stars and the smooth sea appeared a second sky as bright and starry as the other, save that all its stars appeared comets, the lack of a line of division at the horizon could make a man imagine himself in the centre of space, far removed from the earth and every other world, the solitary inhabitant of a planetary fragment.

That last bit comes from Letters on the Herring Fishing in the Moray Firth by Mr Hugh Miller. It was his first publication, and, if you pardon my biased pride, his best. For the first time he presents himself as a man of the people, even embarking on a boat, and for the first time he employed the letter format which would give him fame a decade later and which many say is his most natural vehicle. You must admit that piece about 'an inhabitant of a planetary fragment' is very fine.

He was also one of the few to remark that 'the natural heat of the herring is scarcely less than that of quadrupeds or birds; that when alive its sides are shaded by a beautiful crimson colour which it loses when dead; and that when newly brought out of the water, it utters a sharp faint cry somewhat resembling that of a mouse.' I have heard of how much your nation revers the fears and feelings of a mouse. Would that you held the sentiments of a fish in equal regard!

But no, no, even a herring is not so foolish. However, one day we will disappear and leave your fisher lassies without a home and your coastal towns without trade. No doubt the lairds will prefer this, there is a fish they deem nobler which will bring them the commerce they can profit more from along with stalking of the deer. Remember us then and how you fished us both to exhaustion!

"Hugh Miller"

Damned for a Well-Turned Ankle

He would be damned for a dainty foot and a well-turned ankle. Josep had been the first of many to tell him that as he followed his eye glancing at a foot, naked or shod, under a long dress or glimpses of the young girls playing on the beach. He remembered that time he had seen her after bathing, had watched almost breathless, as she dried her feet with the soft white towel, then applied oil to them. She had looked up at him and he had remembered his friend Josep laughing at him as boys in El Masnou.

He looked at Alia now as she ascended the stairs and thought of her perfect feet, of her delicate step and he started to dream. Where was she going? What was she thinking about? Did she even remember his name?

He had spent the afternoon reading in the bay of the window looking out onto the wide cobbled street and the gated gardens. He had dozed a little and was awoken by the chatter of the seamstresses as they went out on their Sunday visits to friends working in domestic service or family in similar situations. At least, that was where they all said they were going. And unlike most working girls or servants, here they had no need to lie. There was no pressure to attend church or take part in the many religious meetings which took place in Edinburgh on the Sabbath.

Maggie had served him his food and had pestered him at first until he told her that he needed to finish this book and give it back to its owner, and shouldn't she be playing with her friends?

She said she had no friends, well, no real friends, anyway. The seamstresses thought she was too young to share in their conversation and her uncle and aunt were always busy. It had been good of them to take her in when her mother died, but she missed Fife. Did he know Fife? It was the bonniest part of Scotland, she was sure.

He had been lucky to find this lodging. More than lucky, though he seemed to have a knack of finding interesting places to stay in the different cities he had travelled through: the basement flat on Unter Den Linden in Berlin, the top floor attic in the La Rue Sophie Germain in the 14th Arrondissement in Paris. He had encountered this Scottish house by mistake, though, reading the address wrongly. His boss, Mr. Turner, at the printers had sent him there and told him it was a smart, clean place, better than the normal lodgings for skilled labourers like him. He had stayed there once himself, he said, and Enric had only to mention his name and he would be welcomed. When a small portly gentleman had answered the door and assured him that there was no room for rent here, Enric had insisted there was, that he had been sent here and that he was willing to pay above the normal rate. That he had excellent references and good employment at Chambers.'

'Mr John Turner.'

Silence

'MR JOHN TURNER'

The man, who he later learned was called Alec, appeared flabbergasted by the certainty in Enric's tone. However, he had not budged.

Were they turning him away because he was a foreigner? He told the man that perhaps his English was not clear, that he was a foreigner but come to work in Scotland, he needed a decent place to stay, that....

And then there had been those steps on the stairs, those black-clad feet and a command to give him the spare room in the attic for a week's trial as perhaps they could do with another man about the place.

And so here he was living on the edge of the New Town in a house full of women. The long corridor on the ground floor led onto different rooms where the women cut and sewed what seemed to be mainly shirts. Their quarters were in the basement, with a separate entrance. He liked to listen to the girls singing as they worked. He could barely understand the words but that just let him imagine the tales of love and gallantry they must be telling. There was a room at the front where Alec's wife received customers, measured them and delivered the garments.

At the end of the corridor there was a room to which only the Mistress and Alec's wife had access. He had been warned not to approach it and told it was kept locked anyway. On the first floor Alec and his family lived, the next was for the Mistress. Then an attic with several rooms where he had his place. He thought that sometimes he could glimpse the top of the castle from there, but other times not. How was that possible?

'Do me a drawing, please, do me a drawing.'

She was standing in front of him with a scrap of wrapping paper and a pencil.

'Will you leave me alone to read if I do?'

'Aye, though I dinna ken why you would want to spend all day with your nose in a book when folk are up and about in Edinburgh. There is a ball on tonight they say. Mr Mutch John was here yesterday, and some of the lassies told me they were going. Well, they didna tell me but I heard them whispering. The Mistress chased old Mutch out the door though and said we didna need his hats and to be off and to no come back again. The Mistress has a temper, so she has. And...'

'What would you like me to draw?'

'That apple over there. I love apples. Do you like apples?'

'You will have to keep quiet when I draw.'

She nodded and he could see her biting her lip in an intense effort to remain silent. Maggie was one of those children of indeterminate age who alternate statements of surprising acuteness with the babblings of a young child. He had heard that her parents had broken up, the father had left, and the mother was too grief-stricken to cope. So she had been invited to stay. Some of the seamstresses had been taken in to rescue them from some personal disgrace it seemed. Was this a home for abandoned souls? Like himself, he winced. No, it wasn't like that, he paid a good rent and the girls worked hard, this was certainly not a charitable institution.

Alec and Nell, Mr and Mrs Baillie, ran the household and the business. It seemed to do well and had clients from among the cream of professional society. Although Alec had explained to him one night that there were ups and downs and lately they were in a bit of a trough. Perhaps that was why they had taken him in.

He drew the apple quickly enough and decided to give the girl a surprise by drawing her as she stood there in concentrated silence. Mm, he was the one concentrating painfully now; he could do machine parts, plants and even some animals but there was a stiffness in his portrait sketches which baffled him and left him frustrated.

She remained silent when he handed her the drawing. Was she disappointed? Angry? He tried to cheer her up by making the pencil disappear and finding it behind her ear. She shook her head, took the drawing and disappeared along the corridor. What a strange girl!

He thought about the book he was reading. He had been surprised to be informed in the **Preface** that a portion of Chapter 1 had first appeared in *Chambers' Edinburgh Journal*. Perhaps the relationship between Robert Chambers and Miller was closer than he realised. Enric had enjoyed the clear direct style of the text: it was like reading a letter addressed to you by a learned friend. He was surprised too at the interweaving of biographical details with geological observations. So far, he had learned as much about the writer as about his subject, especially in the first chapter. He was struck too that in writing about life and its appearance through time, Miller talked a lot about death, about mass extinctions and the fact of walking over what were literally the graves of a teeming horde of species. Enric was impressed at the commitment to scientific knowledge of such an obviously earnest Christian and by the fact that Miller seemed to have no problem acknowledging the great age of the Earth and the lengthy introduction of species. Yet he did not accept any gradual development from simple to complex organisms and the book argued that the earliest fossils showed as much development as those of later species. An open-minded Christian he appeared to be, yet there were the usual attacks on the stupidity of the sceptics and a fierce social conservatism. Chambers had mentioned the book's great popularity, but he also saw it as defending a position opposite to his own. Enric did not yet see the conflict as he was unsure of Chambers' thoughts on these questions. Both gentlemen probably shared the same political views and enthusiasm for the role of education in liberating the workingman. Educating him to know his place, Enric decided. Why, the book began with an address to young workers, reminding them that '*upper and lower classes there must be, so long as the world lasts*' and warning they would '*gain nothing by attending Chartist meetings*.' Instead, they should cultivate their minds by reading, especially the Bible. Only the quality of the man's prose and his evident curiosity had got Enric past that opening. He thought at some moments that if he were ever to meet Mr. Miller, he would like to shake his hand. At other moments that he would like to give him a shake. However, they would never meet. Enric did not attend church services.

He started at a whooshing and clattering at the window. A black bird, a crow perhaps, had collided against it, nature still not adjusting to glass. He thought of all the adjustments modern life demanded of people and animals. Our lungs were surely not made for all this coal smoke, for example, he thought. And the United Kingdom was the country leading the change while extending its commercial culture around the world. That was one reason he had come here. If this was to be the future, he wanted to experience it first-hand. So far, Edinburgh had seemed like it was still anchored to the past like the Old Town to its castle. Perhaps he should have gone to Glasgow, but he had found it damp and depressing and, in any case, Edinburgh was the centre for printing. He was still hesitating about Chambers' commission as he was unsure what it entailed. If he turned it down, he would have to move on, but that was something he had done many times now. Perhaps too many times.

And here he was reading a Christian book on his day off when he could be out meeting people! That ball, or 'a dancing party' as it said on the ticket he had seen, was organised by a milliner called 'Mutch John' who went to mostly disreputable houses to arrange the girls' headdresses for the event. Perhaps that was why the Mistress had seemingly been so outraged.

'We are not that sort of establishment,' they said she screamed at him as she showed him the door and told him never to come back. The girls had fallen silent but bold, brassy, Nancy Watson had slipped out the back and paid the sixpence the entrance cost, waving the ticket like a banner. 'He says the officers from Piershill Barracks will be attending. I am going to marry me a soldier!' She had laughed but the look in her eyes betrayed her dream to marry. He could have told her where that dream usually ended for the girl, but he kept himself apart from the seamstresses. Enric had had to promise Alec he would have no, how did the Scotsman put it, 'dalliance with the young lassies of the house.' So far, he had scrupulously held to his word, despite some flirting from the girls. But it might be fun to go. He had been so serious since he had arrived. Some frivolity was needed! And Nancy did have very pretty ankles!

He tried to concentrate on the book. Here was an attack on Lamarck and on all who, like him, saw a progression from simple to complex organisms and indeed to the passing-on of characteristics, even character, from one generation to the next. A hunting-dog will squat, Miller agrees, but that is learned behaviour. An animal brought up in a temperate climate will acquire a thicker coat when transplanted to a cold one. But these are all gradations of the same thing. This is not the same as progress. For progress to exist from one species to the next we would need to be able to identify the link between each. This we cannot do. There are no links but a leap between species produced by miracle. His prize-exhibit in the argument against progress was a complex winged fish called the Pterichthys, whose fossil he had discovered himself and whose nature was confirmed by the greatest specialists of the time, Murchison and Agassiz. This complex creature was older than many simpler species, thereby disproving the idea of progress and its substitution of metamorphosis for Creation. His argument was carried home by drawings of the fossil and by his usual delightfully detailed description. You felt you were there with him on the Cromarty shore when he first cracked open the stone to reveal the fossil. You were in the company of a man who not only saw but made you see how things really were, who displayed Nature in all her multiplicity and wonder.

Multiplicity and wonder, multiplicity and wonder... he drifted off and half-awake remembered snatches of his conversations in Fife with Chambers. Then he was on a boat, like the ferry of yesterday, but carrying a St. Andrew's cross on his shoulder. It was heavy and people were pointing at him, but he could not put it down. Then there was music and the skipping of bare feet, a crow crashing against the windowpane, making it shake almost to breaking, then the Mistress, the Mistress.

'Enric! Enric! Why are you calling me?'

'He opened his eyes and she was standing in front of him, her hand just releasing his shoulder. He was shaken, he was confused. He waved her away, 'one moment, bad dream,' he muttered, trying to compose himself. He looked around, checking the furniture was the same, that the sounds from the street were still thrumming as usual. Then he looked back at her and thought, 'I am having a vision!'

He was looking at a woman in her early forties or late thirties. She was dressed in a well-cut black dress with a white lace border showing off her slender neck. Her face was regular, and her raven hair was platted behind her. She had Scottish skin, pale with a slight red flush on her cheeks and without make-up. Her eyes were brown orbs which seemed to drink you in. And oh, those ankles!

She did not appear to be put out at his dazed astonishment. Was that a smile at the corner of her mouth? He made to stand up and as he did so, the book tumbled onto the floor. Before he could react, she bent down and swiftly retrieved it then stepped back to examine it.

'I did not take you for a grim Calvinist, Enric. I thought you Mediterraneans were allergic to its rather strict charms.'

Why was she looking at him like that, probing him? They had barely talked since he moved in and he was given to understand that he was not to approach her. He was generally gone out of the house by the time she rose and at night she would eat in her own apartment. If she had any family in Edinburgh, he did not know. He must be a similar mystery to her. She had asked him after the first week for some details about his life and future plans. He had answered defensively, careful not to say anything that might present any challenge to respectability.

'I will have no drunkards here, Mr Serra,' she had said. And I expect you to treat the rest of the household with respect.'

He had reddened and she had relaxed.

'Mrs Baillie has told me you are very kind with Maggie. That is good. I hope you will be happy here in our country and that it be as generous to you as other countries have been to all the Scots folk who have emigrated.'

And that had been that. She had a quiet authority which imposed itself, but which was not cold.

He took the book from her.

'He is a well-meaning man but only sees what he wants to see and finds what he needs to find. And like many men of goodwill, he does not understand the damage he can do or the hurt he can cause.'

'Have you read the book?'

'Only the **Preface** and the first chapter. It is the same song he has been singing since he first came to Edinburgh. I knew him then.'

Enric wanted to ask her more but did not dare.

'You read a great deal, Enric.'

He nodded, not sure if among non-intellectuals that was praise or criticism.

'And if it is books like this you favour, it must mean you are looking for enlightenment.'

'He nodded awkwardly again. What was she getting at, she was not religious nor a bluestocking?

'You read all these men. How many women have you sought guidance from? How many of their works have you consulted?'

He blushed as he realised the answer. When people said it was an age of sages, they meant men. Not many women published, and he talked to few about serious subjects. He remembered the look on Mrs Chambers' face when her husband addressed him directly and they had both ignored her. Was this an invitation to talk to the Mistress?

If it was, it had been fleeting as she was already on her way up the stairs.

'No doubt you will be off to the dancing, Enric. With a bit of luck Nancy will give you a keek at her ankles!'

The Importance of Landing on Your Feet

The morning sun was peeking over the high tenement walls of the High Street like the rare interloper it was on that morning in 1846 when Hugh came down George IVth Bridge onto the High Street. He spied a tall man of six foot three talking to a beggar who was staring up at the giant as if he had met him at the foot of the beanstalk. Thomas Guthrie!

Hugh waited so as not to interrupt the talk between the two men. The tramp's words were slurred but Guthrie's admonitions in favour of temperance had the solid insistence of distant cannon. The man was nodding his head in earnest acceptance of the minister's words. Hugh saw his friend take a penny from his pocket and pass it to the man. He patted him on the shoulder and told him how much his Saviour loved him. These were not idle platitudes coming from someone like Guthrie.

'Are you coming to visit me, Thomas?'

'Well, I don't know, I have just come up from Johnston Terrace. The church is almost a year old now, but there are still practical matters to be dealt with, building work to be completed. However, I at least have a church, after two years using the Methodist Hall. Not all our brethren have been so fortunate.'

Hugh smiled, happy at the honest humility of the man whose fund-raising had done more to ensure the provision of new churches than all of his colleagues lumped together. Guthrie was a prodigious, energetic preacher whom people loved to hear, and he had raised the incredible sum of 116,000 pounds for the Manse Fund through visiting almost every parish in Scotland. Yet he had not always enjoyed such popularity. In the years before the Disruption, he had often been ostracised for his evangelical leanings. Now, he was the rising star. Like Chalmers he had come to the ministry after first studying science, in his case surgery and anatomy. He had even studied medicine in Paris!

And like Hugh, he was from the Northeast. He was from Brechin, about halfway between Edinburgh and Cromarty. As his father was a banker, like Hugh he had worked in a local branch, and they had got on well from the first time they met. Thomas often dropped into *The Witness* Office. Hugh would find him chatting to his assistant editor, Thomas McCrie when he came in. Guthrie would joke about them being the 'doubting Thomases' in need of instruction from Hugh. He would ask about Lydia and the children, about Church news, about Hugh's health. He never stopped asking and you never stopped wanting to answer and hear the next question.

Even Thomas had been scarred in the internal battles of the Free Kirk in the three years since the Disruption. Hugh liked to think of him as an ally in his struggles with Candlish and with the series of envoys sent by that man: men of business, lawyers, servants of the Lairds like that particularly odious creature in the pay of Buccleuch, and clergymen who urged caution in the editorial lambasting by the newspaper. He was even visited by a committee of 'Friends of the Railways' who asked him to look favourably on the proposed extension of the line from the West End to the North Station through Princes Street Gardens!

Hugh had outmanoeuvred them by taking a stake in the newspaper. It had cost him a thousand pounds and he had had to borrow money and arrange the best repayment terms he could. Of the eleven newspapers established in Edinburgh in the last twenty-five years, only *The Witness* had survived. Surely even Candlish could see that being above party politics was the key to their success. Hugh was still fighting against proposals to appoint an editorial board or a supervising committee and trusted that they would see it was more than a fight for his proud independence. If *The Witness* was directly controlled by a Free Church committee, then any controversy or polemical position would attract public criticism directly to the Church itself. Perhaps their most dangerous proposal was to unite all the Church publications throughout Scotland. 'You would have access to an even wider readership, Hugh, and be part of a greater enterprise,' Candlish had whispered to him while seated at his side at a public event. Would the man never cease in his onslaught? What drove him to this tireless haranguing? Hugh had pointed out that almost half of the Glasgow and Edinburgh publications was already taken up with church news, summaries of sermons and other notices of record. If they were combined the readers would die of tedium. He had already complained about the amount of Church news he had to include, something which made him unpopular with many clergymen eager to broadcast summaries of their most recent sermon or the latest amendment to the parish committee minutes. And if *The Witness* took control of other publications, it would accentuate the growing divide between the Capital and the provinces. There had already been protests at the proposal to establish the new theological college in Edinburgh and not in Aberdeen. 'Those Edinburgh lawyers are getting their fingers into the body of the Kirk,' was a common complaint from aggrieved elders from around Scotland, with what Hugh felt was some justice. Lawyers! How many of the Apostles had been lawyers? He chuckled to himself, thinking he would try out that piece of whimsy on Guthrie.

Yet he had to be careful, even with Guthrie. He was on the Committee with Candlish and the rest and understood the trading which had to go on if he was to succeed better than Hugh did. He was a friend, but not necessarily an ally in all things.

'Do you know Smith, the Governor of Edinburgh Jail?' Guthrie asked, in his typical way of jumping from topic to topic and taking for granted you had access to his thoughts. Hugh confessed that he knew Smith by name only.

'Well, last year he estimated that 740 children under fourteen, about a third of them under ten, had been committed to his prison in the previous three years. Almost six percent of the jail population are under fourteen and a sizeable number are between fourteen and sixteen years of age!'

Hugh waited, unsure of the reaction expected.

'We must do something, Hugh. Not just for these children but for the adults they will become. A relation of mine has started a Ragged School in Aberdeen.'

'A ragged school?'

'You must know yourself that many folk who live in the poorest housing round here can never go to Church as they do not possess proper clothing to attend. These schools are for the ragged, diseased and crime-worn children who would not be admitted anywhere else.'

'What makes you think they would attend? The children of workingmen are often as feckless as their parents and would rather wander free among the tenements than acquire discipline.'

'The love of discipline has to be instilled. We can appeal to other instincts though. On my way over from Johnstone Terrace I came upon a group of these little street Arabs. I asked the oldest, a strapping boy despite his poverty, if they would go to school if, besides the learning, they would get breakfast, dinner, and supper there?

'Aye, I will sir, and bring the hail land too!' And then as if afraid I might withdraw the offer, he exclaimed, 'I'll come for but my dinner, sir!' We will feed them, Hugh, and teach them discipline through Christian love. Beatings are of no use; they get enough of them at home. They will receive good Christian teaching and take that home with them at night.'

'Will the schools be denominational?'

'No, the religious teaching will be Bible-based, but open to members of all churches and of none.'

'The Catholics will never accept that. And they make up a lot of the poor round here.'

'We shall see, we shall see.'

They had been walking down the High Street as they talked and were now in front of Hugh's office. Guthrie accepted his invitation to come in, perhaps hoping for the Newspaper's support for the school project, Hugh supposed.

McCrie was pouring over some proofs for Wednesday's edition when they entered. He was struggling to edit the piece on the Hungarian riots and the news of the Canadian wheat harvest to fit the allotted column spaces. 'Something will have to be cut.'

'Let it be the wheat, then,' Hugh joked. He was in high spirits this morning!

Hugh asked Guthrie about the man he had been talking to when they had met.

'Ach, that is old Tam Donaldson. A hopeless alcoholic but a good man.'

'Yes, a taste for strong drink is the devil's easiest way of getting a hold of a soul. It is a particularly Scottish sin too.' McCrie pitched in.

'No, it is not a sin, nor a weakness, but a disease, Thomas. And you know, when I went to university here not one student was an abstainer and I believe not a single minister of the Church of Scotland is a tea-totaller. I heard you turned your back on strong alcohol as a young mason, Hugh.'

'For my love of books. I couldn't drink, read, and study. Frances Bacon saved me, I suppose.'

'Well, I used to like a dram myself until about five years ago, when I was about 38 and on a trip to Ireland. We invited the coachman in to have a toddy with us. He refused! He told us he would never touch a drop of alcohol. And he was a Roman Catholic! So I thought that if he had the willpower, then I could too.'

'Dr Candlish gives some rip-roaring, God-fearing, hellfire sermons about drink and drinkers. How anyone could sin after hearing one of those, I don't know,' McCrie exclaimed.

'That only increases their sense of guilt and hopelessness, Mr.

McCrie. Our Saviour never won the heart and soul of any man with threats of chastisement. He did it through love. I fear you may find my sermon on temperance too mild for your fiery tastes. It is based on Luke 19:41,

'*And when he was come near, he beheld the city, and wept over it,*'

Even Hugh could not see the connection between this verse and temperance. Guthrie turned to him.

'Jesus saw Jerusalem and wept. Our Saviour, the son of God, wept. That is why He is our saviour; that compassion and human feeling is what gives us hope of salvation if only we will heed His call.

The Ragged Schools and the Temperance movement are both attempts to stop the river before it runs into the sea and is lost. To catch the souls on their way to perdition before they are drowned. An ounce of prevention is worth a ton of cure.'

As often happened when Guthrie talked, the company around him became enthused, even if made up of only one or two others, like today. Hugh's eyes were flashing with the excitement of a student learning from a master, of someone hearing a familiar bell pealing in the distance.

'You are very skilful at taking a different turn on things, Thomas. I am too direct or too abstract when I write. Fervour takes hold or I lean too much on my Augustan masters.'

'We all need a Master, Hugh, a model for our style. Mine's was Knox.'

'John Knox, our holy founder? Of course!' McCrie exhaled.

Guthrie smiled. 'Well, he is an inspiration to us all, but in matters rhetorical I learned from my anatomy professor, Dr. Robert Knox. He always approached a subject from the angle least expected, thereby avoiding all the preconceptions his students held. He used anecdote and examples from Nature. I have tried in my way to learn from that.'

Hugh was almost transported. He banged his fist on the long editorial desk.

'We need leaders, Thomas, we need to teach the powerful the

responsibility they have to help those below them. If they do not, then we will be lost to the Owenites, the Chartists and all the false prophets that lay the blame for injustices on the upper classes. I agree that most people are not poor because they want to be or because they have fewer gifts than their wealthier counterparts. Society and Scotland need us! I trust the Free Church will help us build a community of faith here in Scotland where truth, justice and social order are enshrined in society as in the congregation. God bless us all!'

'God bless us all!' echoed McCrie and Guthrie. And then a very strange thing happened. One that Guthrie would remember for the rest of his days.

The three of them began to jump up and down, laughing and whooping. Then McCrie, a short and rather stout man, proposed a competition to make a standing leap from the floor onto the editor's desk. He went first, failed, and fell back. Guthrie had the advantage of his long legs and he alighted on the edge of the desk before gracefully landing on the floor again. Hugh, always a competitive man, determined not to be outdone and he sprang fairly into the middle of the desk with such force that he split it from end to end!

Guthrie went on to establish several Ragged Schools and the Free Church Temperance Society and was instrumental in bringing about the 1853 Licensing Act forcing public houses in Scotland to close at 10.00 pm on weekdays and all day on Sundays. He knew how far to leap and how to land.

'Hugh Miller,' he said to himself later, 'failed and perished because he could not measure his own force.'

Kindmanunkind

It would be untrue to say that the East wind, once scourge of bonnets and slayer of the old and frail, had deserted Edinburgh, along with the Caddies and the leatherworks at the bottom of the Castle. It would be true to say that it was scarcely noticed and powerless against the smoke pouring from factory chimneys. It could move it around, like a maid clearing the table, but the smoke hung over everything, increasingly infused with the hoppy smell of the city's growing number of breweries.

Enric spent a lot of his time criss-crossing the city looking for and delivering parts, talking to engineers, in addition to his work for Robert Chambers. Some of his workmates had started to look at him with suspicion, as a turncoat, a defender of the workingman become the bosses' ally. There was little he could do about that.

Chambers treated him like a distant friend on his regular visits to Fife. He had travelled to Manchester on three or four occasions, bearing a sealed leather satchel with roughly bound papers. He had caught a glimpse of one packet before it was bundled into the bag and was surprised to observe a feminine hand and not Chambers' own handwriting. He never felt tempted to investigate further as he understood his job sometimes depended more on what he didn't know than on what he knew. His knowledge of French and German was important, however, and he would receive urgent requests to translate the latest scientific papers from the Continent. He enjoyed that as it allowed him to work from home or sometimes in the company's library, in a private compartment at the back.

He realised with a shock that he had been in Edinburgh for almost four years now. He still saw John Arthur from time to time and had even taken up fishing with Archie down at the Forth. They caught little but it was relaxing, and he enjoyed the long ebb and flow of the tide, so different from the comparatively static Mediterranean. Ah, the Mediterranean! Had he deserted it for colder seas, literally become unfaithful to his native shores? Perhaps it was time to go home. His father wrote to him every few months, telling him about the sail-making business and his uncle's poor health. There was work waiting for him there and a position as manager, whenever he wanted it. But the business was tainted in his eyes. No, he would never go back, at least not while his uncle was alive.

Things were stirring on the Continent. He received letters from radical friends promising revolution in 1848. Would he come and join them? He did not think he would. He had tired of radical agitation and become disillusioned about change. Perhaps he was becoming a Scottish Calvinist, seeing everyone as an irredeemable sinner! He smiled to himself at that. No, he was just getting older.

He had become comfortable in his lodgings. Mutch John's dance had changed everything and made him a favourite among the girls, even with wee Meg and above all with the Mistress. When he had paid his entrance and walked into the hall on the High Street, he could tell that this was about more than dancing. A woman had attempted to pull him into a side room, saying they could rent it for 'a wee while, just enough to get properly acquainted.' When he protested he was just here for the dancing, she told him that for a bonnie fellow like him she would lower her price, but that he mustn't tell others or they would all be wanting the same bargain! He had shaken her off and made his way towards where the music was sounding.

He had never seen so many drunk people in his life! Folk were reeling round the room, stopping to drink, and joining the dance again, in a whirl of noise and shouting. Many of the men seemed to be soldiers, and many of the women from the same profession as his accoster. He was about to leave when he thought of Nancy Watson and the girls from the house. Where were they? Suddenly someone tugged at his sleeve. He decided not to respond, sure it was the woman with a special offer, just for him. But somebody yanked his jacket hard and he wheeled round to see Lizzie and Mary, two of the seamstresses. They were crying and pleading him to come with them. 'For we canna do anything, we're just lassies.'

He did not understand what they meant but their evident distress convinced him to follow, the three of them climbing some stone stairs, stepping over and around men sitting as if waiting their turn for something. The men laughed and uttered obscenities to the two women. Enric stopped, ready to face up to them, but Mary almost squealed in desperation. 'Come on, sir, come on, or we will be too late!'

They entered through an archway into a dark greasy corridor. Lizzie took him by the hand and Mary opened the door to reveal Nancy Watson in a state of undress and wielding a glass pitcher to hold off a grizzled, hard-faced soldier.

'I have paid my money and I want my goods,' he was shouting.

'This is her laddie, come to take her hame,' both Lizzie and Mary cried.

'Dinna make a fuss and be off with you before he gets angry.'

The man lunged at Enric. He was drunk and clumsy and in two seconds he was unconscious on the floor, blood seeping from his mouth.

'We had better be going, you can explain all this to me later,' Enric said, taking off his jacket and handing it to the weeping girl.

'I didna ken, I thought he was a gentleman, he talked so sweet. And then he turned on me as soon as I came up with him. Oh, I am sore, I am sore. I am ashamed.'

'Hush, now lassie. We all ken what men like this are like. We maun be off now,' Mary whispered as she helped the girl into the jacket.

And so they had rushed out and down the stairs, across the hall through staggering dancers and down onto the street. Enric had insisted on taking a cab home. This later became part of the legend of the Spanish Caballero and sealed the girls' admiration of him. Little good it did him to protest that he was not Spanish, and that Lizzie and Mary were the real heroines.

Nancy came to see him on his own and said she hoped he would not judge her too harshly and that she felt black-affronted that he had seen her almost without a stich on. He assured her that he had been too busy watching for the man to stir to notice and that it was clear who was the villain here. She took his hand in hers and kissed it.

He had found Nell waiting outside his room when Nancy left. She smiled a strange sad smile but said nothing to him. Now he came to think of it though, it was about then that Archie invited him to go fishing!

When he had come back from work a few days after the incident, he had remarked that the door to his room looked cleaner. The room itself had been tidied and a new rug lay beside the bed. Meg came knocking to say the Mistress had ordered it and arranged for the room to be made a wee bit homelier.

And just then the Mistress herself appeared, signalled for Meg to leave them then held out her hand to shake his.

'I really don't deserve all these thanks and considerations, Mistress.'

She put a finger to her lips, shushing him gently.

'You saved a young woman from violation. There can never be enough thanks for that. And please, Enric, don't call me Mistress, you may use my first name, Alia. And please consider this house your home for as long as you stay in Edinburgh.'

She still kept her distance from him, but occasionally asked how his work was going and about the books he was reading.

One day she asked him if he knew of the work of Robert Owen.

He answered that he had heard the name but knew little of the man or his ideas. Was he a Chartist?

'Well, I don't manage all the terminology, but I don't think so. He has set up factories where people are well-paid and cared for. He calls them communities and he provides education for the children. And that is a good thing. He thinks Britain should become agricultural again and that people should learn to live as a community in a garden.'

She smiled a strange bitter smile as she said this. When she saw his quizzical look, she said.

'I have too much experience of rural life to romanticise it so. And too much experience of people.'

'You must never give up on people, Alia,' he replied. 'For if we give up on people, we give up on ourselves. Times are changing, science and politics will make men, I mean, make society free.'

'You sound like my brother. He wrote to me the other day with plans to build houses to make people free, houses with light and of sound construction. But that is in Canada, and he always was a dreamer.'

This was the first time she or anyone had mentioned her family. He would hold onto this moment.

'And it is all very well to talk about society. In my experience, it is the family that has to change. Owen is right when he says families divide people from one another and lead to the tyrannisation of women.'

Enric was arrested by her passion, by the sense of someone talking of a lost opportunity, a chance forever gone. Like him, he felt, when he thought of home and who he was.

'Don't look so serious, laddie!' She laughed with an enchanting peal of sound that made him think of sunshine flooding into a house.

Her laughter was infectious, and he couldn't help joining in, even if he wasn't sure what they were laughing about.

'But Mr. Owen is a man, and sometimes he acts like a priest. It seems he even baptised someone at one of his meetings recently. And you, as a man, seem to think of society as a collection of men.'

He blushed. She was right, he had just said it in fact.

Then Nell had come in and murmured something about an appointment. Now it was Alia who seemed discomfited, and she left rather abruptly with Nell, tying her hair in a bun as she walked down the corridor.

The next morning as he opened his door to go down to breakfast, he found a page from *The Witness* newspaper from a couple of years ago pinned to the opposite wall. At the top was scrawled,

Do you see what they say of thinking women? She is speaking again tomorrow, perhaps you might be interested. Alia.

The article was entitled, *The Socialists at Church* and had been written by the editor. It concerned a lecture on a book called *Vestiges of Creation* by a speaker called Emma Martin. The editor expressed shock that hundreds of 'respectable church-going people' were prepared to pay twopence to hear Martin lecture on infidel socialism. The editor, Hugh Miller, claimed that Martin was followed by a troupe of young lads with small heads, receding foreheads, and smirking faces, suggesting that 'the door of the monkey-ward in the Zoological Gardens had by some mistake been left open, and that the inmates, escaping out into the open world, had attached themselves to Mrs Martin, and become socialists.'

Enric recognised the caustic tone from the book of Miller's he had read. He also detected fear in these lines, fear of socialism, of atheism, of evolutionary theories, and yes, he realised, of women. Alia was right.

She met him at the foot of the stairs, an expectant look on her face.

'Thank you for the article. And yes, I would certainly like to attend Mrs Martin's talk, if you will but tell me the time and place. Will you be attending too?'

He was surprised when she blushed.

'It would not be prudent for my clients to discover my affiliation to such a movement and nor do I think I would be welcomed. However, if you do go, I shall rely on you for a report of the meeting.'

She handed him a card with the address of a hall near East Claremont Street.

'It begins at 7 pm tomorrow night and will no doubt be well attended, so it might be a good idea to go early.'

'I see,' he said, not seeing anything. 'I was not sure whether you were recommending her talk or damning Mr. Miller.'

'Oh, Hugh has already damned himself, he has become a busy monster, a kind man become unkind. No, it is Emma Martin I wanted you to see.'

He took the card and watched as she passed him on her way up the stairs. What was it about this woman that fascinated him?

As he left the house, he began to wonder about Alia's connection to Hugh Miller. Had she kept the article because of its subject or because of its author?

He was so deep in thought as he walked up the Mound towards the Old Town that he forgot to guard his hat and the East Wind made off with it! Nature demands our respect, even in these sooty industrial times, he realised as he chased after the bonnet, attracting laughter from his fellow citizens.

Letter 14

Sister Cathedral

Yes, there was much to pity and much to admire. Helen Acquroff was a musician, pianist, music teacher, singer and poet who was born in 1831 and lived in the Newington area of Edinburgh. She had been totally blind from the age of eleven but that had not hindered her work in favour of the Temperance movement. Helen would open her packed performances with light-hearted ditties and appeared in concert halls and church premises all over Scotland. The name 'Sister Cathedral' was given to her after an address for Glasgow Cathedral was published, warning the people of Glasgow of the perils of intemperance. He had heard her sing but once, and though he still remembered her sweet voice and her cheerful demeanour he could not rid himself of the irk, like the pebble in your shoe, that dug into him whenever he thought of her.

Some whispered that no good could be expected of the daughter of a Russian-born hairdresser and a Campbell from Nairn. But no, that was not it. We did not choose our birth. It wasn't even the fact that she had had a child born out of wedlock. He could condemn the sin and pardon the sinner, well, depending on the character of each.

She was a member of The International Organisation of Good Templars, who promulgated the legend that the original knights 'drank sour milk, and like them were fighting 'a great crusade' against 'this terrible vice' of alcohol.' Was it this tinge of Romanism which so disgusted him? Perhaps, and because he had fought many battles against Puseyism and the tides of creeping Catholicism washing through the Anglican Church and the British institutions? Perhaps.

He had thought of her when he passed by Greyfriars Kirk. It had been the first church constructed after the glorious

Reformation. The National Covenant had been signed in its Kirkyard in 1638. It was his Zion. His blood was in its soil, the martyrs buried there, the inspiration for his fight.

In 1718 an explosion destroyed the church tower and when it was reconstructed it was partitioned to hold two congregations: Old and New Greyfriars. On 19 January 1845, a boiler flue had overheated, sparking a fire that gutted Old Greyfriars and damaged the roof and furnishings of New Greyfriars. As it occurred soon after the Disruption of 1843, some suggested the blaze was holy judgement on the established church. Hugh had laughed when a divine had blamed the fire that ravaged the Old Town in 1824 on God's ire at a musical performance in the city. Now he was not so sure. He had unsuccessfully argued in his newspaper that the congregations should transfer to St John's Church on Victoria Street where Guthrie had moved as the minister and leave Greyfriars as a scenic ruin. The majority of the town council's members had joined the Free Church and their attempts to frustrate the restoration were one of the reasons it ended up taking twelve years. During the restoration of Old Greyfriars, painted glass was installed at the request of the minister, Robert Lee: this was the first coloured glass to be installed in a building of the Church of Scotland since the Reformation. Hugh was certain that Lee would introduce a service book of his own devising and introduce the practice of standing for praise, kneeling for worship and saying prepared prayers. He had been reliably informed of the man's plans to install a harmonium and even an organ!

In Calvinist Scotland, as in Israel, God had sanctioned no great musicians. Perhaps that was it. Or was it just her name? There was no room for any cathedrals in Scotland.

"Hugh Miller"

Winning And Losing at the Same Time

Hugh had relied on Lydia for supplementary articles and for proofreading work for the newspaper since he had become editor. It occupied her and gave them some extra income. Now, with the growth of the family she said she had less time. She had enough time to become an author herself, however, and under the name of Mrs Harriet Myrtle successfully published a series of children's books.

'She is called Harriet, just like me!' Ha Ha would exclaim when she saw the books and begged her mother to read her favourite, *The Man of Snow*, every evening at bedtime, eventually mouthing the words as her mother pronounced them. Lydia also wrote the only contemporary novel on the Disruption: *Passages in the Life of an English Heiress, or, Recollections of Disruption Times in Scotland*. She insisted on publishing it anonymously. 'We don't want to shock the old ladies in the Church who think that a novel is always immoral.'

'Old ladies like Candlish,' McKenzie snorted.

The heady days of the founding of *The Witness*, then the dizzying clashes and urgencies of the Disruption had faded to a more mundane routine. Hugh felt like he had won and lost at the same time, a feeling that sometimes left him exhausted. He had hammered the opposition around Candlish with a letter as fierce as his one to Lord Brougham.

'Which of you could direct Hugh Miller?' Chalmers had said to the committee once they had all read the letter. They each lowered their heads. Even Candlish.

So he had won. He was still the editor of *The Witness*. He had

had to accept an assistant editor, James Aitken Wylie. Perhaps he had lost. Wylie had been ordained in the Secessionist Church which meant Hugh's diatribes against the voluntaries, or other Christian sects, had to be toned down, though the man was also a rabid anti-Catholic like Dr Begg and so Hugh did find common ground for his ire at the Government's grant to support a Catholic seminary at Maynooth in Ireland. Aitken was a help, it was true. Hugh had had to accept that he could not go on working as before.

Makgill Crichton, the landowner and a lay leader of the Free Church had gone in distress from friend to friend, saying 'Miller is killing himself, working always up yonder. Can no one get him out?'

Well, he was still in. Or was he out?

He needed to work. He needed to make a difference. However, he felt surrounded by increasing disinterest. Candlish and the others were always polite to him, but the Church was becoming closer to the political parties. Chalmers was fading fast, and Hugh understood that with his passing would come the closing down of his influence on the elders and on the ministers of the church.

He was ready for his last epic battle. One he had not foreseen from an unknown enemy. One which would test his much-vaunted defence of the need to accommodate modern science into faith, to look at it as yet another production of the Creator who made us all. Hugh would fight the defining battle for religion. Even if it killed him.

He saw the irony himself. He had been vigilant in watching out for dangerous ideas coming up from below, from the discontented working classes or rural poor. Perhaps that is why he had missed the deadliest virus, one which came from above and worked its way downwards. It could be said to have infected Queen Victoria first. Her husband used to read the book to her in the evening, to keep her abreast of the new science. The new science! The new scourge more likely.

And Hugh had even published an advert for the book in 1844 and a year later short quotes from it. Now by 1846, *Vestiges of the Natural History of Creation* had been published in America and cheap editions were being issued by all and sundry. No-one knew the name of the author, though certain Scottisisms and the clear traces of phrenology running through it persuaded many people it was George Combe. He denied it as did all others named. Even the publisher in London had no idea who the author was as the manuscript was delivered to him anonymously from someone in Manchester. Some thought its hasty jumping to conclusions suggested it was written by a woman.

Sir David Brewster wrote a withering criticism of it as 'prophetic of infidel times and indicating the unsoundness of our general education.' Unfortunately, the harsher the criticism, the more eminent the critic, the more the book's popularity grew. The new class of scientific men, many of them moneyed amateurs, insisted that the book was replete with simple errors and took assumptions for conclusions. The author responded by amending the text and publishing a series of new editions!

It was a difficult book to criticise as it covered so much ground that someone with the specialist knowledge necessary to refute part of it was unqualified to deal with its other claims. The churches had wheeled out their biggest guns, but each contradicted the other and their blasts faded into the unheeding skies. Oxford and Cambridge organised seminars and debates to damn the work, but many of those attending came away with their religious doubts fortified and the cracks in the dam of faith grew wider.

The book put forward a cosmic theory of transmutation as the 'natural history of creation,' suggesting that everything currently in existence has developed from earlier forms: the solar system, the Earth, rocks, plants and corals, fish, land plants, reptiles and birds, mammals, and ultimately Man. In its first editions it claimed that the solar system originated in nebulous clouds of gases that solidified and that life was produced by spontaneous generation sparked by electricity. Again, as soon as this idea was attacked, the author amended it and moved on. Hugh did not feel qualified to comment on these aspects but agreed with Murchison's criticism of the book's insistence on the progression in the fossil records from simple to more complex organisms, culminating in man, with the white European at the pinnacle of this process, just above the other races and the rest of the animal kingdom. Even animals could think, it claimed! He threw the book across the room, alarming Lydia, when he came to its suggestion that the fact of extinction, which can be observed in the fossil layers, suggests that some creations were flawed. How could God make mistakes! He was unconvinced by the author's suggestion that the Creator only established laws that would correct themselves and was not interested in supervising every detail of life at all times. But the Bible taught us that God created every single one of us individually, Jesus Christ died to save each one of us and that we were each made in the image of God. This dangerous book made the crucifixion unnecessary as well as our salvation. It robbed us of our individuality at the same time as suggesting animals as our ancestors. It was ridiculous. It was scandalous. It had to be refuted. But how?

Goodsir too had won and lost at the same time. When Alexander Monro *tertius* finally retired in 1846, John had been appointed Professor of Anatomy at the University. It had been a hard fight. In the preceding years he had published and lectured and kept in touch with all the decision-makers. It had been galling to him to suspect that he had won the election thanks more to his perceived Calvinist orthodoxy than to his technical knowledge. There was still a hint of sulphur associated with Anatomy, with the intervention in the dead body. And just a decade before, James Young Simpson had encountered howls of criticism at his pioneering use of chloroform to dull the pain of childbirth, contrary, many said, to the Biblical curse for women to suffer during labour. John had felt belittled by the need to proclaim the authority of the Bible, not because he did not believe it, but because he did.

He gave lectures on evolution and Man's unique place in the natural world as a complete being independent of the environment to rows of grim clergymen and town councillors as well as the more unruly students. It was the same lecture, at the University, the Royal

Society or at cultural events. Why vary the truth? He was aware of his inclination for matter over style. But they seemed to like it.

'With an animal body and instincts, man possesses also a consciousness involving Divine truth in its regulative principles. But along with this highly endowed consciousness, the human being has been left free to act either according to the impulses of his animal, or of his higher principle. The actual history of humanity, of its errors, its sufferings, and its progress, is the record of the struggle between man's animal and Divine principle, and of the means vouchsafed by his Creator for his relief.'

For more scientific audiences he started with the following:

'In the normal position of the human body the axis of the vertebral column is vertical. No animal form of vertebral column can be elevated into the perpendicular position. In apes, in the so-called upright position, the axis is oblique; and when these animals are on all fours, nearly horizontal. In birds, also, it is oblique. In quadrupeds, horizontal. The human haunch-bone is the only form of haunch-bone adapted for the erect position.'

Edward would have illustrated his talks with funny sketches. John imagined the laughter and smiles of the audience when he produced them extempore. He, on the other hand, gave them the truth and nothing but the solid truth. He argued that the higher truths contained in Biblical Revelation had to be seen as guiding those discovered in the empirical examination of Nature and that Man had been uniquely endowed with the capacity to receive these higher beliefs through his God-given intelligence.

No one applauded these lectures, but several timorous Christians had told him they came out comforted, 'armed for the fight against the infidel.'

He had won. But why did he feel that it was a betrayal of science to enter such a battlefield?

At least he could at last enjoy the social prestige that would come with the post. In 1847 he moved to a house in leafy George Square and waited for the stream of illustrious visitors. Few came and they did not stay long.

People laughed at him behind his back. He was sure they told stories about him and his 'Goodsirisms.' He was presented with an Arabian steed by the Duke of Hamilton. Speaking of horses one day to a visitor to his new abode, he said —' I *love* the horse; I *love* the horse' — laying great stress on the word 'love,' and then added without any pause — 'I've dissected him twice.'

The visitor did not return.

He was aware that he lacked the social gifts to charm. He was no Edward Forbes. Sometimes he felt like an impostor, a usurper. Edward should be here in his place!

If in the years before his appointment to the chair he had written and published voluminously, he was now much warier and greatly less prolific with his pen, as if afraid of risking his position by hazarding the publication of anything rash and speculative. He was now more solicitous about the completion and perfection of his researches than the number and variety of his papers. In short, he published nothing of note for the rest of his life, though he accumulated endless unfinished projects, such as 'A System of Dissections.' This promised work was to form a 'Dissecting Manual,' to be issued in parts, and with plans or simple outline drawings as guides in each stage of dissection, the whole to form a progressive series of studies for the Practical Rooms. Several years elapsed before he made a start, and then only to the extent of a few pages and no more.

In 1848 he was bitterly disappointed and resentful not to be appointed Assistant Surgeon in the Royal Infirmary of Edinburgh just next door to his house and he cut off all future contact with them. At least this explained his depression and sensitive nerves to those friends concerned about his listlessness and almost defeated expression. He suffered from quinsy, dyspepsia, boils, and impaired strength caused by incessant labour and 'neglect of the most common hygiene,' as John Arthur put it to Enric one day after having to help his professor to his bed.

'I don't know what has come over him. There is still no one like him in the Dissecting Room, but the spark has gone out of the man.'

On August 26, 1848, Edward Forbes married Emily Marianne Ashworth, the daughter of General Sir Charles Ashworth.

They Become Water

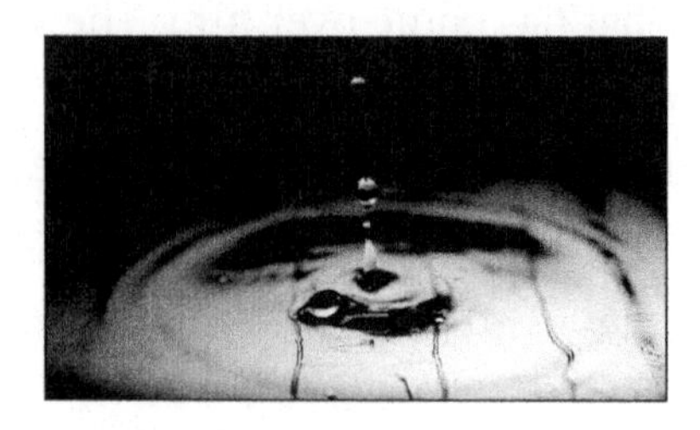

The evening of the talk Enric had slipped out of work early, pleading a translation he had to finish at home and walked down to East Claremont Street. He passed the gates of the Royal Zoological Gardens, which had opened in 1840 in the six acres of beautifully landscaped grounds surrounding Broughton Hall, once the country house of James Donaldson, a wealthy publisher and bookseller.

Enric had never visited the place as he had heard it was like all the other zoos, with the lions, tigers, monkeys and bears cramped in tiny cages. At least the elephant could literally stretch its legs as it carried children around on its back. Only the zoo's polar bears, unaffected by the poor Edinburgh climate and harsh winters, were said to thrive, the rest wasted away. The zoo tried to stay afloat by putting on large-scale events such as firework displays, summer concerts and pageants but from what he could tell, without much success.

As he passed by the high railings, he thought he could hear the whoop of monkeys, the harsh cawing of parrots and he was back in Guiana, the sycamores become palm trees, sweat suddenly trickling down his neck again. He closed his eyes and opened them once more and was relieved to find himself back in Edinburgh, his anti-tropical capital. He wiped his brow and hurried away.

As he approached the hall he could make out diverse groups of people huddled in front of the building, each cluster careful to maintain its distance from the rest and seemingly moving in tandem when a new band manifested itself. 'The radical waltz' he remembered Jacques had called it, sectarian groups of radicals attempting to maintain their own identity in order to preserve the purity of their fight for solidarity and equality. Enric had thought Jacques a cynic, all those years ago in Paris. Perhaps his friend had been right though. Or perhaps he himself had become one. He had grown detached from politics, from the struggle of the workingman, partly through the common disillusionment caused by the flip-flopping spasms of the Chartist movement with its blind belief in the efficacy of presenting massive petitions to a deaf parliament alternating with demands for direct action to wrest power from the upper classes. The Edinburgh Chartists had held a meeting on Calton Hill where they had eschewed physical force, which had earned them the scorn of their Glasgow comrades and caused yet another split in the movement. And what of the increasing number of Chartist churches? Chartist churches! Even if they were just buildings owned by the movement and they called them Chartist Halls of Worship, they were still churches. Could Man never be weaned from the need for a God to serve? Their pastors quoted lines from the Bible showing God's blessing on the poor and on those who earned their daily bread. The Establishment just selected other lines praising the Master and exhorting servants to be faithful and lobbed them back like grenades over a battlement.

He stopped in his tracks, checking himself from falling into the easy anti-clericalism he had encountered in Catalonia and France, remembering the ugly religious fervour of those protesting against the Church. He was doing a lot of checking of himself these days, he supposed because he was past thirty now, and able to shed his skin for one last time before age thickened it. He wanted to be wearing the right one when he made his next move. Where would that be to? He felt he had taken all he could from Edinburgh. Perhaps he should go to the United States, or to Australia? No, the United States had slave states, and he had no knowledge of Australian culture. The world was beginning to feel exceedingly small to him. Another sign of age, no doubt.

The doors to the hall were opened by a stout old lady in a brown shawl. As the groups rushed up the steps to claim the most preeminent seats, Enric hung back and was only starting his ascent when a young woman stumbled and fell backwards, sent skittling by a more robust person. He caught her and was surprised to feel at once how light yet strong her body felt. He righted her and awaited thanks. None came and he was left to watch as she strode up into the hall, catching but a glimpse of her stockinged ankle. He checked himself again then slowly entered through the high black doors. The old woman was holding out a bag for donations.

He dropped twopence in then went to find a seat. The hall seemed to be full and he was resigned to standing when she beckoned to him as she shuffled along the bench. His fallen woman!

'Thank you for catching me. I apologise for not saying it before, but I was startled, and I find it difficult to express gratitude to a man.'

Oof! He felt like he had been drawn in and then subjected to a punch in his chest. He made to stand up and leave but the platform was now occupied by a plain young woman in worker's clothes, introducing the inspiring, the valiant, the worthy EMMA MARTIN!

The whole audience stood up and cheered, especially the women. They all rose, except the strange girl at his side. He looked at her and saw tears in her eyes.

Mrs Martin, a tall lean woman with gentle eyes but a somewhat haggard look was opening a sheaf of papers, laying them on the lectern before standing beside it and only glancing at her notes.

'The people perish for want and you give them MORE CHURCHES! They ask you for bread and you give them more stones. They pine in ignorance and you give them BIBLES.'

Enric was startled by her unabashed atheism. It took him back to those anarchist conclaves in Barcelona where exalted spirits proposed to burn down churches. 'Anem a fer una foguera de hòsties!' He heard shouts, smelled the incense some satirist had thrown on the fire, 'Anem nois,' 'Nois'- boys in Catalan, and the contrast between the male memories and this female gathering brought him back to reality. If what he saw was reality: women in the crowd holding up their hands, forming a triangle with joined forefingers and thumbs. Some were ululating, or was he dreaming again? He was in Africa now, women shouting as their men were taken on board.

He lent his attention to the speaker, whose soft voice seemed to reach to the corners of the hall like an insistent breeze as she waved a book in her hand. It contained, she said, all the evidence that could ever be needed to refute Christianity and to wipe away the generations of superstition and folly it embodied.

'Read *The Infidel's Text-Book*, by my friend and brother, Robert Cooper, and you too can help in the fight against the hierarchy. For do not forget, sisters and brothers, that The Bible is a manual for the oppression of women. It starts with charging Eve with the Fall and sending us to Hell and ends with women treated as unsexed virgins or as prostitutes. We cannot be equal; we cannot be free while we suffer the chains of this iniquitous book.'

The crowd roared and got to its feet again, including the woman at his side. And so the night went on, with Emma Martin's insistent and unwavering complaints about the subjugation of women and her calls for a socialist society making everyone feel that a new world was possible. Perhaps things had already changed outside the doors of the hall! Enric felt that old radical glow seeping through his veins once more. Things could change for the better: we, women and men, could build a new society. How good it felt to feel his cynicism slipping from him like a scab from a miraculously healed wound. He looked around him. People were smiling. Some were crying. He had a nagging thought that this was a religious experience, but he checked himself again. His companion held out her hand and he shook it. 'You see, now, don't you, brother?'

'Yes,' he said, 'Yes.' 'See what?' he thought.

He started to meet Elspeth Grieve regularly after that evening. She was a midwife, working at the hospital but also delivering scrawny babies in some of the poorest houses in the city. She was twenty-seven, with short brown hair and hazel eyes. Enric was bewitched. He would hang around the streets near the hospital just hoping to accidentally bump into her. On the rare occasions the miracle occurred, he stood there like a tongue-tied schoolboy, or offered to carry her packages, then apologised for his presumption, then laughed when she said she would be delighted for someone to carry them. Did it matter to her that the someone was *him*, he wanted to ask her, but dared not. She was not married. She valued her independence. He told her how admirable that was but winced. Why should he object when he had often told women the same thing and felt proud of himself? But he was a man. That had suddenly become a problem, one he had not realised before.

He thought back to his relationships with women, to his mother and sisters, to the liaisons, fleeting and stable, he had had with girls. And he felt ashamed. Sometimes, later, he would tell himself he was overreacting, playing a part, almost. Anything to please her.

She passed him texts by Emma Martin and said they could meet to discuss them. He read them. He would have read the British Museum Catalogue if it meant meeting her. The writings had that soft fire he had sensed at the meeting. However, Mrs Martin had been a Baptist as a young girl and he could not help but feel that her message was essentially religious, even when attacking belief. Was there no escape from faith?

Elspeth was from the Borders, she said, that small strip of territory just an hour or so from Edinburgh that seemed to regard itself as on a par with the Great Wall of China or the Russian Steppes. Scotland was eccentric in its rhapsodising of the sparsely populated south and north of the country and its cultural ignorance of the Lowlands between Edinburgh and Glasgow, where most of the population actually lived. He had met Scots abroad and they mentioned Edinburgh but seemed to identify with the Highlands and a language they did not speak or with Scott's Borders, which they had not visited. They did not mention Falkirk, Linlithgow, Kilmarnock, or Paisley. Elspeth did not talk much about her hometown, her family, her past. She did not seem interested in his past life either.

'The only important day is this one and the ones to come,' she once said to him as they strolled through the Meadows, the fallen leaves crunching under their shoes and black shivering birds perching on the bared branches like punctuation marks on a banner. A banner, that like everything else around him seemed to declare that love was in the air, on the ground, in the faces of the people passing by. Had she squeezed his arm as she said this? He ran his thoughts back, searching for the gesture, trying to remember the look on her face. But it was her eyes that told you how she felt, and he had not turned to face her. What a fool! What if he had missed the key to her heart, what if she had had handed it to him and he had overlooked it? He ran his hands through his hair, searching, searching for signs given from this enigma of a woman. For in many ways she was a conundrum, seemingly so open and trusting, sometimes expressing herself with a simplicity that could sound not only naïve and childlike but obtuse. Yet when he walked back from their meetings, he found that these simple words often contained complicated truths.

Some of her ideas he still found startling. He had heard many radical proposals in the salons and cafes across Europe but mostly from other men and about men.

'We are water, Enric,' she said to him one day while they were having tea together. 'All solids are deposits from liquids, the essence is moisture. The baby is born out of the fluids of the mother.'

He felt ill-equipped to dispute this with a midwife. And her skin grew luminous when she talked about such matters. He almost lost his breath when she leant towards him and looked directly in his eyes.

'We are born from the womb-cave. The baptismal font is an echo of the caves in which the first people lived. Though in general men have taken over religious worship and its symbols.'

'That seems a bit, well, far-fetched,' he said, thinking it was dishonest to dissemble.

She seemed to welcome his dissent.

'Aye, I know it sounds strange, but Emma Martin explains it clearly in her essay on *Baptism as a Pagan Rite*. She points out that the first places of worship were caves and the access to these caves was often controlled and difficult.'

Did she just blush then?

She took a sip of tea and went on.

'The cave is a symbol of the womb. And most religious symbols were equally feminine. But along came 'civilisation' and there was a struggle between the phallus or lingam as a focus for devotion as seen in the last supper and the cross, and the womb-vagina or yoni, as in the pyramids of Egypt, baptism and the caves.

He looked around to see if others could overhear them. Was he becoming 'respectable'?

'Am I boring you?'

'You could never bore me.'

She laughed at that and went on.

'Christ's worship was taken over by devotees of the phallic cross, but the original reality was different. He was born in a cave, then baptised in a river, then buried in a cave, before he rose again.'

'I thought you were an atheist.'

'I am, but society is ruled by rituals and symbols. That is why every society has its priests and its ornaments, both now mostly male. Like that daft phallic monument to Scott in Princes Street!'

She laughed and he did, along with her. But he felt disquiet. He was a man: was there any place for him in her feminine universe?

'We have to cleanse ourselves of the masculine concept of the world. All of us, women and men, because we are both necessary! We must build a new vision.'

She reached across the table and put her hand on his.

'Do you remember in the meeting I asked you, 'Did you see?' This is what I was referring to.'

His face showed a mixture of relief at being included in her world and confusion about what he was supposed to have seen.

'I forget it is not easy at first. Do you remember what the women did with their hands?'

'They formed a triangle.'

'And what is a triangle?'

'It is a form made up of three lines with an apex.'

'Well, it is, from the masculine point of view. An apex! How male! A feminine view would see the interior, the triangular space, not the strong, regular lines. We need those lines in order to have the form but when we focus on them and ignore the interior, we are relegating women's vision. Nowadays people look at pyramids and see only the phallic. They forget that they are constructed caves, symbols of the feminine.'

'What do you expect of me, Elspeth?'

'I expect nothing. We expect things from the future, and we cannot control that, at least as individuals.'

She saw the look of frustration cloud his face. She was being too abstract she guessed. But how many times did women receive philosophy instead of poetry and take it as a sign of the man's worth?

'You are a bonnie laddie. And you have been faithful and patient in these past weeks. You help me say things I have never said or felt so clearly before. Dinna fash, Enric.'

'What did fash mean? Was she dismissing him? He saw a path closing, a gate swinging shut. To his shame and amazement he felt a tear run down his cheek. He wanted to get up, he wanted to leave, he wanted to stay, he had never pursued a woman like this, like a love-struck boy.

Elspeth reached over. She wiped the tear away with the tip of her finger then licked it. She stood up, took him by the hand, and whispered.

'Walk me home, Enric.'

They walked down to Dumbiedykes, not far from where John Arthur lived, though Enric had no thought for him or for any other denizen of this earth. He hoped and feared at the same time, till they came to her close, she picked out her key from her bag and indicated to him to follow her up the stairs. On the third floor they both had to stoop to avoid the low lintel on the door to her corner flat. It was clean and sober, with some orange flowers on a vase on the table and a bed in the corner. Through the window the last rays of the sun were caressing the top of Arthur's Seat.

'I know this is what you want, Enric.'

Again that feeling of being welcomed then rebuffed.

'It is not this I want, but you, Elspeth.'

She smiled and with almost magical ease slipped off her clothes, standing pale and lithe before him. Never had he seen a woman who appeared more woman, he thought, without understanding it completely himself. She moved towards the bed deliberately, like a swan entering the water. He took his boots off and placed them next to the bed then piled his clothes in his usual tidy way next to them. His breathing accelerated as he realised he was taking a step into a territory he could never retreat from.

'This is the time of my cycle, we can be free with each other,' she whispered.

They made love till the dawn peeked over Arthur's Seat. As he felt their loins interlocking and his seed flooding inside her and her release, he felt they had both become water.

'I see, Elspeth. I see, darling. Oh, I can see.'

The Descent from Blackford Hill

Hugh had spent the afternoon walking on Blackford Hill, up through the yellow broom till he was looking down on an Edinburgh suddenly changed. He was spent. He observed black lines of people snaking down towards Newington from the funeral. He could see Leith Docks in the far distance and make out the white rigging of the boats berthed there. The sailing ships were diminishing and being replaced by steamers, poetry replaced by prose.

'Och you were a silly young fellow when you first came to Edinburgh,' he said to himself. He remembered his first view of the smoky city, the tumult on the streets as he walked up to the New Town then how he had almost been assaulted by some street women in the Old Town. He had been saved by Willie Ross, that poor artist taken from him so young. So many gone, so many dying before their time, like his poor father, at fifty years of age, just a few more than Hugh himself now in 1847.

He reached the top of the hill and could make out the Highland Line to the Northwest and the hills of the Borders to the South. He had spent his life in valleys, beside firths, in Cromarty and in Edinburgh. And now both were changing faster than he was, faster than he could. How quickly once you reached the peak of the hill did you start the descent, by choice or not.

He had climbed to compose the report on Chalmers' burial. He wrote his articles walking, but today nothing would come. Hadn't everything already been said about the great man as an academic, a preacher, statesman and leader of the Free Church? Perhaps, but Hugh was the Witness. A witness cannot choose not to testify, to not express what he has seen, even if, as at this moment, he felt bereft.

He headed down the hill past the loch at its foot then up through the Grange and past the throng still waiting to enter the cemetery, past his first family residence in Sylvan Place then, after stopping off at the newspaper's office, home to greet Lydia. The children were waiting for him, aware that something of great import had happened, but unsure what. They seemed relieved and he realised with a shock that they had feared some mishap had befallen their father. Harriet kept her head buried in his shoulder even longer than usual and little William tugged at his sleeve as if to say, 'Don't go daddy, don't go.' He stayed with them longer than he should have and tried to reassure Lydia that everything had gone well and that he had escaped unscathed and steady.

After the children went to bed he waited while Lydia read them one of her stories, then took her in his arms, feeling her body resting against his, supporting him or needing his sustenance? She had not attended the burial. 'I cannot be a hypocrite and acknowledge those who would do you evil, at the graveside of that good man. It would be sacrilege,' she had insisted. He held her tighter, holding onto her as he thought of all the petty sacrifices he had had to make, all the concessions to church politics and the hierarchy. He had done so even under the protection of Chalmers. What compromises would be forced upon him now?

And that night on the 4th of June while the wind tapped on the slates above his head, he finally sat down to write, taking himself back to the morning. He remembered the shock on the faces of all parties at the Assembly of the Free Church when the news of Chalmers' passing was announced. Some bowed their heads in silence, others started to pray aloud, a few stood up and rushed out of the church, to where he knew not. He had been kept informed by a member of the old man's household, his young coachman.

'He's as pale as the watery moon, sir. It'll no be lang noo, no be lang. What am I to do?'

He must bring out the national, even the international resonance of the loss.

'The General Assembly of the Free Church met in Free St Andrews Church at twelve o clock–together with the members of deputations to the Assembly from the Presbyterian Churches of England and Ireland, and also the ministers from foreign parts attending the Assembly; the Moderator, Dr. Keith, and Dr. Clason, conducted the devotional exercises.'

Now, how to bring out the academic importance of their deceased leader? Should he separate the students from the public and the civic bodies? Maintain the hierarchy or stress the democratic mourning?

'The probationers and students met in the hall of the New College, at twelve, where Dr. Cunningham conducted the devotions. A little before one, a large body of citizens, desirous of testifying respect to the memory of the deceased, by joining in the procession, assembled on the south side of Charlotte Square; as did also the Magistrates and Town-Council of the city, in St. George's Church, in the same square. At one o clock, the General Assembly left Free St. Andrew's Church, the Moderator and Office-bearers in front, in gowns and bands, preceded by the two officers of Assembly, dressed in deep mourning, with hanging crapes, and white rods in their hands, and walking four abreast, proceeded to the Lothian Road, where they halted at about a hundred yards in advance of Free St. George's Church. The members of Assembly were followed by the Professors in the New College, in their gowns and bands.'

Yes, that was a good balance. He thought of the Disruption and how important it had been then to reflect the whole of society in a calm, directed order. He went on:

'The ministers and elders not members of Assembly, now left Free St Georges Church, walking four abreast, preceded by four beadles, two and two, dressed in deep mourning, and with black rods in their hands, and took their place in the procession immediately behind the Professors. Next came the ministers of other denominations. These were followed by the probationers and students, walking also four abreast, and preceded by

two officers dressed in the manner last described. Next in the procession came the Rector and Masters of the High School in their gowns and preceded by the Janitor in his official costume; and following in their rear were the Rector, Teachers, and Students of the Edinburgh Normal School, with other Free Church teachers in Edinburgh and neighbourhood. Forming the rear of the procession came the large body of citizens, who had assembled in Charlotte Square, walking four abreast. Thus formed, the procession moved along the Lothian Road, headed by the Magistrates and Town-Council in their robes, the pavement being occupied with solemnized spectators, and every window, being crowded with faces.'

So far, good. Keep the solemn, measured tone. He felt a fit of coughing coming on as the stone dust tickled his lungs and he turned to face the corner to dampen down the sound. He did not want to wake Lydia or the children. She had started to complain in married life about things she had accepted when they were courting, such as his habit of writing deep into the night.

'You have a family now, Hugh. And you, I mean we, are both older.'

Did she not understand that his routine of rising early, then off to work, then meetings and walks, then back to greet the children, left only this time to write? And that the routine could not be changed! It could not, if his life was not to fall into the pit of chaos that he could sense through the cracks in the floor, beneath the boggy marshes in the Meadows or the sewers in the town.

He described the procession from the deceased's home in Morningside to the New Cemetery at Grange, with the hearse drawn by four horses and attended by grooms.

How could he underline the special importance of Chalmers and of this day? Not just to himself, though it was a moment whose consequences he had been dreading. He had been pierced by a new steeliness in the eyes of Candlish, Cunningham and the rest as he greeted them at the graveside. Candlish had started when he saw him and had turned from his conversation with a Church of Scotland minister who Hugh thought he recognised, he thought it that man who was the proud curate of the Duke of Buccleuch. No doubt there in the name of his master, the sleekit fellow!

'Dust to dust; the grave now holds all that was mortal of Thomas Chalmers. Never before did we witness such a funeral; nay, never before, in at least the memory of man, did Scotland witness such a funeral. Greatness of the mere extrinsic type can always command a showy pageant; but mere extrinsic greatness never yet succeeded in purchasing the tears of a people; and the spectacle of yesterday in which the trappings of grief, worn not as idle signs, but as the representatives of a real sorrow, were borne by well-nigh half the population of the metropolis, and blackened the public ways for furlong after furlong, and mile after mile — was such as Scotland has rarely witnessed and which mere rank or wealth, when at the highest or the fullest, were never yet able to buy. It was a solemn tribute, spontaneously paid to departed goodness and greatness by the public mind.'

They told him wordsmiths like him would be increasingly relegated by the new science, or was it art, of photography. People wanted pictures, illustrations. He stood up and started to pace the length of the room to conjure up reluctant words. He would paint a picture that no lens could compete with.

'The day was one of those gloomy days, not infrequent in early summer, which steeps the landscape in a sombre neutral tint of gray — a sort of diluted gloom — and volumes of mist, unvariegated, blank and diffuse of outline, flew low athwart the hills or lay folded on the distant horizon. A chill breeze from the east murmured drearily through the trees that line the cemetery on the south and west and rustled amid the low ornamental shrubs that vary and adorn its surface. We felt as if the garish sunshine would have associated ill with the occasion. A continuous range of burial vaults, elevated some twenty feet over the level, with a screen of Gothic architecture in front, fenced by a parapet, and laid out into a broad roadway atop, runs along the cemetery from side to side, and was covered at an early hour by many thousand spectators, mostly well-dressed females. All the neighbouring roads, with the various

streets through which the procession passed, from Morningside on to Lauriston, and from Lauriston to the burying-ground, — a distance, by this circuitous route, of considerably more than two miles, — were lined thick with people.'

And so he went on, describing the closed shops, the figures dwindling in the distance and the tide of people sweeping into the cemetery, the scarlet cloaks of the magistracy flashing out among the general black, the slow, measured tramp of the multitude. He cried as he wrote down the final sentence,

'It was the dust of a Presbyterian minister which the coffin contained; and yet they were burying him amid the tears of a nation, and with more than kingly honours.'

He wept because he suddenly felt he was writing his own obituary.

He set off in the middle of the night to deliver the article to the printers, his last mission for Chalmers. The clammy darkness closed in around him and he clutched the pistol in his breast pocket, glancing at each passing shadow magnified by the gas lamps.

Lydia found him the next morning in the chair in the sitting-room. She woke him and helped him to the bedroom, undressed him and bathed his face and shoulders before laying him down to sleep. As she crept out of the room she saw nine-year old Harriet looking in, her eyes wide like a mouse surprised in the larder. She took her by the hand, urging her to be quiet and to come down for breakfast. The little girl said nothing.

That was the first time Hugh had not shared her bed except when he was away on his tours or on a visit to Makgill Crichton in Fife. She felt it would not be the last, not because he was growing away from her, though he was, but because she too was on her own journey which he did not seem able to share, as a mother, a writer of fiction, a woman.

Hugh rose and dressed himself around one. The house was empty save for the housemaid who told him the mistress and the bairns had gone out to visit a friend in Morningside. Would he like breakfast?

He shook his head and said he had to go the newspaper and to tell

Mrs Miller he would be home late. He could not tell why he said that.

As he walked up to the office he looked at the people in this world without Chalmers, this world without certainty. He passed by St. George's just as an elder was swinging the door shut.

'Yes, that's it,' he thought.

He oversaw the final proofreading of the paper then retired to his office. There was a package on his desk. He pushed it to the side and took out a sheet of blank paper. He had reduced his contributions to the newspaper and invited others to express their views in order to escape further censure from Candlish and his men on his imposing a single line on the publication. This had not always been successful: some of the contributors, such as Begg, had taken advantage of the opportunity to indulge in the most rabid anti-popery. He was no longer of use to the Free Kirk; no minister ever visited the newspaper and he was aware that Candlish was bypassing him. He had suffered but comforted himself that as long as he was serving Chalmers, he was doing his duty. What now?

His eye was caught once more by the brown paper package with the black stamps. He picked it up and unwrapped it in his usual careful way. It was yet another edition of the book that was taking the decade by storm, *Vestiges of the Natural History of Creation*. Five editions in three years! He began to read it again.

He walked home around nine o'clock that evening, the sun still shining in the long Scottish summer day. He had found his mission. He had found a new community. He would join science and faith and defeat the anonymous blasphemer.

Conversations Among Carnivores

They had been eating and drinking for several hours in one of London's oldest hostelries, the Cheshire Cheese in Fleet Street, at an especially boisterous assembly of the Red Lions Club, yet another association founded by Forbes. It met up at the end of the different professional symposia and congresses held around Great Britain and Ireland in competition with the stuffy formal dinners hosted by the officeholders and dull municipal councillors in the halls of the congress or an opulent hotel. As might be expected from anything set up by Forbes, an invite to the Red Lions dinner was more eagerly sought-after and bestowed greater prestige than the official jamboree. The food was simple, mainly plain roast beef and boiled potatoes and to make that clear the invitations began with the words, '*The carnivora will feed.*' When a contribution met with Forbes' approval, he would gather up his coat tails, wag them and roar his approval heartily. All the other members would then join the roaring chorus. This became so celebrated that the Secretary of the Zoological Society presented the Club with the skin of a lion which graced the President's chair with paws at the elbows and the tail handily positioned so that it could be waved with gusto.

Tonight, Forbes was seated at the head of the table, flanked by Goodsir and other members of the Oernomathic Brotherhood with their scarlet ribbons and silver triangles. Goodsir was smiling: he had been the only one to good-naturedly puncture Forbes' irrepressible flow of ironic self-aggrandisement. The bare wooden tables were simply decorated and the light from the candles and lamps was sent dancing round the room by the low, white-arched ceiling, illuminating that rosy-cheeked fellow there, and this grey-haired bear of a man here. All the naturalists had the healthy air of outdoorsmen and indeed from time to time one would pull out a piece of seaweed from his pocket or produce a snail for his companions to admire.

There was Thompson from Ireland, MacAndrew from Liverpool and five or six sheepish new participants anxious to comport themselves with just the right degree of irreverence while observing the unspoken hierarchies of the gathering. Songs had been sung and toasts made. Forbes had recited one of his specially composed poems for the group and cigars were being passed around. Perhaps because his asthma prevented him from smoking or just because, as usual, the fellow was incapable of sitting at rest, when Goodsir murmured something about a new species of crab he had just dissected, Forbes slipped out through the swing door then reappeared, walking on his hands and with his knees over his shoulders!

'Well, you never saw anything like it!' Chambers exclaimed to the aptly named Lyon Playfair as they were walking back to their hotel later. At the time though, they had hooted and applauded along with the rest of the company and exploded with laughter at the sight of the landlord's non-plussed expression. Could you eject someone for pretending to be a crab?

Chambers had joined the company a little after the others, as he had spent some time in conversation with a tall, bearded man at a corner table. 'A fellow writer and publisher' he said. Playfair had been relieved when he sat down beside him, as a red-haired fellow from Somerset had been trying to interest him in a particular mollusc found only in Cornwall. It was a bivalve, apparently.

'Chambers has returned to our chamber!' Forbes exclaimed. 'A toast to him and Mr Dickens!'

And they all stood to toast to ***Wine*, Love, and *Learning***, the Brotherhood's motto, except for Chambers and the bearded man who was already disappearing through the narrow doorway. And then the speeches had gone on, punctuated by growls of dissent or roars of agreement and the occasional wagging of tails.

Playfair was more reserved than his fellows. Like his brothers he had been sent back to Scotland from Bengal where their father had been Inspector General of Hospitals and had lived and studied in St Andrews and Edinburgh. He had got to know Chambers in Fife. After university he had been appointed manager of a calico works in England and then became Professor of Chemistry at the Royal Manchester Institution and in 1848 he was elected to the Royal Society. He had the open-faced optimist of the northern entrepreneur and the reserve of the Parliamentarian. He was a Scot in England and a Brit in Scotland, a coming combination of the epoch.

Chambers had spent a good deal of time in the great metropolis since he had had to withdraw his candidacy for the Provost of Edinburgh in the 1848 election. The swirling rumours that he was the author of *Vestiges of Creation* had sunk his campaign and threatened to blacken the reputation of his publishing company. He had accepted Forbes' invitation tonight as part of an effort to build bridges with the scientific community, even informally. But he was not comfortable. London society offered him a release from the increasingly stifling air of Edinburgh but at the cost of being an outsider again.

He was still stinging from the attacks. 'Some people will invent stories and scandal just to sow doubts in the mind of the public. I will not submit to this;' he had said in his last stormy campaign meeting. It was necessary for him to lie low for a while. He wasn't safe though, even in London. A year earlier, Samuel Wilberforce, the Bishop of Oxford, had used his Sunday sermon at St. Mary's Church on 'the wrong way of doing science' to deliver a bitter attack obviously aimed at Chambers. The church, 'crowded to suffocation' with geologists, astronomers, and zoologists, was treated to sneers about the 'half-learned' seduced by the 'foul temptation' of speculation looking for a self-sustaining universe in a 'mocking spirit of unbelief,' showing a failure to understand the 'modes of the Creator's acting' or to meet the responsibilities of a gentleman.

'And Lyon, all this because of the mere suspicion I am the author of that book!' he protested to Playfair.

'Yes, but that is what happens when we enter politics. You have to take it as part of being a public man. All my family have paid that price.'

'Your family? Are you related to William Playfair, the architect?'

'Oh no. And he joined the Free Church! I have had to endure much calumny due to that confusion. How can someone be a radical Calvinist and a Classical Architect?'

'Well,' Chambers interjected, 'when he followed the classical Royal Academy building with the Gothic New College at the top of the Mound, the joke went round that no one could accuse him of not keeping up with the times!'

They both laughed, but then Chambers added,

'I am not sure that Camelot is an advance on Athens. What has happened to our philosophical ambitions? Edinburgh is shrinking, sir. It must be said that the arts are not flourishing and even the practical sciences are stagnating. Forty years ago, this meeting would have been held in Ambrose's Tavern in Edinburgh. Now our only cultural export is the Temperance movement!'

Playfair laughed. 'Perhaps we need to look to Glasgow or Manchester and not Edinburgh or London. There are wonderful things happening in those cities, they are the vanguard of the new age of technology. Your health, my friend!'

Their talk was interrupted by Forbes launching into song again. He spoke through his nose and his singing voice was like a bent trumpet heard over a long stretch of sea: sonorous but not pleasant. This was a song it seemed he had composed for the first meeting of the Red Lions and was repeated at every reunion. For the uninitiated there were printed copies on the table. Everyone, even Chambers and Playfair, joined in the chorus.

Hurrah for the dredge, with its iron edge,
And its mystical triangle,

And its hided net with meshes set
Odd fishes to entangle!
The ship may move through the wave above,
Mid scenes exciting wonder,
But braver sights the dredge delights
As it roveth the waters under.
Chorus — Then a-dredging we will go, wise boys!
Then a-dredging we will go.

It was schoolboy stuff but all those round the table seemed to revel in its silliness. Here they were, a bunch of wild young fellows again, men amongst men, ready to conquer the world. All except Chambers, who could not forget the drudgery of his youth and how he had been forced to abandon school and earn a living to support his family. Playfair noted the downturn of his mouth and absent gaze and suggested it was time for them to go back to the hotel. 'Playing the beast is all very well, but progress eschews whimsy and is made through individual effort and through rational argument,' he said as he went to fetch their coats. 'We are getting too old for this,' he muttered to himself, the air of a sober Edinburgh worthy slipping back over him like a second, protective skin.

'I must hang on to reason,' Chambers told himself. 'It will see me through better than this tomfoolery or the superstition of religion. I will defeat the Scottish god and his scorn as well as the arrogant Anglican ministers. Playfair is right. Effort and reason.' It had always been his way. He would not fail.

A cacophony of roars and growls followed them out into the street as the door swung closed behind them.

Inside, the revelry went on for another hour, with people slipping away one by one till only Goodsir and Forbes were left. It was unusual for the Edinburgh anatomist to stay out so late. What was on his mind? Forbes asked himself. Nothing, of course, except dissection and specimens. He must be going.

'I have to be off to bed, John. I am a married man now and Emily will be waiting up for me. She is a good girl but sometimes I miss the bachelor freedoms and envy you, old chap. In any case, I have to write up the proceedings of the Congress. Publish, publish, publish… the endless treadmill they tell us leads to a chair in a good university. I am so desperate that I may even have to accept something here instead of Scotland.

By the by, I have not seen much published by you of late and yet I know you as one who works even harder than I. Something up, old chap?'

Goodsir shrugged his shoulders but with the air of an animal getting ready for a tussle rather than a gentleman showing indifference.

'Well, in Scotland, to the same degree that publication contributes to university appointments, once secured, a word taken ill or a statement suspect of irreligion can dash your career. So better to keep silent. But I am amassing a great body of work which one day will make my name, I hope. And when you are at last up in Edinburgh the two of us will be too strong for the holy whisperers!'

His face was flushed and he seemed anxious to unburden himself of something. Edward had feared this confession for years. It would be the end of their friendship. However, he was relieved when John went on,

'I had four ambitions in life: — to be a great teacher of anatomy, a surgeon of distinction, the founder of a Goodsirian Museum and fourth, to rank as a man of science with the greatest of our epoch. I have had some success in the first, but the second has been sabotaged by the Royal Infirmary, the third takes more time and resources than I possess and so I am focussing on the last at the moment. I feel if I can elucidate my triangular theory then fame awaits. I am still giving the best of myself to teaching, however. I was in Oxford recently and most impressed by their tutorial system. I am trying to introduce it into my courses.'

'Isn't there an opportunity for the Edinburgh students to ask questions in a lecture?'

'Yes, if they are sure of themselves and well-read. But there are not many Edward Forbes!'

Forbes was alarmed by his friend's increasing mania for the triangle, communicated in endless missives whose wavering lines suggested they had been written by candlelight. He stared at Goodsir who was giving him his faithful spaniel look and fingering the triangle that hung loosely about his neck. He hesitated, torn between a desire to say something and his fear of wounding John. Fear of being wounded in return.

'Do you know why I chose the triangle as our symbol? Because I am from the Isle of Man. Our symbol is the three-legged triskelion and I have inherited a fascination with the number three. It gave structure and unity to our meetings. But if I had been from Surrey, it could have been a square.'

Goodsir frowned.

'Are you suggesting my triangular theory is a result of being born under the St Andrew's flag?'

'Come now, Goodsir, of course not, it was just a bit of whimsy.' He made to rustle his coat tails but the look in his friend's face warned him against it. He tried to explain and found himself scratching triangles and squares chasing each other on the song sheet before him.

'John, I don't believe that our structures reflect anything in nature. We perceive but the fragments of ideal forms dreamed up by the Creator. We walk among shadows, incomplete pieces of a puzzle which exists in God's mind. We convince ourselves that this piece will fit, and we change our idea of the whole to accommodate our new discovery. But we fool ourselves. We tend to put shapes on things, old man, like a child in his playpen: today what is a triangle, tomorrow will be half of a rhomboid. You and I have both modified our anatomy in the last decade. We have progressed in our understanding of the skull, for example.'

'Thanks to my research.'

'Yes, John. But that will change with the next discovery.'

He saw that look in Goodsir's eye. The look that said, 'you can talk all you like, you can be as articulate as you want, but I know, and you are just searching.' That quiet arrogance allied to a need for his approval which attracted and repelled him.

Goodsir was not to be shaken off.

'But if you find the same shape throughout nature, not only as perceived but when dissected, it is logical to suppose a unified design and designer.'

'Fine,' Forbes thought. 'I can answer what you are saying and not saying.' That had also been at the heart of their relationship.

'Yes, the logarithmic spiral. Discovered by Descartes and later by Bernoulli. People find it everywhere, especially in the shell of the Nautilus and in Ammonite fossils. But you and I discovered it for ourselves that day I showed you the snails from Arthur's Seat, so it is not only universal but particular to us, my good friend.'

Did he detect tears in Goodsir's eyes? He had thought to bring him back from abstract speculation to the personal, to remind him that the essential pattern in their lives was their friendship. He felt grateful for his companion's unceasing efforts to gain him a post in Edinburgh even if others, including his wife, mocked his 'faithful spaniel.' Now he had only made matters worse. The evening was turning morose. And why was John holding his thumb and forefinger up, pressing the joint between them down with a finger from the other hand? There was no denying it, Goodsir was a case! And he seemed to want to speak as much as he had stayed silent at the feast.

'The recurrence of the same patterns throughout organic and inorganic nature shows a common design, but I do not fall into the trap laid by Hume for those who say it reveals something about the character of the designer.'

Forbes sighed. His friend was in a metaphysical mood tonight. Perhaps there was something happening in Edinburgh that was worrying him. He ordered another port for them both and nodded for Goodsir to continue.

'As you know, I maintain that it is Man's completeness and his independence of his environment that separates him from the rest of Nature, even though he shares many characteristics. Of course, races can degenerate and if we pay no attention to our spiritual part, we may let the animal in us take over.'

'You are rehearsing a defence against the materialists. I did not think they were so strong in holy Edinburgh.'

'No, I am trying to expound my ideas in a way that the ever more powerful Free Kirk can unde..rstand and accept. They are in a panic over *Vestiges* and the evolutionists and see anatomy as a wicked science, profaning the temple of the body and in league with the atheists. They will not accept I am on their side. That has already cost me the Surgeon's position and may yet stifle my research. I have to make their argument for them as they are incapable of making it themselves. They let that windbag Miller publish tales for common folk based on the belief that just because we have not witnessed miracles does not mean there are none. The man draws well and has a notion of geology, but his Creator is too Scottish for me, too unwilling to accept the perfection of humankind.'

Forbes started to pay more attention. When Goodsir made a claim, it was generally based on extensive research.

'So Man is not just a superior animal?'

'A beast behaves only by instinct. It has no consciousness. When a cat is hungry it eats. It does not think about being hungry. An animal species is adapted to its environment and if that environment changes it may become extinct. Man does not so totally depend on his environment. He has also the gift of speech, which is once more not just a change in degree over the animal kingdom but in kind.'

Goodsir was a lion transformed into a man, Forbes thought, though he kept the boutade to himself.

'Moreover, I now know that the human brain is not superior to that of animals just because of its size but *because of its geometry*. And this is what I intend to prove and stake my claim to scientific renown upon. A new anatomy is the key, to demonstrate that the form of the human body is not just fitted to its purpose, to its environment, but is structurally perfect in its design and the perfection of the forms we find in the Universe.'

Goodsir's exposition was cut short by the landlord's presenting them with the bill and explaining it was past closing time. Both men parted at the doorstep, Forbes off home to his wife and Goodsir to the room he had rented at the Society. The bed was still made up in the morning; he slept in his clothes on the floor.

You could never tell with Forbes. He seemed to agree with everyone and was incapable of dismissing anyone. But did Forbes understand him? Did he sympathise? He had been asking himself that question all night into the early hours, broken by the sound of traders wheeling out their carts in the street below. For if Forbes did not sympathise with him in the full sense of the word, he was alone. He was lost. He was a complete failure.

The Lost Idealists

The revolution had failed. No, it was worse than that. The revolutions had collapsed across Europe and even mild Chartism had crumbled. Enric kept the letters he had received from comrades on the continent, describing a crescendo of hope, of joy at the beginning of 1848 and then a crash into bitter desperation. They talked of betrayal, of despair at the failure of class solidarity and fear of what was to come. One of them told him of the death of Jacques in Paris, crushed under the hooves of a cavalry horse. He would never see Jacques again, never discuss Comte and the new age that was blossoming. He realised that the loss of his friend affected him more than the gigantic catastrophe of the defeat in country after country. Jacques would have scolded him; told him this was war and there was no time to cry over casualties. He would have said that Enric was becoming sentimental, bourgeois.

'Et alors, mon ami, imbecile, idiot!' he screamed, shouting abuse at his dead friend. He stomped around his room, glaring at the bedspread, daring the wardrobe to a fight. He felt helpless, he felt betrayed by his dreams of equality, of liberty and brotherhood. He should have been with Jacques. He had not even answered the letter inviting him to come and join him in the conquest of Paris. How could he say he could not do so as he was in love with a girl who would not leave Edinburgh? How to explain that part of him had dissolved in her and he felt her sediment in his blood?

Love, that bourgeois invention! After that first night, he had continued to see Elspeth, sometimes three times in the same week, sometimes not for a fortnight.

'I am an independent woman, Enric,' she had replied when he asked why they did not move in together. And in the mornings she would get up and leave, telling him to make himself some breakfast, unsure if he was invited again that night. He bought her little presents, vases, a pen, hair clasps. She smiled and said, 'That's sweet,' but the gifts would disappear, never to be seen again. She attended meetings on women's issues. She was good with her hands and had made most of the furniture and shelves in her flat. She was studying Russian and it infuriated him as it was a language he did not speak. 'I am writing to Olga in St. Petersburg, in Russian, already!' she gleamed at him one day. No, that was not what annoyed him, was it because she had not chosen a language he could tutor her in? No, it was because she had not invited him to study it with her. She was self-sufficient. He admired her for that but wanted to look after her, to care for her. She encouraged him to go out with others, to do things without him. John Arthur told him he was a lucky man. He didn't feel lucky. He had broken off with her twice. The first time he had felt his heart shattering into small pieces. He had waited for her to contact him then hung around the streets near the hospital. He had finally knocked on her door and been admitted and kissed before she told him she was going out, but he could wait there for her to come back. A similar thing happened the last time although it seemed she had made new friends, 'sisters' whom, she made it clear, were 'not his sort of people.' He never met them but had to sit while she wrote notes to them and asked him to post them on his way to work.

All this was true, he thought, but not the truth. The truth was she was a caring person who would do anything for her patients and their families. He suspected that was where his presents had gone. He had fallen ill once and she had nursed him, made him soup and brought him books she thought he would enjoy. And her voice! She sang radical songs and folk music from the Borders with a voice like warm water running down over your hand. The truth was also that he knew little about her. She was silent on her family, where she came from, except to say that she did not believe the past existed. She was living in the future, she explained, when women would be equal, when the family would not exist. Instead, we would live in a community.

He thought that was ironic, given her fierce independence. When he said that it caused the second rupture. It was also sparked by her refusal to come to his place. 'You will like Alia and the girls,' he said. She had reddened and declared she would not darken the door of a sweatshop, of an establishment run by a woman that exploited women.

'How can you say that, Elspeth? The girls seem happy, and the Mistress was the one who recommended me to go to Emma Martin's talk.'

'The Mistress!' she laughed. 'That says it all. Sometimes I think you still look at things through misty eyes.

And you talk about my reticence,' she had gone on, 'when I know nothing about your past except you were a sailor. I thought you lived for today and tomorrow like me.'

He asked her if she loved him.

'I do love you, Enric. I have given myself to you, at least all I can give. But I love you means I *do* love you. Neither of us knows the future. Just take the moment, just feel my hand in yours and let's just be. Just be.'

'Just be,' but be what? He asked himself. A man acted; a man was nothing if he just *was*.

He was glad to receive a summons to Fife to collect a package for Manchester. Chambers still treated him courteously but distantly. They were sitting across from each other in the bay window overlooking the orchard when he began with his usual indirect probing as to whether Enric had opened one of the packages entrusted to him.

'No, and I have not shown my translations to anyone else, sir.'

He was puzzled by Chambers, who seemed increasingly the picture of the prosperous conservative businessman in his country house, a new curtain here, a new hunting painting there. Yet the articles he translated dealt with radical science and sceptical theories. Enric smarted at the thought that Elspeth was the only person he knew whose way of life matched her ideals.

He was unprepared for the question when it came.

'Do you believe in fairies?'

When Enric did not reply, Chambers went on,

'You know: fairies, elves, ghosts and the spirits of our loved ones come back from the dead?'

Enric did not know what to answer. He knew that in Scotland many people believed in apparitions, the girls at his house often talked about them. He did not want to contradict Chambers over something so trivial. However, he shook his head and said,

'I am not sure I can even believe in the things I see around me and have no time or thought for superstitions. I have seen the harm such voodoo can do in my travels to the tropics.'

'Good. I have decided that the real barrier to progress is not technological obstacles or scientific error but rampant superstition. Sometimes it calls itself religion but that is too big a battle and would involve a social upheaval I am not prepared to countenance.'

Enric sensed there was something more. He waited.

'You have shown yourself to be a trusty, efficient and faithful helper. I hope I too have lived up to my part, giving you employment and time to translate and act as my emissary.'

Enric reddened. Was he being dismissed from his post?

'My dear fellow, what a face! This is not a farewell but an offer to continue our collaboration. This time I must emphasise the need for the utmost discretion, but I am confident enough in you to disclose the nature of the project. In addition to the trips to Manchester I will need you to attend meetings in Glasgow and Edinburgh.'

'Meetings?'

'Well, seances or talks on paranormal phenomena. You not only have a good rational mind; you are a natural sceptic. More to the point, they tell me you are a gifted conjuror and entertain your colleagues with your magic tricks.'

'These are just playful amusements, Mr. Chambers. I fail to see their connection to spiritualist meetings.'

'Conjurers understand how tricks are done. I need you to use your insights into dexterity, manipulation and the technical mechanisms behind illusion.'

Enric was at a loss for words. He felt belittled, demoted from philosopher to doorman. What did he care if the paying public were hoodwinked by the legion of false seers that you could find in any British city, even so-called 'Enlightened Edinburgh?'

'Mr Chambers, I am not your performing ape.' There, he had said it. He had moved from an employee fearful of dismission to a rebel, a proud independent man. He suddenly felt they were both false echoes of the other.'

'Ah, the socialist speaks. I do not mean to change you, Enric. I do not expect you to change me, that is why our association works. I am not your circus master either.'

Enric nodded.

'Though it seems to me that your political ideals have been put on the shelf, for a good while.'

Enric reddened.

'Ach, Enric. I too have cooled towards politics since my debacle in Edinburgh. But I respect you and trust you have some esteem for me. I am asking for your help here. We both believe in progress. Let us defeat superstition.'

He had left the house with two volumes by a writer called Catherine Crowe. 'She lives a few doors down from me in Edinburgh and I cannot risk a public disagreement with her, especially as I have published several of her pieces in the *Journal*. The book is called *The Dark Side of the Night*.

These volumes have gone through three editions in a year, Enric. It is quite the sensation and has almost eclipsed *Vestiges*. I want it discredited, for the public good of course. Read it, attend any lectures on it and check her German sources.'

'Is this really so important? What is one book by a crank?'

'You are too young to have known the precious gem that was Edinburgh. How can we have descended into superstition? Mrs Crowe is a friend of both Dickens and Thackery and this work will make the paranormal respectable if we don't act.'

When Enric did not reply, Chambers went on.

'I realise there is a sort of malign justice in this. That my brother and I have enabled the rapid diffusion of information among the populace for educational and uplifting ends, how we lobbied to remove the newspaper tax and introduced your steam printers has also meant that nefarious nonsense such as this reaches a wide public. I would say we have let the genie out of the bottle, if that was not making use of a superstition!'

And so Enric had nodded and taken the books. He had caught the afternoon coach from St Andrews to the ferry at Largo. The journey had become routine, and he paid no attention to the rolling hills and small villages of east Fife. Just as the coach was leaving St Andrews a man had almost leapt onto it, shouting for the coachman to halt, to let him aboard.

'Goodbye, Sir David!' the fellow cried to a grey-haired old man standing panting against the wall. Tell Makgill Crichton we will all be together in Rankeillor for Christmas!'

'Such energy!' Enric thought to himself as he shifted up to leave space for the newcomer to sit.

The man was wearing a plaid shawl. He was in his late forties, Enric guessed. He could not tell whether he was a gentleman or not as he had learned that being a foreigner blinded him to many of the keys to the British class system. But he trusted his nose. The man smelt of seaweed and sand. He liked that.

The cab jogged on with the four occupants maintaining their equilibrium and therefore their dignity by subtle manoeuvres, holding onto a strap here, clutching the seat with their knees there. The traces of harvested barley insisted by its bitter scent that it had been there and would return the next year. Enric thought of the nodding heads of the grain and felt at one with the countryside in a way he had never done in the sharp-hilled coast he had been raised in. The other two passengers were students from St Andrews and they fell into wide-eyed silence at the mention of Sir David. The other man seemed engrossed in examining shells and fossils that he carried in a canvas satchel. A hammer and some brushes fitted into straps on the bag. It was an ingenious and practical thing, Enric thought, the technician in him responding to neat solutions.

As they were approaching Largo, the seaweed and sand man turned to him.

'Do you know Mrs Crowe, sir?'

Enric shook his head. He realised the man had been looking at the volume on his knee.

'No, I am just returning this for a friend.' He fell silent abruptly. What if the man inquired who the friend was?

However, the man asked if he could look at the book. What if Chambers' ex libris stamp was on it? Enric handed it over, opening it at the Contents page and gulped. The stranger leafed through the book but made no comment other than to frown from time to time and to tut.

'This is all froth and speculation. Sir David Brewster dealt with the apparitions of the dead from a scientific standpoint over twenty years ago in his book, *Natural Magic*.'

'So you don't believe in ghosts, in spectres?'

'I did not say that. I have seen several and recounted my experiences in writing. Indeed, the lady sought me out, as she has pursued anyone who can claim to have witnessed an apparition. I avoided her. This is a difficult subject and a man in my position must not compromise the acceptance of the revealed truths in the Holy Bible by mixing them up with speculations about more trivial, individual experiences.'

And it suddenly dawned on Enric to whom he was talking! Why had he not realised before!

Before he could say anything, the other introduced himself as Hugh Miller, writer, and amateur geologist.

'Enric Serra.'

After running through the standard autobiography a foreigner learns by rote, he asked Mr Miller, 'Hugh' he interrupted him, if he too was heading back to Edinburgh.

Then Miller asked him which part of town he lived in. He mentioned the name of the street, 'On the north side of town, like my place at Jock's Lodge' Miller said. They chatted about the different areas of the city, the up-and coming ones and those in decline. They discovered they both worked in the Royal Mile.

'Yes, I think I have passed you in the street. You generally have a book in your hand, and I presumed you were a teacher.'

When Enric explained he was a printing engineer employed by Chambers, Miller raised his eyebrow. 'He brought you all the way from the Iberian Peninsula to here?'

Enric tried to explain that he had been attracted to Edinburgh thanks to its reputation for cultural debate and by the fact its large publishing companies meant he had a good chance of finding employment. He tried to give an account skirting politics and religion, which was not easy with a man like Miller.

'Well, Edinburgh is not what it was, though it was always difficult for a young man to meet the cultural elite, as I discovered on my first visit to the city. You should have seen the sight of me as I walked up and down in front of Walter Scott's house in the hope of bumping into him!'

'I did the same in Paris in hope of an audience with Balzac. With identical results!'

The two men got on well together. The rough sea made conversation on the ferry more difficult, but when they both alighted from the boat, Miller gave Enric his card.

'I will ask Chambers if he would mind us consulting you on some improvements we are planning in our printing process. It would be well-recompensed. We may not be Chambers', but *The Witness* is a successful publication.'

Enric accepted the card and nodded. Two promotions in one day!

As he walked towards his home Enric stopped short, as if winded. How can I be so shallow? He pictured Jacques running towards him, hands held out as if to catch him and take him with him. He had to blink to make sure it was just his grief speaking. 'Mon ami, mon frère, mon idéaliste égaré'.

Exclusive Societies

The scandal over the money would not go away and Candlish, thanks to his Princeton education and contacts with the Southern churches, felt aggrieved and vulnerable. The Free Church seemed to spend most of its time in infighting, he thought, and this controversy was exploited by his enemies within. Perhaps this was the fate of any radical organisation, at least one without a strong leader or with an egalitarian structure like the Free Kirk. That word, 'free' was a blessing and a curse. At the beginning, it had acted like a shining standard which made the Church of Scotland seem dusty and anachronistic in this democratic age. However, it also made it awkward for the new Church to be associated with less enthusiastic champions of universal liberty. If Guthrie had worked wonders in drumming up the desperately needed financial support from the congregations at home, then Candlish and others had issued similar appeals to brother dissenting flocks in the Empire and the United States. Their call had been especially heeded in the Southern States by congregations of the American Presbyterian Church who were as adamant in their identification with the freedom and independence of the Scottish Calvinists as in their rejection of liberty for their slaves.

Of course, the visit to Scotland and its Capital by the fiery orator and escaped slave Frederick Douglass during 1846 and 1847 still reverberated in people's minds. He had attacked the Free Church and stained them with collaboration with slavery in packed meeting after meeting. He would start his perorations slowly, almost meekly, then build up till he bellowed 'Send Back the Money!' and the crowd started to chant the phrase back to him.

Candlish still shivered with disgust as he thought of it.

And it wasn't even just the hoi-poloi that worshipped him and was thrilled by his renditions of Robert Burns' poems and his admiration for the Bard. *A man's a man for a' that* took on a more dangerous tone when recited by an ex-slave.

What exasperated Candlish even more was Douglass' welcome by people who shunned *him*, one of the leaders of the Free Church! He heard that Douglass had written to his wife,

'*I enjoy every thing here which may be enjoyed by those of a paler hue — no distinction here. I have found myself in the society of the Combes, the Crowes and the Chambers, the first people of this city and no one seemed alarmed by my presence.*'

This was where freedom and democracy led! Yes, he knew he was overreacting, and he was no friend to slavery. But this had been the first great controversy of the Free Church and was used as a weapon against them. Surprisingly, the main ally he had found, the one man of influence to defend him, was Hugh! He did not know whether to be relieved or annoyed.

At the first appearance of the articles in *The Witness* Candlish presumed Miller was trying to win his favour. He even dropped by the newspaper office to see what bounty he might have to trade. He was shown short shrift.

'What a surprise to find you here, Dr. Candlish. Have you lost your way or been attacked by some passing madness?'

Candlish just asked for a copy of the most recent number and made an about-turn. The impudence of the man! He would pay for that!

He was therefore bemused to find not only more articles defending the Church's right to keep the American donations by Hugh Miller, man of the people, but an increasingly dismissive tone then an outright refusal to debate the issue in the newspaper.

The Scots owners of liberated slaves had received a generous recompense from the government for their loss of income. Some considered it recognition that they had been deprived of their legitimate rights, other saw it as a confirmation of their guilt. Lydia had read Mrs Harriet Beecher Stowe and had even thought of writing a Scottish version of her novel with pious Highlanders and the same Christian forbearance. When she mentioned the debate about the slave issue and the churches, Hugh knitted his brows. He was evidently frustrated with her, disappointed. He looked at her, or rather, looked past her.

'I am hostile to the use by liberal American divines of old doctrines applied to a new cause that strike at responsibility, service and the root of all morals. But it is true that while we can compare the supremacy of the Whites to that of the English over the Irish in Cromwell's time and afterwards, Cromwell's despotic supremacy was exercised with a good conscience, which I fear is not the case in the States.'

'But do you really think that the White supremacy in the Southern States will perdure?'

He sipped his ale and looked at her. Before, she would not have questioned him so, she would have corrected his argument but not put in doubt its rightness.

'The chances are all in favour of the Whites from the superiority of race. The Blacks or Half-castes have no person of mark among them. That fellow Frederick Douglass is their most remarkable man.'

'Yes, he was certainly extremely popular when he was in Edinburgh.'

'Popularity is a poor measure of worth, Lydia.'

She grimaced. Hugh would never reprove her in the past. He used to be proud of telling people how shrewd his wife was. Those days seemed to be distant now. There was still love, still respect, but he seemed to her in many ways a diminished man. Bitterness and loss seemed to grow on him like icicles on the windowpanes since Chalmers' death and his exclusion from the inner circle of the Church's elders.

'I met Douglass once and think but little of him, perhaps because he seemed to think so much of himself. Do you know he considered bringing his wife and children over to settle permanently in Edinburgh? Can you imagine where they would have lived, who would have received them once Combe and company had tired of them? No, his colour is not important, he is just another half-educated workingman trying to bring others down to his station.'

She left him to his ale and herring and went to check on the children.

Disappointment and marriage make poor bedfellows, Hugh mused. What was he disappointed about? He wasn't sure. Perhaps it was just that he was no longer young, could no longer measure himself equal to his scientific or literary heroes by loading the scales through adding his future prospects in with his current achievements. He was what he was, not what he might become. That is difficult for anyone to accept. Yet he was not yet fifty and still had a young family. He had time to do remarkable things.

Yes, he was disappointed. *Footprints of the Creator* had sold well, and Murchison, Agassiz and other scientific eminences had praised it. There was even talk of the Swiss expert writing a preface to the next edition. The public had liked it too. Hugh had even been lionised in London's Exeter Hall packed to the roof. Someone else had read the extracts from his book for him as well as his prepared oration. If they could not understand his accent in Paisley, how could he expect more in England? You had to adapt yourself to your audience if you wanted to win them over. He had learned that as soon as he stepped out of Cromarty.

Of course, there was the problem he had encountered with *The Old Red Sandstone*, although multiplied. He addressed himself both to the general public and to the specialists. Geology and the study of fossils was a new and controversial science and he had to proclaim its advances but rest his arguments on solid foundations. His religious peers were suspicious of anything that could put Genesis in doubt and his scientific sympathisers eager to criticise any concessions to faith and to use his apparent concordance with the new theories to advance more radical ideas. Did they not realise the importance of his fight against *Vestiges* and all it represented?

Nevertheless, he could take the criticism along with the praise for the delicacy of his drawings, the precision of his prose. His discovery and definition of a species of Asterolepis had won over Agassiz, who had graciously bowed to Hugh's arguments, even though they overturned his own. The problem was the adulation of the ignorant and the scorn of the knowledgeable. He had thought his use of an evolutionist's conversation with an imagined farmer would serve to elucidate the fallacies in the developmental position. *Superposition, not Parental Relation* he entitled it and in it a farmer explained he had an old midden with generations of dead animals and discarded fish bones in layers according to the time of their deposit. To say that one engendered the subsequent layer would be as ridiculous as supposing that fossils of creatures uncovered in higher deposits were descendants of more recent specimens. Hugh had thought it a pithy exposition of the flaw in his opponents' arguments.

Looking back, he realised he had been mistaken. The scientists laughed at it and the more ignorant of his readers saw his attack on a scientific argument as a licence to attack all science. He had come to understand that the problem of mass communication was the impossibility of knowing your audience, or even of controlling where and in what context your article was published. Many of his articles had been purloined and published in England, Canada, and the United States, and, depending on how they were introduced, earned him the reputation of a radical, a conservative, a democrat, a scientist or the last bulwark of faith against atheism.

There was also the problem of the moving target. Each edition of *Vestiges* changed details, never admitting a refutation but changing the weak flanks of its body for a muscular cartilage which the old arrows could not pierce. To criticise it was to make it stronger. It was a starfish which responded to attack by multiplication.

The clock was ticking, and he still had not written anything for this week's edition. This number might have to contain more Church matter than normal. Well, Candlish and his irksome crew would at least be content, if such a bunch of scheming, ambitious men ever could be!

He thought of the young man he had met on the way back from St Andrews. He had told Lydia as he stepped into the house and divested himself of his muddy boots, that he had met an acolyte of Chambers. He had seen the mark on the book. What was that man up to now?

Hugh had refused to countenance the rumours about Robert Chambers and *Vestiges*. He felt he understood the fellow, he had looked up to him as a young man and Chambers had published his first articles. He had heard of many people asking Chambers if he was the author of that notorious book and they had all come away without a clear answer. Hugh himself had asked him about it at a dinner celebrating the inauguration of the new provost. He had taken the soft refusal and the sideways glance to be the result of Chambers' bitterness at the electoral humiliation. He had not seen him since that night and had received only a cursory thank you for the copy of *The Footprints* he had sent him. Perhaps he needed to visit him, but under what pretext? Then he thought of the fellow on the coach and smiled like someone who has found a lever to move a heavy stone or a twig to clear the mud from his boot soles. Yes, Mr Enric would do. He might also find out what role that man played. No ordinary employee would journey back and forth to St Andrews. Mr Enric did not seem ordinary in any case.

A week passed without reply from Chambers. Then, in an act even more surprising than Candlish's visit to the paper, the door to the office opened and in stepped the publisher! Chambers still had his full head of brown hair, but flecks of grey were appearing, and he was acquiring the more rounded look of many middle-aged men. He was always an energetic fellow, Hugh thought, but today his cheeks were flushed and he had the air of a man just escaped from an ambush or on his way to storm the Castle singlehanded.

'They are the past, Hugh. We are the future. A curse on their pompous, degenerate souls!'

Hugh nodded over to McCrie to tell him to be off and leave the two of them alone. He then fetched some water and slowly poured a tumbler-full for Chambers, who drank it down in a draught and held the beaker out for more. Hugh waited like you do for your horse to calm itself after being spooked by a dog, knowing his demeanour would have more effect than words. Nonetheless, he was itching to know what had brought Chambers to burst in on him like this.

'Excuse my impudence in erupting into your office, Hugh. Most irregular, most unseemly.' He paused. 'Not what a gentleman would do.'

When Hugh waved his hand to indicate that he was welcome and that he was to consider himself at home here, Chambers went on.

'But of course, we are not gentlemen, you or I. And they won't let us forget it. I am sorry, but I was coming down the High Street after one of the most irritating meetings of my life and I thought of you and I and the society we form.'

'The society?' Hugh thought. What can the man mean?

Chambers checked himself for a moment, seeing the bewilderment on Miller's face.

'Yes, laddie. You are a fellow from the North and I from the South, both come to stake our claim in the Capital of our country. And we haven't done badly.'

Ah, the old proud Chambers, marking his superiority by understatement, Hugh thought. He flushed as he remembered the condescending letters he had received more than a decade ago, urging him to rise above the local in his subjects and to eschew any talk of ghosts and spirits. However, he restrained himself from responding with more than a nod of the head and waited.

'I don't want to make too much of it, but we both rose from straitened circumstances by the power of our pens and later by publishing. We both have not formed part of, what shall I say, the literary elite. And we will both be remembered long after these stuffed-up fools have disappeared from the public record!'

'That may well be true, but the true judge of our worth is not an earthly one.'

'No, of course not.' Chambers halted and looked towards the door.

'What spurred your evident fury?' There, he had asked him.

'My own foolishness, I suppose. Cockburn has been chafing me to reclaim what he calls my position in Edinburgh society. I was foolish enough to allow him to put me forward as an ordinary member of The Speculative Society.'

'Those people who meet up at their club rooms in Old College?'

'Yes, they built a hut there when they were founded almost a century ago, and when Old College was built the University provided them with their own rooms to compensate them for its demolition. As ever, they know how to come away with the booty. Like all the other clubs they proclaim their devotion to educated debate and cultural improvement. Like many, they exist for their own advancement, as any grouping made up of members of the legal profession inevitably is!'

Hugh smiled. 'The Adorable Redeemer said, '*Woe to you lawyers as well! For you weigh men down with burdens hard to bear, while you yourselves will not even touch the burdens with one of your fingers.*"

'Yes, very good, very apt. They say most of the highest judges in Scotland are members, though as the list is kept in confidence, it is difficult to confirm whether it be so. I feel foolish, Hugh. And all for wanting to be part of a club that doesn't want me and whose real rules are different from its proclaimed ones. Can you understand that?'

'Careful,' Hugh thought, 'don't be led on here to saying something you might regret.'

'I went for an interview in the Club this morning. Cockburn presented me to the Secretary, then left me alone with the odious chap. He showed me round the tiny rooms and seemed to take pleasure in the fact that the members sign in to each meeting using quill pens and ink. In this day and age! He positively glowed when he pointed out that their meeting hall has no gas heating and is illuminated by candles. And wait till you hear this, my good fellow, there is a portrait of old Lockhart.'

'Sir Walter Scott's son-in-law?'

'Yes, but facing the wall following his criticism of the society! And these are the men running the justice system of our society. Does it not make you tremble?'

Hugh nodded and waited. He did not believe Chambers' ire was fruit of modern disdain for antiquated practises nor the make-up of the courts.

'Then came the interview. My background, which is all a matter of public record, my feelings towards the Royal Family, all very politely done, of course. And then the suggestion that perhaps I, can you believe this? I 'would not feel comfortable in the Society!"

Hugh laughed. Chambers seemed to take this as an encouragement to escalate his attack.

'I most heartily agreed with him and bid him Gooday. He smirked but the fellow does not know with whom he is dealing. For all his smugness, I know the state of his accounts. He and his family are sinking sir, and I can tell you they will sink further!'

Chambers faltered here, conscious perhaps that he had gone too far, Hugh thought. Now was the time to take advantage.

'I wrote you last week, my good friend, requesting an interview about a fellow who I believe is in your employ and whose services I might need. I also of course wanted to hear your opinion on my latest book, that is, if you have had time to peruse it.'

Chambers reddened.

'Of course, sir, and that is the real reason for my popping in here. Why don't we meet in Waterloo Place next week?'

An Unholy Confession

'I dinna understand, I dinna understand what for the mistress is sae fashed with me!' little Maggie wailed as she hid her head in the dark blue folds of Nell's skirt, her face blotched and red and her whole body shaking. Nell had never seen her so upset, not even when they had told her the lie about her parents dying.

'I was just tryin' to help. The mannie had dropped his card and I ran aifter him. But the mair I called tae him the faster he scooted awa. I caught him though, and haunded him the card. I dinna ken whit for he was so scunnered, but though he gied me a richt fierce look, I wisnae feart. He is auld and glaikit and canna hae abody to care a whit for him.'

More tears shook her as she gulped and went on,

'Then the Mistress came running oot and pu'd me awa like a laddie yanking his peerie and gave me such a scolding and then tellt me I am to be aff, that she canna have this happening in her hoose.

When I asked whit *this* was, when I said I was only trying to be a guid lassie and be o' service to the man, she went aff her heid and tellt me I was a besom that couldna be helped. Oh, auntie Nell, she says I maun be awa. Awa where, for my ain parents are deid and this is my only hame?'

Nell let her go on, then took her by the hand and led her into her and Alec's quarters, signalling to her husband to leave them alone. Once he had closed the door, she took a cloth and dipped it in the basin then wiped the girl's face.

'Dinna fash, lassie. I will talk to Alia. She was angry. We all get angry sometimes. It will pass. Now why don't you lie down on my bed with the big pillows and have a wee rest. I will make you some sugar barley water and bring it to you in a wee while. Dinna be feart, lassie, the mistress doesnae mean you ony hairm.'

Nell slipped out of the room a few minutes later and tiptoed down the stairs to find Alec waiting for her.

'What on earth's the matter? It's a good thing our own girls are at their cousins.' What has got Maggie into such a state? What has the lassie done?'

Nell recounted what had happened. It had been at best an embarrassing mistake to show one of the Mistresses' 'special customers' that he had been recognised. This man had requested extra privacy, it seemed. However, the slip didn't merit such a response. 'Alia's no been herself lately,' she said.

'Maybe the man was feart Maggie was trying to blackmail him.'

'He must know our reputation for confidentiality. It is what sets us apart. And when I let him in, I kept my eyes down, as instructed.'

'Well, but that might explain why Alia was so worked up. You need to talk to her, Nell. Poor wee Maggie looked such a sight when you came into the room with her. It's no' fair. Something has to be done.'

However, when Nell went to Alia's rooms, there was no answer to her knockings or calls. She went to take the barley sugar drink to Maggie and was glad when Alec said to let the girl bide with them that night. The seamstresses had been let go early that day: that must mean the man was more important than she had realised.

'You stay with her, Alec,' she whispered. She took her key and walked down the stairs and along the corridor, swept the curtain aside and inserted the key in the lock of the brown varnished door. She went in, hoping that Alia was there. The room seemed empty but in the grey light that seeped in through the top of the frosted windows she could see that everything had been turned upside down. Two large white candles lay teetering on the edge of the table, and she rushed over to set them aright. The coffer with the implements lay ajar, the low chairs were awry, and the portrait of Madame Corbett lay face down on the floor! Nell gasped. She called out for Alia but there was no reply.

As Nell stooped to pick up some of the leather implements and place them back in the coffer, she heard Alia's voice. Yet it sounded like the voice of a much older woman.

'I will right things. Just leave me to do it.'

Nell looked over to the woman in the black dress in the corner half-shrouded in gloom. She walked over to her and was shocked to see her tousled hair and her face streaked with tears.

'Oh Alia,' she sighed. At first the other woman held out her hand as if to ward her off, but she soon desisted and let Nell take her in her arms. They both cried together. Nell did not know what was wrong, but Alia's distress was her distress just as her happiness had been for all these years.

'I am sorry for what I said to Maggie. Is the wee thing alright?'

Nell nodded then took Alia in her arms again.

'We are finished, Nell. The whole business is gone, and all because of me.'

'You are the most unselfish woman I have ever known. I don't know what's wrong Alia, but we will get through it together. We always have, we always will. Now let's get this room sorted and then we can have a cup of tea and a talk, just you and me. You will feel better when things are in their right place.'

'Aye, aye, perhaps.'

They both set to work, putting things away. Alia beckoned for Nell to help her right the portrait and they lent it against the wall.

'Let's turn it round, I am that lady no more,' Alia said and as they did so, Nell felt a page in their lives was turning.

Once they had restored order, Nell noticed a long ribbon of cloth, black on one side, white silk on the other. It had a red heart pierced with an arrow at each end and in the middle. She wound it up and looked over at Alia.

'I will tell you all about it. Can you bring some tea in here so we can be alone?'

When Nell returned with the tray of tea and sandwiches, the room looked brighter as the last low rays of the evening sun streamed in through the windows. Alia had tidied her hair and rinsed her face. She still had a vulnerable look on her that Nell had not seen since the troubles of their first times together at the time of the Great Fire.

Nell poured the tea and waited. Alia took a sip but refused a sandwich.

'Have you seen this man before, Alia?'

'I have seen him, yes, but not for a long time. He is perhaps the reason I am here with you in this house. And now it is fitting that he will be the one to push me out.

But let me tell you what happened. I received a note from Mutch John saying he had a special client for me, someone who would pay whatever I asked. That rascal is trying to get back into my good books after the failure of his latest social. Well, I would normally not accept a recommendation from the likes of him, but the money was attractive.' She faltered, and Nell added,

'And business has been very slack recently and mainly for garments at the cheaper end of the scale.'

'Yes. So, I agreed. I was told he wanted to enter and leave discreetly.'

'Which is why we gave the girls time off and you told me not to look at him.'

'Yes.'

'But we forgot Maggie.'

'Yes, we forgot Maggie. But her mistake only served to infuriate him the more. He was already seething.'

'What made him so angry? And what was so special about this appointment? He didn't ask for sexual favours, I hope.'

'No, they come for submission, and it is made clear that is all they get. But he wanted a ritual. He brought his own clothes, 'vestments' he called them, a short white robe like the priest wears in Catholic services, that ribbon thing which he kissed and wore around his neck and down his front. He had a bottle of what he said was Holy Water. He told me to cover my hair and then he knelt before me and said he wanted to confess to the Virgin. The Virgin! I would have laughed if I could have!'

'Well, you have had stranger requests than that. What happened?'

'He confessed and asked me to chastise him with the whip and say, 'I forgive you in the name of the Virgin' after every declaration.'

'And what did he confess to?'

'The usual: lust, greed, pride and dishonesty. He grovelled. He was knelt there, bent over, his surplice thing up, so I could whip his bare back. His head down.' She stopped, her face suddenly white.

'And then he said, ′And the prostitutes, the temptress whores. ′

He asked for more punishment and forgiveness and for me to douse him with the water.

′And the girls, the servant girls and their mothers. ′

Here Alia almost wailed.

'What is it lassie, what is it?'

'I recognised him. He has changed a lot, is so much older, but it all came back to me. And at the same moment he looked at the portrait then up at me. He called me a blackmailer, said I had enticed him then and now and had ruined his life, taken his wife and sent him on a mistaken path. And now I would pay!'

'Did he try to assault you?'

'No, I stepped back behind the table. He went wild, stripping off his vestment and flinging it back in his case, knocking the candles over and tipping the portrait down. He was foaming at the mouth, out of himself!'

Nell took Alia's hand and held it tight. 'Alec and I were here; you should have called us.'

'No, it was clear that this man's fists are his tongue and his power. He called me all the names he could think of, told me I didn't know who I was dealing with right now, but would soon find out I had tried to blackmail the wrong man. He had come to entrap me, he said, all this was just to ensnare me. I would find out what justice meant soon. And out he stormed. When I heard Maggie calling after him, I feared he would assault her. And I am afraid I took out my fears on her. When I said she would have to leave, it is because we will all have to abandon this place.'

'Why?'

'Because he will come for us. He will persecute us. He blames me for losing his wife and for my dealings with Veitch and Combe. He made all that clear, saying he served the most important nobleman in Scotland, and he would crush me.'

'Well, we have influential friends too, Alia.'

'No, Nell, we have influential clients, who will cease to be both at the slightest hint of scandal. We must prepare to move on.'

'Why can't we just keep the tailoring business?'

'You know very well we have no money to tide us over the downturns. And everything is increasingly mechanised or made cheaper in the colonies.'

'But what will we do, how will we live?'

'Well, we need to close this room down. Give the girls time to find other work. We own this property.'

'*You* own this property, Alia.'

'*We* own this property, which is worth a bit. We can sell it and move out of Edinburgh. You and Alec and I can find some work, and we will not do too badly.' Here Alia began to sob again.

After a while she calmed herself and then looked up at Nell, her eyes shining. 'Never bow down, never apologise.' Remember what my grandfather taught me. I have had enough of this life in any case. Abusing pathetic men is no longer to be excused as just retribution. I was becoming bitter, hard and unfair. Yes, we will move on.'

Now it was Nell's turn to look disconsolate. What about her daughters and their schooling? How could she explain the sudden move to them?

'Nell, this had to end one day. Respectability was bound to come after us sometime. We must just get on with it.'

Alia reached up to take down a series of silk drapes from the wall.

'Come on, let's get these things packed up. I can get Mutch John to sell them for us. We have to open this room, make sure the girls and customers see it is just ordinary so as not to damage the valuation. Better to start now while there is no one about.'

They worked on until almost midnight, wrapping things up in the rolls of brown paper they used for the garments they delivered. Alec came down to say that Maggie was sleeping and what was happening? Nell sent him to make some supper and told him to take these things down to the cellar and place them by the door.

And just before the clock struck twelve the three of them sat round the table in the kitchen, feasting on the cheese, mutton, and kale that Alec had got ready. Alia left for a moment then came back with a bottle of claret.

'To our new life!' she toasted.

Alec and Nell clinked their glasses. They all smiled even as they heard the cold north wind rattling the windowpanes.

Letter 15

A New Edinburgh

In 1842, George Rennie, MP, a sculptor specialising in lascivious nudes, was the first to announce the establishment of a Scottish settlement in New Zealand. 'We shall found a New Edinburgh at the Antipodes that shall one day rival the old,' he declared. He proposed to send a cross-section of Scottish society, a mix of classes, as if replicating Scotland could be done without taking into account the foundational aspect of the Kirk. The new Free Kirk staked its claim as the rightful Church of Scotland, not just within its borders but around the world and soon wrested leadership of the project from Rennie, who had the good sense to withdraw. This would be a golden opportunity to emulate the Pilgrims who had taken Puritanism to America and establish a new Scottish Jerusalem on the other side of the planet. Captain William Walter Cargill, who had served with distinction in India, Spain, and France, took charge and set about organising the expedition of the good ship, John Wickliffe and a smaller vessel, the Philip Laing. Hopes were high that spurred on by the clearances and the high unemployment in Scotland, suitable Calvinists would sign up en masse.

However, for all his qualities, Cargill was no Moses, and when the John Wickliffe left Gravesend on the 24th of November 1847, and the Philip Laing departed Greenock three days later, the former carried Captain Cargill, only 97 emigrants and a large quantity of stores. A majority of her passengers were not from the Free Kirk, but members of the Church of England, showing how difficult it had been to persuade enough Scots to leave everything for a foreign country. The Philip Laing was only a little boat (450 tons), carrying 247 passengers. In charge was the Rev Thomas Burns, the nephew of the Bard!

Life on board the Philip Laing was as disciplined and

ordered as was to be expected from enthusiasts of the new Kirk. The emigrants rose at 6.30 am, rollcall was at 7.30 am, then quarters were cleaned. Breakfast followed, then morning worship at 10.30 am. There were 93 children under 14, so they had school at 11 am under the supervision of the schoolmaster, James Blackie. Lunch followed, then, after free-time, school was recalled at 4 pm. Steerage passengers had tea at 5.30 pm, the cabin party at 6.30 pm. Evening worship brought the day to a close. Weekly rations for the steerage passengers were: 5 1/4 lbs hard ship's biscuits; 3 1/2 lbs flour; 1lb beef; 1 1/2 lbs prime mess pork; 1lb preserved meat; 1lb rice; 1lb barley; 1/2 lb raisins; 3 oz suet; 1 pint peas; 1 oz tea; 1 1/2 oz coffee; 3/4 lb sugar; 7 oz butter; 1/2 pint vinegar or pickles; 2 oz salt; 1/2 oz mustard; 21 quarts water; 3 1/2 pounds potatoes. The Greenock vessel arrived three weeks after Cargill's ship. Two sets of barracks were built, one for the Scottish, the other for the English colonists. The Philip Laing barracks were much larger and divided into three: married couples in the middle, unmarried men and women at separate ends. Partly prefabricated cottages had been brought out for the leaders, and these were erected.

The first choice for the name had been 'New Edinburgh,' until William Chambers argued that the prefix 'new' was already overused in North American provinces. Chambers suggested that instead the township should be christened 'Dunedin,' a more poetic name for Edinburgh, in his view. No-one thought to question a Gaelic name suggested by a non-Gaelic speaker, for a settlement that owed more to Lowland Scotland than to the Romantic Highlands. No-one pointed out that the colony was to be established in a country with the offending 'new' in its name!

The new city's surveyor, 25-year-old Charles Kettle, wanted to transform the area into 'the Edinburgh of the South.' He placed the Octagon (Dunedin's town square) at the heart of the city, with Moray Place shaping the outer part of its thoroughfares.

The town's axis, George and Princes Streets, were named after their Edinburgh Hanoverian homonyms despite the hilly geography of the new settlement bearing little relationship to the Scottish capital. Rev Burns was Dunedin's first appointed minister and became the province's most influential religious leader. He was an enthusiastic supporter of the policy which saw a local river renamed Clutha after the Gaelic name of the Clyde, and with the authority of his link to his departed Uncle Rabbie, inspired the naming of cities such as Mossgiel, Musselburgh and Bannockburn!

The first note for the new settlement was struck by Captain Cargill, the 'father' and leader, when he addressed a united meeting of his pioneers: *'My friends, it is a fact that the eyes of the British Empire, and I may say of Europe and America, are upon us. The rulers of our great country have struck out a system of colonisation on liberal and enlightened principles. And small as we now are, we are the precursors of the first settlement which is to put that settlement to the test.'*

"Hugh Miller"

The Tramp and the Lady

Elspeth had shrugged her shoulders, stopped off at two public fountains to wash her hands and feel the sting of the fresh water on her face before she reached the West End, empty save for a few street cleaners and vagabonds. She was used to deprivation but the depravity she had been forced to witness last night had left her feeling as hollow as a barley husk blown across the late autumn fields. Dr. Tait had sent a messenger to her to say a woman he had observed in the Lawnmarket was due. The woman was penniless, but Tait promised to find some money for Elspeth if she would only go. There was something in the tone of his missive that hinted at desperation, at despair.

Normal despair was a flimsy thing compared with the grim blackness she found when she had ascended the stairs to the fourth-floor apartment just before midnight last night. She had clambered over the usual inert bodies on the stairs, people with the air of someone recently evicted or waiting to enter the flats, she could not tell, a fug of alcohol fumes and tobacco hanging above them like a shroud.

'I've come for Agnes MacPhail,' she said as she pushed her way up the stairs. She felt the eyes on her leather bag and waved it about as if to say, 'No drink here!' A woman spat at her. Why would someone spit at a person they do not know? She was just asking herself that question when she found the door, and relieved to escape the squalor on the stairs, stepped into hell.

The room was dark, illuminated only by a candle on a shelf and scattered embers in the fireplace. There were two mattresses, both stripped bare of bedclothes. There was literally no furniture, save for the remains of a wardrobe that had been scavenged for firewood. Two men and a woman sat in the corner, drinking whisky. The woman was stark naked, just like her pregnant companion on the other mattress. Elspeth discovered that the furniture and then the women's garments had been sold during the day to pay for whisky.

'You havetae wet the bairn's heid,' a man who said he was the new bairn's father, slurred. It was indeed customary for the neighbours to be invited to toast the new-born with a dram. Only this time the drams had all been drunk before the baby's arrival. And when the money ran out, they sold the furniture, including the beds. And then they sold the women's clothes. There were no garments or towels for the expected child.

'Could you spare a shilling?' the other man asked her as she made her way over to the woman raving on the corner mattress.

'Ach, I am dying, my heid's sair and this bastard bairn is still kicking me. It will be my ruin even afore it is born' the pregnant woman screeched, her round belly glistening with sweat and snot in the subsiding firelight. The other woman was almost comatose but grasped an empty whisky bottle in her hand like some token guaranteeing her entry to a better place.

Elspeth roused the man slumped on the floor by the harpy's side and sent him to find a pot to boil water. 'And if you are not back with it in ten minutes, I will call the police and denounce you all for public indecency. And they will listen to me. Now off you go!'

She told the woman in labour that Dr. Tait had sent her. The woman said her name was Agnes, and she was awfie sorry. She hadna meant to drink at all. She had lost a boy in childbirth two years ago and she was feart, terrified it would happen again. The man came back with the pot and some water and they put it on the fire to boil as Elspeth got her things ready. She could hear a fiddle playing an Irish air from the flat below as Agnes began to wail and her breathing became heavier.

The two men and the woman had passed out, lying in a tangled heap together, leaving Elspeth to deliver the baby without help. It took all night. Agnes cursed her, thanked her then cursed her again when she told her there was no more whisky. At last, just as the morning wind was rattling at the few remaining panes of glass in the windows, the child arrived. Alive, but looking like a blueberry. Elspeth cut the cord then handed the baby wrapped in a cloth she had brought with her to the exhausted mother. She stayed with them both till the father stirred. He began to cry too, with happiness, he said that his bonnie bairn had arrived. This called for a celebration!

Elspeth slipped out before they robbed her of her belongings and started to walk. She headed down to the New Town to get away from the squalor of the High Street closes. Normally she disliked the sterile avenues of this quarter, but it was just what she needed today. She walked round Charlotte Square, its empty magnificence almost obscene compared with the poverty she had come from. After the first complete tour, she kept going almost as if she were winding the world into her. Elspeth did this when she was unsettled, an adult version of her childhood habit of touching all the walls of the schoolground to give herself some feeling of control, grounding. She needed to feel the ground beneath her feet right now, to have some sense that she controlled the direction she was going in, even if it was just around in circles! It wasn't just the scene of degradation she had witnessed that made her feel as if she were losing her way. The endless round of repeated battles, birthing babies to poverty-stricken women who already had more weans than they could care for or sometimes care about, the lack of support from the authorities and the often open censure from the Church for her refusal to distinguish between wedded and unmarried mothers, all these things were knocking her off her feet. Perhaps it was just tiredness; no, it was weariness, which was another step up, affecting not just the body but the soul. And then there was her relationship with Enric. Where was that going? She had tried to make her aversion to marriage clear, she had fought to keep private space for herself by going to classes, meetings and sometimes even inventing friends. Enric made her feel good and he was a decent man. But the recent turmoil in his lodgings had stirred the unspoken question of why they didn't just move in together and that was a question she did not feel ready to answer, or even properly ask.

She looked up and imagined Enric marching in front of her, his shoulders straight, his magician's hands at his side, a tall, slender, elegant figure. But he was marching in front of her. She could overtake him but then he would be behind her. How could they fall in step and walk side by side with such different gaits, such divergent paths? She knew little of his past: she had seen some photographs of his mother and father, and a view of a bay dotted with sailing boats. She had found unintelligible letters written to him in different languages, to people she could never talk to. He had travelled the globe but seemed reticent to talk about it though she seldom asked about his voyages, so as not to invite questions about her own past. But could you live without a past, disdaining the present and trusting in an uncharted future to make everything right, to make your life worthwhile?

And now he kept insisting she should come and meet his 'other family.' She had invented excuses and tried to explain she did not want to be seen as half of a couple, half of anything. A meeting with them would make her that, did he not understand? He did not and truth be told, Elspeth was not sure she did, either.

Lost in these thoughts she was just wheeling round into Charlotte Street when she heard a thump and what looked like a sack of potatoes tumbling out into the street. She looked over to see a dishevelled figure in an ill-fitting brown overcoat semi-unconscious on the pavement. His feet were still hidden inside the doorway and he seemed to be at peace, making no effort to stir himself. Elspeth looked around to see if others had noticed but the street was empty. She hesitated, telling herself that this was not her concern, but finally walked across to the doorway, cautiously observing the immobile figure.

She stopped and listened and could hear hoarse breathing.

There was still no response to her offers of help. She could see the thinning long straggly hair, revealing scalp covered in sores. The man appeared to be about forty years old or so. When she got nearer her nose wrinkled at the stale smell emanating from his body. She hoped someone else would come along, but no one appeared. 'Ach, he will be fine, someone will help him in a wee while,' she told herself. Then she looked down and saw a rat scuttling beside the foot of the building towards the body. She shrieked and threw her bag at it. The rat took fright but some of her papers were strewn on the pavement and she chased them like a cat catching moths. A groan brought her attention back to the supine figure.

'Are you alright sir?' She leant down and shook his shoulder. He stirred. She peered into the dark hall behind the open door, 'Anybody there?'

Just as she was asking herself why this should happen to her on this morning of all mornings, she felt a hand gripping her ankle. She screamed and looked down.

'Help me, madame. I will be fine if you can aid me to sit up.'

She stepped over him and went into the house. In the room to the right there was a couch which seemed to serve as a bed and there were pillows and bedclothes piled high at one end. She took two pillows, put them both under his head. 'How heavy his head is!' She found a beaker of water and gave him some to drink, drops dribbling down his chin and onto his soiled shirt. As she was wrestling with him, his arms around her neck, a man, a tradesman on his way to work, she supposed, appeared.

'Help me,' she pleaded. The man nodded for her to move out of the way and he hoiked the supine figure up like a roll of carpet. Elspeth pointed down the hall and into the sitting room and she propped up the pillows behind his back on the sofa.

'I hae to be aff, I will leave you to look after your faither.' He was gone before she could explain. When the door boomed shut, she felt alone in a tomb. She looked down at the stranger who seemed to be recovering his awareness. Around him lay papers, piles of books and on a nearby table what seemed to be bones and preserved pieces of animals and plants! There were some pyramid shapes on a shelf beside the window. The room smelled of formaldehyde and bleach, which took her back to the hospitals she worked in. The fireplace had obviously not been cleaned and set in days. Where was the domestic service people who lived in these smart houses depended upon? Had he been abandoned, locked in here?

'I am sorry if I have caused you distress.'

He was speaking, softly, but with a firm voice.

She held the glass to his lips again, but he grasped it in his white bony hand and sipped from it. She noticed how fine his fingers were and how graceful the arc of his hand was as he placed the glass on the table. Who was this man?

'I will leave you now, sir. If you tell me whom I can contact I will send a message to them to come and care for you.'

He started, as if receiving an electric shock and made to stand up.

'I must be off to my classes. I will be late. I must be off.'

'Your classes? It is 6 am. Where are the classes?'

'At the University. I am Professor Goodsir. I must be there. I need to prepare my lecture.'

She pointed to the clock on the wall to emphasise it was much too early. He nodded and sank back into the sofa.

'Who should I contact? Family? When does your domestic staff start work?'

'To avoid visitors, I go to bed at 8.30 pm.'

A weary breath, motes of dust floating before the window.

'I rise before 5 a.m.' He coughed without covering his mouth.

'In this way I get five hours work done before Edinburgh has breakfasted.'

He looked as if he had often gone without breakfasts, Elspeth thought.

'And I dismissed the servants months ago so I can dress or work at any time without fear of intrusion.'

There was a look of pride on his face, like that of a man who on his own has discovered a remedy to a fundamental problem overlooked by everyone else.

'Well, you shouldn't be on your own, Professor. Whatever caused you to faint could happen again.'

'Sit with me. Just for a while.'

Elspeth had been dreading this request. People seemed to sense her instinctive helpfulness and they could not resist taking advantage of it, she told herself. And people trusted her. Like this strange man obviously did. She supposed the fact that she had remained at his side and was talking to him now inspired confidence.

'Well, I will bide for a little, but I too am tired. I have been up all night.'

'No need to talk, we can just sit till I can get back on my feet again.'

'Is there a scullery? Shall I make us some tea?'

He nodded and pointed over to a green door at the back of the room. As she stood up, she gave a wry smile. Here she was, off to the kitchen, doing a woman's chores. And she spent half her life boiling water in saucepans and kettles, usually not for tea, however.

The kitchen was in even more disarray than the living room. The stoneware breadbin lay open and she could smell the mould before she looked at it. A basket of eggs hung from the ceiling, empty shells mixed in with the rest, flies crawling all over them. There was some loose tea in a bag next to an empty kettle. The fire was almost dead, but some embers still resisted extinction. Here was genteel deprivation, in some ways worse than the scene she had witnessed that night, as it was self-inflicted. Perhaps she was being unjust, perhaps this clever man was trapped in a web as perilous as the whisky of the poor.

When she took the tea back into the living room, he was asleep, snoring loudly with his mouth open beneath that enormous nose, looking like a seal washed up on the beach. She sat down and sipped some tea, but instead of reviving her, somnolence crept over her, dragging her down into its arms.

He woke her about an hour later, according to the clock.

'Miss, Miss. I have to be going and cannot leave you here.'

She looked up and saw him looming over her and schoolgirl dreams of being found in her hideaway by a friendly giant flashed through her mind. She took a deep breath and waited for the dream to dissipate but he was still there.

She managed to nod her head and reach down to pick up her bag. The room became clearer and the giant stepped back. Now it was his turn to offer her a glass of water.

'I would like to thank you for taking care of me. I do not know your name.'

'Elspeth Grieve,' she answered.

He reached into the inside pocket of his jacket.

'No, sir, I neither want nor need your money.'

He stood there with his bony fingers stuck inside his pocket.

'I am a midwife, and you are a Professor of Anatomy,' Elspeth said, as she stood up. I have some questions about female physiology and would be grateful if we could have a conversation about them.'

Goodsir smiled. This woman had fire in her, and she was as concerned about her work as he was. He also realised with gratitude that she had neatly cancelled his debt and put them on equal footing. He was not the weakling rescued from the pavement. He was a gentleman again, and she a lady.

The Secret Agent

Candlish had decided to stroll the short distance from Fleming's house in Walker Street to his own home in Randolph Crescent. It was a cool, fresh night, with occasional gusts of wind lifting discarded papers in scurries over the grey cobbled roads, like flocks of gulls disentangling themselves from the rippling sea. At least he told himself that is what they looked like, as he searched for striking images for his next sermon. We must make the Bible new, he often said. This is an age of invention, of progress, and preachers cannot just intone the same old verses from scripture at educated congregations like those of the Free Kirk, made up of professional men and educated women, people on the rise in business and industry in Scotland. If Guthrie had sewn up the appeal to their sentiments, he would catch their imaginations and their thirst for social approval.

The Free Kirk had tried to identify itself with education, with its ambitious programme of school building and its founding of colleges such as the one in Aberdeen and above all, New College, at the top of the Mound in Edinburgh. It had been a rocky road, with some, like Miller, arguing against denominational schools and problems with chairs at New College. Candlish had hoped to be its Principal upon the death of Chalmers and had indeed been appointed. However, poor Alexander Stewart, the man chosen to take his place at his parish of St. George's had passed away almost immediately! Was this a sign from God? His congregation thought so, and they pressed him to return to them. He had obeyed, but still regretted missing the opportunity to make an impression on a wider range of souls than his parishioners.

It would be his, one day. He had promised himself that.

And Fleming, what was to be done about him? It was already a source of some scandal that the Professor of Natural History at New College maintained that Noah's flood was a local deluge and not a worldwide catastrophe. He had just been questioning Fleming about this and had to admit that the man knew his geology and was able to defend his position ably. He also seemed to have no doubts about the authority of the Bible.

'There is no contradiction between science and Christianity, my dear Reverend Candlish. In fact, as Professor Goodsir argues, the existence of science is a product of Christian belief. Look outside the Christian world and you will find no technological research or scientific inquiry. We need to celebrate that fact.'

'Ah, Goodsir,' Candlish thought. Did Fleming realise he had uttered this defence along with an ode to the sacred mission of anatomy in response to criticism from the Free Kirk, with Candlish to the fore? The fellow was only trying to protect his job. He had thankfully published little since then. It frustrated Candlish that he could rein in outsiders but not those dangerous characters within the Free Kirk. True, he reflected as he crossed Melville Street, he had neutered Miller in *The Witness*. It seemed the man had now turned to autobiography, an inexhaustible subject, especially for a person with that fellow's immense self-esteem!

Then there were the tricky questions of death and of the age of the earth. With breath-taking naivety, Fleming sent out his student clergymen to teach and preach that death and pain had existed myriads of ages before Adam, and that the starry heavens and the earth are millions of years old! Such dangerous speculations! Does the man not realise that houses generally collapse from within and not from the buffetings of external forces!

It was Chalmers' fault, he grimaced to himself as he walked along Drumsheugh Gardens, the cobbles glistening in the full moon and the gas lights winking from the windows. The old man's first profession as a mathematics professor had led him to encourage academic research, even into sacred matters. Look where that had got him and the Kirk! His sermons and writings were once as popular as the works of Scott, now no one read them and those that did talked condescendingly of his 'good intentions.' And now the Free Kirk, which had prided itself on the intellectual quality of its ministers, was struggling to deal with the latest advances in geology and natural history, many of which were defended by men such as Fleming from within its own ranks.

He was mulling over how best to confront the rising tide of doubt and secularism in Scottish society when he noticed a carriage waiting just outside his door. It was a splendid version of the Clarence coach, known as 'growlers' because of the sound they made on cobbled streets. As he drew nearer, he could make out a coat of arms on the door with the motto '*Amo*.' Ah, the Duke of Buccleuch! Some joked that instead of meaning '*I love*,' the motto signified '*Master*.' Surely His Grace had not turned up unannounced at Candlish's humble abode! Candlish rushed up the stairs, glancing at his reflection in the curved pane of the dining room window. He looked a sight, but he would have to do!

As he was fumbling with his key, Mary opened the door.

'You have a visitor, sir. I escorted him to the sitting room.'

'Yes, I can see I have a visitor, lassie. Why did you not send for me immediately?'

He shuffled off his coat and left it on the floor in his rush to receive the august guest.

'I really am most sorry; I do wish I had been informed earlier of your Grace's kind wish to bless me with the honour of your presence.'

The white-haired figure seated in the comfortable armchair next to the fire chortled. 'He chortled!' Candlish would later exclaim.

'I am sorry if there has been a misunderstanding, Dr. Candlish. His Grace never makes an unannounced call, save to members of his closest family, or equals. Did your maid not tell you it was just my poor self, his curate?'

'But, but….' Candlish was lost for words and turned round to find the crimson-faced maid standing at the doorway, waving his coat like a lifeguard using semaphore to warn a ship of oncoming rocks.

'Tea, Mary!' he shouted.

'What can I do for you, Reverend Hardie? You should have made an appointment.'

Hardie realised he had discomfited his host and strove to make amends. He needed his help.

'His Grace was talking of you just the other day, Reverend Candlish. Said it was a pity for the spiritual health of the country that you had to relinquish the highest post at the New College. 'Scotland needs more men like Candlish in the forefront of civil life,' I believe were his exact words.'

'Most kind, and completely unmerited,' Candlish replied as he held out his hand to welcome this snake.

They indulged in small talk while the maid appeared with the tea-set and served each of them, Hardie refusing the offer of a home-made scone. 'I have renounced the pleasure of the pastry shelf for the good of my constitution,' he explained. 'His Grace insists his staff look after their health. 'We cannot care for our Master if we do not care for ourselves,' were his exact words.'

'Very wise, most sagacious,' Candlish replied, wondering if his legs were long enough to enable him to kick the smug dolt into the fireplace. He blushed at the violence of his reaction.

Hardie sipped his tea. This visit was not going well. He had called in on the spur of the moment and thought thus to preserve the confidentiality of their conversation. Candlish was thought of as a dangerous radical, closer to the dissident evangelical sects than the established church by many of Hardie's colleagues. It was risky to be seen to consort with him. If news ever got back to His Grace!

In an attempt to make peace he started to discuss the growing crisis in the Crimea and the possibility of war!

'It is to be hoped the Earl of Aberdeen will move with his wonted security as Prime Minister.'

Candlish almost retorted that it was the good Earl's cack-handedness which had given impulse to the Disruption, but he understood that Hardie was simply talking about anything to re-establish a climate of confidence between them, and he exchanged the usual platitudes about the burdens of responsibility and the duties of the Empire with his visitor.

Once civility had been regained, Candlish addressed his visitor directly.

'Is there something I can do for you, Reverend, something that requires this private meeting?'

'Frankly, there is, Dr. Candlish.'

Let's see what you have, Candlish thought. Hardie ran his hand over his hair like a man about to step out into a storm and went on,

'Unlike some of my more prejudiced brethren I do not rejoice in any scandal or reprobation that may be associated with your church. As far as I am concerned, a slight on any Christian body, save of course the Church of Rome, is to the detriment of the entire community of faith.'

'Are you referring to the attack by the materialists over our defence of Genesis?'

'No, that is a question where you and all the Christian congregations stand more or less united. It has come to my attention sir, and I beg you to excuse the crudity of my expression, that you are operating a bawdy house right here in Edinburgh!'

'I say, sir. How dare you!'

'Please my friend, I am only reporting the rumours that have reached me. I thought it necessary to bring them to your attention speedily and confidentially, that you might act to extirpate the tumour.'

'This is most unsettling. I beg you to continue.'

Hardie bent down and picked up a small attaché case from which he extracted a sheet of paper with the name of a property not far from Randolph Crescent, down towards Stockbridge.

'The Free Church inherited this property. It consists of three apartments in a four-apartment building.'

'Yes, sir, if you say so.'

'The ground floor and two upper floors of the fourth property are occupied by a bawdy house.'

'That is impossible sir. The municipal authorities would not permit it!'

'Oh, it is a sly operation, hidden within a business which purports to be an honest shirt makers.'

'I shall investigate. But you say that the Free Church is proprietor of this business. I find that hard to credit.'

'No, sir, your church owns the deeds to the other three properties. The ownership of the bawdy house is claimed by a Miss Thompson, who says she bought the property almost thirty years ago. That may be true, it may be false. However, the public will not look at such niceties if it learns there is a house of ill-repute in the building. I myself have witnessed the activity and unmasked the fraud, in an incident which no gentleman could bear to recount.'

'What are you proposing we do?'

'We cannot easily prove these claims without revealing the sordid commerce being carried out there. I have given the matter great thought. I recommend your church to petition the authorities for the whole building to be classified as residential property and explain that the commercial activity of one unit is prejudicing the value of your portion, without formally mentioning the sexual traffic. Keep the focus on the financial question, is what lawyers I have consulted, in the strictest confidence, have advised.'

Hardie sat back and a look of compassionate concern almost hid the smug smile on his face.

'Well, I will have this investigated and if there is the slightest hint of impropriety, we shall act as you suggest.'

Hardie reddened, conscious he had not convinced Candlish. Did the word of a Church of Scotland minister stand for nothing? He was about to protest when that day's copy of *The Scotsman* caught his eye and he remembered their opening conversation. It was a desperate gambit but worth a try.

'I am sure you understand that no one sins in isolation.'

'We are all sinners, sir.'

'Yes, but when we give way to temptation the sin comes calling again and vice flourishes.'

Candlish shifted in his chair. He wished Hardie would not speak in riddles.

And then, as if conveying a state secret, the minister leaned forward, looked to left and right as if to make sure they were not being overheard, and whispered.

'They are harbouring a foreign agent, a Russian spy!'

'Come, come sir, this is the stuff of a penny novel! Explain yourself, please.'

'Well, an agent I hired to follow the fellow and his mistress, — yes Dr. Candlish, a fallen woman, — recovered a letter from this harlot to her lover, written in Russian! He is a Spaniard, by the way! He resides in this bawdy house. In the missive, which I have had translated, she confesses that her anti-bourgeois principles and rejection of what she calls the 'religious patriarchy' means she doubts she can share his project, that the Revolution will have to be won by women now that men's efforts have flagged.'

'This is extraordinary!'

'She says she may have to take action herself and does not know if she can ask him to walk the same path.'

'Why does she write in Russian to a Spaniard?'

'Because obviously it is not really to him! She mentions someone called Olga in St Petersburg, whom I take to be her supervisor. Nevertheless, her lover is a dissolute fellow, a drinker, an agitator. He had to flee first Spain, then the German states and finally Paris, pursued by their security services. I have a full report.'

Hardie flourished a file, whose front cover featured a single staring eye. Candlish still felt this was some melodramatic fiction.

'This is disturbing, but the United Kingdom is full of seditious exiles. Some of them are indeed dangerous, such as that Marx fellow. However, this is Edinburgh, it is not even Glasgow; what harm can he hope to do here?'

'You are too trusting, sir, too trusting. The fellow has charm, it seems, and can win the confidence of people of all classes. What if I told you he has insinuated himself into Chambers' the publishers?'

Candlish sat up, his crest of hair making him look like a startled cockatoo. Hardie seized his chance.

'And not only is he employed by the firm but over the last few years he has made secret visits to Robert Chambers' country house in St Andrews. He has even stayed overnight there. In addition, he has been discovered making covert trips to Manchester!'

'Robert Chambers! That is indeed more alarming. Did you know I always suspected him of being behind *Vestiges,* though Fleming says I am mistaken?'

'Yes, I am of the same opinion. But it is extremely hard to prove, and he is a powerful man beyond the direct influence of either of our congregations. There is a danger closer to home, however, and the real reason I am reporting this sordid affair to you and asking for your help while offering our cooperation.'

Hardie pronounced cooperation with all the attention and care of a child sucking the last juice out of a sweetie. He almost choked when Candlish responded,

'I can't see the need for any cooperation. Should such suspicions have any foundation, it would be sufficient to pass on the information to the authorities and the fellow will be dealt with as he was in Europe.'

Hardie gulped, but then looked Candlish straight in the eyes like a poker player producing his trump card.

'Of course, and we would do so had we not been informed of something which cautions against such a step.'

Candlish held his breath. What wild accusation was the fellow about to make now?

'What would you say if I told you this agitator, this foreign agent, on at least four occasions has been discovered visiting the offices of *The Witness*? He has even been seen supping in private with its editor!'

'With Hugh Miller?' Candlish laughed out loud. 'Really, my dear sir, the idea of Miller in cahoots with a Russian spy is just too ridiculous for words!'

'I did not say he was 'in cahoots,' as your American friends might, though some of his articles in the paper, while characterising the Russian Empire as barbarous, argue that democracy weakens the European powers' strength.'

Here Hardie pulled out some cuttings from *The Witness*, waving them as if to waft his argument over to Candlish.

'The Russians detest radicalism. However, they are keenly interested in sowing confusion, in fanning the flames of dissent. Since this agitator has been in Edinburgh, Chambers has moved towards materialism, and it seems you have had some difficulty in controlling the strident arguments of your editor. And Miller has been seeing Chambers regularly in the past several months.'

Candlish averted his eyes from Hardie. He was not sure what was happening here, but he felt at a disadvantage, that Hardie had known from the very beginning where the conversation would lead.

'Dr. Candlish, think back to your most recent dealings with Miller. Have you found him changed?'

Part of Candlish told himself that this was absurd. Miller had changed, but only by becoming more cantankerous. It was true that many in their church wondered if his continual scientific speculation was really a defence of or an attack on their faith, despite his declarations of devotion. Before Hardie said it, however, he reasoned that whether true or not, the diffusion of even a rumour would be damaging to the Church. The connection to the house of ill-repute could be dealt with, but this was a question he had no practice in handling. He looked over at Hardie, with what he hoped was a calm, controlled expression.

Hardie smelled panic, and a shiver of pleasure ran down his spine.

'We can come to some arrangement. If you do what is necessary to close down the tailor's shop, I will deal with this foreign troublemaker. Just keep a close eye on Miller and avoid any favourable mention of Russia in the paper.'

'This is exceptionally good of you, Hardie. Forgive me if I ask why you are making such an effort to help us? Our two churches literally face up to each other on the streets of Scotland and in the hearts of their members. What has driven you to assist us?'

'We are Christians above all, Dr. Candlish. And my Lord the Duke of Buccleuch is anxious to promote peace throughout the kingdom and in the hearts of his Christian countrymen.'

'Yes, most noble sentiments.'

Candlish waited. The coal sparked in the fireplace and the wind rattled the panes. Hardie's face grew sombre and later Candlish would reflect that this was the first sincere thing his visitor had said.

'And I admit that we all receive blows in our past which may take years to overcome. When we can return them and do so with justice on our side, it is a sweet recompense. I shall say no more. I bid you goodnight, Dr. Candlish.'

Letter 16

Riderless Horses

The great frowner: the sage of Ecclefechan, Scottish misery on two legs, but at least Thomas Carlyle and his heroic visions offered a thoughtful analysis when he complained we were living in the Mechanical Age where our moral worth depended on nothing more than utility. He was more and more under the spell of German metaphysics, however, and tended to confuse heroic defiance with truth.

Robert Owen and his acolytes continued to enthuse the workers with utopian dreams of godless equality, but at last it seemed Chartism had collapsed under the combined weight of its internal contradictions and its despicable aims. Electoral power is illegitimate without the responsibility that the ownership of property confers! With the help of the Great Redeemer, and the shock produced by the events on the Continent, the Chartists had been vanquished. Or so it seemed.

Chalmers had once been seen as a sage, a prophet, even, with his vision of society under the tutelage of the Kirk. Now almost no-one read him and the Disruption had been just that. The Free Church had enamoured the up-and-coming middle classes with its offer of quick promotion to elderhood but failed to attract the lower classes or the aristocrats. People prizing respectability above all else had little time for philosophical speculation. They craved comfort and comforting.

Now a grocer's son from Haddington was preaching the Gospel of what he called Self-Help. Samuel Smiles was one of eleven children, raised by their widowed mother despite her relative poverty and overcoming endless tribulations with a belief in good works and God's bounty that would have seemed almost scandalously Roman Catholic at times, if not for the emphasis that God only helps those who help themselves and thus there are the deserving and the undeserving poor.

The insidious idea that man can save himself, at least in this life, by the sheer force of hard work had first been proposed by the Combes and later taken up by a man called Emerson in New England. And this fellow, Mr Samuel Smiles, had welded it to the list of the demands of Chartism: universal suffrage for all men over the age of 21; equal-sized electoral districts; voting by secret ballot; an end to the need of MPs to qualify for Parliament, other than by winning an election; pay for MPs; and annual Parliaments. All of these things should be available to people of good character, he argued.

Character! What did that mean? Were you born with it? Did you have to earn it? Was it bestowed on you by others, like the references required when applying for a position? Hugh had followed the Romantic idea that the child is father of the man and written endlessly about Cromarty and its influence on him. He had believed his character came from not just his own, but from Scottish history. What if a purely Scottish history was at an end? Both Carlyle and Smiles lived in England.

He had not pretended to be a sage or a prophet, but a mere witness. However, sometimes he felt the age was looking away from him, leaving him pointing frantically to incidents only a dwindling few thought worthy of notice, distracted as they were by heroic enterprises or by pulling themselves out of the water. The horses had been let out. And they were riderless.

"Hugh Miller"

The Limits of Reason

'And they told me I was musical! Can you imagine that? I had almost believed everything they said based on my wonderfully wide forehead. It seems I was a natural genius, a prodigy! What man could resist such flattery?'

They both laughed, making the flasks of water on the table tinkle.

'And dashed if I wasn't disappointed! But I can't sing a note or keep a tune, so I am afraid I turned my back on phrenology.'

Chambers laughed then took a sip of water.

'But Hugh, even the Bible has inconsistencies.' Chambers halted, aware that he had perhaps gone too far for his companion.

'What I mean is, we shouldn't let a particular discrepancy discredit the fundamental truth of the whole. I am grateful to phrenology, it made so many things clear to me. How I am like my brother and how we are different. My tendencies to worry and to overwork.'

'I agree, but it overlooks our essential individuality. We are each created individually by God and these systems tend to forget that fact in the name of homogenous classifications.'

And so Hugh and Chambers went on talking throughout the afternoon. They fenced and challenged each other as two working intellectuals, practical men of ideas. Their first meeting had been unfruitful, and both had privately decided not to renew the acquaintance when Hugh had started to talk about his boyhood and how he had felt cut off from his fellows except when he regaled them with adventure stories. Chambers had responded with enthusiasm and echoed his experience. And so they were off, two old schoolboys talking about village life, their struggles to educate themselves, business success, rivalries, how they hated their teachers.

'Ah, but I was so poor I became hard and distrustful, Hugh. I have cut myself off from my fellow man and feel alone now even in company.'

'I walk and walk and search for fossils which are tokens of death. We are all marked by our childhood.'

However, such solemn moments were occasional interludes in lively banter-filled discussions. Once William Chambers looked in, surprised at the roars of laughter from the conference room. Robert's face lost its spark, and he became the serious burgher in an instant.

Why does William look so alarmed to see me here? Hugh asked himself.

Generally, they were left alone. They talked about everything though Hugh noticed when he introduced ideas from the *Footprints* that Chambers avoided direct comments and often led the conversation down other routes. Chambers also seemed bored at any mention of *Vestiges*. This was frustrating for Hugh as he sought vindication for his onslaught on it, confirmation that he had triumphed. He did not receive it from Chambers or from almost anyone else. He felt like an Arthurian knight lost in the green wood, hearing the clashes of arms but with no worthy opponent to face up to him nor followers to cheer him on in his quest.

One day Chambers gestured for Hugh to stand beside him and to look out onto Waterloo Place. It was a bright, windy afternoon and the street was full of carriages and people making their way to and from the railway station. A red-haired old woman was weaving through the throng trying to catch her wayward terrier. A fruit seller wearing a white apron and a black bowler hat was holding an orange in his hand and some small children stood nearby, wondering at it and perhaps hoping he would be distracted and they would have their chance. There was a steady thrum of voices and engines, some of it an insistent throb from the printing machines.

'Even the sounds have changed since we first came to Edinburgh,

Hugh. It was the shout of the caddies and the clip clop of hooves then. The steam engine has changed all that. Things move at an inhuman pace now.' Chambers had a faraway look in his eyes as he said this. He was a young man again, just setting up his stall on Leith Walk.

Hugh became young too, then the rage of the middle-aged man at time's increasing indifference to him flared up.

'Yes, and distances have shrunk. Look at all those busy fellows coming and going to Fife and West Lothian every day. And to London and beyond. Long journeys that we once made by boat and now by that mechanical monster, the train.'

'We are getting old, I fear, Hugh.'

'No, the world really is changing fast, but we are still full of energy. You and I can work as hard as any of these young pups.'

A maid came in with tea. The men moved away from the window and sat down in two facing armchairs next to the fire. Hugh was flattered at being treated so informally and in some confidence by Chambers. This was the type of intercourse with a cultivated, professional person he had craved but been denied since he arrived in Edinburgh. He hoped his eagerness did not show.

They moved on to talk about future projects. Chambers told Hugh, 'under the strictest confidence' that he was interested in doing something to combat the rising tide of superstition.

'I have recently joined with Chapman in London to reinvigorate *The Westminster Review*. We differ in politics, Hugh, and I do not expect you to be a subscriber but regret that a magazine devoted to freedom of thought and reform can no longer be published in Edinburgh.'

Hugh was about to remonstrate, but Chambers went on, 'Perhaps you will at least agree with me that it sometimes seems the decline in established religion has been accompanied by a corresponding surge in spiritualism and belief in fairies and goblins. Instead of…'

'Instead of in revealed religion?'

Chambers face reddened. 'Well, of course, but also instead of science and rational discourse. We must hold on to reason or we are lost.'

For the first time in their conversation, Hugh became passionate. He started to stride up and down the room, his mane of hair catching the light pouring in through the high windows.

'Do you comprehend how frustrating it is to be always caught between religious people fearful of any discussion of science, who view anyone who engages in scientific contemplation as opening the castle gates to the unbelieving mob, and the scientific materialists who seize on any acceptance of a part of their argument as an acceptance of the whole! They are crushing me between them.'

'I can sympathise. I gave a talk on the geology of cliffs a few years ago and am still feeling the daggers of one party and the other in my back. But there is another problem.'

'Go on.'

'You and I are seen as not to be trusted by the devout, as you say, but also as baffling by the untutored and as amateurs by the professional scientists. They point to our ungentlemanly origins, lack of academic training and take that as sufficient reason to pour scorn on our arguments.'

'This struggle is what tires me most. It is like walking through a bog towards an ever-receding mountain.'

Chambers nodded.

'You are a fascinating man, Hugh. Why don't you write about yourself? Your rise from the poorer classes and your professional career are emblematic of present-day Scotland. And it might make people more sympathetic to your religious and scientific endeavours.'

Hugh blushed.

'Thank you, but I could say the same.'

'Well, I am working on a volume about Burns, that old staple, though I still admire him, and he remains the only national Bard we have. What has happened to poetry in this country? We have the likes of Gilfillan and Alexander Smith, but they are spasmodists and their measure has no measure! The English poets like Tennyson speak for us now.'

'They pretend to. But good poetry, like the Bible, goes beyond logic. Mr Mathew Arnold may be clever, but he simply serves up doubt in rhyming stanzas.'

The fire suddenly blazed, stirred by a draught down the chimney perhaps. Both men looked into the glowing coals and saw their pasts, their departures from the village and now their daily professional life as the coals darkened into black again.

And so they went on talking, each taking pleasure in seeing themselves in the other. However, such illusion cannot last even between brothers, as Robert and William had found out. It was a pleasant way to pass an afternoon though, and Robert was about to propose the next meeting when Hugh leaned forward in his chair and said in the way of a man taking a pebble out of his shoe,

'You are a neighbour and perhaps a follower of Mrs Crowe, aren't you?'

'Well, a neighbour, certainly, and she is a very pleasant and interesting woman, if a little diffuse.'

'How can you defend reason and her? You have her book.'

'Well, she presented me with a copy. I have your books too!' Chambers could not help himself, but immediately regretted the riposte. Miller was a sensitive man; he must not forget that.

'How did you know I was in possession of a copy of her book?'

Miller now told his version of the meeting in Fife with the Spaniard.

'That was my motive for wanting to see you a few weeks ago. I wanted to have your permission for him to advise me on some changes to our print operations. However, we got to talking and it slipped my mind. Would you have any objections to him lending me a hand? I just want to ask his opinion; no labour would be involved.'

Chambers was nonplussed. Enric had said nothing about meeting Miller. Had it just slipped his mind, or was something being trammelled? He decided to find out and pressed a buzzer. When

Johnson came in, he requested him to find Enric and bring him to the meeting room.

While they waited, they talked about printing and of the future use of photography in publications.

'You could have your photograph on the title of *The Witness*,' Chambers exclaimed.

'Why on earth would I want that? Our readers have enough shocks to put up with in their daily lives already!'

'But you are *The Witness*, man. People read the paper to study your observations, people from all walks of life, like me, for example.'

'That is very flattering, but fortunately not feasible and just as well, as my wife thinks I look a terrible sight in these old clothes. She would die of shame if I were captured in my plaid and rough shirt. Lydia would never let me out of the house again!'

They were both still chuckling when Enric was shown into the room. He looked less smart than normal, Chambers thought, and ill at ease, even. Was he right to be suspicious?

Hugh also noticed the lack of the easy confidence that had impressed him on their first meeting in Fife and a change in Chambers' demeanour. Were the two men colluding against him?

Thus the opening exchange of polite greetings appeared stiff to all three and Hugh was quickly reminding himself that he no longer needed the excuse of this man's technical collaboration in order to renew his acquaintance with Chambers. For his part, Chambers was beginning to ponder all that Enric knew about him and his endeavours and ask whether and how he might keep his distance from the fellow. At least that is how it appeared to Enric.

'You need my services, Mr. Chambers?' His Latin inflections sometimes made it difficult to know if Enric was asking a question or stating a fact.

There was a pause, the pulsation of traffic noise grew louder. Hugh decided to break the silence.

'I may be the one who is in need of your help, sir. Good to meet you again.' He held out his massive hand and shook Enric's.

'I see you are both old acquaintances,' Chambers muttered.

'No, just that time on the crossing from Fife,' Hugh said, 'Though I think our paths have sometimes crossed on the High Street,' he added.

'Let us all sit down, and I shall ring for more tea.' Chambers pulled up another chair between his and Hugh's and signalled for Enric to join them. Enric was still not comfortable with the tea ritual. Give him coffee anytime!

Once all were seated and served, Hugh went on to explain the nature of the technical question he was concerned about and Enric, looking over at Chambers, said he would be happy to help, but was not sure if he had the time to do so.

There was another silence. Chambers looked at them both.

'Of course you have time. I will not be needing you as much as before, Enric. It would be good for you to diversify your efforts.'

A shiver ran through the room. 'You are more like Candlish than I thought,' Hugh found himself thinking.

Enric blushed and nodded. He proposed that he come to Mr Miller's office on the following Thursday afternoon. Miller accepted, looked up at the clock on the wall as if he had just noticed it and declared that he must be off.

When they were left alone, Enric looked at Chambers.

'Have I done something wrong, sir, something to annoy you?'

'No, but there was something about your air when you came in, something about the way Miller had changed too, that did make me wonder if I have been wise to put so much trust in you. And your translation of the German sources for Mrs Crowe's book are basically done, so perhaps it is the time to bring our special collaboration to a close.'

Enric's face turned a deathly white.

'You too!' he gasped. 'The persecution has got to you too! It is implacable, merciless. I cannot take it any longer, I ….'

Here Chambers interrupted him. Perhaps this rational creature was just another excitable European. He must calm him down.

'What do you mean, persecution? I have only intimated that my reliance on your extra services may be coming to an end. You will still have your post at the printshop, my good sir.'

But Enric was not to be consoled. He took his handkerchief out to mop the sweat from his brow and stared at Chambers, as if attempting to peer into his mind.

'You are not in league with the Minister?'

'Enric, you are not making any sense here. Take a deep breath, calm yourself and tell me what is troubling you so.'

After a moment, with his eyes fixed on Chambers, Enric began to talk of the persecution, as he called it. Worse than the Inquisition, he said.

He explained that for the last several years he had rented a room in a house on the edge of the New Town. The ground floor was a tailor's, employing seamstresses who specialised in fine shirts. The girls who worked there were all well-paid and excellent workers. The Mistress was a most extraordinary woman, not easy to get to know, but who was respected and loved by all the staff and for whom Enric had come to feel an almost filial devotion.

'You mean you admire her?' Chambers asked, sure that the younger man was victim of romantic turbulence.

'Oh, no, she is single and as they say of her, singular. I have a friend, Elspeth, whom I have been seeing for several years now. It is not that, sir. It is not that.'

'Then what is it? What has happened?'

Enric explained that he was not completely sure but that several months ago now, the Mistress had had a falling out with a customer, an important minister of the Church of Scotland. The man had promised vengeance, that he would sink her. And he was doing it. The local bank had cut off their credit. One by one, their suppliers had pulled out of their contracts and several clients had explained they could no longer wear the shirts with the distinctive crow motif on them.

'At first, we thought these things were just the chance misfortunes any business has to face, but it has become clear that there is a directing hand. Last week the city authorities declared the property to be a house of ill repute. But how can that be, sir, when I live there and have never seen an untoward act?'

Chambers waited. He poured some more tea for Enric. I should at least give him a hearing, he told himself. But be on your guard man!

Enric seemed calmer. Then he began to speak again, moving his arms in a most unsaxon way, Chambers thought. Why had he never noticed that before? He became more and more unsettled as Enric declared that it seemed this man's malevolence was everywhere. They had encountered difficulties when they tried to sell the property. The business had plummeted. The girls could not even find work elsewhere and now here was Mr Chambers prescinding of his services!

'I regret these difficulties, but why do you not just change your lodgings?'

Enric jumped up and strode round the room. He seemed furious.

'How can you, a Scotsman, say that to me?'

Seeing the dumbfounded expression on Chambers' face, he went on, drumming his fingers on the table as if calling the troops to battle,

'I have studied and tried different systems of life, from anarchism in Catalunya to socialism in Germany. I believe in liberty and equality, but above all fraternity. Yes, you may smile, but your scientific and rational endeavours will take us all there, even if it frightens you. Reason is democratic, my good sir. But for the first time in my life, I have encountered these values outside a political system. You Scots still have something of the clan in you, I have found a community here and I will not abandon it. These people, the Mistress, Nell, Alec, the girls, little Maggie, represent my community and I will not forsake them.'

These remarks winded Chambers like a punch to the stomach. It was the first time that Enric had not just reported or explained but had declared his own opinion, and not one gleaned from books. This was not academic speculation but raw intelligence. He plumped himself back down on his armchair and wiped his brow. He closed his eyes and saw copies of the *Westminster Review* flicking through space, words like 'constitutional reform' 'rationality' and 'equanimity' dripping from them. He imagined the magazines with their smart covers and blank pages lying scattered on the floor as the words drained out into the street to be stamped on by the crowds of passers-by. And if Enric was right, did reason lead to a democracy more radical than anything dreamed of by the Chartists? Had he devoted his life not to enlightenment but to destruction? He pinched himself and saw Enric standing in front of him, a glass of water in his hand.

'Take this, sir. You have had a turn.'

Silence fell on the room. Even the noise from the street had subsided and the printing machines lay idle.

'I am sorry; I have been unkind, Enric. Let me see what I can do to help you. I will contact the agency I used to investigate you before our first interview. I can promise nothing, but if this woman is as blameless as you say, this is indeed a persecution, though if it is a minister of the Church I must act with caution and maintain my anonymity so I must insist this remains between us.'

'I understand and thank you. Am I to continue with my work for you?'

'Yes, of course, though in a slightly different role. I want you to report to me on what Mr Miller is up to. Is he still content with his Church? Does he still hope to vanquish the theories of development? I look forward to hearing from you on this. Oh, and I still want you to go to several spiritualist meetings and report on them to me: the type of people who attend, what happens, the claims they make, etc. I want to expose these charlatans. Do you think you can do that?'

'As long as it is not to spy on the person but report on his ideas and concerns, yes. But you will help me at the house?'

'Agreed. Can you write down the address for me to give to my agent?'

Enric wrote it on a yellow sheet of notepaper and handed it to

Chambers.

'Thank you for your help, sir.'

As Enric closed the door behind him and walked down the stairs, Chambers looked at the address. His eyes widened. It was the residence of Madame Corbett!

Lost on Portobello Beach

There were four of them walking like scarecrows escaped from the fields, she told herself as she raised and waved her arms, watching how they seemed to join onto his in the air. To her delight, he too maintained his arms aloft and they all advanced towards Portobello beach with the Spring sunlight casting both their bodies' shadows on the sandy track. Some people came onto the path from the beach and she lowered her arms. Her father was a public man, she could not embarrass him. Harriet was thirteen years old now and conscious of the privilege of walking out alone with an adult while her two brothers and sister were left at home, even if her mother had secretly insisted she go alone, leaving her building a play fortress with Hugh and William.

'Go and walk with your father, he has something to show you,' Lydia had whispered, helping Harriet on with her shawl, the red one grannie had brought from London, and calling after her father not to be impatient, that they would be down presently.

He had held the door open for her and then the front gate, as men did with ladies. They had even taken a cab from Jock's Lodge down to Portobello, sitting side by side and she feeling high up above her normal station in the world. Travelling down on the border of girlhood. At least that was how she remembered it all those years later, in Australia. She kept that day with her like a picture scrap of her time with her father, before he deserted her.

He was in a jovial mood. *My Schools and Schoolmasters*, his autobiographical sketches, had just been published. He had heeded

Chambers and he felt the book was good, it was, well, just, he told Harriet. That may have been true, but the writings she cherished were his letters to her. Especially the ones where he described things he saw on his travels and told her how he was feeling or wrote poems to her and then confided he could not explain such things to her brothers. She was his special child. She had always known that and had made efforts to hide that knowledge from her two brothers and Bessie.

They walked hand in hand now down to the shore as he pointed to the bony fingers of rock formations that had been uncovered by the sea. He told her that some of these went south as part of the coal seams and others halfway to Glasgow! He had traced their path as far as Linlithgow, someday he would take her with him on an expedition, if her mother agreed, of course.

Her father had spent most of his time in the house in the last few days, since the incident, the one she was not supposed to know anything about but which she had heard Maisie the char gossiping to the next-door maid about. Why did adults think children were deaf or could not unpick their code?

'A sodjer... followed her hame…drunk…Gied her a richt fricht, maybe just what she's needin', if you ask me.'

'Shush, the lassie's listening, she's a sleekit one.'

Harriet suddenly remembered how flushed her mother had been. She had waited till her husband had come home, sent Harriet off to bed and then talked in loud whispers. After a few minutes, loud shouts and bangs resounded and then her father stormed out onto the street followed by his wife, pleading with him to come back, to calm down, that he was not a young man anymore. Instead of pacifying him for some reason these words just served to inflame his temper and it was only when her mother said he would cause a scandal that he came in again to the house. They argued a bit more, Harriet was not sure for how long as she kept drifting off into sleep, but she heard her mother climb the stairs and her father's study door slam shut.

Since then, both of her parents had started to criticise their home, how small it was, its poor location, neither in town nor in the country, how the fire smoked, every day a new complaint. What were they getting the children ready for? And now this trip to Portobello.

They walked down to the south end of the shore, the dagger of Berwick Law pricking the sky in the distance then wheeled round, so the Firth was on their right, and she could see the smoky chimneys of the Kirkcaldy mills writing sooty scribblings in the sky far away across the water. Her father picked up some flat stones and sent them skipping across the sea. She hooted and told him how strong he was. He was the strongest father in the world! He laughed but she could tell she had made him happy. She ran up to him and buried her face in his shoulder. He held her to him for a minute then stood back and said, 'You are growing up fast, Harriet. You will make some fellow a happy man soon!'

She blushed. Why did he say that? How could he be so silly? She ran off, throwing down the stones still left in her hand and didn't stop till he cried for her to come back, to come back, he had something he wanted to show her.

She did not return but slowed down, waiting for him to catch up to her. She had observed how her mother did that, striding off when she found their father too infuriating. However, it did not seem to work when she did it and she had to surrender and go back to him. He was looking at her with a puzzled expression, obviously waiting for some explanation for her abrupt flight. An explanation she was unable to give for so many of the feelings that seemed to be sweeping over her these days like the waves over the defenceless shore.

'What did you want to show me, father?'

Now it was his turn to stride off, forcing Harriet to do the chasing.

'Come on then, lassie.'

He would never understand women! He stopped. He had just called his daughter a woman!

'How would you like to live beside the sea?' he asked her as she caught up with him. 'Like I did when I was your age in Cromarty.'

Cromarty? She did not like Cromarty. Her father talked about the close little community of his youth, but all she had seen on her last visit was a grubby decaying industrial small town. She especially disliked her Grannie Harriet. The old woman smelled, though Harriet couldn't say that, and she was always telling stories about ghosts and fairies and haunted houses. 'Your father has a gift, he can see them, has been able to since a boy.' What nonsense!

But Portobello wasn't Cromarty. It was an up-and-coming area, full of professional people who liked the opportunities it offered to buy or build good-quality housing at a much lower price than in the crowded city centre. Margaret Symonds, who went to the same Bible study group as Harriet, had recently moved there and had told her it was a bonnie place with a much better class of people than Jock's Lodge. Harriet had taken the comment as an attack on her but now she reasoned it could be seen as a recommendation from one popular girl to another.

So she said that she had always liked the sea, at least the Firth of Forth, if not the northern waters. Her father tutted, that look of baffled miscomprehension which she increasingly witnessed clouding his eyes.

At last they came to the rear of a big house, much larger than where they lived now. Her father opened a gate in the wall and beckoned her to follow him into the overgrown garden. There was a large tree, a chestnut, he pointed out. It would be good for swings, she was thinking, when he tugged her arm and pointed to some outhouses in the far corner. 'I could convert them into a museum for my collection,' he said. Her mother laughed when Harriet told her that. 'That is so like your father, not even seen the house yet, and only thinking of his fossils.'

Harriet blushed. She wanted to confess that she had only thought of the swing, but instead laughed in a knowing fashion along with her mother.

After inspecting the garden her father produced a grey key, strangely small for such a big house, Harriet thought, as he twisted it in the heavy lock to open the white painted door at the back of the building. He paused once the door had swung open as if listening for intruders or trespassing animals and this made Harriet feel as if she were taking part in some great adventure. Later, once furnished, she would recall how immense this house had felt to her this day, how her heels had echoed as she passed over the bare planks and how she had chased after her father. He had climbed upstairs, and she heard his steps then silence. Had he been hiding from her on purpose? Did adults do such things?

She apportioned rooms in his absence, that one for her brothers, the other for Bessie, this one with the silver mirror still on the wall and the inset wardrobe would be hers. She was aware that none of this would happen, but one day perhaps she would have her own house and she would really choose. Was that what being an adult meant, to choose?

As she was pondering this she saw a figure at the bottom of the garden, a dark-haired woman in a black dress and shawl. She seemed to be about to come up to the door. Was she a neighbour? Did she own the property? Had she lost a possession, as she had the look on her as she approached of someone trying to recover something. Or at least, that is how Harriet later remembered her. The woman who had lost something.

Her father had left the outside door ajar, and Harriet went to it, whether to close it or to greet the visitor she never discovered, as the woman reached it first.

'Hello,' she said in a voice that was at once firm yet inviting.

When Harriet echoed her greeting, the woman explained that she was interested in property in the area. Was this house for sale? There was no small talk, no complimenting Harriet on her shawl, no questions about what school she went to, what her name was, nothing. The woman was intent on finding a property, that was evident.

Before Harriet could answer, she felt a hand on her shoulder. It was her father.

'Go upstairs and wait for me, child,' he said. 'I will be back shortly.'

'Hugh,' the woman said and turned to go.

Before Harriet could react or say anything, her father, yes, her father, walked down the path behind this strange creature and waved to Harriet to go inside. She was dumbfounded, but she obeyed.

She watched them both exit by the garden door and thought what to do, what to do? She heard the stairs calling to her, and she bounded up them to a window at the back of the top floor. She could catch glimpses of the top of her father's head in the dips in the wall as he passed, she supposed with the woman, back down the passageway to the beach.

If she stood on her tiptoes, she could just make out the two figures walking to the shoreline in the direction of Joppa. They stopped, she advanced, he followed, she advanced again, and so on. Now they were far enough away for her to make them out without stretching but soon became two indistinct dark blobs. She was accustomed to her father greeting unknown people in the street or being accosted by them. He was a public man, she knew that. She had been jealous of these strangers as a child for taking him away from her. But this was different. Her father had said nothing to this woman, he had simply followed her. What did it mean?

Out on the rocky beach Hugh attempted to keep his companion at his side without raising his voice or attracting others' attention. He was flushed and emotions that he had thought conquered came rushing over him along with memories of his youth, of Willie Ross and of those first callow days in Edinburgh. He had not sought her out, it had been she who had found him, there had been no impropriety, no unfaithfulness to Lydia. But oh, how his heart raced!

She answered none of his questions about where she had been in the last thirty years, was she married with a family too, where she lived now. All were met with replies like, 'It is of no matter,' 'It is of no concern to anyone but myself,' and petitions for him to leave her be. Why had she not gone up to the main road instead of the shore if she wanted to leave him behind?

A flock of seagulls sitting on the sand swept up into the sky as they approached, and he remembered that flurry of birds in his heart when he had first fallen in love with her. He also recalled her rejection of him, and bitter saliva rose in his mouth. He was shocked at himself, all these years later, still with the sting of rejection. Was that why he had followed her out of the house, to tell her she had been mistaken, unjust? He wanted to tell her how successful he had been, how he had a beautiful, talented wife and a lovely family. How he was famous. How he was a fool, he realised. All the frustration of his youth, not just in Edinburgh, but as a struggling poet, a folklorist, a damn banker for goodness' sake! seemed to be encapsulated in the shape of this graceful middle-aged lady carrying with her in her steps along the shore what he might have been. Why would she not stop so he could tell her this? A revelation needs to be shared or it is not revealed. She was the only one he could share this with, except for Willie Ross, and he was gone into that abyss of the youthful departed.

Suddenly she stopped, wheeled round, and addressed him directly. Short wisps of black hair rose up around her breeze-kissed face.

'You have done well, for yourself, Hugh, as I always knew you would. Life has been kind to you, it seems, even if you seem to me sometimes to have become unkind, but who am I to judge?'

He had heard that reproof too many times to be surprised.

'I have done what I could, Alia. We are all fallen creatures and I may not have risen as far as you.'

She reddened. He had her touched her, wounded her even. He winced.

'Alia, let us not meet each other again with reproaches. We are both, I am sure, different people from those innocent youngsters who met on the Mound all those years ago.'

'I had my innocence stolen a time before that,' Alia thought to herself, but retained the retort. Men never understood, and when she tried to talk about it saw any complaint about their brutality as directed at creatures less noble than them. The very act of confiding in a man seemed to reassure him that he was not like these beasts who molested women. She had been shocked by this when one evening she had attempted to talk in confidence to Enric, a man of wide sympathies, but still, she found, a man.

'Very well Hugh, but you continue speaking of the period when we knew each other in ways that I do not recognise, and which often offend.' She paused and turned to look out over the sea.

'But you are right. This is a chance meeting, and we should part as we did the last time, as friends. No doubt you can still recite *The Castaway* to me as you did then. You see, I took you seriously, I listened to you.'

'A chance meeting? So, you did not come looking for me?' As soon as he said it, he blushed.

'No, Hugh, I came looking for a house. I had heard that property was for sale and as I must sell my current home in the centre, I thought I might have a look. But it seems you have got here first.'

'Yes, we have just a few details to clear up with the solicitor and we are anxious to move. I want to be beside the shore, to hear the waves roar again at night. And my wife, Lydia, is eager to move.'

'Your daughter is an attractive girl. Your wife must be very beautiful!'

Hugh faltered, unsure what to say. Alia burst into laughter, the wind carrying it away like birdsong.

'I am sorry, Hugh, I am just teasing. I am sure the lassie gets some of her looks from you. She has your eyes and your mouth,' she hastened to add. He smiled and made a gesture of surrender, as if to say, you had me there, what can I say?

She allowed him to walk at her side as they retraced the route he had taken with his daughter just a short while before. He thrilled as he looked at Alia, her strong gait, her raven locks and fine hands. She was older. That was obvious; that was irrelevant. A cloud dusted over the sun as he glanced up at it then at her, suddenly feeling as if he was following his younger self along the beach, ready to correct any awkward admission, guileless confidence, or over-needy petition. Ready to give the right answers this time. He listened to his mature voice uttering words his younger self had not written yet and understood we can never retrace our way, never say what we should have said. When we age we lose track of ourselves.

She was talking to him more freely now, her shawl slipping down over her shoulders. He established that she had never married and had no children and directed seamstresses in her own business. He told her that his mother was still alive, that he was getting old, that his recent book had made him think about Edinburgh, about how it had declined in importance, how hard he had worked, in short, the things we all say when we meet someone again.

He had the feeling that she was holding something from him, some worry, some project. He inquired again.

'Alia, while I can be persuaded to believe in happenstance, you have said you have been in Edinburgh all these years without us coinciding. Forgive me, but our meeting today must be beholden to more than the movement of the stars or just plain luck. Why did you come to see me?'

She started to protest, but then bowed her head.

'Your church is trying to evict me.'

'On what grounds?'

'That my business is conducted in a residential property which damages the rights of the neighbouring dwellings, which they own.'

'Well, I am sorry for you, but this is a matter for a solicitor and not one I can have any control over. I don't see what I can do to help you.'

'You never see, you never make the connection!' she exclaimed. He was alarmed by her vehemence but stifled his protests and gestured her to go on.

'This is part of a campaign. My customers have deserted me, the bank has withdrawn my credit and I received a missive yesterday questioning my ownership of the property. I cannot fight this on my own. I am in a desperate plight.'

'But what has that got to do with the Free Kirk or with me?'

'They are coming for you too, Hugh. I don't know why, but there is an alliance between your church and the Church of Scotland. No,' she said, placing a hand on his arm. 'Listen to me. Look into the contacts between your Reverend Candlish and that snake, the Reverend Arthur Hardie.'

Hugh felt confused and even irritated. That Alia had come to see him because of some wild conspiracy theory!

'I have had problems with Candlish and am all too aware of conspiracies, but none which could have involved you. What possible link could there be in his mind between you and I, with all due respect, Alia? I can't see any trace of a plot there at all!'

'I did not mean to speak of this. I understand it sounds fantastical. But I am suffering from persecution and you will too. There is no one more blind than the one who think he sees! And you see nothing, just as always!'

Hugh laughed, to try to defuse the situation.

'What don't I see?'

'What about Willie Ross, poor Willie Ross, who loved you. Did you see that?'

There was a sucking sound and a grating roar as the retreating wave sequestered the gravel from the shore. His past was bleeding away. That he had been stabbed by Alia, whom he had dreamed of meeting again, that it had to be her who punctured his illusion of certainty and solid judgement only increased the pain. Why did she have to be the one who had taken the last stone out of the dike and let the sea of doubt in? He was speechless.

She wrapped her shawl tightly around her shoulders.

'Goodbye Hugh, it was a mistake to come. I will fend for myself, as always.'

With that she dismissed him with a brief crisp wave of her hand and headed up the beach to the town, disappearing into a tree-lined lane leading to the main road. A tall slim fellow turned into the lane a few steps behind her. It was Willie Ross, walking away with Alia like all those years ago! Hugh staggered as a stiletto knife pierced his brain like an electric shock.

'Willie!' he cried. 'Alia was wrong! Of course, I understood your love. Of course, I know now who those drawings were!' He had always known, which is why he had so forcefully denied it.

He closed his eyes and picked up some sand, feeling it run like time through his hands. 'I am finished with autobiography,' he told himself. 'It is revelation without divine inspiration.' It had been an act of foolish pride to publish his life story and to talk of Willie and others. But what was left him? He had neither the stamp of clerical authority nor the certitude to speak directly on theology. He was a witness, he had forged his life around that fact, but what was left him to bear testimony to? There was nothing new, just old battles unsuccessfully fought. He thought of *Vestiges*. This time, he would conquer it, this time he would win back science for faith, even if it killed him. But his next book would not be about him or his struggle. It would outdo that heathen tract in its science and breadth.

As he walked back up the beach, he saw the tracks in the sand of Alia and himself, crossing each other at times, overlapping. He scuffed them then shrugged. That was over now, so much vanity, so much vanity!

His eye was caught by a black pebble, a small round stone. He picked it up. Harriet would like it, he thought, automatically. Harriet! She must be worried about him; she was on her own in a strange house too! He hastened up the shore.

When he got back he found Harriet sitting shivering on the step. She looked at him and realised she had lost her father. He never did give her that stone.

Alarming Revelations

Enric must have visited half of the dusty halls in Edinburgh and quite a few dark echoing rooms in Glasgow too in the last months. Each time the ritual was repeated: a host of folk huddling in the doorway, most trying to look as if they were attending by accident, a few illuminated souls commenting loudly on last month's session, making sure that any newcomers understood who the founders of this particular group were, martyrs who had suffered for the cause. As he came to recognise the faces, he realised several attended a chain of meetings and he was relieved that his serial appearances were not a motive for surprise.

At first he had chafed at Chambers' commission to read up on and attend the meetings of the Mesmerists and Spiritualists in Glasgow and Edinburgh as well as to look up the German sources of Mrs. Crowe's *The Dark Side of the Night*. It seemed a trivial task, below his merits. How many people could be taken in by such nonsense? Did anyone know about these beliefs, especially in Calvinist Scotland? He was soon disabused. His workmates showed more interest in the pamphlets he was reading than they had for the Chartist material he had previously devoured. And the meetings were all well-attended. Indeed, it seemed the new belief had spread from Protestant New England in 1848 to the United Kingdom, and principally to the Dissenting towns of the North of England before making an electric leap to Scotland. It spread throughout the industrial towns, skipping over the countryside. Why was that? Elspeth said that it gave comfort to Calvinists trembling before the consequences of their sins, as it seemed to promise a more benign afterlife, where your friends came and went and could talk to each other. Enric had taken that as a jest, as she had become ironic recently, making fun of his attempts to analyse political movements and scientific advances. 'Man voodoo' she called them, appropriating a word he had taught her. She did that increasingly, echoing back phrases he had used, teasing him, seeming to almost dare him to answer back. He never did. However, the more he thought her words over, the more he agreed. How else to explain the queues of regular kirkgoers entering heads-down into the meetings and asking for their departed brother?

There were meetings in genteel homes too. At the first, in a smart new tenement in Eyre Place, he had been seated next to a man who identified himself as an engineer, though he would give neither name nor place of employment. When Enric probed his reasons for belief in the transmission of messages to and from the departed, he answered that it was just like a spiritual telegraph, and if anyone had tried to propose the electrical transmission of messages just a few decades ago, they would have been met with the same incredulity the uninitiated bestowed on this new form of communication.

He was struck by the constant calls to the scientific nature of the occult, by explaining communication with the 'other side' in technical ways. The bumps, rappings and table movements were all mundane mechanical manifestations of the departed. He thought that once again people could cope with neither pure religion nor pure science and both Chartists and Spiritualists relied on a variety of combinations of the two. This thought came to him after he had had a talk with Miller, who had insisted, as he did with his customary vehemence, on the bright alliance between geology and Revelation.

John Arthur said it was all that Mr Dickens' fault, with his *Christmas Carol* and the ghost stories he published in his magazines. And it was true that there seemed to be a boom in such tales of spirits, elves and fairies. Among the more educated classes the book by Mrs

Crowe had caused a sensation and become the subject of much after-dinner talk, it seemed. Chambers told Enric that he had had to ban the subject from his table as talk of it upset his wife. It made her think of their lost babies without offering the comfort she got from religion.

'A spirit is not a soul, Robert. It consorts with ghosts and vagabond creatures. I will not hear of them at all, no not at all.'

Enric was stung to find that Chambers had been right: his knowledge of sleight of hand and illusionism had made him a good detector of fraud and deceit. He still laughed at the memory of the woman with the 'extra hand.' She had slipped a glove over her naked foot and dexterously raised it above the table in the darkened room, stroking the hair of her terrified neighbour while the others in the room trembled at its mysterious appearance. He had been tempted to stand up and yank the glove off but handling a lady's ankle would have been unseemly and, in any case, marked him as a sceptic.

After every meeting he wrote up his experiences, under the headings of *Venue, Name of Medium, Composition of Attendees, School of Spirituality, Type of Apparitions, Tricks Detected.* By the end of two months or so he had filled thirty folio pages. He realised that he was grateful for this work. It distracted him from the steady disintegration of his little community and the increasingly stormy relationship with Elspeth. Edinburgh was telling him to move on, he felt. But he had done that so many times before. Was there to be no resting place on this Earth for him?

He had requested an early evening meeting with Chambers, and he awaited it eagerly, hoping that he might also hear of some measure taken to protect Alia's household from further harassment. He had started to avoid her eyes when they met on the stairs at home, or just walk out the door past her as she stood in the empty workshop like the captain on a sinking vessel.

He had sent in his report and was expecting a series of keen detailed questions from his employer, but when Chambers came into the room in Waterloo Place, he seemed distracted. However, once Enric launched into his report, he found he had awakened all the man's powerful curiosity and had him taking copious notes, probing the technical details, interested in the audience's responses and declaredly triumphant when Enric explained pratfalls, when someone had denounced a fraud and above all when Enric explained how the deception had been perpetrated.

'By Gosh, that is cunning!'

'The brass neck of the fellow!'

'This is particularly good, sir, this will do splendidly. It will give life to an otherwise rather dry peroration on the virtues of reason and the dangers of superstition. I have been using the tales of people such as our friend, Mr. Miller, of Highland fantasies and witchcraft, showing how most of the witnesses are unreliable and the work a projection of the fantasies and fears of the writer. But this is drama, this is action, this is what I need!'

Enric was pleased at first by such praise. Then he began to ask himself why a man normally so sparing in his compliments was bubbling over with enthusiasm. It was for distraction. He felt it as he looked Chambers in the eye as the man was gathering his notes together.

'You can do nothing for me and my friends?'

Chambers grimaced.

'I don't know how, Enric, but she has won herself some enormously powerful enemies. She is the first person I know of since the Disruption to unite the Church of Scotland and the Free Kirk in a common cause.'

'She is innocent, she has done nothing.'

'I am too old to believe you have to have done something to be found guilty by the powerful. Yes, Enric, even conservatives such as I can despair at the cruelty of those who hold the keys to social advancement. But to have both Dr. Candlish, the most important figure in the Free Kirk, and the Reverend Hardie, Chaplain to the Duke of Buccleuch, the richest landowner in Scotland, in alliance against her is more than a misfortune, it is a calamity. And I can do nothing.

These two men each wield more power than I do and together, they are invincible. I am sorry, my lad, but my advice to the lady is to leave, to quit the city and probably, Scotland.'

Enric slumped down in his seat. Chambers fetched him a glass of water and as he drank it tried to comfort him.

'I am a dreadful coward I am afraid, Enric. Though you must have guessed that.'

Enric's silence was taken as acquiescence.

'How many men would have published not only anonymously, but with the secrecy I have employed through your help? How many would have dissembled even to his closest friends and family, till the secret became a second skin he could not tear off without rending himself apart?'

Enric looked at him and suddenly realised what his role had been for all these years. He understood that he had always understood, just refused to look it in the face. Like he had done all his life. He was a coward too! And he felt that ache in his chest at the mention of an imprisoning secret.

'Did you never open the satchel and peruse the manuscripts?'

The offended look on Enric's face made Chambers apologise immediately. Perhaps to make amends he made an admission he would make to no one else for rest of his life.

'I am the author of *Vestiges of Creation*, Enric. Only my brother, Mr Ireland in Manchester and my wife, who copied out the manuscript in her own hand, know. And now you do. A mark of my trust in you. To reveal this would be to ruin me and the business.'

Enric felt overwhelmed. He did not want to be the keeper of someone else's secret. And he felt stupid for not having inspected the text or spoken more fully with Ireland in Manchester. He had remained the simple postman!

'Have you read the book?'

'Only snatches. Though its argument is in the air we breathe. Miller is obsessed with it and sees the author as his enemy. My partner,

Elspeth, has read every word and is an enthusiast, though she thinks that its focus on man and the reduction of Nature to a series of laws shows, as she put it, 'a typically male-centred rationalisation.'

'Hmmph, my wife has said the same thing! Well, my next work may be just as masculine, I cannot help it, but it will knock these spiritualist charlatans for six. It will also have to be published anonymously and I will trust in you, my friend, to lend me a hand in delivering it to the publishers. I have come to depend on you, Enric. I am only sorry I cannot do more to aid your friend. I am not as powerful as others or myself dreamed.'

This last remark brought them both back to a silence which laid its fingers on their shoulders. It caressed Chambers with the gift of his revelation to Enric, in having opened a small breach in the wall he had laboriously built around himself. It pushed down on Enric till he felt the bones in his spine ache, if he had a spine! Chambers' revelation was unwelcome to him, like fresh vows made by a disloyal friend which are felt as a burden and not as a warm reaffirmation. Enric made to leave, to make his way home and think what to do for himself and for Alia. He had told himself that Chambers would help her in ways that he as a foreigner could not. Now he felt that it had just been prevarication, he had not been brave. But what to do?

As he was reaching for his satchel, Chambers produced a black card embossed in gold letters.

'I received this earlier today. I cannot attend but would be grateful if you could. The fellow was highly recommended by Mrs Crowe who talks of him in the most glowing terms. It will be my last special commission for the book, Enric and if you can carry it out, I will be happy to reward you sufficiently to be of use to your landlady. I can say no more.'

Enric took the card. It announced a séance, or what it called *A Phantasmogenetic Encounter*, chaired by a Mr Daniel Dunglas Home. There would be physical manifestations of the '*subliminal uprushes*' from the unknown. Finally, it announced, Mr. Home would perform a levitation, carried aloft by the spirits!'

'I would not trouble you with yet another meeting of the hopeless, but they do tell me he is something special. Before I finish my study of the supernatural deceivers, I would like to have this man's performances examined by someone of your acuity. He has received glowing recommendations from the principal scientific authorities in the land, more enthusiasm than my works ever received! Will you do that for me, Enric?'

'Of course, I am at your service. As always.' Enric took the card and left, walking down onto the teeming thoroughfare and then through Clyde Street and onto York Place and the New Town. Something was broken, he told himself. And perhaps it cannot be mended.

Robert Chambers stood at the window, watching the crowd, wondering how many of them had read *Vestiges*, how many would read his new work. He liked to think of readers as individuals, like that tall fellow there in the grey overcoat. He told himself that was the key to his success as a writer. What would that fellow think of the new work? Would it make him turn to reason? Would it make him turn against faith? What responsibility did a writer have for the effect of his works in this, a democracy?

He was toying with these thoughts, rolling them around like a sweet lozenge on his tongue when he heard the door click open. It was his brother, William, looking flushed, no doubt from haranguing the workers in the print shop.

'Ah, there you are,' William said, as if Robert's presence in the building was a rare event.

'I am, as you can see, William.' Robert waited, guessing if the reproach or the request for more material would come first. However, this time his brother surprised him.

'Is it too late to cancel the publication of the latest edition of that damned book?'

'Don't worry, William. It has an autobiographical preface, but it is general, and no one can identify me by it.'

'You are a fool, Robert. A multitude of people are convinced you are the author, only they can't prove it in court. But the damage to our reputation is real. Can you not cancel the latest edition? You have said your piece.'

This was of course not the first time William had entreated him to desist with *Vestiges*. Well, he just wouldn't. However, there was an edge to his brother's voice, an urgency not often there except in moments of real family crisis, such as during their early business struggles, that caught his attention.

'What is it, William? What has happened?'

'That minister. The preening fellow who calls himself the curate to the Duke of Buccleuch, Hardie. He came to see me at home last night, *in incognito*, he called it, though he left the Duke's coach in plain sight in front of my door.'

'What has this to do with me?' But Robert's voice trembled as he spoke. It must be to do with that Alia woman.

'He came to tell me we have been heavily compromised and that he came in friendship on behalf of Lord Aberdeen.

'Aberdeen? The Prime Minister? What on earth can he possibly mean?'

'We are harbouring a spy. A Russian agent. At a time when we are about to go to war with that country!'

'This is ridiculous, and if it came from Aberdeen it can only be the result of the tussles between Palmerston and Russell. A spy? Who does he mean?'

William produced a handwritten document in Russian, seemingly titled 'Olga.'

'What is this?'

'It is a communication with a Russian in their language, containing socially inflammable views and mentioning us and the contacts of an accomplice with us. I do not speak Russian but have no doubt what Hardie says is true: you can see our name at the bottom of the first page.'

'This is extraordinary, but perhaps the writer is a subscriber to one of our publications. I know no one who speaks Russian.'

'Are you sure? A gift for languages is a promiscuous one.' William paused, then went on,

'And the writer is, shall we say, the intimate consort of your cosmopolitan friend.'

'Enric? This is absurd. He is a foe of regimes such as the Russian or Louis Bonaparte's in France. He has had to flee from several of the most repressive governments on the Continent!'

'Have you never asked yourself how likely such an escape is, not just from one but from several police authorities? Have you never asked yourself why the French let him go?'

'The French? Now you are telling me he is a French agent! This is absurd!'

'I am telling you there is reason to believe he is in direct or indirect contact with the Russians. And what matters is not whether you believe it, but that according to Hardie, Buccleuch and Aberdeen do. Do you need me to tell you that public perception is all? Do you realise the damage you have exposed us to?'

'What does Hardie want?'

'What does any Churchman want of you, Robert? Why do you think I asked you to cancel the edition?'

'I cannot do that. Ireland has confirmed to me that the books are already printed. But Robert, I am not such a fool as to think I can take on these people and I care deeply about the firm. Why else would I have gone to all this trouble to guard the identity of the author? I can provide a solemn promise that it will be the last edition and that I will not do anything to promote its greater diffusion. They will have to accept that.'

'Mm I will try my best. But he is a snake, a most repulsive, bitter chiel. There is one thing more, of course, brother.'

'You mean Enric.'

'Yes, he must be gone immediately. You must publicly cut him off.'

'I could have done that this morning. Now I am tied to him. He can denounce us.'

As Robert sought for the right words to explain his predicament he felt like that person in the séance with the hand of a spirit reaching for his throat. It was more the pallor of his countenance than his words that persuaded his brother not to insist.

'We will have to find another way. Let me think. I promise to give this my deepest consideration. Now leave me alone, Willie. I need to recover and see my way forward.'

Strange Forms of Life

'Lilly,' that it appears was my first word. I was two and my mother used to take me out into the countryside and the coast bordering Anstruther. I loved flowers, it seems, and creepie-crawly beasties as well. My mother would lay me down in a daisy-spotted field and whisper to me to sit there silently till the singing of the birds and the buzzing of insects returned. She loved me and would tell me the world was beautiful, that everyone was beautiful if we just knew how to appreciate them.

Of course, I could not tell the Aesthetic Club that. And I have a certain duty to science not to descend into mere sentiment or opinion. So my first paper to them, on the *Principle of Beauty* made reference to the usual Greek classics. I believe my most useful contribution was the citations of work in the German language.

Do you speak German? I learned it on a holiday spent in the Black Forest, with a tutor, so I could understand the museum descriptions and attend natural history lectures. A curious people, the Germans, so organised and yet so Romantic at the same time. You can tell a lot about a people from their language, I think. The French, so precise and inflexible, the Italians so musical and emotional, and the Spanish, half European, half Moor.

And we Scots? We hang on to vowels which the English left behind centuries ago and have imported just enough French terms to render us even more incomprehensible without adding precision. However, I am boring you. And this is not what you came for.'

Indeed, it wasn't, but nevertheless, Elspeth had sat in silence listening intently. She admired intelligence and Professor Goodsir was as famous for his erudition as for his strange ways and his capacity never to speak without authority though in the soporific tone of a sleepy bluebottle. He had invited her over to his house, to thank her, he said, for her help on that day he had found himself so strangely indisposed and to talk to her about the female anatomy. Better to do it in private, he had suggested, though she was welcome to bring a companion. And his sister would be in the household.

It was the sister, Elizabeth, who had opened the door to Elspeth. A small, severe woman who looked as if she had been born wearing black and to whom Elspeth's red shawl and brown dress evidently seemed to be a provocation.

'My brother is expecting you. Please be so good as to follow me,' she had said as her eyes scanned Elspeth through the lens of her own respectability. She turned and led the way in. Did she know that Elspeth had already explored the apartment?

It was in a much better state than when she had last been there. Elizabeth had evidently been assiduous in sprucing up the room, with no sign of blankets and the dust mostly removed from the shelves, save round some of the bone specimens and the pyramids above the fireplace. Such territory was evidently out of bounds to all except the Professor. Elspeth was accustomed to making rapid inspections of rooms to provide her with clues to the status and condition of the woman she was come to help in her labour. But this was a man's room without feminine touches. She noticed a pile of books and picked out the name of Newton. Skewed on top, as if added at the last moment, was a heavy Bible.

Elspeth accepted the offer of tea and waited while Miss Goodsir fussed about in the kitchen. She was tempted to tell her where the tea was kept but decided to desist from mischief. She had looked forward to this meeting. As a woman she was barred from anatomy classes using human bodies and though she had much experience with dilated vaginas in the birthing, she wanted to know more about the structure of the bone and muscle in women before they were pregnant and about the placement of the uterus. Even Enric had been shocked when she had talked to him about it and told her he knew not where to find such information, before scurrying off to ply Chambers with more man-data.

The tea and the Professor came into the room at the same time but by different doors, causing a moment's embarrassment over which to acknowledge first. Elspeth decided to greet the Professor, leaving his sister stranded with a shaking cup in her hand. He stepped out of the way to make it easier for the cup to be placed on a side table but did so with such little grace that the table tumbled, and his sister spilled the tea as she jumped aside. It took a good few minutes to re-establish calm, and once both seated and with fresh tea, the sister beat her retreat, leaving the door ajar.

Goodsir had attempted to make small talk in order to overcome the jitteriness spread around the room by his disapproving sister.

'Do you really ken who this lassie is?' she had questioned him that morning as she tidied the room, he wincing as she moved his things and stowed away the bedclothes.

'Do you ken whit kirk she attends? I thought not. Are you aware it is irregular to invite a woman to your apartment and positively reckless to talk to her of anatomy? Aye, I ken, you say she is a midwife, but is that a respectable profession?'

'The fools ask the same question of anatomy! Lizzie, if you don't wish to be here, I shall happily greet the young lady on my own.'

The threat had done the trick, as he knew it would.

And now he was talking about beauty, for reasons he at first did not understand though ruefully quickly grasped. For he found the young lady to be possessed of features which while soft, expressed a confident openness, her eyes telling you she understood you and was interested in all you were saying. Some men would just say she had perfected a good bedside manner, but Goodsir felt it was more than this. And her hands were delicate with fine long fingers. He found himself glancing at people's hands, comparing them, censuring and admiring them. He was proud of his own hands and their dexterity. Old Forbes had delicate fingers too. They should form the society of handsome hands! He blushed as he thought how silly he was being. She had that effect on him.

He found himself confiding in her about his childhood and his mother, and then whimsical boutades about languages and peoples. Enough of that!

'I want to express my most sincere gratitude to you for your help during my sudden indisposition,' he said.

'And add to it my appreciation for your discretion. I feared gossip about it and have heard none.'

'Well, I only hope you are in ruder health now, Professor. I was glad to happen by, but that fellow who helped you in was the real hero. Sometimes the kindness of strangers is what holds a society together.'

Why had she said that? She realised she was trying to be as abstract as he was, highfalutin talk! Be yourself, Elspeth.

Elizabeth had retreated into the small dining room across the narrow entrance hall, leaving both doors ajar. She had not had time to tidy it in her quick clean-up, indeed she had added to its jumble of clothes, papers, half-washed plates and periodicals highlighted in slow succession by the waning afternoon sun. She made a space for herself on the brown leather sofa. It had come from their father's surgery in Anstruther. Part of her was glad John had kept it, part of her pricked by a stab of envy.

'No matter, and dinna be a silly lassie,' she murmured. Like many people who lived on her own, she had begun to talk to herself, even hold arguments!

She strained to pick up snatches of the conversation from next door and suffered the embarrassment we all feel at the sound of an unsociable man trying to be amiable. She caught sight of her own severe features in the dusty mirror in the corner and tutted at the effect feminine beauty can have on even the most serious man. He had been talking about their mother. He had never talked to her about mother or their times among the daisies!

But now the more normal drone had taken over as he switched to professorial mode. Elizabeth stood up and slipped into the hall to peek through the crack between the door and the jamb and could see her brother holding up a large notepad. The girl appeared to be taking notes. She sighed with relief and went back into the dining room, letting her shoes slap against the floor to remind them of her presence. She opened her pocket-bible and began to read her daily text and sank back down again onto the couch.

Her movement precipitated a cascade of newspapers with a sound like pigeons taking flight. Oh drat! The unopened sheets slid across the floor and lost their order, if they had any. Most of them seemed to be copies of *The Witness*. At first, that surprised her till she remembered that this Free Church broadsheet also published news about the Established Church. Yes, there was a column on the last General Assembly. And it seemed to be a straightforward account, not a sly attack. That was one thing about Miller, he always attacked head on or not at all.

She spent the next hour or so perusing the issues which tended to have an item of news in one number followed by a related letter or column in the next, and then a response to that in the subsequent numbers. Sometimes, she suspected, Miller provoked the controversies himself. If not, why would he print such stinging attacks with all the details of their animosity towards him expressed in their own words? She followed the latest controversy with his erstwhile ally, Dr. Begg, a most fervent Protestant and rabid anti-Papist. Nothing to object to there. However, the correspondence almost reached the level of a flyting! It seems the conflict had arisen when Begg tried to poach Miller's staff along with the list of subscribers. Begg and his allies denied this, and Miller printed their letters, then published his own replies and the replies to them through several numbers.

She was struck by one letter from a Mr Nichol, Begg's associate, attacking Miller:

...no man who dares to differ from you appears to be safe, and most men feel that, for aught they know, it may soon be their turn to be dragged before the public in the columns of your newspaper, in which, whatever injury may have been done to individuals, no apology, as far as I know, has ever graced its columns.

I have heard you say that The Witness never sold so well as when you slew a man... You say you are glad of the opportunity of converting 'secret unfriends' into open opponents. I have never fawned upon you, and then ridiculed and mimicked your peculiarities afterwards, as I have often seen others do ....'

And back and forth on all sorts of topics and with all manner of debaters. Lord Aberdeen continued to receive regular batterings, except when it came to the conduct of the conflict with Russia. Elizabeth flicked through the endless reports from the front line and from European courts drawn from the pages of *The Times* and other broadsheets. These seemed to increase in volume as the conflict decreased in size. It occurred to her that this was an extremely effortless way to fill a newspaper! No doubt that was just her feminine aversion to politics and statesmanship.

She tiptoed out the door again. It seemed her brother was responding to questions from his visitor, sometimes asking her for more details, sometimes scratching sketches on his notepad. He was at his best with an applied student, Elizabeth reflected.

On her return to the sofa she picked up another issue from the floor. Ah, it seemed Miller had discovered Begg had succeeded in publishing a rival newspaper, *The Rock*. She almost laughed out loud when she read the attack on the traitor!

'.... *Be it remarked, too, that The Rock, if successful, will be a most important newspaper, seeing that, even should it be of no use whatever to Protestantism itself, it will be of great use indeed to a most excellent Protestant, and enable him, added to his other editorship, to double his already large income.'*

This was most unchristian, but what could you expect from these fellows who had rebelled against the Established Church! They would consume each other like jackals, that's what would happen, she had always said that. 'Haven't I always said that? You have.'

There she was, conversing with herself again! Well, the Minister had told her it was only a problem if you didn't realise you were doing it.

She heard a chair scrape back and rose to check on what was happening in her brother's room. It seemed now it was the young lady's turn to be drawing, it looked like various positions of a baby's head. Elizabeth stepped back without making a noise.

'You should not be so squeamish. Your father and two brothers were medical men. Yes, but MEN, Elizabeth!'

There were still several newspapers littering the floor, with two or three seeming to make a bid for freedom by hiding under the dining table. As she got older all types of inanimate objects appeared to have the power of secreting themselves and to turn up in places she could have sworn were not where she had stowed them. She got down on her knees, reached under the table and caught them by the tails, so to speak. 'There, got you!' She laughed to herself as she took her booty back to the settee.

Her eye was caught by a letter from Sir David Brewster. A sound man and perhaps the most eminent scientist in Scotland. He had been a good friend to their family and to John when he had studied in St. Andrews. Even if he was a Free Kirker.

The letter recounted a visit together with Lord Brougham to a séance in London. There had been rappings in response to questions, a table had moved, and an accordion had seemingly played some tunes on its own.

'God help us!' Elizabeth exclaimed.

Brewster went on to say that although he could not explain all the marvels he witnessed, he was convinced the medium had used his feet to move the table and that he had in fact manipulated the accordion. The man had also left the room several times, probably to secrete things on his person and no one was allowed to look below the table.

Elizabeth was shocked, not by the fraud of the so-called medium, but by the fact that this séance had been attended by Lord Brougham and such an eminent scientist as Brewster. It seemed Mr Faraday had attended an earlier session! And there was not just scientific interest in the question. Mrs Aitcheson at her Kirk Bible study group had even suggested to her that the Bible gave sanction to the idea of spirits and demons. Thank goodness her brother had his feet on the ground! Rappings! Levitation!

It was when she was stacking the papers on the sofa that she noticed an item ringed in ink. Tears ran down her face and onto her dress as she read it. The world disappeared.

• • •

The two medical practitioners in the next room were in a world of their own, each taking pleasure in talking to another odd fish. Like the Professor, Elspeth was used to being looked upon as the strange one, saying things that made others ill at ease and saved by her expertise and sense of duty to her profession. She had never had a conversation alone with a man like this. Goodsir had never conversed in private with a woman on such matters. It was thrilling.

And Elspeth felt at ease listening to Goodsir, who talked about the human body as if it were a plant or some species of butterfly. He talked of the Perimetrium, the Myometrium and the Endometrium; of dissections he had performed on different female bodies and discussed some abnormalities of structure in that zone, of possible deformities due to their age or stature or stage of gestation. As usual, he was thorough and clear. He illustrated his talk with sketches and answered her questions as if she were a colleague or a favoured student.

However, as the conversation proceeded, there were moments when Elspeth recoiled a little, not from embarrassment or distaste for the rather antiseptic tone of his explanations, but with some resentment at having to receive this instruction from a man simply because women were excluded from advanced medical studies. 'Keep calm,' she told herself.

Her ears pricked up when the Professor began to talk about the normal triangular form of the uterus and, in medical language to discuss whether the vaginal opening should be seen as oval or triangular.

'Triangular,' she said. 'In my experience, at least, though in labour we can perhaps talk of a dilated oval.'

Goodsir nodded, unusually giving way to a junior colleague. He admired her practical experience, her first-hand knowledge of the human anatomy and a part of the anatomy that he had little contact with. Moreover, she was someone he would never talk to again and that gave him freedom, perhaps. Elspeth too was flushed at the confirmation of her belief in the triangular structure of the female organs, of the 'cave' as Emma Martin would call it.

She had hesitated to mention such an unscientific point. However, her response seemed to trigger something in him. He glanced towards the pyramids on the shelf.

'Do you know the whole human body is a triangular structure containing a series of pyramids such as the uterus in women, but other structures in the male? I have demonstrated as much down to the level of the cell but have now unearthed new proof. Shall I explain it to you?'

Explain! Here she was back to the position of servile woman. She reddened. It was worse: he was quitting the specific uniqueness of the female, once again suggesting that the male was the prototype, the female the copy. Nevertheless, she nodded her head.

'I have been examining the tendon and the fibres that connect it to the bone.'

He picked up a bone from a nearby table and handed it to her.

'As you can see, I have inserted black bristles in the holes where the fasciculi are, the bundles of fibres which connect the bone to the muscle. And what can you see?'

'They form triangular shapes between them!'

'Well done! Not everyone sees it straight away, but the different bundles of minute fibres criss-cross each other at the apex of the triangle. Even our nervous system is structured in the same way the Egyptians built their pyramids!'

Taking Elspeth's silence as acquiescence he held up his hand and bent the phalanges of his long thumb towards his palm.

'Do you see the triangle?'

Without waiting for her reply, he went on to explain with all manner of diagrams and references to different organs that he was convinced we were all made up of crystals, that the human body was a triangle, that in fact all organic creation was made of triangles, he had even triangled a tree by including its roots in the diagram. His eyes began to gleam and sweat appeared on his brow.

If Elspeth had been impressed by his calm exposition of the uterus and vaginal structure, she now began to worry for the man's sanity. She did not take in all he was saying but she recalled the time as a child she had been hemmed in a corner by an old lady who needed to tell her how the cows were talking to her and the terrible things they were saying.

When he began to talk about electric fish and that he had specimens sent to him at his own expense from around the globe and how he proposed to investigate the spark of life in them she turned to look towards the door.

She did so just in time to see Miss Goodsir rushing into the room with a damp towel in her hand.

'Please leave us alone, Miss Grieve. You have overexcited my brother, and he is not a strong man.'

She nodded towards the hall and the main door. Goodsir made to stand up, but his legs would not support him.

'He collapsed while giving a lecture last week. Oh, learning will be the death of you, John. I beg you to leave us alone, Miss. Please go.'

Elspeth scuttled out of the room like a scalded cat and stepped out onto Charlotte St. Before her the Square loomed up and she began to walk quickly around it, to ground herself, to bring her sanity back. For she too felt sent awry by the Professor's discourse, not just by its fevered manner but by its content.

For what had seemed comforting at first in his identification of the triangular shape of the female reproductive organs had given way to something near despair when he had identified triangles in everything, even trees! What if the shapes we put on things have more to do with us than what is really in Nature? And if so, then the shapes we see will be determined by the most powerful, by men!

Well, she knew that already, she reminded herself as she approached the far end of the Square. But she had thought that Emma Martin had deciphered the true geometry of human existence in the feminine triangle, in the cave. Now it seemed just another illusion. She was lost among a world of shape makers, a maze of cracked mirrors.

Back in the apartment Elizabeth was mopping her brother's fevered brow. He tried to push her away at first but then sank back in the chair. He was breathless as if having just climbed a mountain and his eyes were glazed over like someone exposed to blinding sunlight.

'Oh John, John. What were you thinking of! How could you belittle yourself to that girl, raving away at her? What must she think? I didn't hear much, but triangles! It is against religion! What is happening to all you scientists? Spirits, shapes? What happened to reason?'

'Beauty,' he muttered.

'And I have lost one brother to science, I can't lose two. John, I saw the article about Harry's expedition. They found some kitchen utensils. That does not mean he is dead; it cannot mean he is dead.'

He reached up and pulled her down to sit by his side. They cradled each other and wept.

The Day of Humiliation

They had met on Waterloo Place, but this time Hugh had not been visiting Chambers. Enric had just left the publisher and was hurrying home to think about his offer. Both men seemed put out by the accidental meeting.

'Good afternoon, Mr. Serra. I trust all is well with you on this special day.'

Enric ignored the last part as he had no idea what was special about the day, except for his own private eviction.

'I have decided to forget *Vestiges*, Enric.' Chambers had said, once they were seated in the chairs beside the fireplace. The curtains were drawn in the room, which Enric found unsettling, reminiscent of when a corpse is exposed for visitors before the funeral. He turned to look at Chambers.

'My real work is my debunking of spiritualism, and my explorations of natural philosophy have become a distraction. I will not be giving the latest volume any attention or promotion. I am grateful for your help with the new undertaking and I plan to attend a séance myself soon now that I know what to look for and cannot be easily hoodwinked.'

How could a man give up a decade's work like this? Enric was still lost in thought when Chambers lowered his voice and almost whispered.

'I have a favour to ask, Enric.'

Chambers looked straight into his eyes as if searching for something there, some sign of deceit, perhaps.

'I realised the other day that you have been poorly paid for your extra efforts. I propose to rectify that. Yes, man, I know, you accepted the work and do not wish to renegotiate. That honours you.'

'If you don't have work for me, why pay me more?'

'Ah but I do. I would like you to help Mr Miller, at my expense.'

'But he is at work on what he sees as the definitive demolition of *Vestiges*, his third and deadly onslaught he called it to me the last time I saw him.'

'I need him to be kept busy and am happy for him to spend his ammunition on a book which I feel may be old science now, despite this latest edition. Help him with his researches. I trust you will not reveal the secret of its authorship?'

Enric reddened. So that was why he was being offered an increase in salary! He felt like telling Chambers to go to hell with his bribe, and his job. However, he thought of Alia and the people he lived with and decided to reflect a little first.

'Why would Mr. Miller accept the help of a materialist, a radical like me?'

'You will have to win his confidence in the same way you won mine. And I made use of your talents even though I was and am aware of our deep philosophical and political differences. He will be happy to use you. He has told me that this new attack will go beyond geology and require a knowledge of ethnography, comparative religions, racial theories and politics. He has limited experience in these. So, yes, I think he will be glad to be able to call on your aid.'

'Until he has tired of me.'

Now it was Chambers turn to redden. There was an awkward silence, then as if by magic, Johnson appeared. Their interview was over.

'Spend as much time with him as your printing labours allow. I will tell Johnson to make sure you are rewarded. Thank you Enric. I wish you goodbye. He handed him a brown envelope which Enric dropped into his satchel, dismissed as he had seen others sent away.

He was still smarting as he rushed out into the street and literally bumped into Miller. He asked himself what brought the man away from his office on a working day. The door he had stepped out of had a sign indicating it was the entrance to *The Waterloo Rooms*. When Miller saw Enric looking up the stairs, he blushed, and said,

'We all have our weaknesses, Mr. Serra.'

'Enric, I beg you.'

Damn, this was awkward. Had he discovered the good Christian on his way back from a romantic rendezvous?

'I have a weakness for Panoramas and Dioramas.'

'The painted spectacles of historic events?'

'Well, they are more dynamic than that. This diorama is of the lands of Hindustan and one hears the strange music of those people and the murmuring of the vast crowds on their way to the temple. Most dramatic, most dramatic. They propose future spectacles on the Holy Land and the Russian War, once it is over.'

'I saw one once in Paris, the Battle of Austerlitz! They do make an impression.'

'I am ashamed to say that on my first stay in Edinburgh in 1824, a Panorama of the Battle of Trafalgar made more of an impression on me than the more spectacular and real great fire in the Old Town.'

They were walking along side by side as Miller made these remarks, striding along at his usual brisk pace. Or was he trying to escape Enric?

'I can see no harm or shame in visiting the spectacle.'

'Well, that is most liberal of you. But many of my fellow kirkgoers disapprove of all forms of artistic entertainment, even of music and theatre. And today is not a day to attend such shows.'

'Forgive me, but it is a Wednesday, not a Scottish Sunday.'

'Yes, but have you remarked how quiet the streets are and that the shops are closing early?'

Enric realised he had been so taken up with his own worries that he had not noticed.

'Of course. Has the Queen died?'

'Good gracious, no, how could you think such a thing! This is a Day of Humiliation, convoked by her very much alive, Majesty, the Queen Victoria.'

'I am sorry, I don't understand.'

'Well in non-Popish countries we don't have endless religious feast days. As you know, in Scotland, for example, we do not celebrate the Pagan feast of Christmas, although the Episcopalians still cling on to it. We do however have special days of Thanksgiving, where we show our gratitude to the adored Creator for some mercy He has bestowed on us, and days of Humiliation when we beg His aid and accept our sins that He may help us. A few years ago, at the height of the Irish famine, there was a day of Fasting and Humiliation.'

'And why did the Queen call for one today?'

'Oh, for the Russian War, that we may deserve victory.'

'Is its observance mandatory? They are still at work in the printer's, I believe.'

'Well, no, the whole country can't shut down, but special religious services are held and the civic authorities take part in solemn parades. In London the Queen led the procession followed by the Anglican bishops and the members of the Cabinet and their wives. It is quite a social occasion, unfortunately. I am just off up to the High Street to see what Edinburgh has put on. Would you care to join me?'

The wind tickled their backs as they continued up over the North Bridge towards the Old Town. As they turned the corner up past the Tron Kirk, shouts and curses could be heard from the nearby closes.

'The Irish,' Miller almost spat. 'They and their Church inhabit another country and only obey Rome. I went past their chapel in the Cowgate this morning. It was empty save for a few old women. Some of the protestant Voluntary Sects refuse to follow the dictates of the national government too, feeling their independence would be compromised should they do so. But we are all citizens, subjects of the Queen, and men are dying for us!'

Miller's outrage was cut short at the sight of the civic authorities, the Provost, the Councillors, and the local guard, standing in solemn silence while a prayer was read out by a member of the Established Church.

The doors to the Tron Kirk and the Cathedral lay open and Enric could see that both were packed. At the door of the Signet Library, lawyers in their black gowns stood to attention and on the Lawnmarket a troop of soldiers were ranged in files with their flag waving quietly in the light wind. There was silence, broken only by the cooing of the pigeons on the rooftops. Silence.

Until a keening voice cried orders for them all to stand at ease, to make way for their General. People looked around with disquiet then down to a nearby close from where the sound was issuing. Out came a young man dressed in a red jacket and with a ragged pair of trousers, bare at the knees and with no shoes.

'Present arms!'

'It's daft Peter!' the man next to Enric cried. He walked up and down, imitating the unsteady step of the young man.

'The laddie's no right in the heid!' shouted his companion, rolling his eyes and sticking a finger in his ear.

'Collons ! Fils de puta, cabróns !' Enric swirled round and raised his fists, which was sufficient to send the two gentlemen scurrying off, muttering deprecations against foreigners, especially Germans.

He made to chase after them but was checked by Miller's strong hand on his shoulder.

In the meantime, the laddie was parading up and down before the dignitaries a few yards in front of Hugh and Enric.

'Sergeant Major!' he cried.

'At your service, Captain,' Hugh replied, saluting him slowly. The fellow walked towards them through the parting ranks of black-coated citizens and smiled at Hugh.

'Do you hae ony o that guid bried ye gied me the last time?' he asked.

Hugh nodded and held out his hand then led the lad away and

down towards the printshop in Horse's Wynd, only a few hundred yards away.

Enric thought he should make himself scarce as there were murmurings in the crowd nearby.

'A Russian spy, that's what he is. Did you hear him speak?'

He could see Hugh and his companion in the distance, and he followed them. He had been surprised at himself for the rush of blood to his brain. Was his flareup the result of righteous indignation, or had he just been looking for a release from his frustration with Chambers and with the falling apart of his life in Edinburgh?

He thought of his last conversation with Elspeth, which made him think of an empty fireplace with traces of where the flame had once been but with no warmth to give, cold, listless. She had packed up all her books and pamphlets by Emma Martin and her group and given them to the local chapter of the Socialist club. She had told him she no longer believed in dreams. Where did that leave them? Time would tell, she said, time would tell.

And Alia also seemed different, as if she were living in another place. Perhaps she was trying that out in her mind, as it seemed the only alternative to a costly legal challenge to the Free Church was to accept the miserable sum they were offering in return for ceding them the house and to move out. Alec and Nell were already arranging to move back to Fife to stay with a cousin in Kirkcaldy where Alec said the floorcovering business was flourishing. 'Lots of work for us both,' he said.

When Enric caught up with Hugh he was sitting on the steps leading to the printshop, talking to the boy who was munching on a piece of bread and cheese.

'Go and see Dr. Guthrie, tell him Hugh Miller sent you, Peter,' he was saying.

'I will, Sergeant, I will.' And off he wandered without a glance at Enric.

'And they tell me I have a temper!'

Enric lowered his head.

'I am sorry. I don't know what came over me.'

'Well, we often act based on what has touched us in the past. When I was a young man in Cromarty a young boy, Angus Mackay, with mental difficulties, would follow me from the bank where I worked all around the village. The other boys would make fun of him, imitating his stuttering walk behind my back. I have never understood the cruelty of poor people to other poor folk. Angus would wait for hours for the coach to arrive when he was told I was coming back from Inverness. He liked to be called Captain, so I guess that is why I bestowed that name on poor Peter. Angus taught me kindness and constancy. He lives there still and greets me when I go back and smiles with a glee that would light the sky when I call him Captain. At some moments I was glad of his company, of his appreciation, for there were times in Cromarty I felt an outcast and terribly alone.'

'Loneliness walks with people who have deranged or damaged minds,' Enric said. 'When I was lonely, I thought of how these people must feel, condemned to ostracism by society.'

Hugh looked at him. He remained silent and waited. Enric lowered his head.

'I was in a circus. No, not one with animals but with dancers, jugglers, and acrobats. I don't expect you to appreciate it. But it was my first real family after ruptures in my household at home. They taught me to do tricks and we travelled all over Europe. Monsieur Rinaldi, the boss and the strongman, was married to Madame Hortensia, the contortionist. They were both in their late forties and had a sixteen-year-old boy, Fofo, who was, as they put it, 'special.' I was frightened by him at first, as he could be unpredictable. At times he would get excited and start to snap his fingers faster and faster till they bled, saying he was going to set the world on fire. At others he would take my hand and sing to me in a strange keening voice that pierced my heart. And how he could laugh! He seemed to take to me. And I, after a time, to him. I was his only friend. He would hold my jacket while

I performed and carry my bag when we went into a new arena. One day, he was lost.'

'Lost?'

'We were performing in a fishing village on the Cote D'Azur, and I missed him. I went through the town and as I was approaching the beach, some local boys raced up past me from the shore, whooping and screaming about 'le fou noyé.' I found Fofo floating face down in the water, his leg wound round by a boat cable. The boys said he had drowned after following them into the sea. But I knew he was frightened of the water. I even had to hold his hand when he took a bath. The police sided with the boys and that night we were chased out of town and told never to return. I left the circus not long after that. I couldn't bear to think I was entertaining people who could do such a thing. I couldn't bear to see how his parents cried night after night.'

'That is a sore heart speaking, my friend.'

Enric smiled. It was an expression he had not heard before, Scottish, he supposed, and it seemed exactly right. That sense of fit can bind us to a place, and to a person.

'Mr. Miller.'

'Hugh, I beg you, too.'

'We come from different worlds, and we are headed in different directions. I want to be frank with you. Mr Chambers has no need of my help in research now and has told me I am free. He even suggested he would have no objection if I lent you assistance with your researches. I prefer to be as open as I can with you.'

Hugh looked him up and down, seeming to check for what was behind these words. Was the man playing with him? He understood that the fellow's sympathies were not with the Kirk. Well, he had been tricked by many a coreligionist. A declared atheist could not be worse!

'Well, Enric. The book I am working on will contain talks I am to give in London and here in Edinburgh. There is nothing secret in the matter and my arguments have been rehearsed many times and tried out in the newspaper. You may be of use to me.'

'I will not try to influence your arguments, just provide you with proper intelligence. I owe that to intellectual truth. And you contrary Scotchmen interest me, so let us see if we two intellectual misfits can do something in the spirit of the Edinburgh I came to find.'

'As I wrote just the other week in the newspaper on the disturbances in your country, Spain is a country of anarchists and assassins. I will just have to hope you are only the first and trust you are a gentle one! Let us see what you can do for me.'

'To enlightenment!'

'To the eternal glory of God.'

They went into the office together just as the bells marked the end of the Day of Humiliation and the crowds disbanded and went home, comforting themselves that their efforts would count for something.

Peter spied a man leading a horse along the Cowgate. He walked up and took the animal's tail in his right hand.

'Giddy up, Giddy up, all the way home.'

Jericho

Nell told her it was normal that the dreams had come back.

'We have all had a shock. Why if Alec had left Leith Wynd two minutes later, he might have been crushed beneath the collapsed wall too! Those poor souls. Twenty of them taken. Who would have thought a wall that had stood there for centuries could just collapse like that? It made you wonder if the Castle is safe. Who is to say that one day the toffs in Princes Street Gardens won't be flattened like pancakes, just as those poor folk were? And the fallen wall had closed off the path from the High Street down towards Leith, past Calton Hill. Though the railway would do that for good, they said. Did Alia know they were going to move the Trinity Church, that old fancy one, with the paintings in? Alec said some wanted to stick it in the place occupied by Burns' monument up on Calton Hill. They wouldna dare. The Masons would stop them, at least those in his lodge said so.'

'I haven't dreamed about doors since I was a young girl, and I don't see the connection between them and tumbling walls.'

'It's that none of us feel secure. And if the city walls can collapse then we can't be sure of anything. The doors were off their hinges, you said, and you were floating down the Forth on one of them while folk waved to you. Where were you going?'

'To the open sea, I fear,' Alia answered.

They were in the back room, packing up the curtains and the furniture that Nell and Alec would not need in Fife, working together like in the old days. In the old days they had been young women, and the ups and downs of life had served to propel them on with more force into the future. Now they seemed like obstacles announcing an oncoming canyon or sheer wall.

'Why don't you come to Kirkcaldy with us, Alia? Just give us a wee while to get on our feet then I am sure we can find room for you. And it's not such a bad place. Alec is fair excited about the thought of going back to Fife. He says the fishing is magic! Men, what are they like!'

Alia tried to laugh along with Nell, but they both knew it was forced gaiety. And Nell had mentioned Alec, but not her two daughters, Mary and Katherine. Because she doesn't want to bring up poor wee Maggie, Alia realised. What was to be done with the girl who didn't belong to anyone?

'What will we do with the lassie?'

Nell looked at her as if to say, you cannot expect me and Alec to take her, we have enough to deal with.

'Aye, Alec and I were talking about her last night. We cannae send her back home as she doesnae have a home. And if we send her out on her own then we both know what will happen to her. We cannae do that.'

'But how can I take her if I don't know where I am going? And I don't know if I can be a mother to anyone. I am a solitary bird.'

'Solitary birds fall from the sky, Alia. And no one notices. But you are not alone. You have Alec and I and the girls.'

'I have you, or I have Maggie. One or the other.'

This was the first real argument they had had in thirty years and that, more than the subject, was what tore deep into their hearts.

They began to talk past each other, to suddenly find the contents of the next packing-box deeply fascinating.

Alia found a notebook she had taken with her to England all those years ago in her voiceless time. It was in a brown leather bag, and she tarried several minutes in opening it.

There were rote phrases, like 'I am very well, thank you,' or 'May I have some more tea,' 'I am tired and need to go to bed,' 'Thank you for being so kind,' and so on.

There were some drawings too, dresses with a button missing, an umbrella, a question mark above a post-box and many other commonplace things or places she must have needed to ask about.

She flicked through till she came to the end, and there she found drawings of crows, of a girl alone in the middle of a crowd of harsh-faced men, and a woman holding a Bible and pointing towards a small man in a top hat. There were a couple of letters pinned to the back of the book but she focussed on the images, reminding her of those that peopled her dreams nowadays.

She wondered what sketches would fill such a book at this moment of her life. She closed her eyes and thought, mindless of Nell chattering on about the quantity of stuff they had amassed and what to do with it.

Women walking in groups up the hill towards Princes Street, each one trailing a thread and their clothes unravelling as they distanced themselves from the house till they could be glimpsed semi-naked and shivering at the top of the slope.

A small woman looking up at the towering figure of a white-haired clergyman with claws for hands.

An empty house enclosing an empty heart.

Och what was the use? This was childishness and she was no longer that innocent girl taken from her mother and brother. She leaned forward to put the book back in its leather casing. As she did, she felt the folds in her tummy and the loose skin on her arms. She was a middle-aged woman now and was losing her looks. Perhaps that was what explained her abandonment. She had relied on beauty and beauty was leaving her, off to bestow its charms on the next young enchantress. Her merchandise had devalued. Yet she had never sold her body, save in a sense, to Combe. The men who submitted to her were not allowed to approach her. But yes, they submitted to a beautiful goddess. Frumpiness could not command anyone.

She was wandering, letting herself be led along by scattered thoughts down avenues that led nowhere. That too was a sign of age, she supposed.

She came to herself when Nell asked for her help in tying up a parcel.

'My daughters' old clothes. Maggie should have them.'

Alia held down the string with her finger while Nell made the knot, moving with the slick dexterity of a dressmaker.

A dressmaker. And what was Alia? Not a mother, not a skilled craftswoman, not even a proprietor now, it seemed. A mistress of nothing and no one.

As they were concentrating on tying the knot, Alec entered. He was looking for Maggie, who it seemed, had had one of the tantrums she excelled in recently. She had run away from him like he, she said, was running away from her.

They were all talking about the lassie and where she could have gone when she appeared, hand in hand with Enric and a tall, attractive woman.

'Elspeth and I caught this young fugitive and thought we should bring her back to you before she reached the Border. She said she was off to England to stay with the Queen!'

They all laughed, except for Maggie and the woman. The girl was clutching her hand as if it was a lifeline.

'Maggie, we are glad to see you back. Now let me say hello to your friend properly.'

'I am Elspeth, and it's alright. Maggie is just a wee bit disconcerted. I am happy to hold her hand.'

So this was the woman who had stolen Enric's heart! Alec, Nell, and Alia all said 'Pleased to meet you' almost at once. Alec slapped Enric on the back, for some reason.

'Please come and sit down, Elspeth. It's good to meet you at last. I am only sorry that with everything so topsy-turvy we cannot make you more comfortable,' Alia said. 'Though I am sure that is not important to you.'

Elspeth blushed and then assured them all that no, of course it was not. She would like to see Maggie's room as she had been told it was especially nice.

'Of course, of course. Maggie, take Elspeth to your room while we make some tea. We will see you in the kitchen as it still has all its furniture.'

Once left alone with Enric, Alia waited. Enric glanced in surprise at a room he had never visited.

'We did not mean to come but Maggie would not let go of Elspeth's hand. It was lucky we chanced upon her as she was weeping and out of herself. She might have got run over, the way she was rushing out onto the road in her haste.'

'Do you know what distressed her so?'

'Well, she wouldn't say anything to us at first but then she blurted out that she was sad because she knew her parents weren't dead. Katherine had told her. It is the first time I have heard of a child crying because her parents were still alive!'

'That wee besom! Katherine heard me and her father talking but she promised she would haud her wheesht. I am sorry, Alia.' Nell beckoned to Alec, 'Come and give me a hand with the tea. What a to-do, what a mess.'

Enric and Alia stood near the curtainless window, with their backs to the packing cases. The room already had the odour of a warehouse. Alia put her hand on Enric's shoulder in an unusual gesture of closeness.

'Elspeth is very beautiful. And she seems kind. And strong. Her own woman.'

'She is all these things.'

He said this without flourish, with what seemed almost sadness in his voice.

'She is leaving you. She has that look about her.'

'How can you tell? Even Elspeth doesn't know it completely, but I can sense it too. And I am heartbroken. I work harder and take on these research projects to keep myself from thinking about it, to, how can I say, close the window or seal up the cracks in our relationship.'

'Have you talked with her about it?'

'Well, Alia, like me, Elspeth will read anything, will debate and discuss everything from the price of bread to the names of the planets. Unlike me, she feels even more than she is capable of saying and that stops her from talking about deeper things, as if words might kill the feeling. I am just the opposite, am often not able to feel something until I can say it. And when I say something, even as a question, it becomes what I feel and so I don't speak in case my words take on a life of their own and carry me with them. The curse of us would-be intellectuals!'

'Words are seldom the solution to anything, I have found. The fact of talking is what is important, if the other is really listening. I am listening, Enric. Just say whatever words come to you and let them disappear into the air.'

He turned to look out of the window onto the grey cobbles below.

'I thought I had found another country where I could anchor myself. I thought here was someone who appreciated what I had to give, saw things in me I had not seen, and completed me with her difference. Now I fear I am being exiled once more.'

'Go on, Enric.' She stood at his side, her eyes on the street and the trees swaying in the East Wind.

'Have you ever been swept across a border into a foreign country where you don't want to go? I have, and sometimes even crossed those frontiers myself in a vain hope that the country I needed was there, in France, in Austria, in Germany. I was up on the Pentland Hills on Sunday, and I swear I could see England just across the Border. The border seems so near! Elspeth and I are skirting it daily and I am so frightened that we will end up on different sides. I am sorry, that sounds fanciful. I suppose I just feel like I have felt for years, a wanderer, an exile, from home and family and love.'

He leant against the window and Alia could see he was crying as the glass steamed up and droplets ran down it.

'I am so sorry, Enric. And I am envious too.'

Silence, save for the neighing of a horse and the curses of his driver.

'You see,' she went on, 'I have never loved. Something was killed in me when I was taken across that border as a girl. And when I thought I could love, the man I chose had no love of the type I needed to give me back. And thus I have stayed here, stuck on my perch, watching the world go by. Admiring the shiny baubles of the world, laughing at people's folly, following the fortunes of a few and wishing them well, half-hoping they would see me, really see me and call on me to swoop down and go with them. But I can see over those borders and what frightens me, is that it is just like here!'

They were both speaking in exaggerated tones, and they knew it. They were giving each other permission to say things they would never have to take back, to express thoughts that had been seeping out of them in broken cries, quick complaints.

Their conversation was cut short by the sound of screaming and kicking from upstairs. They both ran out of the room and towards the commotion. Maggie's bedroom door was open, and the entrance was strewn with broken toys and shoes and clothes. Enric recognised his portrait of her torn on the floor.

Elspeth was trying to contain the girl who seemed be having some kind of seizure, her face bright red and her body writhing, with sounds sparking out of her like water dropped in hot oil.

It was difficult to make out what she was saying but Alia caught one repeated line.

'Nobody wants Maggie. Nobody.'

'Maggie, my wee lamb, calm yourself. We all want you.'

Alia's words had no immediate effect but gradually the girl's fit subsided, either reassured by Alia's gentle insistence, or perhaps just through exhaustion.

Enric picked her up and carried her to the bed and Nell came in with a hot facecloth and towels and a sweet drink. She waved her hand behind her back, urging them to leave the room.

'The bairn needs space, some quiet and rest. I will sit with her.'

'Are you leaving me after all?'

'No, Maggie,' Alia said. 'We will leave the door open so you can tell we are just down in the kitchen. I will come up and see you in a wee while. Now rest, my dear.'

When Alia, Elspeth and Enric stepped into the kitchen they found Alec nervously pacing up and down before a table strewn with pots of jam and half-made sandwiches. There was more butter on his trousers than on the bread and his clumsy attempts to scrape it off meant the floor was dotted with grease.

'Oh, the poor bairn, how is she?'

As Alia was explaining how they had found Maggie and that Nell was with her, Elspeth put her head on Enric's shoulder and began to sob. He held her then helped her into a chair while Alia handed her a handkerchief.

'It is my fault. I think I was flattered that the poor wee soul took to me so much that I encouraged her. And when she said she would come and live with me and Mr Enric could visit us, I laughed, and then tried to explain that I had no room for her in my house. She kept asking why? I said I was going away. 'Like everyone I know. Does no one bide in their hame ony mair?' she said. And then she suddenly went wild. It is my fault, the poor lost thing.'

Alia noticed Enric wince as he listened to Elspeth.

'You weren't to know about her situation,' Alia interjected. 'And Maggie says the wildest things. You are not to blame, Elspeth. Alec, come and help me clear up the stuff from the floor.'

As the door clicked shut behind them, Enric took Elspeth in his arms. She began to cry again.

'I feel like Maggie,' he said.

• • •

Maggie was sleeping or at least lying on the bed with her eyes closed. Alec made to say something to his wife, but she shooshed him.

'Dinna be making promises we canna keep, that disna help anyone.'

Once they had tidied up the room, they all stood around, uncertain whether to withdraw and if they did, who should stay with the girl. As they slipped out, Maggie stirred and opened her eyes. They all moved back into the room like shingle following the waves.

'We are here, Maggie,' said Nell.

'Where is the lady? Where is Elspeth?'

A whisper came from the darkened hall.

'I am here, Maggie, and tonight I will be biding upstairs with Enric, so as to be close to you. So dinna fash ony mair my wee dove. I will bring you your breakfast in the morning.'

'Alec and I have to go and fetch Mary and Katherine from their cousins, but we will be back tomorrow morning. We are not going away!'

'And you can come and sleep in my room,' Alia added, surprising the other members of the household. The Mistress always kept her room as a space apart. Maggie was aware of the honour and held out her hand to Alia.

Alia spent the evening in her room watching Maggie playing with some toys the girls had given her, with the child's facility to forget and to live in the moment. Alia and Enric and Elspeth were lost in thoughts of past moments that were gone forever.

Alia felt that her conversation with Enric had exhausted her even more than the scenes with Maggie. She had talked! How she had talked! She hoped it had helped him as much as it had unsettled her.

In the room upstairs Enric and Elspeth made love. Like lovers do before they part.

Telltale Time

How long was a day? Time was stretching and contracting around him. He peered through the small window and spied an unruly column of soldiers extending accordionlike along the end of the street on their way to the barracks. He sat down and tried to concentrate on his work. He was convinced that the days in Genesis referred to geological periods: that was the testimony of the rocks. But there was more.

The problem causing his brain to explode was that there was so much more. It all revolved around time. He could show that the seas that had covered much of inland Scotland had taken aeons to subside. If we knew that the shores of the Solway Firth still lay where they were when the Romans constructed Hadrian's Wall, then change obviously happened at much longer intervals.

Time was becoming of personal concern too, as it does to anyone in their fifth decade with children, especially one as young as four. Would he live to see his sons and daughters married, set up in the world? Time and aging. Would he have the strength to continue fighting with words, pushing the Church and society closer to God? And was eternity endless time or the absence of time? So many questions, sending his brain buzzing like a bluebottle in a jam-jar.

He had to finish this chapter of the book in the next few days, as it was to constitute the talk he had been invited to give in the Exeter Hall in London. Five thousand people had already confirmed their attendance, which proved to him there was an audience for those who rejected secularism but who supported scientific advance, like he did.

He was tired. He became weary now faster than he used to. Random thoughts pushed their way into his brain like the wheedling beggars in the High Street, not catching your full attention but refusing to be ignored. 'Concentrate, Hugh.' Suddenly, his eyes stung. What was that smell? It seemed like a mixture of burned tar and cinders with a dash of lemon! A premonition of hell?

'Lydia! What in the name of Mr Johnson's cat is that?'

No reply came and Hugh dropped his pen and stomped down the stairs, holding onto the handrail so that he could descend faster without stumbling. He strode into the dining room and found it vacant save for the table set with the best crockery and a bowl of raisins and another of sliced onions. What was going on!

'Lydia!'

He ventured through to the kitchen to find his wife, his oldest daughter, Harriet, and Agnes the cook all reading instructions from a green paper. Lydia was holding a bottle with the prestigious brand of *Scott and Orr, Dundas Street*, up to the light.

The three looked round when Hugh entered the room.

'Agnes says we need to add sugar to the rice. I can't get her to accept that a Bengal Curry is a savoury dish. However, the instructions say nothing on the matter.'

'It is a sair waste o' a guid bit of lamb, sir. But gin it hae raisins, it maun be sweet, dinna ye think, sir?'

Hugh reached over for the paper and tutted a few times as he perused the instructions. They read more like a proclamation than a recipe, describing the properties of the different spices, the tamarinds, cumin, and *Scott and Orr's* own secret ingredients, 'Making this repast of the Maharajahs your private emissary from the glorious Orient.' Once it described how to add the powder to a lamb stew, of the rice it simply said, 'Rinse the rice then immerse it in water and boil for twenty minutes.'

Hugh did what men do. He read the instructions out loud three times, put the paper on the table, then walked back to the dining room, calling his wife to follow him.

'Lydia, can you tell me what this curry nonsense is and what you and Harriet are doing in the kitchen.'

Lydia glared at him and then put her finger to her lips.

'I beg you to keep your voice down. Harriet will hear.'

'Hear what? Am I to be silenced in my own house?'

'*Your* own house? It is *our* house. And in any case, it is because we are leaving for our new home in Portobello that Harriet wanted to have a dinner on one of the few evenings you are at home.'

'Harriet wanted to have a dinner? She is fifteen years old!'

'Exactly. And she wants to be treated as such and not just as another of the children. William is twelve, but behaves like an infant, Bessie at nine, is well, Bessie. A ray of sunshine, frightened of nothing, but a child, like Hugh.'

'Hugh is only four, what else should he be?'

'No, they are all fine, well nearly all. William is a contrary creature who doesn't seem to understand more than how to exasperate his teacher. And don't smile, Hugh. For all the rebellious schoolchildren like you who succeed, there are ten that don't.'

'I stand corrected. But what does all this have to do with curry?'

'Well, Harriet saw an advertisement the other day for it in your newspaper and had been reading about India and the missions there. She begged me to buy some and said that she thought you would like it as you have been talking endlessly about the Hindus and the Buddhists and the Mahomedans in the last few weeks. Although I know what she really wants is to be able to boast to her schoolmates that she has tasted exotic fare. But that is what it is to be fifteen.'

'I was fifteen and never had a dinner.'

'You were never fifteen Hugh. You went from boy to man. Let your children grow at a natural pace. Even though you see little of them.'

'I see them on Sundays.'

'You see only God on Sundays, and when you do find time to take them out for a walk, you lecture them.'

'Lydia, do not take the Lord's name in vain! Call me when I have to present myself at the curry ceremony, but I beg you to temper your language!'

He retreated upstairs into the large booklined room he used as a study and paced up and down, hoping to calm his agitation. To no avail. Lydia had been increasingly short with him in the last few months. He had tried to placate her by buying the house in Portobello after the incident and when she repeatedly said she yearned to live beside the sea once more. Still she was not satisfied.

He could tell that she was disappointed with their social circle, or lack of it. He had never had many friends and he had fewer every day. 'Why do you have to see every conversation, every article, as a combat?' she had exclaimed a few weeks ago. Her dreams of social prestige when she had first come with him to the Capital had disappeared, leaving a trace of bitterness in her eyes and in the curl of her mouth when she addressed him.

When he had refused an invitation to the Duke of Argyll's home in Inveraray, her fury had known no bounds. Well, so he had thought till he received the onslaught of her frustration at his refusal to accept a knighthood. It had only been a rumour, a sounding out, he protested, but she reacted as if he had slammed the door to good society in her face.

She had even suggested that his latest venture was a mistake.

'You tried to demolish *Vestiges* in *Footprints*, Hugh. The public has moved on. You need to think of what will sell.'

'What will sell?' As he paced up and down this phrase rang in his head like the Tron kirk bell. 'Think what will sell like the Tron kirk Bell, A bell tells what it's told. And in the end, time takes its toll on us all, like the tales we tell, though they do not sell. Think what will sell…'

He was almost chanting, repeating these nonsense lines to himself. He stopped and leaned against the wall. The world was slipping beneath his feet. He was even starting to distrust Nature and his trusty rocks. Fossils were multiplying, time was stretching further and further back and letting him slide between the cracks.

'A bell tells what it's tolled.'

'Stop it Hugh, stop it man.' Was he becoming so alone he only had himself to talk to? Chambers still received him occasionally, although when he suggested meeting to talk about a philosophical question, the publisher usually replied that he should discuss it with Mr Serra, 'as he knows more about it than I.'

Guthrie too had become an infrequent visitor, though was always warm when they did meet. Makgill Crichton had died at fifty, just under three years ago, worn out by work. And to think the poor kind fellow had feared for Hugh! Lydia had stopped urging him to work less. Hugh did not know whether to be pleased that she seemed to understand how important his labours were, or to give in to the suspicion that she no longer cared. She had her own publications, her own little troupe of female friends who met for teas and literary talks.

And the children. He was still learning to be a father after all these years. His own father had left him so young that he had never finished the course. Children nowadays seemed so different, fascinated by the latest mechanical toy or, as he had heard someone call them, 'gadgets.' The children talked about London as if it were closer than Cromarty and the boys had those stories of the Wild West, which was more familiar to them than Fifeshire! He was getting old.

He heard the sound of a gong. A gong! And Harriet calling to him. He walked down like John the Baptist into Herod's banquet.

And indeed, it was like a scene from the Scriptures, almost a parody of the illustrations in their volume of Kitto's *Pictorial Bible*! Harriet was dressed in a shapeless red gown and was wearing a headscarf and a sort of veil. William sported a small black hat with no rim and with a picture of an elephant pasted to its front. Little Hugh had a band round his head with a feather sticking out of it, as he had insisted that was what real Indians wore. And Bessie! She was wearing a turban made from a tea towel and her face was stained brown, with streaks of red and yellow running down it. Thank goodness Lydia and the maid were their usual selves. Hugh was about to ask if they had all gone mad when he caught Lydia's look.

They sat down around the table and Hugh gave thanks then waited as Harriet and the maid served. Harriet explained that people in India only ate rice and had never seen a potato. William went into fits of laughter at that. A look from his father quietened him. Harriet said she had read that Indians ate with their hands, but her mother had told her there were some standards you had to respect. William asked if this was a Christian food, and if not, did eating it make them into heathens? The food itself was blander than Hugh expected, and the rice stuck together, and Bess spilled hers all over the floor. Hugh complimented Harriet on her idea, told her she was getting quite grown-up and that now he had two ladies in the house.

Lydia asked him to tell the children about the diorama on Hindustan. Did he think it was realistic? 'Well, I coincided with some gentlemen of the Scots Guards in the Waterloo Rooms and they assured me it was, with long plains interrupted by mountain ranges. William perked up at the mention of soldiers. He alone liked living so close to the barracks and would salute the men in uniform he encountered in the street.

'So Hindustan looks like Palestine!' Harriet said, and she fetched Kitto and flicked through the well-worn pages till she came to some biblical landscapes.

'Well, yes, I suppose it does, though the Hindustan mountains are higher and rougher, and it is not as fertile.'

'And is that why the Garden of Eden was not there but nearer Palestine?'

Hugh tried not to laugh at the sight of his daughter speaking through a flimsy veil.

'Yes, the Garden was in Mesopotamia, not too far away from the Holy Land.'

'And what do the Indians look like? And why do all the races look so different?'

'Because people are like pan-bread, and some get toasted by the sun!' William interjected.

'I have a fool for a son, God help me,' his father thought, though was careful not to reveal anything more than a slight grimace, what Lydia called his Cromarty Banker's face. His son knew that tick too well, and was silent from then on, sitting with his head down, counting the grains of rice on the carpet and assembling them into troop formations.

'Jesus looks like me!' Bessie suddenly exclaimed in the way she had of bursting in on conversations with the wildest ideas.

'Perhaps his mother Mary, did, as a girl,' Lydia said, signalling to her husband to pass over the blasphemy. Things were getting out of control. Why did this man not just learn to play with his children?

But Bessie pointed to a picture of Christ entering Jerusalem. He was bearded and a man, but yes, he did have her eyes and pale skin, they all had to admit.

'Bessie, that is just a painting, we don't really know what the Saviour looked like,' Harriet lectured her, hoping she sounded as authoritative as her father.

Lydia beckoned the maid to clear the table, like a woman signalling for help on a sinking raft. Another lecture! Why could they not just be children dressing up for fun! She pushed her chair back and went over to young Hugh and took him by the hand, then called to Bessie to come out for a walk with her.

'I shall leave you three older ones to continue the seminar. Once I have washed her face, Bessie and Hugh and I will go up to the Queen's Park to feed the swans. Perhaps *they* will appreciate the rice!'

Once the door had banged shut behind them, Hugh proposed to William and Harriet that they sit down in front of the fire, so they could talk about these important questions.

'The reasons why people look so different across the world has puzzled many great thinkers, William. And whether the Saviour resembled our portraits of Him has been a great source of debate, Harriet. As usual, our religion gives the answer to both questions.'

William tried to look interested but was really wishing he could have gone with his mother to the pond. He could have thrown stones at the swans! Harriet did not have to feign interest: she was captivated by her father's attention. She slipped her veil off and looked up to him and waited for his explanation. Should she fetch her notebook?

'Some people, such as a man called Professor Knox, think that human beings are what is called a genus and that the different races are all distinct species. So dogs would be the genus and a Labrador and a Spaniel two distinct species of dogs.'

William nodded his head emphatically. If he seemed to understand, perhaps his father would stop. Harriet asked her father to go on.

'I disagree, we know that dogs can breed with other dogs, so you can cross a terrier with a spaniel, for example. And men and women from different races can marry and have children, which cannot happen across species. So Man, like dogs, is a species and the different races are variations of the same species.'

Hugh could tell that even Harriet was having trouble following him, but he found it helpful to try and explain these things to her. They were complex and he needed to be as simple as possible in his public talks. He also felt proud to be able to address subjects that the more prudish of his peers would not have discussed even with other adults.

His son was imagining a dogman or a mandog. Would they talk or would they bark?

'So why do the races look different?' Harriet asked.

'Well, in fact the answer to that goes together with the real image of Christ. Does our Saviour look handsome in this painting, William?'

'Yes, yes, he does.' More nodding.

'It would be strange indeed if God had created Adam and Eve ugly or that God had taken on a human form in any way less than the most handsome. Even nowadays the natives of the Caucasus are considered the fairest in the world. And they come from Mesopotamia, and down to Israel. We can see from paintings in Egyptian tombs that before the influx of the negroes, the Egyptian was also very handsome. God always creates the perfect type first.'

'So the painting of our Redeemer as a fair-haired man with white skin is correct?' Harriet said this then held her breath.

'Exactly, daughter. Exactly! You are as smart as your mother and far cleverer than your father!'

Seeing the despondent look of his son, Hugh asked him. 'Now, what happened to Adam and Eve after they sinned?'

William's face brightened. He knew the answer to this one.

'They were expelled from the Garden of Eden.'

'Yes, and then they wandered the face of the earth. The Caucasians stayed around Europe and the stronger races pushed the weaker ones farther and farther out. The further from the centre, the more degraded the humanity, till you encounter the negro tribes in Africa with their sooty skins, broad noses, thick lips, projecting jawbones, and partially webbed fingers. And on to the very south of that continent, where we find ourselves among the squalid Hottentots, repulsively ugly, and begrimed with filth.'

'And the Indians?' the boy asked.

'Well, if you look at the Globe you will see India is halfway between the Holy Land and Australia. The antipodean aborigines are of the lowest, most sunken type, completely black and small in stature. Therefore, what must the Indians look like?'

'Brown and not too small!' his son replied.

'Quite so! And they have the advantage of a culture of some artistic merit and some economic success in the past, which helped arrest their degradation. They will not disappear as the most degraded races are bound to. But they have no Christianity. Perhaps someday you, William, or you, Harriet, will bring the knowledge of the Lord to them.'

Hugh left the two children in the care of the maid, who whined at her kitchen minging with those foreign potions. He just had to go and jot this down. It would form the basis for his talk and become a chapter in his opus major, *The Testimony of the Rocks*. Time seemed an ally once more as he sank into his chair and proceeded to write. The time would come, surely, when Men would marry faith and science and see the providential patterns in Nature. 'Now, concentrate, Hugh, tell the tale of creation and the testimony of geology.' He bit his lip and wrote on.

The walls around him dissolved and he was looking down on fields of tall grass and glimpsing herds of antelope, cattle, and here and there sheep grazing. It was the Tertiary Age, and their fossils show God had created them just in time for Man's subsequent arrival. Time was measured, one day of whatever length succeeded another according to God's plan. And Adam and Eve were not born in a hostile wilderness, but in a Garden.

Now the two stories below him sunk into the ground, the house was demolished, and they were all gone. Stuart Street and the Barracks ceased to exist.

Lieutenant Colonel William Miller would go to India and serve in the army there. He would die aged 51. Harriet would emigrate to Australia, and die in Adelaide at the age of 44, surrounded by her husband and four daughters.

Young Hugh would become a geologist like his father and die after falling seriously ill with typhoid contracted during fieldwork on the Old Red Sandstone in the north-west Highlands in 1896 aged 46.

Only sweet, carefree Bessie would live to be older than her father was at his death, dying at the ripe old age of 74, though her life would be blighted at the end by the loss of her son in the First World War. We all slip through the cracks of time, even Lydia, despite her attempts to shore herself up against oblivion by endless publications of her departed husband's writings. Eternity eats us all up, Christians and Jews, Hindus and Muslims, swallowing us like the sunken rock formations and the fossil beds. Time takes its toll.

The Age of Ugliness

The Aesthetic Club had baulked at first at his request to devote two sessions to the subject, but out of whimsy or to avoid confronting a man famous for his obstinacy, they had finally ceded. He said he wanted to take Hay's recent book, *The Geometric Beauty of the Human Figure* in a different direction. He had supplied anatomical information to Hay for the book and this had started his speculations on the subject, he explained. David Ramsay Hay had triumphed as a young man as the interior designer of Abbotsford. Now, like everyone else, he was trying to turn art into science, nature into geometry.

Goodsir had begun in a standard fashion, outlining Hay's formulae for the conversion of regularity and harmony into beauty, then discussed the rejection that we all feel for dissonant sounds or skewed lines. Several in the company yawned, as Goodsir had already given a talk on Beauty. He was never the most electrifying speaker, Sheriff Gordon mused, his glance escaping out into the gorgeous dusk.

However, of a sudden, in the hotel room overlooking Princes Street and the Castle, as the Spring evening ceded to the night and each of the streetlights were lit, he startled them all. He produced a large sack, put his hand into it and placed an enormous toad on the table.

'Behold the toad, gentlemen, the Bufo Bufo, or as we say in Fife, the puddock. The stuff of both folklore and art as the epitome of ugliness. And in the next two evenings I want to talk about '*The Aesthetics of the Ugly*,' Yes, gentlemen, there is such a thing. Our German colleague Carl Rosenfranz has even published a paper with that title, where he takes the points I am going to make even further. Some people say we live in the Age of Ugliness. I want us to discuss what that means.'

There was some uncomfortable shifting in seats, signs of embarrassment from his colleagues. Was this a joke? Was he trying to shame them with their own caricatures of himself as the ugliest man in Christendom?

The toad quivered, the room lights glinting off its dry wart-pocked flesh. It had been consuming a fly and remnants of the hapless insect still dangled from its mouth.

'Look out, it is going to escape,' little James Ballantine shouted, shivering in disgust.

'I say, old man, frogs are one thing, we all kept them as boys, but the bulging eyes and stumpy face of this creature is repellent,' Dallas, said. It takes me into unpleasant places in my mind, into what I call my unconscious.'

Goodsir just smiled as if to suggest that was his intention and clamped a hand on the toad's leg to stop it leaping off. Piazzi Smyth, the Astronomer Royal, would later insist that the professor and the amphibian shared the same facial expression. 'You should have seen the pair of them, Jessie,' he said to his fiancée when he called in on her on his way home.

'Please, Charles, you will put me off my sleep!'

Goodsir did not deny the ugliness of the creature. Indeed, he almost seemed to glory in it, relating descriptions of toads throughout history. He pointed out its stunted features and even its unpleasant croak. When he picked it up with both hands and held the twitching beast out in front of each of them, some feared they were about to witness a live dissection, given the professor's renowned love of the practice.

After a while he put away the toad and handed it to his assistant, John Arthur, Ballantine thought he was called.

'Most of you, gentlemen, reside like I do in the New Town or in the pleasant suburbs of the city. Mr Ballantine here, one of our most gifted artists and experts on stained glass, as well as a poet of some standing, was born in the slums of the West Port and knows well what ugliness poverty brings. Perhaps for this reason he understands beauty. What do you think, James? Do we need to understand ugliness in order to comprehend beauty?'

This was more like it. They began to discuss in a livelier fashion. They even accepted that the ugliness of the modern factory or of the steam train could be seen as a kind of contemporary beauty. Goodsir did insist a little too much on the magnificence of the opened skull, but the man could not help himself!

'However, we are talking about what we can see and the visible effects on us. It's what we *don*'t see but which our brain apprehends that affects us in ways we are not aware of. In this sense, beauty and ugliness are the same. They function as stimuli on the unconscious mind. Despite your neighbour's and friend's Hughes Bennett's insistence on tracing everything to the blood, the nervous system is the key, Goodsir,' Laycock insisted.

There was silence in the room for a moment. The two men were rivals for the soon-to-be vacant chair of medicine, Hughes Bennett representing the French school and Laycock the German. There is nothing more bitter than a competition for a university chair, as Goodsir had found to his cost.

'Well, I can see why those Pre-Raphaelite bounders call their female subjects, 'stunners,' Dallas joked. Their beauty certainly reaches all our organs in a variety of ways. And they are surely reacting to the ugliness of the English industrial scene.'

There was polite laughter here, but at least the tension had been defused.

'I agree with you about a thirst for beauty in reaction to surrounding ugliness,' Goodsir countered. However, that is not what I am trying to convey, rather that beautiful things can be ugly as well as the opposite. I hope to demonstrate that more fully in the second meeting. Goodnight, gentlemen, goodnight.'

He closed the talk that night by declaring that in the next session he would make the toad beautiful. They all laughed, telling him there were some things that neither poetry nor the new sciences could do.

Goodsir felt triumphant. John Arthur noticed his renewed confidence and felt reassured. The master was back!

It was, of course, his meeting with Elspeth that had made him reflect on ugliness and beauty. Her image stayed with him, even though he doubted he would see her again. Indeed, he had no wish to do so: beauty is troubling, it gets in the way.

About a month later the Club met at the Princes Street hotel. The custom was for about the twenty or so members to reunite at one of their homes. Goodsir alleged some works at his place and the members accepted his excuse with alacrity. He sent John Arthur ahead to get the room ready.

He went over with Bennett, famous for having located leukaemia in the blood. A good man and a friend of Forbes too, though not a member of the Brotherhood, preferring the more traditional Masons.

'How is Edward? Still working as hard as ever?'

Goodsir answered that he believed their friend was working on a guide to the flora and fauna of the Southwest of England.

'I have heard Professor Jameson was visited by his doctor twice this week.'

Despite himself, Goodsir could not help looking eagerly at Bennett.

'You know, even if the time has come for him to step down, I am not confident they will elect Edward.'

'He is the best qualified, he loves the University, and he has the energy that the post needs.'

'Well, John, you don't need me to tell you that the best man does not always get the job. You were passed over a few years ago and I am beginning to think from the increasing smugness of Laycock's greetings to me that I may be losing my own race. But come, it looks as if others have arrived before us.'

Indeed, he could see Ballantine and Piazzi Smyth talking energetically at the main door. The astronomer was pointing towards Calton Hill at the other end of Princes Street.

'Hello, gentlemen,' Ballantine greeted them.

'Charles was just explaining the ball he has had installed on top of Nelson's monument to give a time signal to the ships in the port of Leith.'

'Really? What time will it mark?'

'Well, one o'clock of course, Bennett. Otherwise I would need a lot of levers or a lot of balls!'

And laughing, they all made their way up the stairs.

The curtains were closed and the gas lights cloaked with covers, giving the room a ghostly air. Impatience ran around the room like the snapping of branches in a storm. 'Where the devil is Goodsir?' people were muttering. 'And why are we sitting in the gloom? We have come to a talk, not to a fairground.'

Goodsir entered a few steps behind his three companions.

'Good evening, gentlemen. I apologise for my tardy arrival, but I wanted everyone to be here before we start our discussion. In our last meeting we discussed not just beauty as a response to ugliness and examples like the stained-glass work of Mr Ballantine or the Manchester paintings of the Pre-Raphaelites, but also my contention that the ugly could be beautiful.'

'If it is in the dark, like this, you mean?' someone called out from the back of the room.

'No, just the contrary. Patience, please, gentlemen.'

Chairs shifted; people were muttering. He was losing his audience. Why had he tried this piece of showmanship? Forbes had suggested it, but he was not Forbes!

Last time we examined the 'ugly and venomous toad,' as Shakespeare called it. The epitome of ugliness which stirs rejection and even dread in people. Now let us look at this creature once more. Mr John Arthur, please.'

At Goodsir's command his assistant pulled back some curtains to reveal a table. The light flooded in to reveal a small pond of water, with the toad sitting on a rock. And next to the creature was a little pile of precious stones, rubies perhaps, with the light glancing off them and the toad and, as Ballantine later recounted, establishing an unconscious link between the two. Some in the audience gasped, there were a few, 'I says,' and 'Och aways' but the display made its impact.

'You may now remove the toad and restore light to the room.'

While this was done, Goodsir took out some notes and then began his talk. He argued that despite Hay's principles and calculations, beauty was not absolute and, he wanted to stress, neither was ugliness. We were all prejudiced by our past experience and the culture we lived in. The discussion gathered pace, with some championing immutable standards of aesthetics, others, like Laycock, defending the influence of our chosen philosophy over our tastes, but overall, the evening was a success.

Goodsir stood up and raised his glass.

'It is customary to accompany our talks with a dram and I would like to close this evening's discussion with a toast, one which I hope will move us to reflect on more than abstract aesthetics and puddocks.'

Such rhetorical flourishes were unusual in Goodsir and the audience fixed their attention on him.

'I referred to the slums and the smoke-filled infernos of our cities in my last talk. We must admit that landscapes were pleasanter in bygone times, our towns more picturesque, and that country people have an attractive ruddiness that the factory worker has lost. Yet, we are the most advanced and prosperous society that the world has ever seen, gentlemen. This is the age of ugliness. This is the age of prosperity and progress. I offer a toast to Ugliness!'

'To Ugliness!' And they all rose to toast, even those like Ballantine, who denied it later. Why did we do it? Laycock asked himself afterwards. Perhaps we need to come to terms with the ugliness around us, and the ugliness in ourselves. He was startled when he realised that appreciation of beauty had never made him feel this way.

'Edward would have been surprised to see how I pulled it off,' Goodsir thought to himself as he headed down the stairs towards the door of the hotel and homewards. As ever, he was careful to turn his eyes away from the hall mirror.

He thought of Piazzi Smith and the one o'clock ball. How would the sailors see it on a foggy day? Really, the man had wasted his intelligence since he had been appointed Astronomer Royal for Scotland about nine years ago. His observatory on Calton Hill had been taken into administration for lack of funds just when he was appointed, and he had had to do his work elsewhere. He was interested in the pyramids and in a recent talk had suggested that their dimensions were based on the God-given 'pyramid inch.' Among other things, this made him a fervent opponent of the metric system, which he saw as a tool of the French radicals. That just showed how a key insight, such as the recognition of the importance of the pyramid, could be led off into political and social byways. He himself had to take care to focus on physiology.

Goodsir felt strengthened by these talks, a respected part of the Edinburgh scientific community. He must get on with his work now, produce the definitive theory of the triangular nature of the body and the cell. He must work harder.

He did work harder, but not on his theory. Sure enough, Jameson's health was in steep decline. If he resigned his post, then the Trustees would have to appoint a substitute. They were reluctant to ask for the resignation of the venerable professor and Hughes Bennett whispered that some wanted delay in order to put forward their own candidate. John Goodsir offered to impart the next term's lectures on behalf of the ailing professor, free of charge! Unsurprisingly, the council and the trustees accepted.

The dying professor's son turned up at Charlotte Street with a bundle of yellow papers.

'My father's lectures,' he said. He seemed distant, a little put out.

Did he expect to inherit the position?

Goodsir thanked him but insisted on preparing his own classes.

'If I read these out, the gap between your eminent father and my poor self will be all too evident,' he said. Both knew that classes written thirty or forty years ago were useless, or worse, as Darwin had complained before abandoning medicine at Edinburgh. The son thanked him and left; the papers tucked below his right shoulder like a fardel of kindling.

Goodsir robbed hours from his dwindling account in the bank of days. If he could present a modern view of Natural History then that would make it easier to present Forbes, one of its leading lights, as the natural successor. He did not ask his friend for help. He was too busy and would only have made a fuss. Goodsir hated fuss.

The lectures also gave him a chance to defend the good name of anatomy against the criticisms of the Free Kirkers. He skirted round zoology and the principles of classification and concentrated on the psychological conditions of man as compared with the brute. Science was a moral enterprise! He consoled himself that this alone justified his decision to compose the lectures afresh. It was a high price to pay: at the end of the course, he was shrunk in features, worn in body, shattered in nerves and, as his sister confirmed to anyone who would listen, 'an almost helpless invalid.'

Jameson passed away in April of 1854. Goodsir regretted his death as he had been good to both Edward and he when they were just beginning their careers. Part of him was thrilled, however, and he had to restrain himself from talking about the future while colleagues were still mourning the past. Luckily, as Lizzie said, he had a face like a wet Sunday and only when completely animated did something approaching joy betray itself.

He began to discreetly look for accommodation for the future professor. Edward told him that he wanted to live close to the sea, both for his family's sake and to facilitate his dredging expeditions. Goodsir spent his Sundays walking around the Granton and Leith streets. He had given up finding somewhere suitable when he came upon a small cottage only two hundred yards from the beach in Wardie, about two miles from the centre of Edinburgh. It was not advertised for sale but was obviously empty. This suited him as Forbes had still not been offered the position. What if the Town Council promoted one of their own?

He heard with alarm that Hugh Miller was being touted as the new Professor. 'He is the most famous natural historian in Scotland' they said. 'And his extensive private fossil collection would complete the one gathered together by Jameson.'

'But he is not even a scientist!' Goodsir exclaimed to his colleagues. Bennett agreed with him but said not to worry in any case. The appointment had to be approved by Lord Aberdeen, the Prime Minister. 'After all the insults the Cromarty man has directed at him over the years the Forth is more likely to dry up than that to occur.'

'If you say so, Bennett. I know nothing of politics so will just have to trust to your experience.'

He did what he could, though, to promote Edward's candidature.

Goodsir insisted on accompanying his sister to Church every Sabbath morning and encouraged her to talk to the worthies in the best pew while he did his best to canvas the minister. The problem was the Free Church held the majority on the University Trustee Board, but what could he do? He kept his eyes and ears open for news of other pretenders. John Arthur was extremely useful in this, chatting to his fellow class of municipal and university servants, all keen to show they knew who the coming man was.

'It's no' a question of faith, sir. Nor of reputation,' John Arthur explained to him as he was washing down that morning's corpse. 'The town councillors hold the sway and they only care about one thing. Sillar!'

'Are you suggesting bribery?'

'No, no, not at all. Just that they will choose the cheapest candidate. I hear the man in charge of the appointment, Baillie Fyfe, offered it to

Professor Trail on condition that he gave half his stipend for the first year to the Jameson family so as to spare the council the compensation money they owe to Jameson's heirs.'

Goodsir's heart stopped.

'Of course, Trail sent them packing, said he had never heard the like.'

On May 3, the appointment of Forbes to Natural History Chair and Regius Keeper of the Museum, as well as his induction, was announced.

Goodsir almost cried with joy, the pent up wishes of so many years releasing themselves. He saw the two of them as youths, walking along the shore, then now, as they would be, reorganising the Museum, publishing, researching together, making that claim for greatness that had eluded him on his own.

Then he received a telegram from Forbes declaring he would have to decline the offer. The council had made the appointment conditional on immediate acceptance and, instead of his duties commencing as normal in the new term in September, on immediate uptake of them that very month. 'That means finishing my lectures in London, handing over to my successor, packing up my goods, arranging for the sale of my house. In short, it is impossible. Could you perhaps give these lectures for me?'

John knew he couldn't. His heart would not withstand more work. His heart was letting down his friend! And in any case, he suspected the council would not have him. He had offended them by denouncing the strict religious orthodoxy tests all professors had to pass. For the first time in his life, he said no to Edward.

There was silence for a few days. John despaired.

On the 15th of May, the largest lecture hall of the University was filled to overflowing. Crowding the benches were youths who had heard of the fame of the great teacher and who had come early to make sure of catching the first accents of his voice; others having long known and studied his works, now hurried to see the man who had instructed and delighted them. Here and there, too, among the crowd was an older head, one that had been young when Forbes himself was a fellow student in the same classroom many years before. At the back of the room, a few feet apart, sat John Goodsir, and Hugh Miller.

A Fearful Symmetry

Elspeth had been frightened at first as Alia led her and Maggie down to the Dean Village. Its towering tanneries and decaying mills were like massive beehives with gaping holes in their walls, revealing families shuffling about, cooking, washing themselves or just staring out onto the weir and at the carts bearing goods up to the city centre. It was part of and apart from the city, down in a valley carved by the Water of Leith on its determined way from the Pentlands to the shore.

The mills had once provided all of Edinburgh with flour, until the arrival of steam-powered competitors. The tanneries still worked, but it was a filthy job, and the famous waters of St Bernard's Wells were now avoided by those in search of a limpid bath and a pure pale complexion. The path down to Stockbridge still had its charm, however, especially for Alia. She liked to walk the sun-dappled track while she listened to the rooks in the towering trees on the steep banks. They were up above, looking down on the New Town, while she breathed in the scents of the last of the wild garlic on the riverbank, in the city but not of it. She felt most at home there, reminded of Inveresk, in the countryside but comfortingly near the anonymous metropolis.

Coal Nell, an old woman in a chestnut brown dress who sold fuel, had called to Maggie. Alia had smiled and told her to go and say hello to the old lady. The dame kept a barrel of water and a cup to offer refreshment to the passing schoolboys. Maggie hesitated but then gave way to the endless flow of compliments from Nell calling her a bonnie wee thing, a princess, even!

Elspeth and Alia stood side by side watching the exchange of pleasure between Maggie and the old woman.

'The four ages of woman!' Alia joked to her. But Elspeth refused to laugh, and Alia reminded herself not to be whimsical with someone she didn't know, someone who also seemed a serious person. They had both sat on the bed with Maggie and played with her, a strange experience for all three. The girl had calmed down now, though whenever one of them left the room for a moment she would become agitated or lose concentration on what she was doing. It was a sunny day and Alia had proposed this walk, 'just the three of us.'

'We will come back here, though, Mistress?

'Of course we will, you silly lassie.'

'And Elspeth too.'

'Elspeth is always welcome, now get your boots on, it's muddy down there.'

When Maggie came back, Alia suggested they walk down to Stockbridge.

'Just beyond the bridge the burn curves and there are swans in the calmer water. And, as luck would have it, I have the rest of the bread that Maggie didn't eat this morning!'

Maggie whooped and skipped off down the path in front of them, looking back from time to time, stopping to pick up sticks to launch into the burn and letting them catch up with her.

'I have just met you, Elspeth, and I don't want to pry or say anything that could maybe fash you.'

'Well, we have just met but I feel as if I have known you a long time, through Enric.'

'Likewise,' Alia answered. Emboldened, she went on,

'Can I ask you why you never paid us a visit before? I made it clear to Enric that you would be welcome.'

Elspeth started to reel off the same excuses she had always given to Enric when refusing his invitations to meet his 'other family': that she was busy, that it was better to keep some part of each of their lives separate, that, 'I did not like you.' There, she had said it.

The air around Alia suddenly got colder like it does in Scotland when a cloud covers the sun. There is no residual heat in the earth, no bank of warmth except on the few bright days in full summer. Alia pulled her shawl around her.

'I did not like you because I did not know you.' Elspeth added, hurriedly.

'Ach, Elspeth, even wee Maggie could do better than that.'

They were approaching the bridge and Maggie was standing looking back, with all the impatience of a child who feels the special day running through her fingers, who craves her next dose of happiness.

'Come on Elspeth, hurry up Alia, the swans will be awa and we will no' see them!'

They both quickened their step.

'Just forget it, forget other people and what they think,' Alia told herself. 'Never bow down, never apologise.' But she was hurt as we all are when someone described to us in the glowing terms Enric had used of Elspeth, rejects us. Old hurts, old slights, from the villagers in Inveresk to the coal miners, from the snobs in Bath and even some clients in Edinburgh when she passed them in the street, came tumbling down around her like horseflies disturbed in the harvest, stinging her, making her want to seek refuge.

Elspeth tapped her on the shoulder and looked at her.

'I have hurt you. I did not mean to. But I never mean to hurt people, yet I do, especially Enric.'

'Just haud your wheesht, I don't need any more grief in my life just now.' Alia picked up her step and went to hold out her hand to Maggie. The two of then walked in front of Elspeth, crossing the river via the bridge and then down and round as it curved towards Dean Bank.

In front of them were three swans, one in the water and two waddling about on the bank. Alia reached into her bag and handed some bread to Maggie and to Elspeth, motioning them to go down to the water and feed the birds.

'I'll bide up here, I'm not so keen on big birds.'

Maggie shook her head as if to say how could anyone not want to feed the birds. Elspeth took her hand and led her down to the river, her words to the girl drowned out by the splashing and flapping of the startled swans' return to the water.

'They are goin' awa. They dinna like me.'

'As Alia said, don't be a silly lassie, Maggie. Show them the bread and they will soon be back.'

Maggie held on tightly to Elspeth's hand as she started to feed the swans, tossing lumps of bread onto the water to flow down to where the birds sat. Elspeth encouraged her, told her not to be feart of the swans, at least while she had bread. 'They are only dangerous when they have weans, they are very protective.'

Alia could not help the bitter thoughts running through her brain. Years looking after Maggie and already forgotten by her and replaced by Elspeth! 'Ach, who is being silly now?' she reproved herself.

As the supplies of bread were running out, a black terrier suddenly jabbed its nose through the bushes behind Alia and sprinted down to the riverbank, barking and heading for the swans, causing the birds to scuttle away then to take off in an ungainly hurry, and spattering Maggie with water. She turned to bury her head in Elspeth's skirt, crying for her to tell the ugly dog to go away. Elspeth shushed her and said to stand still and the wee beast would run off on its own. She then brought her back to Alia and the three of them sat in a circle on some logs locals must have arranged on the bank.

They sat in silence, each deflated for a different reason. Then Maggie stood up and waved her arms, in imitation of the swans.

'Let's all fly away!'

Despite her insistence they would not join in her game.

'You cannot fly away, Maggie.'

Alia and the girl swivelled their heads to look at Elspeth as she said this. 'We are not birds. And I have tried to fly away, but it doesn't work.'

'It was just a game; I was only pretending.'

They both smiled at the strange mixture of childish matter-of-factness and budding adulthood.

'How old are you, now?' Elspeth asked.

'I am just turned fourteen.'

'But she has been kept as a pet by the girls, looked-after and spoiled,' Alia interjected, whether in reproof or in excuse, was unclear.

'You have been happy, Maggie, which is the important thing. Enric often talked to me about you and your own way of saying things.'

'I *was* happy. We all were. But I dinna ken whit for I was tellt that my parents were deid if they werenae. It came as an awfie shock to me. I ken it sounds daft. And I feel like I canna be a wean ony mair, but dinna ken how to act as a grown-up. Mibbie Alia is right, I have been kept in wee girl's claithes, hand-me-doons from Nell's dochters and outfits made for me by the girls. No ony mair, no ony mair.'

We all feel the fall from childhood to maturity at some point in our life, that door clicking shut behind us, that moment when we suddenly understand things, often whispered to us by our bodies. Some fight against it for years. Maggie did not have that luxury.

'You don't need parents, Maggie. I never had a father, and I was taken away from my mother.

Maggie looked up at Alia, her eyes seeming to say, why are you talking to me like this now? Is this what being a grown-up is all about?

'You need to learn to be strong.'

'You need to learn to be weak, but with the right person,' Elspeth suddenly said, stroking Maggie's hair with her long slender fingers.

'I too had no father and I lost my mother, or she lost me, it is the same,' Elspeth added.

Maggie looked from one to the other, wondering which was saying the stranger thing, frightened by the fact of them saying it as much as by what it meant. But also experiencing that short rush of gratification we all feel when people use words to say what they mean and not what they want us to hear.

'How did you no hae faithers?'

'Well, everyone has a father, I suppose, but mine left my mother when I was a bairn,' Alia replied.

'Like my faither?'

'Yes, Maggie, like yours.'

'And your mither couldna take care of you?'

'No, I was taken away from her and sent down to England. That was the worst part, thinking that she didn't want me, worse than if she had died. That's what you were feeling when you found out yesterday that your parents were still alive. But your mother wasn't able to look after you. I am sure she tried her best. And we all love you, Maggie.'

'Aye, but it's no' the same, is it?'

It was Elspeth's turn to speak now.

'My father was there, but he wasn't there. That can be just as bad. He worked as a coachman and spent his days travelling, except when he was home, when he spent them and our pennies on drink.'

'And did your mither run awa?'

'In a way, she did. She wasn't a wife to him nor a mother to me, once that man took advantage of her.'

Alia pointed to the swans come swimming back. It was one thing to open the door to adulthood to Maggie, it was another to push her into the cellar.

'They will be expecting bread, let's go back home and not give them false hope. Come on, Maggie.'

They walked back along the riverside and up the steep brae to the New Town, with Maggie in the middle. They were lost in thought and scarcely acknowledged the calls from Coal Nell to have a wee sup o' water.

They told Maggie to meet them in the kitchen in half an hour. Enric was nowhere to be seen and it seemed Alec, Nell, and their girls were out for a walk too. For the first time Alia and Elspeth were alone together. Alia was heading for the stairs when she felt Elspeth tugging at her sleeve.

'Please, let's have a cup of tea and a talk.'

Alia continued on her way.

'Please, I need to make a decision and I would appreciate your help.'

'Why should you look for help from someone you don't like, someone you had decided against without even meeting them?'

'What you said down at the burn makes me think you will understand my situation. Talk to me, even if only for Maggie's and for Enric's sake. And I will not trouble you further.'

'I will be down in a few minutes. Get the tea ready.'

A few minutes later Alia stepped into the kitchen and found the teapot, cups and saucers daintily laid out on the table. Elspeth had a natural grace in everything she did, evidently. Except in her way of speaking.

'First of all, Alia, I want to apologise. I did not mean to hurt you and, ... please let me go on, it was not you I disliked but what you represented.'

Alia's first reaction was that the insult was only being compounded. She kept silent and poured the tea. There would be time enough to throw the girl out on her ear.

'What I represented?'

'You see, I chose to work as a midwife as I thought it freed me from serving men, made me and the women stronger. I saw how many of the pregnant girls were giving birth in ignorance in the midst of dirt, while their men got drunk, like my father.'

'I don't see what that has got to do with me.'

'Well, I heard about you from the cousin of one of your girls, she told me how you gave work to women, helped them, paid them fairly. How the girls all admired you.'

'And I am to be blamed for that?'

'Then I discovered that it was a front for your other business, for, well, prostitution. I was disappointed in you and upset that Enric either ignored it or was too blind to see what was happening under his nose.'

On another day, Alia would have sent her packing. On another day, she would have taken her down several pegs. She had not been talked to like this since that fateful encounter with Hardie. She would not bow down but she held herself back.

'I suppose you understand the nature of my commerce with men?'

'You are not talking to Maggie, now. Of course I do. You are a beautiful woman, and no doubt men pay a high price for your favours.'

'It is irrelevant if they did, though I can tell you I have never had physical intercourse with a client. Nor have any of my girls! I will only contradict you on one point. The tailoring business was not 'a front' as you put it, and my other activities served to keep it going. How else do you think it lasted so long? Enric was not privy to my private affairs, and they were conducted so discreetly that Maggie was not either. Now if you have insulted me enough, perhaps it is time for you to go. I can take abuse from the likes of the Reverend Hardie, but not from someone like you, someone who could so easily be in my shoes.'

'What do you mean?'

'I mean that it is time for you to go. You may bid goodbye to Maggie first. I will take care of her from now on.'

'No, what did you mean by 'abuse from the likes of Reverend Hardie,' do you know him?'

Elspeth's hand shook as she said this, and a small puddle of milky tea slipped across the table and slowly dripped over the edge. Alia handed her a tea towel.

'I knew him when I was a girl. He determined my fate, as a child, and now at this moment.'

'Mine also.'

At that, the two women fell silent. Such symmetry can inspire intimacy or distrust. Alia was heading for the latter while Elspeth suddenly felt the bond of female suffering growing between them both. That had been the glue that had kept her life together. She had lost it recently and perhaps this more than anything else explained her disaffection from events and from Enric. As they were staring at each other, Maggie came in, swiftly followed by Enric. They stood together at the doorway as if impatient for news. Alia beckoned the girl to come to her.

'Maggie, I cannot talk to you right now. I want you to know, however, that you will stay with me. I cannot have you taken from your folk, abandoned. And I will do my best for you, if you will let me.'

Maggie buried her head in Alia's shoulder. She did not look over at Elspeth.

'Enric, could you take Maggie up to your room for a bit, do some of those magic tricks she loves, then bring her back down here for a bite to eat. I have something to show Elspeth.'

Once they had gone, Alia led Elspeth along the corridor to the almost empty back room. She turned the portrait around.

'That is what my clients paid for. They did not touch me.'

But Elspeth seemed not to care.

'Please tell me all you can about your experience with Hardie, then I will do the same. This is important, Alia. And forgive me for judging you.'

Alia briefly related her life in Inveresk, her brother's misfortune, how she had been taken from her mother to England. She even mentioned her time with Andrew Combe, without naming him, and seeing Hardie again in Edinburgh. She had thought herself free of him, she said, but he had appeared as a client and on recognising her and fearing blackmail, had attacked first. He had ruined the tailor's business and was forcing them out of the house. There was nothing to be done.

'That's what I thought when I left my home. My mother was employed by him to do occasional cleaning at the Manse.'

'So was my mother!'

The symmetry now seemed to unite them both.

'And, well, he took advantage of her. There is nothing unusual in that, as we both know. What was strange was that the more he abused her, and he *did* abuse her, the more devoted she became to him. Perhaps the years of abuse from my father had made it seem the only way she was special, in how much mistreatment she could take. Sometimes I thought she was flaunting his abuse to my father, as if to say, this is what a real man can do! I know that seems perverse.'

'I have some experience of submission, though little understanding, but it may be you were right.'

'I was fifteen when it happened.'

Elspeth paused, unsure whether to go on. Alia took her hand in hers.

'I feel so ashamed. I have never told anyone this.'

'There are things you cannot say until the time comes to say them. Something tells me this is the time, for your sake and I think for Enric's.'

'Enric? Yes, perhaps. I thought I could live in the present and block out the past, but you are right. When people talk about a weight on their shoulders, they say it without thinking what it is really like to have one. It is wearing me down.'

She halted again and Alia was repenting her interruption when Elspeth continued, almost like a jolted horse, her eyes wide, her nostrils flaring.

'I spent as much time as possible at the school and with friends in the village. People were nice to me, but I still had to go home at night, still had to do my best to stop the house turning into a midden. And things started to get worse. My father, my father was drunk and weeping one night. I tried to console him, to tell him things would get better, when he put his hands on me, told me I reminded him of my mother when she was young.'

'And you felt ashamed? It was not your doing.'

'Well, from Eve's day to now women have been made to feel ashamed for men's passions as if there is something about being a female that declares you guilty. But let me go on. I escaped from my father and in the morning he seemed not to remember that anything had happened. But I knew if I stayed it would. It was useless to talk to my mother, though I tried. One day she came back from the Manse with a new shawl. She had a parcel with her, and she told me to open it. I did and it was a red velvet dress which she said was a present from the Reverend Hardie for me. She insisted I try it on, and I am afraid

I did. I was vain, like young girls often are and so wanted to be pretty.'

From the corridor they could hear the kitchen door opening and the voices of Enric and Maggie, like coins spilling down an alleyway. Elspeth seemed to be searching for words. Alia gave them to her.

'And your mother took you to the Manse in your pretty dress to say thank you to the Minister.'

'How do you know?'

'I was your age when I was taken into the Hardie household.'

Now Alia was the one lost for words as images of Inveresk, of her mother, of that man and his wife danced through her brain. Elspeth squeezed her hand and the two of them caught sight of themselves in the wall mirror, looking like copies of each other, their knees together, their simple dresses flowing and their hair loose and over their shoulders. Elspeth went on,

'I was worried, suspicious even, but my mother told me how beautiful I looked. She never said that normally, she was always criticising me if I tried to make myself look pretty. Anyway, I went with her to the Manse. She took me into the living room. She told me to be nice, she, she left to fetch something, she said, and then a door opened, and he came in. I was terrified.'

Elspeth was speaking in a whisper now and not looking at Alia, almost as if reading from a text in her head, one she must have recited to herself many times.

'He complimented me. He asked me to stand up and let him admire me, to walk up and down. I did, hoping my mother would come back in. And then, and then he did the strangest thing. He asked me to lie down on the couch. He told me he would just say things to me, all pleasant things, he promised. I had only to look at him. And, and oh, this was the strangest thing, I had to not say a word, rather I had to mouth my replies, but as if I was mute! As if I had lost the power to speak!'

'Oh, the evil swine!' Alia could not help herself. Elspeth looked over, as if awakened. But she bowed her head and forced herself to go on.

'He told me I was prettier than the finest ladies in the Duke's household. He insisted I mouth, 'Thank you, sir.' He complimented my figure, my hair, my legs and then my feminine parts. And I thought I would scream and run out of there when I saw him touching himself. I opened my mouth wide and no sound came out. I was struck dumb! He seemed to notice that, and he became, well, more agitated. I don't know how, but I forced myself to get up and run to the door. It was locked so I turned round and took the door he had entered by. I could hear him gasping as I left. I wandered up and down staircases and finally found my way to the back door. I ran home. I changed clothes, threw the dress on the fire, and left. I vowed never to return, and I haven't. I swore never to think of that man, or pronounce his name and I haven't, until today. I don't know why I mouthed the words; I don't know why I even sat on the couch.'

Alia stood and raised Elspeth to her feet. She put her hands on her shoulders and then caressed her cheek, Elspeth leaning into her hand like a cat in want of affection.

'I found out my father died two years ago. I felt sad that I had abandoned him, though I realise that is just another sign of my oppression, of his abuse.'

Alia stroked Elspeth's hair.

'Never bow down, never apologise. A man taught me that. A good man. For there are good men. Good men like the one you have, Enric.'

Letter 17

Little William

What would be his legacy? What, apart from his works as tribute to his Redeemer, would he hand on? Journalism was ephemera, and he felt increasingly that his geological explanations were but arguments with a sceptical public or, as the very nature of science suggested, an invitation to future refutation in the name of progress.

There were his children, but they were more the legacy of Lydia; she took charge of their education and the moulding of their characters. Ach, he was becoming bitter, disillusioned sometimes. And what was in a famous name?

Celebrity had finally come to Hugh Miller as a journalist and a nature writer. He had enjoyed the recognition but could not help but grimace when he thought of the years of fruitless toil to make his name known, first as a poet and then as a compiler of local traditions and stories. Scottish poetry was in the doldrums and either there had been a glut of local tales or folk preferred the Borders and the Highlands to Cromarty!

When Lydia took to novel writing, she eschewed the disapprobation bestowed by her peers on fiction by publishing her novel, Passages in the Life of an English Heiress, or, Recollections of Disruption Times in Scotland, anonymously. She might as well not have bothered, as the book attracted little attention. And when she did meet with some renown in her stories for children, it was under a pseudonym, Harriet Myrtle! For all her insistence on the propriety of genteel anonymity, Hugh suspected she wished to flee from association with the Miller name and all the controversy surrounding it. There he was, bitter again.

Another Miller, William, was enjoying greater fortune with lasting literary fame. He had dreamed of becoming a surgeon; however, ill-health and poverty had shattered that ambition.

Instead, he became a wood-turner and cabinetmaker in his native Dennistoun, Glasgow. He turned to poetry, like so many educated artisans, and like so many of his fellow Scots, focussed on children's verse. His poems appeared in magazines and newspapers and attracted greatest attention in the popular collections of Scots poetry and song, Whistle-binkie. As his dedication in the book Scottish Nursery Songs shows, he trusted in his own literary immortality, 'To Scottish mothers, gentle and simple, these nursery songs are respectfully dedicated, not fearing that, while in such keeping, they will ever be forgot.'

Hugh's son William had been born around the same time as the most beloved of the Nursery Songs, appeared. Perhaps this explained the boy's lasting delight in the ditty and his identification with his namesake. No, no, not with the Miller name, nor with the writings of his father or even his mother, but with Wee Willie Winkie!

Wee Willie Winkie rins through the toon,
Up stairs an' doon stairs in his nicht-gown,
Tirlin' at the window, crying at the lock,
'Are the weans in their bed, for it's now ten o'clock?'

Hugh complained that the poem only mentioned one parent, the mother, at the end. Was there nothing safe from his bitterness? It was no longer his concern, either, that Scottish poetry seemed increasingly confined to the province of the nursery. In any case, no doubt the work of Aytoun, Gilfillan and Alexander Smith would hold the sway and claim lasting renown for adult verse.

"Hugh Miller"

The Year Edinburgh Lost Its Reason

Just as the spirits had instructed her, she divested herself of her clothing, offering each garment to them. She caught sight of her naked body in the mirror and shuddered, then told herself that for a woman of sixty-four, she had nothing to be ashamed of. Her belly was still smooth, and her breasts only sagged a little. The blue veins on her legs were what caused her most distress, but they, like all the rest of her, her wispy hair, her wrinkled shoulders, would soon be invisible. How she would laugh at them all! They who had mocked her, buying her book to scoff. But their scoffing had bought her this fine house in Northumberland Street, so justice had been served.

She had been disappointed in De Quincey, who had called her mad. The fellow was jealous, obviously. It had been over forty years since his *Opium Eater* had gained him notoriety and it was he, in fact, who was a pathetic creature, hanging on the heels of his betters, hoping for scraps. She had also been stung by the remarks reported to her from that odd Danish fellow, Christian Andersen. He had come upon her and her friend Tess as they were inhaling ether at a rather lovely Edinburgh party. It was quite the thing, nowadays, but perhaps not in herring-soused Copenhagen. He had called them two mad creatures and said they smiled with open dead eyes. Well, the truth was, they could hardly see him. In any case, she and Tess were writers on the occult and more interested in the attention of the spirits. However, the spirits had not visited them that night, despite her wearing the amulet and when she got home, performing the rituals. They were fickle, the spirits were, and only responded if you served them appropriately. And you never knew when you had offended them, till your cat died, or the milk in the coldbox went sour. She had told people to pay them more respect, like they did in Germany. The problem with Edinburgh was its reverence for hard science, for machines that made steam and noise, for the things of everyday experience. The interest in the other world was reserved for the peasants, especially for the Highlanders. How blind a university education can make men! People laughed when she said that but she won her point, oh yes she did, when she produced her trump card: Hugh Miller! One of the most learned men in Scotland, one who revered science, but who had never been to university. And he believed in ghosts and spirits. People who knew him had told her so, though on the only occasion she had met him he had evaded the subject, talking of his large head and phrenology but telling her he was really the wrong man to ask about such things. What was he hiding from her?

No matter, no matter. Concentrate Catherine, concentrate. It was time to go out before the spell lost its powers. What was it the spirit had said? 'Beautiful one' he had called her. No, Catherine, concentrate. Ah yes, the visiting card in her right hand and the handkerchief in her left. The spirit had said it could be a silk or cotton handkerchief. But no black on it, not even in the embroidery. The only one she had been able to find had been a present from bad old Major John, her fool of an ex-husband. In Bristol people had told her leaving him would mean she would never again be received in polite society. It was true she had had to move up to Edinburgh but here she was, living in the smartest street. Though some of her neighbours avoided her salutes. Perhaps she would drop in on them tonight under the protection of invisibility. Oh, how they would be startled when the door opened of its own accord, the candle floated from the table to the hearth and they felt a tickle on the back of their necks!

She was a silly girl! The spirits surely had not offered her this privilege to play party games, even though it must be said they did a lot of that themselves at séances. She would stay in the street this first time, get her bearings: as an invisible creature you could not expect a horseman to veer out of your way, or a child not to throw a ball that might come straight at you. No, being invisible, like being visible, evidently required practice. People did not think of that, well she hadn't either, to be frank. Perhaps it explained why ghosts were always bumping into things or knocking things over. She was learning so much already. Should she look in the mirror again before going out? No, that would be to disrespect the powers.

She had been pleased and disappointed to find the street empty. It was late on a dark February night, but normally people would be coming back from dinner parties or a concert at this hour. Perhaps the spirits meant her to walk right out in the middle of the road and they were keeping it clear for her. The spirits were so kind. When her son was cruel to her, they had comforted her, told her that men were such blockheads, only women were granted true visions.

Brrr. It was cold! She hadn't thought about that either, just taken for granted that the suspension of her visibility would also cancel other bodily sensations. But no, her ankles felt the night breeze lick round them. As she walked along the street, she felt the cobbles pressing coldly into her soles. She looked to her right and saw a pair of red velvet curtains being pulled shut. She thought she recognised the Chambers' housemaid. The girl obviously couldn't see her. She raised her arm and waved, just in case there was someone at the adjacent window. Waving! There she was again, acting like a visible person!

She reached the end of the street without encountering anyone. Well, anyone except for the tabby cat outside number 14. By the way it looked at her she could tell it was not just a cat. Should she sit down beside it and enter into conversation? No, she could do that at home. She waved the visiting card at it, so it would see her address. It ran off. Must be a male cat.

Perhaps the dearth of humans meant she was meant to meet spirits tonight. Well, that made sense. She could encounter humans while respectably dressed. Who might they be? She hoped there would be no dead children. Though it would be good to make their acquaintance and be able to contact their parents and comfort them. She tried to give comfort in the children's books she wrote, even if Mr Dickens had suggested she had done so for an easy market. Him, of all people, to criticise someone for writing what was popular! Perhaps if she told him about her gift, he would write a story about her. He was a good writer, even if she firmly believed, as she had told Tess, that he had copied much from her *Susan Hopley* novel. Who else had written a crime novel before her? There she went again. Concentrate, Catherine, concentrate. She almost cried then, remembering how her mother used to scold her as a child with that phrase. Oh, it all enters, all stays there. She must ask the spirits if they still took the hurt around with them or did it slip off them like her clothes?

She could hear voices from the other end of the street, and someone had come out of number 17. They didn't look like spirits. Oh well, she would just have to make do with her neighbours. Make do! They were the cream of Edinburgh society, even if sour cream, for her. She walked steadfastly towards them, opening her legs, letting the breeze caress her sex. Oh, it was exhilarating to be invisible! She should have acquired this knowledge before. Before she was old, before she was alone. Who could she share it with now?

At first she had refused to believe they could see her. She had attempted to ignore them and walk past them, but Mr. Chambers' housemaid had thrown a coat around her and his coachman, his coachman! had carried her up into her own house surrounded by the others, more concerned to keep her out of view of any passers-by than worried about her dignity. How had they got into her house? How had they been able to see her?

She had thought about that for days, at home and now in this refuge. Some refuge! She had finally understood that the door had been ajar and offered no resistance to them. And she remembered she had opened it with one hand while holding the card and the handkerchief in the other. When she slipped out onto the porch, she had changed the card into her left hand and the pocket handkerchief into the right! That was why the spell had not worked! There was a logical explanation for everything. Not for them, though; they would not listen to reason and had shut her up here before shipping her off to London.

They left her on her own most of the day and tried to make her eat. Spirits do not need food, she said. She could not eat or that would make them feel they were right.

And they had bound her after she tried to stop them feeding the fire. Use wood, she had begged. I cannot have coal; I cannot have anything black in my presence! I will tell Mr Chambers to have them stop, to do his best to silence the wicked gossip in the press. He will do it. He is a reasonable fellow and not uninterested in the night side.

Chambers had replied to the first three letters from Mrs Crowe until he realised his soothing words only served to confirm her delusions. So he suggested she take the waters at Malvern and excused himself from further correspondence, citing an impending visit to the United States.

'Better say Brazil,' his wife had said. 'The United States is not as far off as it once was. She can probably fly there on her broomstick.'

He had laughed but then used his disapproval frown on his wife. As usual, to no effect. Anne had given him fourteen children, three of whom had passed, and though they both had gone through difficult moments, she was his rock. No, there was nothing rocklike about her, his staff, perhaps, or his refuge? The one who knew all his secrets, who rarely judged him. She had the quick wit of the Glaswegians and, in private, would give her no-nonsense view of those around him. She had liked Enric and told him he was foolish to give in to the pressure from his brother. She had always considered Catherine Crowe to be, as she put it, 'away with the fairies, but no' the ones she wants to be away with!'

They had been talking about his latest secret work, the still untitled book attacking belief in an otherworld, a sort of Chambers *Traditions of Edinburgh* but this time with tales and unmaskings of the spiritualists, the table-rappers, the voodoo merchants, and their like. He had been amazed at how numerous they were. Scratch the surface of even genteel society and you would find a woman convinced she was sterile because of a charwoman's curse, a man who crossed the road to avoid a red-haired person with a limp, people who assured you they did not believe in ghosts only to tell you about their encounter with one! Some of those who had embraced the message of *Vestiges* would still turn to blind belief in fairies to explain events. Even in good old rational Edinburgh wiser men than he betrayed their education by penning off an area of knowledge or investigation for the supernatural. He had some choice anecdotes for them in the book. Several important people would be revealed for the credulous fools they were. Which was why, he insisted to Anne, the book had to be published anonymously. She had accepted but announced copying it all out was beyond her now, she wasn't the lively young thing he had married, and her eyes were failing her. Well, he would deal with that when he finished it. He only had one more case to investigate. And it was a corker, he told Anne.

He had just come upon that expression and found himself repeating it at every opportunity. One had to learn novel words, keep your style modern. Miller needed to learn that, he thought. Why had he thought of him now? He had of course not had news of him from Enric though he knew Miller was working away at his latest onslaught on *Vestiges*. It tickled him that he was using material harvested for him by Enric to knock down the development theory. Well, let him try! The man had a knack for choosing combatants he could not defeat because they were backed by more powerful forces than he, or because they were expressions of a public that was either above him in class and means or whom he disdained for their poverty. Why was he being so harsh? At least Miller was a sounder man than that blowhard, Wilson, who had died just recently. Yet Chambers had volunteered to chair the memorial committee to the professor and to steer the erection of a statue to him in Princes Street. You had to play the game. Why was he so harsh on Miller? They were both from poor provincial backgrounds, both self-made scholars and men of business. However, they were headed in different directions. History would judge, he supposed. He trusted it would keep its light on his own strivings in favour of modernity and leave the doomsayers like Miller and Carlyle behind.

He was plucked out of these reveries by the maid's announcement that a gentleman had come calling. His card was elegantly embossed with what looked the arms of the Earl of Home, and had a strange, soft velvety feel. Chambers was sure he felt a sharp electric shock when he took it in his hand. It dropped to the floor and when the maid retrieved it for him, he felt no such charge.

'Mr David Dunglas Home.'

'The gentleman said he was recommended to you by Mr. Lyon Playfair. He says he would be honoured to make your acquaintance and is in Edinburgh for a few days. He said...'

'That will be sufficient, Agnes. He has obviously made an impression on you. He must be a dashing fellow. Ach, don't blush, lassie, I am only teasing. You may show him into the drawing room.'

When Chambers stepped into the room he found his guest seated at the piano! He was just starting to play an air, *Ca' the yowes tae the knowes*, the tune that had been performed at Robert's wedding reception. Was this coincidence? The pianist was a handsome young man, in his mid-twenties perhaps, smartly dressed in a dark suit but wearing a rather racy cravat and with a prominent moustache. He smiled over at his host and played on until the end.

Once the recital was over, he stood up and bowed to Chambers. 'Your favourite tune, I believe, and that of Mrs. Chambers.'

The man had a strange accent, lowland Scots tinged with an American twang and even a hint of London. Perhaps this was what distracted Chambers and made him overlook the sheer cheek of the fellow, coming into his house and playing his piano. Anne would have had him sent away for that!

'Thank you for receiving me, Mr. Chambers. I do hope you may forgive my forwardness in presenting myself directly here, but you were unable it seems to come to my séance in Eyre Place. I trust your Catalan employee was sufficiently impressed, even though it was a rather low grouping. I have been fortunate enough to have been sought out by people of the highest class and even Royalty from all across Europe. The recently enthroned Empress Eugénie has requested my attendance for a consultation this summer in Paris.'

As he said this, the young man walked about the room, taking possession of it. He picked up an apple from the fruit basket and bit from it, the sound seeming to reverberate against the windowpanes.

'You have some doubts. Your book, *The History of Superstition*, aims to bury spiritualism with the same sweep as your *Vestiges* undermined Genesis.'

Chambers sank down onto the red damask sofa. He was not at all taken aback by the allusion to his authorship of *Vestiges*, but he had only decided on a name for his new book a few days ago. How on earth did this fellow know it? It was uncanny.

He scanned the room. No, there were no papers here, the visitor could not have come upon anything in his brief time in the house. 'Possess yourself,' he whispered.

'I will not mention the names of your lost bairns. Out of respect. But they need you to talk to them.'

'How dare you, sir! If this is some trickery such as the magic hands or table-rapping, I beg you to desist and not to besmirch the names of my beloved departed in a conjuring trick.'

The man only smiled in a way that seemed to say, 'I know you; I will not be put off by bluster, we can understand each other.' And then the miracle happened. One that Chambers would witness in later seances in London with this man, and in more pronounced form. However, he saw it, there in his own room, in his own house: Dunglas Home levitated! Only about a foot above the carpet, but he rose up. It lasted only a few seconds, but those seconds changed Chambers forever.

'What does this mean? What are you trying to demonstrate?' He thought of the Apostles when Jesus stepped from the boat onto the waters. But this man was no new Christ. To keep a hold on reality, he rang the bell and called for tea; he needed to take stock, to get back to himself. When Agnes came in, he marvelled that it was only ten minutes or so ago that he had dismissed her. She seemed different, she seemed to be looking at him oddly. He ordered the tea and turned around to find Dunglas sitting at a table and beckoning him to join him. The fellow had taken possession of his house! He had taken possession of him, he almost felt.

'Robert, I may call you Robert, may I not? Thank you. I came to see you today, or rather I was sent to visit you. By whom? I don't know, but I have always followed the calls of the spirit, from my native Lothians to Massachusetts, then to London and who knows where next. Today they sent me here. They said, this well-meaning man is about to commit an act of folly from which he would never recover. And no, Robert, I am not come in the name of religion to admonish you, but in friendship and concern from one spiritual traveller to another. For that is what you are, Robert, a cosmic traveller. You proved it with *Vestiges*. No ordinary man could have written it. It is the most important book of this century.

And your use of scientific experiment is keenly done. But Robert, does your wife love you? Of course she does. How do you know? By her acts and declarations. It is not a scientific knowledge, but it is true. Many years ago, those who testified to the existence of meteoric showers were laughed at. Now we know they were in the right, because of repeated reporting of the phenomena. We know that human beings can observe and report facts with reasonable accuracy: when large numbers agree in a report, we accept its substance as established. You proceed in this manner in your business and in your civic life. Yet when testimony of spiritualism is offered by people of sound mind and solid education in country after country, you dismiss it because it cannot be verified experimentally. This is unreasonable behaviour, and it deprives science of knowledge concerning types of phenomena to which the experimental method cannot be applied. Such testimony should be accepted as a valid and necessary instrument of investigation. That is what the spirits wanted me to communicate to you. You saw my levitation a few minutes ago. I don't understand it myself, but I know it happened. As you do. I ask you for the sake of your future reputation, for the sake of your lost souls, to consider this and to abort that work. I am in Edinburgh for a few more days and will be happy to invite you to my meetings in London whenever you are in the Capital. Consider me your spiritual friend. However, I ask you to keep today's encounter a secret between you and me. This is the only time I have ministered to an individual and should others hear of it I would be pestered beyond extenuation.'

And with that, the young man stood up, picked up his hat and held out his hand to Chambers. When Robert shook it he felt the same electric shock, though amplified, that he had experienced upon touching the business card. He watched the door close upon his visitor, lost for words, unable to react. When Agnes came in she called for her mistress and they both insisted on him taking to his bed.

'He has got a peely-wally face on him, Mistress Anne. It's like as if he's seen a ghost!'

That night, as the clock struck three, Robert slipped out of bed, put on his dressing gown and slippers and descended to his study. He retrieved the manuscript of *The History of Superstition* from the bureau and took it over to the main fireplace in the drawing room. He watched as the yellow flames licked round the pages, probing the words for the sweetest morsels, and bowed his head in memory of his departed children. He thought of all the experiences he had gone through, of the tussles of his life, of his path to this moment and realised that the natural order of things was in fact just that, an order ordained by nature. He thought he could catch glimpses of the spirits in the yellow flames. From now on he would serve Immortality and the Hereafter. He closed his eyes and felt himself levitating.

Sic Itur Ad Astra

'Do stones just roll down hills of their own accord? Did the boulder you find one day at the foot of Salisbury Crags just decide to explore the Queen's Park?'

Harriet looked up at her father. Here he was, putting her to the test once more. Here she was, not wanting to fail him again. Her mother just sighed when he asked such questions, as if to say, 'don't ask me things you already know the answer to.' Her brothers were too young or too stupid to respond to such questions without expecting a prize, an apple perhaps, or the best one, the tap on the head that told them they could be off without further quizzing.

It was especially hard to answer as she was trying to keep pace with him as he strode up through the Queen's Park towards the Canongate on his way to the office, holding onto her bonnet for dear life and hoping no one saw her tripping along like a puppy after her master. He had taken her with him after her mother had complained about always having the children round her.

'Isn't it gravity that makes them fall?'

'It is gravity that means they fall rather than rise. But not all the rocks fall, otherwise we would be walking through rubble. Those that do, tumble down because of their geological make-up, they have been designed at some point in the past to behave like this in the future. The wind that shook them comes from a pattern of currents that depends on the sea and the coast. He who created the world, created these conditions. He is the power behind whatever happens.'

Harriet bit her lip. This seemed obvious, so why the questions?

And why was he asking her?

'There are some people, Harriet, who believe that things just happen, that we cannot know the causes, or at least the reason for the causes, but must just observe patterns, tendencies. They remove the Creator from his creation and replace him by laws. They replace Providence by accident. And they call that science!'

'If someone does not love you, does that mean the Creator has decided it must be so?' She thought of Thomas Balfour at the kirk. He ignored all her proposals to share the Bible or to help distribute the prayer books. But her father was off in front of her, his head literally in the clouds scudding down from the hill.

She looked at his hunched figure and caught the sight of passers-by nudging each other as if to say, 'there goes the famous Hugh Miller.' She was proud of him, but, like her mother, increasingly concerned at his fits of bad health and his black moods. He had been borne up into high spirits at the hope of acceding to the chair of Natural History, his mother had told her. They had argued at tea the other night when Lydia had criticised the new Professor, Forbes. Her father exploded,

'He is a good man, an industrious worker and a brilliant teacher. That he has powerful friends and is loved by all is not his fault. The fault is mine for not knowing how to courie up to the right folk.'

Her mother's face had blanched. Later she called Harriet through to her study and pleaded that her father had not meant to be so brusque.

'He feels shut out from the religious community and now from the academic and scientific one. The few Edinburgh intellectuals that received him, like Mr Chambers, have dropped him. He is lonely, Harriet. He who courted his own company up in the Highlands feels bereft of friends in the city. We must be sweet to him. Strong men like your father can break more easily than softer spirits, like a tall tree in the storm does while the sapling bends.'

Harriet had noted that last phrase down in a yellow-bound jotter in which she collected sayings and poetic quotations. She would need them when she became a writer, she thought. A writer, like her mother, but for adults. Then she had felt guilty at turning grief into poetry. But was that not what her mother was doing? And if her mother saw that her father needed help why did she leave him on his own so often? Why did they no longer share a bedroom? Being fifteen was proving more difficult than she had expected. She was still treated as a child when it suited her parents then asked for the understanding of an adult when one of them behaved badly or said something spiteful.

As her father was getting ready to go up to the office, her mother had pulled her aside and whispered to her to go with him. 'He won't let me, and I don't want him to be alone. Mr McCosh has upset him and he needs a calming influence.'

'Ugh, Mr. Soor Ploom McCosh! Harriet knew she shouldn't laugh with her brothers and sister as they all sucked on the sweeties the old gentleman would hand out whenever he visited. They were green balls, with bits of hair from his pocket and scraps of the paper bag sticking to them which he doled out in an evident bid to keep them quiet while he talked with their parents. They would run up to William's bedroom and sit in a circle on the floor, their mouths half open as they sucked and competed to see who could reduce the ball to a speck without chewing. Young Hugh always cheated, and Bessie just took her own good time, as with everything. Harriet liked to win then felt stupid, playing such games at her age!

And so here she was, traipsing up through the Canongate, wondering what she would do at the office. If Mr Fairly was there, he and her father would discuss practical matters concerning printing the next number. That would be boring. If he was not, then her father would check his mail, write some replies, put the finishing touches to his main article. In both cases she would be invisible, sitting with her nose pressed against the window, watching the passers-by and the folk coming out of St Giles and down the High Street. They were dressed in gayer clothes than she and her mother wore. Sometimes Harriet wished the Free Kirk was a little freer in its dress code!

Hugh looked round then stopped to let Harriet catch up to him.

Poor girl, she would be bored waiting around the office. He also felt guilty for talking to her about science and philosophy. But who could he talk to? Lydia was becoming irascible, and this morning's talk with McCosh had been a disaster. Hugh had shown him the article he was composing on Comte and discussed the dangers of these positivist thinkers. Enric had given him pieces by Comte, underscored from previous readings in someone else's hand. Enric had insisted that you could disagree with the French sociologist, but you could not ignore him. Hugh had been taken aback by McCosh's acceptance of such writings as part of scientific progress. 'No doubt, they need correction, but that will come. And his division of the three distinct stages of civilisation is interesting, don't you think? He also musters a huge amount of data to support his argument. The days of relying on samples from your backyard are gone now, Hugh. Science is scouring the globe to find evidence to support its theories.'

Perhaps it was that last remark that had stung hardest. Forbes had dredged the Mediterranean and clambered up Alpine slopes for specimens. Hugh had got as far as Devon. But hadn't Forbes declared in his inaugural lecture that Edinburgh with its hills, valleys and coastlines supplied all a man could need for the study of nature?

How could it have come to this? How could he be reduced to explaining his ideas to a fifteen-year-old girl, to sporadic conversations with McCosh and Guthrie, and worst of all, to the readers of *The Witness*? He had few illusions about the intellectual worth of journalism. You only had to look at journalists to see what superficiality looked like when it was wearing trousers! He talked to that strange Spanish intellectual vagabond, Enric, of course, but more like Christ conversing with the Pharisees than in comradeship. Enric's materialism was only redeemed by his idealism, but idealism for what? And the man was indeed an enthusiast of Comte and the French. He even read French novels! Hugh had determined to make the most of his diverse knowledge despite the differences between them, but to be on his guard against the temptation to see intellectual speculation as a good in itself. Speculation! The word itself was tinged with ambiguity and the stink of the marketplace. He thought of the scribbled comments on the notes on Comte Enric had given him for his article and felt a soft voice whispering to him in his head. 'Shush,' he told himself. 'Shush.'

Harriet's face was flushed from the effort of catching up with her father. He stopped and pointed out Moray House and told her about the old Duke of Argyll and his exultation at the execution of his rival, Montrose, and how he and his men had stood on the balcony and spat at the captive being led to the executioner. 'Such cruelty in Christians is difficult to comprehend, daughter.'

They both paused, imagining the hot exchange of insults, the bloodied Montrose on the gallows carriage. Hugh decided to bring the conversation back to the present.

'The Canongate has squares behind many of these houses, while the High Street up the road has closes. There is a proposal to incorporate the Burgh into Edinburgh. It makes sense, I suppose, but what will happen to its squares and its Tolbooth if it is absorbed? They may all be swept away in the name of progress, or to build yet more breweries!'

She did not laugh. These were old men's jokes. She was staring past him up to the Tolbooth building featuring the Canongate's motto, *Sic itur ad astra*. She read it aloud and looked at him quizzically. Was she deliberately asking him a question about a language he had refused to learn?

'Well, my dear, you know I have no Latin. It is a language mainly used to exclude the workingman from education and as mumble-jumble by the Papists. I do know this phrase, as nothing resists real curiosity. It means '*Thus shall you go to the stars*.' It is from Virgil, Harriet. The heathens only had the stars to go to. We have heaven.'

He was aware he had given her a riposte instead of just an answer, but a fifteen-year-old could be a trying creature!

Harriet remained silent, merely staring up at the letters and mouthing the phrase. Inwardly she saw herself looking out from her bedroom window at night at the shooting stars above the smooth dark estuary, its waters like silk cloth stretched out to the horizon. She dreamed of going to the stars. Did that make her a heathen? She shrugged her shoulders. She was tired of sermons.

They continued on their way in silence. Mr Fairly greeted them when they stepped into the office but said he was on his way out to a meeting in the town council. 'The edition is ready, Hugh, except for your column. I presume you have it with you.'

When they were left alone Hugh explained that he had some changes to make to the article but that should not take more than an hour. No doubt Harriet had brought a book with her. He was so used to taking a volume with him wherever he went that he took it for granted for everyone. She replied that she would write to Granny Fraser in Inverness. It was her birthday next month.

Hugh nodded, and sat down to work, leaving Harriet to seek out pen and paper. Practised in the art of not disturbing her father when he was composing, she looked in drawers and stood on her toes to peer into tall shelves as quietly as she could, but to no avail except to annoy him. There are few things more irritating than distraction caused by a well-meaning person, as your unease is compounded at the sense of unfairness of chiding their movements. Hugh tried to concentrate but finally stood up, walked over to a bureau and extracted pen, ink and paper. 'You may stand at the window over there. I find it easier to write sometimes that way.'

Harriet held the pen, but no words came. She saw images of falling stars, smiling friends, her refuge in the garden when she needed to be alone, her mother altering a dress for her, her granny in her house in Inverness. She could see, but not think. And you can't write images down, unless you could draw, like her father. She felt him standing behind her and she shivered. Please don't let him scold her.

'I can't write either, dear. It happens to us all. Let's look out the window at the people passing by. Tell me what you see.'

She hesitated then pointed to a group of two women and a child carrying some flowers. Hugh asked her where she thought they were going. Perhaps to the hospital, she answered. Or to visit a soldier in the Castle. Or to Greyfriars graveyard. And where were they from? I don't think they are city folk, she replied. Perhaps from East Lothian. Their shoes are too polished to be from the city. And what are their names? She invented names for each of them. Then they repeated the game with others in the street. She loved her father when he was like this but drew in her breath when she realised how long it had been since he had played such games with her. Perhaps that was what to expect as you grew up, but he did not seem to play with her brothers and sisters as much either.

'We can use words to describe things we already know, or which the people we are talking to already understand. Images are for the totally new or not yet understood things.' He was looking beyond her, into the street, when he said this. 'There are two types of Revelation, the spoken, and the visual. That is why Genesis describes the original creation in images, like a diorama, unfolding in seven stages. God must have revealed it in images, in visions to the authors of the Bible. That is what I will have to do in my book, paint a picture of the different geological phases of creation, not tell people things or attempt to argue with them, but make them see. Give up my old rational style and become a prophet, like Milton.' He smiled ruefully and squeezed her shoulder. 'Your father is too good at arguing and not good enough at seeing, isn't he?'

She shook her head, but realised he was not really speaking to her. Something had gotten hold of him; he was composing, he was working out ideas that had lain buried inside him she realised when she told her mother about it later. There was a new force about him, a new energy. She did not understand then that it was the last fire in an erupting volcano. And what if she had? And what if she had?

But oh, how he burned that day. 'And we classify things, normally in threes. That is why I disagree with people like Comte, who use that same triple structure, but don't realise it is a God-given capacity. We are created in His image, above all in how we think. God prepared the ground in earlier phases of creation. The beauty of the seashells you collect on the beach, Harriet. They were created beautiful before Man was there to admire them but in harmony with the tastes of the Creator. What does that mean, Harriet?'

She felt herself lifted by his enthusiasm. 'That we have the same appreciation as our Creator.'

'Yes, exactly. We value harmony like He does. We are made in His image and likeness. And we construct like Him, we improve what we find. As a geometrician, as an arithmetician, as a chemist, as an astronomer, — in short, in all the departments of what are known as the strict sciences, — man differs from his Maker, not in kind, but in degree, — not as matter differs from mind, or darkness from light, but simply as a mere portion of space or time differs from *all* space or *all* time.'

She found these very words in the book that killed him, when her mother published it after his death. But then it had seemed like a private revelation, one that linked her admiration of the stars to her God. She felt thrilled.

'God is a stonemason, just like you, father!' They both laughed with giddiness at the thought. She could tell he was pleased by her happy, quick response.

'Well, he was a much better one than me, my dear.'

The flames had abated, there was a moment of quiet while he seemed to reflect on what he had said, before bursting out again with renewed energy.

'Of course, Genesis is also about the future, not just an explanation of the past. Man had to be made in the form he was so that God could appear as the second Adam in the form of Jesus Christ. And after Man in the image of God in Genesis, to God in the image of Man in the New Testament, we are heading for God and Man intertwined at the day of Judgement. It is all preordained. I believed this before but until now I found it hard to reconcile suffering and injustice with predestination.'

She had lost him again, but she felt the magic of the spell he was casting. He was ablaze, he was the shooting star right now. He paced up and down the office, running his hands through his mane of hair.

'And it is Geology that reveals all this to us in pictures, Harriet. This is the testimony of the rocks.' Three years later she would find in the book of that title, almost word for word, his declamation to her that day,

'*As certainly as the dynasty of the fish was predetermined in the scheme of Providence to be succeeded by the higher dynasty of the reptile, and that of the reptile by the still higher dynasty of the mammal, so it was equally predetermined that the dynasty of responsible, fallible man should be succeeded by the dynasty of glorified, immortal man ; and that, in consequence, the present mixed state of things is not a mere result, as some theologians believe, of a certain human act which was perpetrated about six thousand years ago, but was, virtually at least, the effect of a God-determined decree, old as eternity, — a decree in which that act was written as a portion of the general programme. In looking abroad on that great history of life, of which the latter portions are recorded in the pages of revelation, and the earlier in the rocks, I feel my grasp of a doctrine first taught me by our Calvinistic Catechism at my mother's knee, tightening instead of relaxing. 'The decrees of God are his eternal purposes,' I was told, 'according to the counsel of his will, whereby for his own glory he hath foreordained whatsoever comes to pass.' And what I was told early I still believe. The programme of Creation and Providence, in all its successive periods, is of God, not of man.*'

Last glorious memories of a loved one are often not really the last, but the image we choose to keep. Harriet would carry the picture of her father composing with her as solace for the betrayal to her of his suicide. Someone so inspired was not for this life, she told herself and others.

She also tried to extract comfort from the 'cosmic Calvinism,' as she thought of it. All our sorrows are subsumed in the grand march towards our union with Jesus Christ at the end of time. Some days, that worked, more often she just despaired.

She also shut out of her mind the picture of her father sitting slumped in the office chair, his head between his hands. He was exhausted, consumed by his efforts. She had stood there, aghast, wondering what her mother would have done. She had been saved when the door opened and a tall, handsome man had entered. He introduced himself as Enric and sent her to the coffee shop next door for something to revive her father, while he loosened his tie. When she came back her father was better, and after sipping the coffee, wanted to stand up. But Enric urged him to rest.

Perhaps to distract her father and to keep her amused he produced a coin from her ear, then a card from under the papers on her father's desk. Harriet was enchanted and laughed like a young girl. Enric smiled too. Her father gave no response but asked Enric to escort his daughter home.

'Fairly will be back in a minute. I am quite recovered. And I need to be alone to finish my article. Tell your mother I will be back before eight. And Enric, I thank you for your help to my daughter. Call back another day, when I am restored.'

He would brook no resistance. When they had left he took out his article. He added the names of the venerable Edinburgh Chair of Logic and Metaphysics, Sir William Hamilton, of Harriet Martineau and George Henry Lewes to the list of the damned with the Frenchman, whom he satirised as,

.. '*the terminator of religion, the iconoclast of metaphysics, the apostle of positivism, and the regenerator of the future belief of the world. The pangs and throes of the human intellect are now safely ended; the fortuitous evolutions of the universe have produced Monsieur Comte, who has fortuitously produced the positive philosophy, which, in its turn, is fortuitously to produce miracles of so extensive a character that we are tempted to say a few words in apology for the older philosophic faith.*'

After Hugh's death, when asked for warning signs of his mental decline, McCosh cited his conversation with him about Comte. 'It was in the stars,' Harriet heard him tell her mother.

We Are We At Last

The fat Forth flipped like a silver fish as they made their way down the long sloping road to Granton. The sun had come out to bless their expedition on this July morning in 1854, sprinkling its rays on the waters as they parted to reveal a pod of dolphins at play, cutting the green-blue sea into a mosaic of mirrors. Since his return to Edinburgh, Forbes had supplemented his weekly lectures with Saturday excursions of almost two hundred eager students, all armed with hammers, chisels, and a cold collation. Sometimes, as today, they were accompanied by Professor Balfour and a hundred or so of his biology students, making up a posse of searchers for the living and the dead. They had been to the North Berwick coast and to Cramond. Goodsir occasionally came with them, as he did the last time, to relive their dredging and foraging on the Burntisland shore. 'The Thane of Fife,' Forbes had called him and reminded him of that day over ten years ago now when he had stridden down the beach to meet them after riding from Anstruther.

'Here we are today, a Fifer and a new Edinburgh man to raise our standards on an island halfway between both!' Forbes was in great good humour, despite the cough and weariness that would force him to cut short his attendance at the British Association's congress in Liverpool. When anxious friends fussed, he would just shake his head and murmur, 'That Mediterranean colic I caught in Greece' and take a swig from the milky quinine mixture that seemed to accompany him everywhere these days. On the way back to Edinburgh he had stopped to rest at Sir William Jardine's house in Dumfries, but with such bad luck as to be caught out walking in a downpour which had soaked him through. No matter, he was back in Edinburgh now and both he and Goodsir felt glorious. His lodgings in Princess Street meant they were neighbours, though John was not one for entertaining much and even preferred to meet in the rather decrepit oyster rooms at Ambrose's Café Royal than to receive his friend at home.

Edward's wife and children would be arriving in a few days' time, so this was perhaps the last of the two men's bachelor outings. Both were wearing the scarlet ribbon and triangle and shining with the delight of feeling young again without having the cares of actually being so.

'Youth is best enjoyed by the old!' Forbes joked. Their banter was interrupted by petitions from the different dredging teams to come and help identify their haul. Forbes had a gift for nudging the students towards the right answer, focussing on the grounds for their identifications rather than the result.

They looked back at Edinburgh as the ship began its docking manoeuvres at Inchkeith. The constant flow of steamers into Leith Docks and the hundreds of tall chimney stacks spewing smoke into the air reminded them of an Edinburgh they paid little heed to in their hermetic world. However, though they were free from commerce, from the scraping and the grinding labour of the factories, few men laboured harder than Forbes, Goodsir and their fellow scientists. Working ceaselessly had almost become a badge of honour among them in a race to see who could endure longest. Goodsir was already yawning on this fine morning, having, as usual been up working since dawn. He was brought to sharp attention by the sound of whooping and splashing from the other side of the boat. When he and Forbes rushed over they were faced with the spectacle of one hundred or so naked boys jumping into the waters to swim the last yards to the shore, their garments stacked in heaps on the decks.

'Hooray for the savage savants!' Forbes shouted. Goodsir put his hand on his friend's arm, anxious lest he follow the students. But

Forbes was already thinking of organising his troops and he climbed down from the boat and made his way to the end of the dock. He then gathered students together in groups of twenty or so and gave each unit instructions on what to look for: kelp, crabs, different specimens of snails, mostly the invertebrates that he felt most knowledgeable about. He insisted that he would ask them for a detailed description of the terrain in which they had discovered the specimens. 'Habitat is all, gentlemen. It determines the characteristics of the species. Botany and zoology both follow the same principles. Happy hunting!'

Goodsir observed his friend and could see the young boy in Forbes and imagined him as a callow youth on his native Isle of Man. Edward had been confined to bed with a series of illnesses then, but had learned to observe, to draw and his love of nature, he said, was what had saved him. John turned and gazed over to the East Neuk of Fife and his hometown. They had come so far to this small island to be together. It felt good. It felt right, preordained, even, but not in the harsh mechanical Calvinist way. They would do so much now, starting with a reorganisation of the specimens in the natural history collection.

As they clambered up to the top of the island, John mentioned the collection. Edward paused, perched upon a boulder like a cormorant about to take flight.

'Do you know, I have been pleasantly surprised by how good it is. Jameson has made some clever purchases in the last few years. It just needs some reorganisation, and I am happy to contribute specimens from my own findings. No serious teaching institution can be without a top-class museum. People need to see the order in creation, even those who read the scientific papers need to have the connections between rocks, plants and animals made manifest. They must be led away from wild speculations or ignorance and given proper guidance. That is our task, John.'

They lingered and let the soft breeze run its fingers over them as they looked down on the suddenly quiet multitude poring over inlets, chipping away at basalt shelves, and felt that their lives had not been wasted. A pair of puffins flew close by, seemingly oblivious of them. Forbes' face was flushed, whether from the climb or from the heat of thoughts racing through his brain. John suggested they sit down, then pondered aloud,

'I have been thinking, Edward, even brooding on one question that neither you nor I have addressed. What is the place of Man in this collection? Should he be included in a collection of Natural History or excluded from it by his divine nature? If he is included, how can we arrange the exhibits to show how all development leads to him? And then there is the question of the different races. How would we scale them with regard to each other?'

Oh, that thrilling 'we'! Never had he used it to mean the two of them in tandem, instead of just them as part of a scientific community, or perhaps, he and Forbes as two individuals. Now *we* meant a team, a partnership, at last. He waited for his friend's response.

'Well, old man,' Edward replied, 'I think I have a way round that. You see, nature is not a mere mechanism, obeying laws and producing certain results, but it is a great visible manifestation of the ideas of God. No one part of creation shows more than another of the wisdom and goodness of the Creator. The snails you and I found on Arthur's Seat, the kelp these boys are harvesting, the bodies you dissect, all conform to God's will, they all make manifest the design of their author. Of course, they are not complete signs, but types or symbols of the thoughts of the Creator. Humans will never discover a complete genus, it is a perfect form in the mind of God alone, and we see but its shadows in the species all around us.'

Ah, the magic pronoun had become just a routine plural again! John felt crushed, but he must not lose the connection. He also felt his faith in pure science undermined. This was not science, it was poetry. Was there a contradiction in that? He was about to bring up the idea of triangles as the basic structure but suddenly felt that geometry was a crude way of understanding nature. And Forbes had not talked to him as lyrically as this since their days in Lothian Street. Here they were again in the flat: two friends amazed by the possibilities of science and the multiplicity of creation. Only *he* understood his friend; only *his friend* understood *him*. 'Go on, Edward, go on.'

'How many and how curious problems concern the commonest of these sea-snails creeping over the wet seaweed!'

Edward opened his palm to reveal a small peaty-brown mollusc.

'In how many points of view may this fellow's history be considered! There are its origin and development, the mystery of its generation, the phenomena of its growth, all concerning each apparently insignificant individual; there is the history of the species, the value of its distinctive marks, the features which link it with the higher and lower creatures, the reason why it takes its stand where we place it in the scale of creation, the course of its distribution, the causes of its diffusion, its antiquity or novelty, the mystery (deepest of mysteries) of its first appearance, the changes of the outline of continents and of oceans which have taken place since its advent, and their influence on its own wanderings. Some of these questions may be clearly and fairly solved; some of them may be theoretically or hypothetically accounted for; some are beyond all the subtlety of human intellect to unriddle. We should not be afraid of mystery. That's what I want our collection to show, and what I want to introduce these boys to, not the dull relation of facts, nor the desperate clinging on to liturgical fancies, but the wonder at the heart of creation that only we, now, in this age can at last have access to. We are a privileged species at a privileged time, John. And I feel that my long-awaited appointment here in Edinburgh is a confirmation of that and the challenge of my lifetime is to grasp it with both hands. Exciting days, my friend!'

They talked on, discussing the practical questions of the display, of the preservation of exhibits, of possible purchases. Goodsir had a network of agents furnishing him with specimens from around the globe. He had recently started to receive a steady supply of electric fish and eels and their price meant he was a valued customer who could ask for favours on more common items. Forbes had contacts in London, and they were talking of making up a common list and an organised search for the choicest examples, when they were brought back to earth, or at least the speck of the island, by Balfour's foghorn voice.

'Inspection time, come on, sirs!'

When they arrived on the dock the foragers had laid out their findings in columns, following the taxonomy taught to them by their professors. Forbes inspected the students and their catches like a general reviewing his troops and their kit, pronouncing himself well-pleased and exclaiming what an excellent bunch of students he had and how it confirmed the rightness of his choice to come back to his alma mater. Then he gave the order to prepare for their voyage home and they waited while the boat was loaded and the students counted on. The three professors were the last to embark and Forbes chatted effusively to Balfour, perhaps to counteract any impression of rudeness at having ignored him earlier in favour of Goodsir. Without Balfour's participation, trips like this one could not be afforded. When the biologist gave him a series of short replies, Forbes feared the worst and started to apologise for leaving him alone with all the students.

'They must have harassed you endlessly. I know how tiresome young enthusiasts can be.'

'No, not at all, not at all. I enjoy their questions. It is just that this place dampens my spirits.'

'Really? But it has such a variety of rock, plant and animal types in such a small area.'

'Well, I realise this may be improper in a scientist, but I shiver every time I step down onto the island. This was a place of pestilence. During every plague or outbreak of epidemic in history, people have been isolated here and left to die. Perhaps there was no other option, but I still think of the abandoned souls.'

'It says much for your humanity that you think of them. As a Manxman, I know what it is like to be marooned on an island when disease strikes. Cholera ravaged our community in the 1820s when I was a young lad. But it was overcome by science, as these scourges are; we must not forget about that.'

'Of course, of course,' Balfour nodded. They could tell something else was still troubling him.

'The night before I come to the island, I always dream of the two bairns and their mother abandoned here on the orders of King James IV at the end of the fifteenth century. Did you know about that?'

'It features in a chronicle by a man from Pitscottie, not far from my hometown, if I am not mistaken,' Goodsir broke in.

'Yes, Robert Lyndsay. He relates how the king commanded that a mute woman and her two infants be transported to this island in order to ascertain which language the bairns would grow up to speak isolated from the rest of the world. This speech, they thought, would be the 'original language,' the 'language of God.' Some say that when they fetched them off years later the children spoke good Hebrew, or what sounded like an archaic version of it. I still dream of those bairns watching the supply boat leaving them behind in silence and their poor, desperate mother. If I believed in curses, I would avoid this place. But enough melancholy, gentlemen, our crew is waiting!'

Once they had cast off, Forbes requested the captain to sail around the island before making for home. Goodsir only thought about that later, when the entire day would take on for him the air of a ritual, the air of farewell. Edward stood up on the bridge, pointing down to the boys and signalling whose turn it was to speak. Hopeful seagulls hovered and hooped above his head and seals slipped down from the rocks as the boat skirted the rocky shore. He pointed to a redhaired freckled lad, Hugh Morrison, Goodsir thought he was called, and asked him what could explain the variety of molluscs or plants they had collected on the same island. The lad gave him the answer he was seeking, that it was due to the different heights, below or above sea level and the sustenance thus provided.

The boys were all seated in rows on the deck of the ship, many of them still eating their potted hough sandwiches and sipping from clay bottles of ginger beer, some of them with that fire in their eyes that freedom and discovery bring to us as youths. There was a gentle swell in the sea, almost as if the planet was breathing and the questions and answers took on that rhythm.

A lanky boy with dark heavy eyebrows and with his shirt still open over a hairless chest raised his hand, then when Forbes nodded his head, sprang to his feet.

'What is your question, Mr Nairn?'

'Do you think there have been new species, sir? Could that not be the explanation for the differences between the specimens?'

'That is a burning question, congratulations. I would call on Professor Goodsir to respond, but as his answer would mirror mine, I will simply pull the academic trick of giving my own opinion but leaving the responsibility to other wiser men, such as the good professor! However, John, if I stray too far from your views, please indicate it.

Perhaps new species were created before the advent of Man. However, we have no positive or available evidence of any having appeared within the human epoch. The constant increase in new species is due to the increase in our knowledge and our ability to explore further and further, higher and deeper. Assertions such as those made by the author of *Vestiges* about the creation of animals by electricity are rubbishy.'

Edward waited for the last term to ripple through the boys' minds. He was adept at inserting slang or unorthodox terms into his lectures, to seem like one of the people, an amateur searching for knowledge, John had often thought. Here he was, doing it again. John could imagine the boys imitating him later. 'Oh, that is just rubbishy!' they would say, to any proposition, then laugh with those in the know and at outsiders. Just as he and Edward had done as youths.

'Not only because we are uncovering more species, but also because we can demonstrate that here in northern Europe there are species which are unknown in the fossil record, we can be led to believe these discoveries, in the Hebrides or in Patagonia, are proof of the creation of the new. However, gentlemen, that proposition, is still rubbishy. My research has convinced me that these newcomers are just colonists from older centres, moving here or there since the commencement of the human epoch under pressure of the climate, the environment and even of man's activity. There are no new species. The parsons are wrong when they cling onto a calendar of few thousand years but correct in the essential. There are new varieties of the same species but no leap from one species to another.'

John tapped Edward on the shoulder and pointed behind him where the dolphins were doing their dance again. As they both looked round, he caught sight of the reflection of their faces in the water. You could not tell which was which!

John wrapped that day up in his memory and stored it away like one of his prize specimens for his own private collection. In the years afterwards, he would take it out and unwrap it, see Edward laughing at the diving boys, observe him perched on the boulder at the top of the hill, feel the heat of his gaze as he talked about what 'we' would do. John appropriated that pronoun for himself and Edward from then on and scarcely used it except in reference to the two of them. Everything he did was in the name of them both. After Edward's death John lived on as the reflection looking for the lost mirror.

When they had disembarked and the students had been dismissed, the two of them bid farewell to Balfour and headed to Wardie near Newhaven to inspect the cottage John had found for Edward and his family. When she was presented with it a week or so later, Emily found it dingy and dark but accepted it with the good grace she always showed when faced with her husband's life, his choices, his activities. She and Edward soon used it as a base for their Sunday walks, especially to their favourite place, the Dean Cemetery and its panorama over the Forth and Fife. The children too, liked Edinburgh and were sad when their father left them on his next journey. He went to Liverpool at the end of the summer and made his friends anxious. He made them laugh too, when he appeared dressed as the Scottish Lion and launched into a mock defence of the rights of the Scots. On his return to Edinburgh he worked on the next edition of *The New Philosophical Journal* and prepared the winter term's lectures as well as working on the Collection and keeping up his professional correspondence. He complained about chills and fevers after the soaking at Dumfries and when the University reopened on Wednesday, November 1, his hand shook as it rested on the lectern. Hugh Miller had attended several lectures as an auditor and, in an admiring article in that month of November in *The Witness*, wrote that '*the interest of his original descriptions was almost lost in the admiration of the beautifully graceful forms which seemed to arise, as if by magic, from beneath his long and delicate fingers, and how a murmur of applause was not refrained from by his admiring audience, spectators rather, they might then be called.*'

John came to see him on the Friday the 4th, to beg him to give up the lectures and the organisation of student matriculations.

'Are you the pot or the kettle, my good man?' was all he replied. 'I have taken on this post, perhaps too speedily, but this is my life's work and I intend to make a success of it.'

On the Sunday, Dr. Bennett was called to the cottage and detected a slight fever and an accelerated pulse. Forbes was too weak to walk to the Dean Cemetery with his wife. Nevertheless, he insisted on going to the College the following day and lectured till Wednesday. He agreed to suspend classes till the Monday, but on the Saturday was forced to write to Balfour to ask him to take charge of his students for a while. The fever continued to increase and, on the Sunday, he experienced severe back and kidney pain. He was increasingly obsessed about the *Journal* and his professional responsibilities.

On Monday evening, with a hand that could scarcely hold the pen, he wrote, in hardly legible characters, his last note: —

'*Monday evening. — DEAR BALFOUR, — I am completely shattered for the moment, and don't know how to get on with the Journal, being so ill. Could you look in upon me and advise. Come here, i.e., Wardie. I am still in my bed. — Ever, E. FORBES.*'

The splitting pain from his kidneys became more acute on the Tuesday, and when Balfour visited, Forbes was unable to speak. At his side, then and since he had taken to his bed, was John Goodsir. Balfour thought he looked as if in as much pain as his friend. Over the next days, Edward's condition worsened although with several short revivals that gave him hope, he said, that he would overcome this attack as he had done others.

He referred to his having been overworked, and to the anxiety the Town-Council had caused him by insisting on his leaving London so hurriedly to lecture in Edinburgh. He brought this up time and again, sometimes humorously. 'The bailies have killed the goose that laid the golden eggs.'

When John was bathing him, Edward held his shoulders and looked past him as if there was a further landscape out behind him then smiled and whispered in John's ear,

'I am off, John. Please tell everyone that I was not ambitious, I hoped and wished for the Edinburgh chair because I thought I could do good there.'

On the Friday he asked for his children. He kissed them and then requested John to 'Be kind to my wife and the little ones.' When Emily came back after handing over the children to her cousin, Edward held onto her hand and winced whenever she had to leave the room. The pain seemed to disappear afterwards but was replaced by an increasing sensation of suffocation. On the Saturday he fell into silence, only stirring when he overheard the doctor discussing ideas for treatment with Goodsir.

'That will do, Bennett, no more of that.'

He seemed lost in speechlessness, and it was only later in the afternoon, when Emily took his head again in her arm, did he open his eyes and smile, and signed to her to kiss him. To her inquiry if he still knew her, he could only faintly whisper, 'My own wife.' Another hour crept on, during which he said nothing, though his eye showed that he remained in the full possession of his faculties. And then, as twilight was deepening into dusk, his spirit passed imperceptibly away.

John Goodsir took over his friend's Natural History lectures so as not to leave his students untethered. His colleagues said that labour became a monomania for him. He died thirteen years later, in that same cottage in Wardie where he had moved after Edward's death, after being carried, paralysed from the lecture hall. He left most of his work unfinished and unpublished. He was buried beside his friend in Dean Cemetery, and under an identical obelisk, featuring the logarithmic spiral. Visitors often confuse the two. 'We are we at last,' John might have said.

Letter 18

The Kilties

Assynt, August 20th, 1852.

'Harriet, you, William, and Bessie are the public for which I write; while poor little Hugh, who is, I suspect, not intelligent enough to feel any interest in papa's adventures, must be regarded as that ignorant, but not uncared-for, portion of the community which education has not yet reached. I broke off late on Saturday night in the little inn of Huna; the Sabbath morning rose clear and beautiful; I never saw the Orkney Islands look so near from the main land; their little fields, at the distance of many miles, gleamed yellow in the sun; and the tall Old Red Sandstone cliffs of Hoy —cliffs nearly a thousand feet in height —were sharply relieved against the sky, and bore a blood-hued flush of deep red; while the Pentland Frith, roughened by a light breeze, was intensely blue. I walked on after breakfast to the Free Church, and heard from Sir Macgregor two solid, doctrinal discourses. The congregation, however, was very thin; but I ought not to judge of it, I am told, by present appearances, as many of the men connected with it are at the herring-fishery.–Still, however, it is only half a congregation at best, the other half congregation of the parish being in the Established Church. Papa and his friends could not help being Free Churchmen, as you will learn when you get older; we could not avoid the Disruption; but papa does sometimes regret that the Disruption should in so many parishes have, as it were, made two bites of a cherry; that is, broken up into two congregations a moiety of people that would have made one good one, but no more....

I took the mailcoach from Wick very early on Monday morning, and travelled on, for the greater part of the way, under the cloud of night to Helmsdale, where I passed a day. On the morning of Wednesday I walked on along the shore from Brora to Golspie, and saw at a place called Strathstever a cave high up in a sandstone rock, to which ascended a flight of steps. A high wall fenced round the bottom of the steps, but I contrived to climb over it; and, ascending to the cave, found it to be in part the work of nature, but also indebted to art. The space within was about the size of a rather large room, and there was a range of seats cut in the live rock that ran all around it. I was told that in the days of the late duchess it used to be the scene of many good picnics; and as it occurs in a sequestered corner of the old coastline, with wild shrubs hanging from the rocks all around, and with a green, level strip of land and the wide sea in front, one could, I dare say, take one's dinner in it very sentimentally. I passed Dunrobin Castle on my way; it is an immense pile, on which there has been expended money enough to purchase a large estate. But though a part of it —the part papa remembered of old —be very ancient, and though the additions be in the newest style, the general effect is that of a very large, fine upstart modern building. The new has swallowed up and overborne the old. I had to rise at a little after four o'clock next morning, to take the mail-gig from Lairg to Assynt, and reached the former place at breakfast-time, passing through a fine valley, which opens into the sea, at the Little Ferry, for about sixteen or eighteen miles. Along the flat bottom of this valley the sea must once have flowed, and the precipices along its sides are very steep and abrupt, as if they still retained the forms given them by the waves; but the bottom is occupied by rich corn-fields; and cottages and trees appear where once canoes may have been. 'At Lairg I used to be well acquainted, but it was long, long ago; and the people whom I knew were all away or dead. On my way to Assynt I saw a gentleman in a kilt, and, before the gig came up to him, set him down from his dress as an Englishman. And an Englishman he was, who had come out to the road to get his letters. As a general rule, Scotchmen — save pipers, who are paid for it, and soldiers, who can't help it — don't wear the kilt.

Papa

Forgiving Time

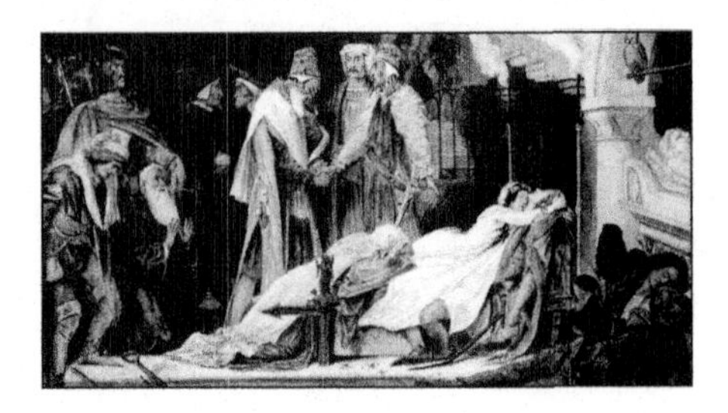

Once you let someone in, you cannot control when they will come, or when they will go. Maggie now slipped in and out of Alia's room, leaving her things on the sofa, on the bed and on the table beside the window, like a cat extending its territory. The rest of the house was almost empty, most of the furniture, linen and kitchen utensils packed and stacked in the back room. Where would they go?

Alia seemed unworried but Nell was frantic.

'We are off to Fife next week and I cannae go without knowing what you are going to do.'

Alia seemed dazed, talking as if nothing had happened. Enric came and went from work and Elspeth visited, sometimes staying overnight. The household was like a great ship becalmed at sea, waiting to discover if they would be released or sunk by the storm looming on the horizon.

On a grey Tuesday morning when the haar from the Forth was slipping its cold fingers into every nook and cranny of the tall apartments in the New Town, when the ghostly shadows of seagulls swooped and soared in front of the windows, Maggie decided she wanted to go back to bed. That way, she could watch Alia when she came back and learn how to mimic the movements of a graceful, grown woman, one like she had decided she would learn to be. She had tried all Alia's combs and brushes, even painted her face with her rouge, and walked up and down in her smart leather shoes. Alia had shrieked the first time she came upon her 'all dolled up,' as she put it. Maggie could not understand why. Hadn't they told her she would need to grow up, that she was no longer a wee lassie? Alia had taken her to the bathroom and scrubbed her clean and raw, telling her she never wanted to see her painted face again. But if it was so wrong, why did Alia have all these fancy clothes, shoes, and paint?

What would she do till Alia came back from yet another walk with Elspeth? They spent a lot of time in each other's company, Maggie, thought, for two women who did not like each other. She picked up the vanity mirror and made grown-up faces in it as she rested her head against the pillows. She held a handkerchief she found under them and tucked it into her sleeve as she had seen Alia do, discreetly, elegantly. She had to make four attempts to get it all the way in without forming a bunion in her wrist or sticking out like a piece of stuffing from a rag doll. When she got tired of that she tried to find new patterns in the wallpaper, but there were no dragons or strange flowers to be found. She was getting bored! There was a small cabinet beside the bed and Maggie noticed the top drawer was slightly open. It was normally locked, but Alia must have forgotten in her rush to go out. What treasures might it hide? Maggie got out of bed and knelt, then slowly tugged it open, dreaming of jewels, or at least of photographs of elegant men and ladies. However, all she found was a brown paper bag containing a couple of old notebooks. They had Alia's name on them, in letters of a younger hand. And inside, there were sketches of people and strange phrases. She climbed onto the bed and flicked through each pad, wondering what they were about and why they were locked away. Oh! The downstairs lock was being turned; it was Alia. Maggie stuffed the books back in the bag and once more into the drawer. How open had it been exactly?

She slunk out of the room, deciding denial was better than being found on the scene of the crime. Perhaps Alia would not notice. In the hall she could hear Elspeth's voice. She had been working irregularly recently and her timetable was not that of most working folk, Nell had explained to Maggie. Maggie leaned over the banister and tried to catch what the women were saying to each other in half-whispers.

In fact, neither Alia nor Elspeth were aware they were whispering. They had lowered their voices as they sat on a bench in the park and a woman passed by, then just kept on. In any case it was as much an inward conversation for each of them as a dialogue. They had decided to fight. Elspeth had taken Alia's motto to heart.

'We have little to lose, Alia. And Hardie is afraid of scandal. What can he do if we both bang on the door and tell him we will denounce him if he does not stop this persecution and compensates you for your losses?'

'What can he do? He can have us locked up, beaten up. It's his words against ours and he will claim the fact that our charges come years after the events we allege, and that we know each other, is proof of our connivance, of conspiracy to slander him. People will scorn at the poor midwife delivering children out of wedlock and the Madame who is down on her luck. It would be suicide. We would be asking people to accept the word of women, and that counts for nothing, as you and I both know.'

They both fell silent then turned to look upstairs, alerted by the creaking of the banister.

'Don't you know it's not right to eavesdrop on people?' Alia almost hissed as she climbed up the stairs, determined to chastise the little besom. But when she saw the fear in Maggie's eyes, she just tutted and waved her away.

'I need to change, Elspeth. I will join you in the kitchen in a wee while.'

However, only ten minutes had passed when Alia appeared, wearing the same clothes as on their walk. Her face was flushed, and she seemed unable to speak. She pointed to the teapot and Elspeth poured her a cup.

'That little minx has been rummaging among my things again, thank goodness,' she exclaimed at last.

'Thank goodness?'

'Well, she opened a drawer and must have looked at some notebooks I had in England. I think I told you about them and my dreams.'

Elspeth nodded. She noticed that Alia was clutching two sheets of yellowed paper.

'They were pinned inside the back cover of one of the notebooks. I had forgotten about them. I found them in Mrs Hardie's room when I was packing to leave Bath. I was more like Maggie than I care to think, I suppose, and I didn't even read one but just kept them. I found them on the floor next to the bed just now.'

Alia read the letters aloud, skipping over the details which would mean nothing to Elspeth or of no relevance to their case. The tone was Hardie's signature mixture of haughtiness and grievance.

'*I have been more sinned against than sinning, Susan. And I have fought against the weakness of the flesh that the Lord has chosen to burden me with. Moreover, you aligned yourself with the devil through your neglect of me and my needs. Our moments of intimacy were cold and granted as a duty and not as gift from you. And these servant girls will be taken by some rough farmhand, in any case. It is better that they taste some refinement, that they learn from someone with education. Few of them uttered one word of complaint to me.*'

Alia paused then turned to the second letter.

'*You maintain you ran off with the Thompson girl, alleging her youth and that she was under our protection. I told you I would never interfere with a girl taken in under our own roof and I am promising it here in writing. If after this, you and that little hussy do not return to Inveresk, then I will know her virtue is just an excuse for your wilful desertion of your husband. And I say hussy, because I have seen the way she walks, the way she looks at men. She comes from wanton stock. I would not have been corrupting her. In any case, she is not so young. The age of consent in Scotland is twelve.*'

Elspeth reached across the table and put her hand on Alia's.

'Wait, there is one more piece. '*If you abandon me I will have to satisfy my needs. I am a man, after all. If nothing else will move you, think of your return as protecting the innocence of the young maidens of Scotland!*' I think he was starting to rave here, and the letter ends in rambling statements, promises, threats of every type. I think I am beginning to feel sorry for Susan Hardie. Perhaps I misjudged her. Though she did betray me over the rapist.'

'Are the letters signed and dated? Good. This proves your story and lends credence to mine.'

'Well, they are a step forward. But it would be important to have something more to pressure him with. Something that backs your testimony up, Elspeth. What if your mother calls you a liar? She may, if she is still dependent on this monster.'

They were still talking about twenty minutes later when the door was pushed open. In came Nell and Alec. Nell looked nervous but Alec was beaming. Behind him was a third figure, a man of stocky build with raven black hair. When he came right into the room, Elspeth remarked his dark complexion, with some pock marks on his face and the darkest brown eyes that bore right into you. Alia fainted.

• • •

She came to herself on her bed, with Nell holding a cold compress to her forehead and her brother seated at the foot. Nell started to cry, to say she hoped Alia wasna angry with her, but she had decided to write to Roddie. He had told her to contact him a couple of years ago if they were ever in serious trouble.

'Well, this is trouble. And it is serious, Alia. And if you dinna mind me saying, it's the first time I have ever seen you at a loss, dithering over what to do. You willna listen to me and I thocht, I ken someone who can help, and who she *will* listen to. And here he is, here is your Roddie.'

When Roddie spoke, Alia felt confused. He still sounded like her brother, but he had taken on a Canadian accent and it made the shape of his face look different to her as he talked. She noticed the foreign cut of his clothes. He was smartly dressed and had an air of solid success about him. He was still handsome but had aged. Why did that surprise her? She had seen photographs taken in recent years, but he was different in the flesh. Her vanity made her worry about how she looked to him and several minutes passed. So it was only after a few minutes that they began to talk properly to each other. Then the doors opened.

Roddie explained that Nell had told him all about what had happened. He had arrived from Liverpool three days ago but had spent that time in Inveresk.

'Inveresk! I have never been back there, and we both said it would be unsafe for you to go. Why on earth did you set foot in that place?'

He smiled. 'The world moves on, Alia. Inveresk is really a suburb of Musselburgh now and folk come up and down to Edinburgh and beyond as if they were crossing the road. Hardly anyone knew me, till I sought out poor old Campbell Fraser in his butcher's shop.'

'The lad whose jaw you broke?'

'Aye. He is a goodhearted soul and he forgave me. He introduced me to his friends and we had a couple of cheery nights. Our house is still there and the Manse too, though it is empty now as the vicar comes out from Musselburgh. It felt good to be back and to be forgiven, Alia.'

'Forgiven?'

'Ach, Alia, when I came out of prison and down to Edinburgh, I was a hard, bad man in many ways. Maybe not as bad as I liked to make out, but I threw my weight around a bit. And building houses and running a team in Canada also thickened my skin at times. Luckily, Hamish was there to keep me centred. I have thought before of coming back to visit here before I get to be too old. I am not one of those desperate Scots exiles that sit around extolling the virtues of the auld country. If Scotland really had so many advantages people would not still be escaping from it. But I felt I needed to see Alec and Nell, meet their girls, and spend some time with you. And go back to Inveresk and make my peace. I would like you to go back with me and make your peace too, Alia.'

'Well, if it's so important to you, I will come to take a look at the village.'

'No, Alia. I mean to Canada, to make your peace with Jessie. She is an old woman now and growing frail. I know you have written to each other and exchanged explanations. But I knew when I got on the boat home and I felt it even more in Inveresk, that you need to be there. And the good of forgiveness comes not from being forgiven, but for doing the forgiving yourself.'

Alia bowed her head. 'You will need to give me time, Roddie. This is overwhelming. I have a lot to think about right now, a pressing problem with Hardie and with losing this house and my livelihood.'

He squeezed her hand. 'If I can sort this out, will you come? No, don't answer that, this is not a bargain. I want you to decide to come. Now, Alia, I have changed from that wild boy that Hardie saw. Except he does not know that. He was frightened of me, and I am sure I can frighten him again. I gather Mr Miller has made quite a name for Cha as the licentious madman. Let's make use of that.'

'Let's talk about all this, Roddie. But I hear noises from the kitchen. Tonight, we will celebrate your return and I will introduce you to Enric and Elspeth and Maggie.'

And what an evening they had of it! Alec and Nell decided to make this their official leaving party and produced a steak pie and several bottles of claret. Roddie had purchased some ham and some whisky and brought with him a jar of the famous maple syrup which especially delighted Maggie. She abandoned Elspeth and sat next to him all evening. Elspeth set out the table and decorated the room with flowers from the back garden. She and Enric joked and flirted like a newly met couple and Alia felt a release of joy that she had not experienced in years. And when Enric was not dallying with Elspeth, he only had eyes for Roddie. He was literally enchanted with him. 'Your brother is the only type of person I like better than an honest

Scotsman,' he whispered to Alia. 'And what type of person is that?' 'An honest, hard-working, talented Scotsman who has travelled. They are the ones on whom the fame of your nation really depends! Now a toast to the traveller!' And they all raised their glasses, even Maggie, who was given some of Nell's home-made ginger cordial. The songs began, as at all Scottish parties, and they all did a turn. Roddie's singing voice had not improved over the years, but he sang a Canadian air that had them all dreaming of dark forests. Elspeth sang a Border ballad, full of honest lassies and brave laddies. And Enric sang a piece he said was about the song of birds and though they could not understand Catalan, there was birdsong clearly in it and an emotion in his rough voice that melted their hearts. He lifted them all out of melancholy by immediately producing an egg from Maggie's ear and saying that his song had made her into a bird!

It was time to retire; Maggie was losing the fight to keep her eyes open. Elspeth had to work early the next morning and insisted on going home. Alec and Nell went off to catch the last boat-train from Granton to Burntisland. Alia escorted Elspeth to the door, leaving Enric and Roddie in animated conversation, like two old friends who had met again by surprise.

'We must hold onto joy, and each other.' Elspeth said as she hugged Alia farewell and stepped out into the street. Alia watched as she disappeared into the evening mist, amazed at the change in her. 'To hold onto joy, and each other.' Well, that was certainly a more optimistic motto than 'Never bow down, never apologise,' but could she make it her own?

When she went into her room, she found Maggie already asleep in her bed, the poor wee darling. She had to remember now that whatever she did would affect the girl and she thought of her brother's talk of forgiveness and of growing a thick skin. Perhaps she too needed to forgive people: Susan Hardie, her mother, and above all herself for climbing into a shell and never coming out. Yes, she would try to forgive them all. All except De Quincey and the Reverend Hardie.

Crumbling Rocks

It was like a tapeworm in his gut, slowly consuming his insides. But now the beast had lost its force and he hoped to be left without the burning sensation in his stomach that flared up every time he was attacked from within. When *The Rock* foundered in November 1855, Hugh wrote '*A newspaper without a distinct necessity is a thing begun in folly to end in failure.*' His gut twisted as he examined the column in typeface, anxious to print it before Fairly could intervene. *The Witness* had seen off its most dangerous rival publication, set up by that traitor James Begg and fellow stalwarts of the Free Kirk, zealous of Presbyterian purity and kicking against Hugh's insistence on opening his newspaper to the world and to science. Begg had been publishing a magazine called *The Bulwark* for several years and was one of the founders of the Scottish Reformation Society, now just five years old, and made electric by the man's energy. Hugh's mistake had been to allow Begg to contribute articles to *The Witness* in an attempt to appease Candlish, but even he tired of their relentless anti-Catholic focus. Hugh approved of the man's adoption of Chalmers' social vision and his promotion of the Colonies, cheap, solid homes for artisans that would soon dot Edinburgh. However, as he said in the article, '*Some people do not understand how much talent and effort is needed to publish a successful newspaper.*' Hugh's private pain had first seeped into the public sphere when he had accused Begg in print of trying to steal his staff and his subscribers' list and every few months *The Witness* answered letters from Begg complaining that his latest public appearance had not been given the full coverage it deserved. Now whose turn was it to squirm?

The wind was racing up the High Street that dull autumn day, banging on doors and rattling windows and when the office door opened Hugh started, ready to close it to keep out the cold blasts. However, it was not nature at work but Candlish, who now was divesting himself of his cloak and trying to rearrange his crested hair. He had not visited the office in years; Hugh put down the article, taking care to cover it with some other documents.

'To what do I owe this honour?'

'Come now, Hugh. We know each other too well to stand on ceremony. I was just passing on my way to a meeting and thought I would call in.'

Candlish was a bad liar and he stood there like a cardplayer waiting for his opponent to rescue him by wilfully playing a bad hand.

'Then what can I do for you?'

They passed the card back and forward several times till Candlish seemed more at home and could show what else he was holding.

'The meeting I am on my way to concerns the winding-up of *The Rock* newspaper. I know you never approved of it, Hugh, but we need as many soldiers as we can muster in the fight against false dogmas and materialism.'

Hugh resisted the urge to show him the article on the desk. 'Did Candlish have no other form of expression than reproach?' he almost blurted out. But no, he would not fight him any longer. He was weary and he also felt a duty to the Church and even to the man who had supported him in the days of the Disruption.

'Perhaps the time was not right, perhaps Dr Begg lacked prudent counsellors. It is difficult to strike exactly the right note with the public. However, I am sure the Lord has other work for him to do.'

Candlish sat down and examined Hugh in the way he did a sinner come to seek salvation. Hugh had aged, he seemed to carry his size instead of wearing it as he used to. His hair was as unkempt as ever but thinning a little now. He stooped. But there was no repentance there, no submission to authority, to the hard lessons time teaches us all, he mused.

'Do you think you have struck the right note with the public, as you put it, regarding the current conflict with Russia? I have received endless complaints about the harshness of your criticism of our forces and their generals.'

'I have been cautious, and my columns are mainly drawn from the London *Times*. I do not think I am more critical than the mass of the population.'

'When have you ever been swayed by what the mass of the population thinks? Are you sure you are not influenced by a closer quarter?'

Here we are again, both men seemed to think at the same time, no more cards, just a face-off. Candlish was angry, but more with himself and with that self-important fool, Begg, than with Miller. Nevertheless, he had to take his ire and frustration out somewhere. And he had received a letter from Hardie yesterday, informing him of the success of his moves to empty the apartment and asking about the spy. Any communication from that odious man irritated him even more.

'I beg you, Dr. Candlish, not to come here with glib insinuations. Speak clear, what quarter do you allude to?'

As Candlish outlined Hardie's information and accusations against the Spaniard, he felt once again how ridiculous it was. If it could be proved, the security services would have been called. And it was true that *The Witness* had mainly just echoed other paper's views of the War. If there was any real criticism to be made, it lay there.

Hugh looked grave, like a man at sea who smells the storm coming and is too far from land. His demeanour changed of a sudden, however, and he began to laugh out loud. 'Enric, a spy? In Scotland? And at a religious newspaper? You have been reading too much Dickens, sir. It is true he is a materialist and some kind of European socialist. His views represent much of what I attack and am battling against in my latest book. However, he has been open about our differences and if

I am to defeat our intellectual enemies, I must understand them. He performed the same role for Robert Chambers and as far as I know that solid citizen has not taken to wearing balaclavas and extolling the Czar.'

It was Candlish's turn to make an about-turn. He stood up. He walked over to Hugh and held out his hand.

'Perhaps I have been ill-informed. And Hugh, despite all this, in spite of our disagreements and the conflict with Begg, know that I admire you. We were friends and allies once. May the Lord grant each of us the generosity of spirit to become so again.'

Now both men were discomfited like unseated cavalrymen looking round for their horses.

Hugh nodded. 'May the Lord do as you wish.'

As Candlish pulled the door open, he turned to face Hugh once more. Why did he do this? he would later ask himself.

'You are engaged upon yet another attack on *Vestiges*, I believe, though I am afraid its rudimentary materialism is about to be superseded by even more nefarious publications. You must ready yourself for the fight against those who deny the existence of any purpose to creation and to individual life. I read the talk you gave in London last month and there is a breadth of argument and amplitude of sources there which is new in you. It does you credit, and if this fellow has furnished you with such information, then perhaps he deserves some too. Chambers seems to have thought as much of him as you do. *The Vestiges* is a dish full of the same ingredients though seasoned differently. Think on it, Hugh. I bid you goodbye.'

Hugh did not really take in that remark, anxious as he was to sign off tomorrow's edition for copy. He thought about the visit though, and what Candlish had intended by it. He had banned the chief elders of the Free Kirk from entering the premises after their attempt to unseat him as editor. Was this a gesture of renewed comradeship by the Doctor or was he just emphasising his authority and right to go where he pleased? Perhaps with the fall of Begg's publication they had decided they needed Hugh once more. There was one way to see, to put them to the test. He would publish the article and see what they would throw at him: grenades, or flowers.

He met Fairly on the way out and they chatted about the edition, about the weather and their families. As he headed down the High Street, Hugh was stopped dead in his tracks by a knife piercing his skull. He had to turn his face to the wall and hold on to a doorpost to keep himself afoot. He waited several minutes for the pain to subside, as it had on other occasions, then looked around to see if he had been noticed. No, no one had stopped or come over to him. He decided to have a coffee to put him on his feet again and crossed the road at the junction between the Tron Kirk and the North Bridge to an establishment that offered tea and coffee and light refreshments. It was on the site of the bar where he had seen the badger-baiting all those years ago. Why had he thought of that? He walked to the back of the room, past the round brown tables to a corner seat where he could sit in private. He ordered his coffee then closed his eyes and tried to relieve the pressure on his brain. It was then that Candlish's parting words swam into view, like headlines in the newspaper. He thought of those lines of Comte with the annotations. They were not in Enric's hand. He thought of the reference to the Frenchman's work in *Vestiges*. He saw himself seated in Waterloo Place, taking tea with Chambers and his heart began to beat as if trying to break out of his chest. He then heard Enric's voice, adding to his nightmare. He gripped the table, willing himself back to reality then felt a hand on his forehead. He opened his eyes to find Enric really standing over him.

'My friend, what is wrong with you? Can I get you a glass of water? Do you need a physician? Mr Fairly told me you might be here. What is the matter?'

Hugh mumbled 'water' just to get Enric to leave him. When he saw him at the counter fetching a glass, he struggled to his feet. It felt like he was climbing Arthur's Seat with a heavy weight on his back. As he was about to reach the door it opened and in came Alia and a man whose face he thought he recognised. It couldn't be!

They put him in a coach and the three of them, Roddie, Alia and Enric accompanied him to Portobello. Hugh only opened his eyes after they had passed the Queen's Park and were heading down by Jock's Lodge. He indicated that they were home now, and he would leave them, and seemed further confused when both Alia and Enric insisted that he had moved house and was now living beside the shore. He would have leapt out of the carriage, but Roddie's strong grip held him fast.

'How have you all conspired against me?' Hugh whispered at last.

'No, Hugh, there is no conspiration.' Enric answered. 'My lodgings are with Alia here. I know you were acquainted but that was long ago. We have barely discussed you. And Roddie is just come back from Canada to see his sister.'

'His sister?'

'Yes, Hugh, I am Alia's brother. Life is more complicated than in books. I was Charles or Cha when you knew me, but that is an old story, one that does not fit in your scheme of things. I am sorry to find you so disturbed. We will get you back to your family and then leave you. You will not have to worry about seeing me again.'

'Why did you not tell me when we met in Portobello that he was your brother, Alia?'

'I could tell you had already had more of the truth than you could take when I talked about Willie. But it is no matter. I came to you for help. I was wrong to do so. We all have to help ourselves. Now we are approaching your house so try to compose yourself before we stir your wife and family. Enric will go in with you as he has already met them. You need to rest, Hugh. Enric has told me how hard you work. Rest, and stay with your family. Goodbye Hugh.'

Hugh let himself be helped from the carriage by Roddie.

'Thank you, Cha,' he said. 'Please forgive me.'

'It was a long time ago, man. Get strong, treasure what you have.'

Enric had rapped at the door and then entered with Hugh leaning on his arm. Harriet was the first to see him and she called for her mother while she herded her brothers and sister into the drawing-room urging them to hurry but to take care of the good furniture.

Lydia appeared at last, her face pallid and with the look of one who had witnessed this many times before.

'Please help me take my husband upstairs to his bedroom. He needs rest and will recover there.'

As they climbed the stairs Enric could not help asking himself why they could not have gone to a room on the ground floor and why she had said *his* bedroom and not *our* room. Hugh sank down on his bed like a sack of potatoes dumped in a shed. Enric had never seen this vigorous man in such a state of abandonment. He made to leave, but he felt Hugh holding onto his arm.

'Go back to my office and ask Fairly to let you take your papers. Begone from my life and tell your friends I will not be blackmailed. If Alia and her brother, whatever his name is, cross my path again, they will regret it. I have never uttered a threat against a person in my life before. But I am badly used, and justice is on my side. God has a destiny for you, Mr Serra, and I am sure it will be a suitably bad one. Now leave me.'

Enric made to remonstrate but Hugh was shaking, his face glistening with sweat. His eyes were burning, reflecting a consuming inner fire, he later told Alia and Roddie.

'Very well. I wish you a speedy recovery.'

He walked past Lydia and out of the door and down the stairs. Harriet was standing at the foot, but he did not return her welcoming smile. Mrs Miller had not said a word while her husband attacked him and had only bowed her head on his departure. A strange family!

Hugh allowed his wife to help him undress and to close the curtains. He said the light hurt him.

'You cannot, we cannot go on like this, Hugh. You are losing the few friends that were left you, along with your health. I will not ask that you think of me, but have pity on your children who depend on you for their well-being and who need a father who is with them in body and mind. I will bring you something to drink in a few hours.' And with that she left, instructing Harriet to get her brothers and sister ready to go out for a walk.'

'But it is cold, and the wind will carry us into the sea!'

'What a fanciful mind you have, child. Now do as I say. Your father needs quiet.'

As the door slammed and the family stuck their heads out onto the cold grey street, Hugh tossed and turned in his bed, panic extending its grip round his neck.

He was being literally harried till his flesh came off in flakes by Candlish, Begg, Chambers and a host of others, each one taking turns handing the lash to the next, each one's face contorted with exaggerated scorn while his assailant cursed him.

'You thought to undermine my authority,' Crack!

'You mock me and the League in your rag!' Crack!

'I know every word you are writing. And did you really think you were my equal!'

He jumped out of bed and went to the window, convinced he had heard someone in the garden. After standing trembling in his nightshirt, he went back to bed with a new terror oozing through his brain like molten metal. It was not the likes of Chambers and Begg he really feared, or even Candlish. He thought of Alia and then of her brother. Could the characters in your books come back to demand retribution? If you knew your characters like no one else, they might know your secrets, your weaknesses too. How did he defend himself from them?

He reached under the bed to clasp the cool barrel of his rifle.

'Let them come, I am ready for them.'

Tara

Elspeth had never seen Enric so upset. The four of them had gone directly to Hugh Miller's office where a surprised Fairly had allowed Enric to collect his books and papers. He asked if Enric thought Hugh could receive a visit, 'When he has these attacks, he often needs to spend days in isolation, so I don't know whether to go.'

Enric was finishing bundling up his things and the others were already waiting impatiently in the coach, when Fairly threw his grenade.

'They say you are a spy.'

'What?' This was the second shock Enric had received that day and he was still dazed from the first.

'They say that is why Chambers banished you from his office and why he sent you here.'

Enric later told Elspeth that was the moment he had decided to fight.

'We need to get to the root of these calumnies.'

He had determined to go and see Chambers but realised that he would be denied permission even if the man was in Edinburgh at the moment and that he could lose the last job that was left him.

'It is the Reverend Hardie we have to attack,' Alia said, with that new steely look that came into her eyes these days.

Perhaps only now did Hugh's business partner feel he had the liberty to attack, Enric had told himself as he stood in front of the office door. Well, he would not take it.

'I have lived in Scotland for ten years and people still look at me when I speak a foreign language or read in one. The boys at the printing shop joke with me about my uncle the Czar, but that, I thought, was just teasing. Now you come out with it directly. It is true that Mr Chambers sent me to Mr Miller, perhaps because he was enchanted by my work. But he lost any interest a while ago and I am not in any correspondence with him now. Everything I discussed with Mr Chambers and with Mr Miller was in the strictest confidence. I am not Mr Miller's enemy and regret he sees me as such. I hope his health improves and now I am happy to bid you too goodbye, sir.'

That was the first door Enric had slammed behind him in many years. He had the feeling it would not be the last. He was breathless, perhaps because of the long speech, perhaps because some of his optimism had been knocked out of him, he later confided to Roddie when they took a walk around town and ended up in the snug bar at Mathieson's. They both remarked on the irony of the foreigner showing the Scotsman round his capital city.

'It is much changed since when I lived here. All these new suburbs, and the Old Town is a husk, the poverty and overcrowding even worse than when I left. When its heart was burned down in the Great Fire, they talked about refurbishing it all. The biggest change is George IV Bridge and Victoria Street going down to the Grassmarket. All very elegant but the nearby tenements are still falling apart. The rich have all escaped.'

'Like you to Canada!'

'Yes, I suppose there is a danger for a country if it exports so many of its people.'

'It seems to me that Scotland is one of the few cases in history where a nation can industrialise and the people still remain poor. In Germany and Northern Italy, even in the Basque country and to some extent in Barcelona, there has been a steady rise in the standard of living. Industrialisation doesn't seem to have done that here.'

They went on talking about the mysteries and contradictions of Scotland and Roddie answered questions about Canada. Like others, Roddie found it difficult to understand why Enric had come to Edinburgh and why he had stayed so long.

'I don't know how you can even stand the weather!'

Being in Matheson's and answering such questions carried Enric's mind back to that first conversation with John Arthur. How long ago all that seemed, how young he had been in spirit and in body!

'I had too much sun as a youngster, so it's only the darkness of the winter here that bothers me. I came because I had read about the Edinburgh Enlightenment and in Paris people sang the praises of the intellectual culture here. And I felt sure I could find a job.'

He took a sip of his ale and placed it back on the table. He enjoyed the heaviness of the pint, its quiet thump when he set it down. Roddie looked over the table at him.

'Aye well, Edinburgh is full of breweries, but I don't think that is what brought you here or is keeping you. And you yourself have told me of the cultural decline of the city. What was it you said about the magazines?'

'Oh, that the only cultural organ still published here is the *North British Review* by the Free Church. Even Chambers' *Edinburgh Journal* has dropped the city's name and the *Edinburgh Review* is now published in London! Hugh, I mean Mr Miller, is convinced that Edinburgh is just a provincial town now. But I need to forget about that mad fellow.'

'It took me a while and he hasn't forgotten about me! Ach, I should not joke, we left him in a sad state. Go on with telling me why you decided to move to Scotland.'

'Well, the reasons that brought you to a place are often not the ones you find when people ask. Have you not felt that in Canada? Do you just tell people you love building oval houses and the wood is in plentiful supply there?'

'Yes, I do. I don't tell them I was running away from a hard, cruel place, from a land where people didn't love me, where because of one mistake I was an outcast.'

Roddie paused then insisted, 'So why did you leave home and come to the other end of Europe? Why are you still here? Are the police in Europe after you?'

'No, no, it's not that!'

'Well, you would not be alone if they were. I have some experience of that myself. So?'

Enric had to stop himself from crying. Why had no one ever just asked him these questions before, or at least others like this? He realised he had been hoping for someone to do so, someone he could trust not to judge him. He realised with a shock that perhaps that was why he felt he could tell Roddie but not Elspeth. Perhaps it was because he knew Roddie would be off back to Canada soon, but no, there was something in this man's nature that called to him, that said he would understand.

At the same time Alia and Elspeth were making plans to travel down to Inveresk and the Borders. Roddie had offered to pay for a coach and they decided they needed a couple of days.

'We may have to hunt him down,' Elspeth said. They were both excited, freed at last by having made the decision.

'You and Enric seem to be getting on better,' Alia said.

'Yes, though it is not completely right. Sometimes I feel he is holding something back from me.'

'That is always possible with men. But forgive me, Elspeth. Might it not just be that you still feel the weight of the secret you were carrying around and see others as hiding something away too?'

'Perhaps. But have you noticed Enric never uses both his surnames?'

'Well in Scotland we only have one. So that must be the reason. What is it again?'

'He received a letter from Barcelona last week, addressed to Enric Serra i M A R I S T A N Y.' Elspeth spelled out the last word.

'Well, if you can't even say the word, there is your explanation.'

'You don't use your Thompson surname when you can avoid it.'

Alia's face reddened. It was a hard but fair riposte. She was about to hit back when she remembered their new resolution to 'hold onto joy, and each other.' She made some more tea, took a sip and told her own and her brother's story. She talked in fits and starts, at times drying her eyes, at times letting Elspeth take her hand. As she told the story, she realised she was forgiving people, even forgiving places. Not her bastard father nor De Quincey nor Hardie. But all the rest. It felt good. Why had she never told her story to anyone except Nell before?

When Enric and Roddie got back they found the two women changed in some way. Elspeth noticed that there was something different in Enric.

'Roddie, I have told Alia our story. I am sorry if you feel I have betrayed you.'

'Ach no, Alia. It's a cliché but Hamish taught me that the truth does set you free. I am glad you did. It means you have found a friend.'

He turned to Enric.

'Now man, go on, tell Elspeth what you told me. She needs to hear it. Alia and I can go into another room'

'No, I would like you to stay. I may need help. I am such a coward sometimes and what I have to tell you frightens me. Can we sit beside the fireplace? It is where families talk in Catalonia, that may help me.'

It took a few minutes to arrange the chairs and move stools and tables out of the way so the four of them could sit down. Elspeth's face darkened as she imagined the most terrible secrets: murder, adultery, robbery. No, no, she whispered to herself, Enric has always been straight and gentle with me, though Nell told me about his fight at the dance. She looked over at Roddie and he signalled to her with his right hand as if to say, stay calm, just listen.

Enric started to speak. He looked at the floor as he talked, occasionally glancing up at Elspeth and shifting in his seat as if wounded.

'I received a letter last week which means I have to make a decision; one I have been putting off for years. My father is unable to go on with the family business due to his advanced years. The family want me to take over, as the new Hereu. Enric began to speak in a mixture of Catalan and English. He was losing control.

Roddie interrupted him. 'Let me explain to the lassies what you told me about that. It seems in Catalonia the eldest son inherits everything; the rest get nothing. The younger brothers have to devote themselves to other business and commerce. Enric's older brother has just passed away and now his father expects him to return and take over the family concern.'

'Thank you, Roddie, please intervene if something I am saying is not clear. My father started a sail-making business over thirty years ago, taking advantage of the clothmaking expertise of the Barcelona area and the bay of El Masnou where boats can take anchor safely. It has done very well.'

He looked up.

'Ah, Elspeth and Alia, I can see you think this is just about me wanting to shirk my duty and that after all there are worse things than an inheritance to bear. I wish it were so simple. You see, like my younger brothers I went to seek my fortune on my own, training as a naval engineer and working for different shipping lines. I was one of the youngest technical navigators in Spain. And then my cousin, Joan Maristany i Galcerán, persuaded me to join him on his own boat, to sail to Guiana and make our fortune. Even as a boy, he was wild, a crazy fellow. We gave him the name everyone calls him by, 'Tara.' It means crazy, mad, in a sick way, and he has lived up to it. He was much younger than me and his father was funding the expeditions; I thought, and I think the family hoped, I could control him.'

Enric was sweating now. The room was dark and full of flickering shadows from the gaslights. Elspeth drew her shawl tighter around her shoulders.

'When we got to Guiana, he produced boxes filled with cheap glass jewels, beads, for what they call in Spanish the 'táctica de la chaquira.' That means the ploy of attracting people with shiny beads and objects. We went deep into the jungle and tried it out. We made friends with the natives that way, won their confidence. At dawn on our third day, we rounded up the women and children, the young boys, a few grown men. We shackled them and marched them back to the ship.'

Elspeth made to stand up, to leave, but Alia put her hand on her leg to urge her to stay still.

'I can still hear them wailing. The voyage back was terrible. We sailed to the West Indies and sold them there then bought goods with our loot to sell in Barcelona. That trade has gone on to these days although my cousin has moved onto Peru and if slavery is banned there he has plans to go to Polynesia. There is no limit to his greed and cruelty.'

'When I got back to Catalonia, I told my family I was leaving, that I wanted no share in the business, in the money, in the nice houses they were building for themselves. My father promised me I could work in the sail-making business. But how can a business that is built on funds from slavery be ethical? I looked around for something else to turn my hand to, but when I examined things closely, I saw that everything was built on some type of slavery. I, I had a breakdown, a mental collapse of some kind and then one night, when everyone was sleeping, I just left. I left the Maristany surname behind. I made my way towards the French border, and it was there I joined the circus, the only slavery-free business I could find, I told myself.'

Elspeth kept her head down and Enric could not make out her expression. Alia looked straight at him and bowed her head as if taking on part of his burden.

'When I left the circus, I decided to seek out thinkers who defended the rights of all, man and woman, educated and uneducated. I found very few and most of them were consumed with hatred for those of their comrades who disagreed with them. I met a Scotsman in Paris. He seemed a free soul. And I came here, a corner of Europe where no one would know me, no one would come looking for me. And you know the rest. Now they want me to go back. They say the business has faltered and only I can save it. I still love my parents and my sisters and brothers and have stayed away because I told myself that if I went back and met Tara again, I would kill him. But I realise I am a coward. Perhaps that is the real reason I am here.'

There was silence, like the stillness that comes after the occurrence of some great calamity, the death of a relation, the demolition of a building, the sudden firing of pistols. At last Roddie stood up and put his hand on Enric's shoulder.

'Mr Miller's Calvinism has affected you, my friend. Or rather the whole mad Scottish obsession that we are all born guilty, can do nothing to escape our fate and must accept the preordained judgement of God. I felt cursed for years till a good man showed me that virtue does exist, that we can be straight and honest. We do not need to be trapped in the mire we were born into or were foolish enough to step into. And we need to be modest about what we can do. The Tuscarora tribe who inhabit the lands around where I live in Canada, have a saying, 'Man has responsibility, not power.' It seems to me you have done what you could with the power you have, and you have accepted your responsibility for what you have done and what's more, you are acting honestly without the bribe of salvation. But it is good you have let go of your secret, Enric. Secrets kill people.'

Alia looked on with amazement at her brother. He had adopted more than a different accent in Canada. She felt she was called upon to say something too, if only to make Elspeth's lack of response less wounding.

'Roddie is right, but we are at least responsible for recognising what we are doing and not justifying it through the faults of others or by calling virtue in ourselves what we call vice in them. I have come to realise that was what I was doing in carrying on my private profession for all these years.'

She sighed and looked at the two men. Both were grave as they took in what they all had said. Suddenly the silence was shattered by the sound of a chair tumbling backwards.

'These are all just words, replacing old lies with new ones. Enric, I cannot forgive you! Not a word of this in all the time we have known each other, just magic tricks and intellectual fancies. I am sorry, I cannot forgive you and know I won't forgive myself for not doing so, but it is impossible. Those poor women and children!'

And with that Elspeth rushed from the room and once again there was a slamming of doors and a crashing of hearts.

Scepticism on a Plate

The bee kept crashing softly against the windowpane in fuzzy panic, distracting him from the contemplation of the garden and drowning out the soothing sigh of the waves on the shore. He had tried to liberate it by opening the lower part of the window but whenever it could be persuaded to cease searching for the crack in the invisible wall it flew back once more, to almost exactly the same spot. At first this bothered him so much he was forced to stand up and take a walk around the room. He did this constantly nowadays, when the noise of the children disturbed him, when someone knocked too hard at the door, when he could hear the loud whispers of Lydia talking to the servants, trying not to molest him, she said, but what was she really saying to them?

Why did the stricken insect bother him so? Ah, he remembered: just yesterday he had written a fine paragraph. It had cost him two hours work, but that was not unusual now. And it wasn't yesterday, he supposed, but yesternight, as he could only really write after dark now. Perhaps that was not true, just that writing at night meant he could avoid the dreams and the people who came to visit him and those who beckoned him from beyond the glass to come and walk. Well, he couldn't avoid them completely, they increasingly stepped out of his dreams and left clues of their existence in papers that had been moved, cups overturned, little notes that resembled his own hand but were full of things he would never say.

'*And yet it may be remarked that such of the lower animals as are guided by pure instinct are greatly more infallible within their proper spheres than the higher, half-reasoning animals. The mathematical bee never constructs a false angle; the sagacious dog is not unfrequently out in his calculations. The higher the animal in the scale, the greater its liability to error.'*

'*it may be remarked*,' that was good, his old Augustan style, abstract but not too impersonal, lending objectivity to what some might regard as mere opinion. But here was the '*mathematical bee*,' another fine phrase, putting him in the wrong. The ungrateful creature! No, no, Hugh man, the next line got you out, '*within their proper spheres*'; a study in Portobello was not the bee's '*proper sphere*.' He sat down again, relieved. Why did these details concern him so? Why did he doubt himself so much? Why was so much he was writing becoming an argument with himself rather than an attack on *Vestiges*?

If '*within their proper spheres*' saved his defence of the accuracy of instinct, it led to questions over the influence of those spheres, those environments, on the creatures that inhabited them. And that led away from unique creation of every species by God to the development theory. He stood up and paced about again.

How many species were there? People like the late Professor Forbes seemed to find new ones every day. Perhaps that proved his own defence of unique creation: only God could conceive such multitudinous diversity, and it was He, after all, who created the environment. God could stop now, as His purpose in preparing a home for Man was done. No newly created species had ever been found, they were all there in the fossil record, till…till they weren't, and the Creator snapped his fingers and established new conditions and their corresponding creatures, ones not derived from the previous inhabitants of the Earth. That was the testimony of geology showing the ordered emergence of new species of animals and plants with clear breaks between the three great ages. The botanist or zoologist was so easily overwhelmed by profusion that they could not stand up to the infinite series proposed by the atheist. '*Every plant and animal that now lives upon earth began to be during the great Tertiary period and had no place among the plants and animals of the great Secondary division.*' There, he had taken out the '*it has been remarked,*' from that sentence. It was a fact; one he would stake his life on. One he had staked his life on.

He picked up a sheet of paper and slipped it between the insect and the pane then flicked it till the bee was swatted down and could fly out through the raised bottom. He smiled. He felt relieved, released somehow, as if he were the bee.

His uncle James had had a collie dog in Cromarty. While everyone had remarked on how smart it was, how adept at picking up new tricks, how it looked like it understood you as it peered up into your eyes, it was then that he noticed all the mistakes it made, the false paths it took, the way it scurried about trying to remember where it had hidden its favourite stick. Error and intelligence go together. Wasn't that the lesson of Adam's fall? Did it mean the more intelligent you were, the greater the sinner too?

He laughed to himself in that strange bitter way that had taken over him these days. Well, he hadn't been a great sinner, so what did that say about his intellectual capacity? He had battled a bit as a youngster, picked fights with anyone who wouldn't run away, but he had confessed to that in *My Schools and Schoolmasters*. He had left out his visits to the theatre with Chas, but then it didn't fit, it was not intellectually coherent with his arguments about the working man. Had that been wrong? And there was that woman he had met on the road to Cromarty, a woman of the street. She had given him succour and he had even written about her. Well, not all about her. It was scientific truth that interested him, and he had never knowingly betrayed it just as, since he came to live in Edinburgh he had not betrayed the principles of his religion. Careful, Hugh, careful, you are getting too intelligent there!

Chas, Alia and now Enric. Characters in the fiction of his life, those stories we tell ourselves and others or choose not to tell. Was he just a character in other people's stories? Bah, he was beginning to sound like Gilfillan, that complicated sophist. How he had laughed when McCosh had read out loud from Aytoun's satire of the poet, *Firmillian*! It really was too cruel. He liked McCosh. He was the only one of the old friends, save for Guthrie, who came to visit him out of more than social duty now. Though he sensed he disappointed McCosh, that the man felt he contributed more than he received from their intercourse.

Perhaps he should turn back to poetry. Since perhaps the death of Burns or at least the demise of Scott, there had been no national Bard, despite the number of pretenders like Alexander Smith, or Gilfillan or Aytoun. He shook his head as the temptation tickled his hair like a teasing lover. He thought of Willie Ross and how he had finally mustered up the courage to tell Hugh that he was wasting his time as a poet, that his strengths lay elsewhere. Poor Willie. He had heard that Forbes had described him to Goodsir as 'always poetic but not necessarily aesthetic.' Well, that was a typical dismissal by a gentleman of someone from the lower classes. It stung him though, coming from Forbes.

There was a knock at the door and the housemaid entered. A new one, it seemed. Jennie, was it? He pointed to the table he wanted his tea set down on and waited till she had left before he checked the door was closed fast. He was not sealing himself in but trying to keep the others out. He looked over at the chimney grate to check there were no footprints there, then checked himself, shocked at his fancy.

He had left poetry behind and moved on to defending John Knox and the true Calvinism. Oh, those heady days before and after the Disruption, tumbling opponents of the truth and of Chalmers with blows of hammering prose. It had all gone awry with the passing away of the old man. How he missed Chalmers' hand on his shoulder, his soft quiet encouragement emitted in short phrases like blossom flying down on the breeze. No one praised him like that any longer. Lydia would sigh when he talked about Chalmers as if to say, he is gone now and, in any case, no one reads him, he is like the Scott Monument, imposing but somehow stuck in another time, when Scotland was gothic, was heroic, not commercial and thrusting as it is today. And what had he and Chalmers achieved? They had not only split the Kirk in two, but split it from the country, making both congregations just one more option in the spiritual marketplace.

He had been a workman who wrote poetry, then a banking clerk who wrote journalism, a layman who spoke in the name of divinity and now just an amateur writing about science. Yes, he knew that was what they said, and perhaps they were right. Perhaps he was not really anything. When thoughts like this assailed him, he would remember his father alone in the pitching cabin in the North Sea, himself until the end, undiminished by the hostile elements. Or was that just how he wanted to remember him? Early death has the advantage of fixing you unchanged in people's memory, he supposed; it defines you, sharpens the blurred edges. He felt increasingly like a smudge on life, something that people could see but not make out properly, an irritation, an almost-thing. He must stop now; this was just aimless rambling.

His head ached and his lungs were burning. The stonemason's disease they called it. Why did people think that the simple act of naming something made it better, made it easier to bear? There was no name for what he was feeling right now. Perhaps he should call Lydia, have her soothe his brow with a cold compress. He made to stand up but slumped down again. No, she would just insist that he stopped working, or worse, she would bring the children in to 'cheer him up.' The three youngest ones were a mystery to him; he hoped they were happy and would grow up to be fine adults, but he did not really recognise himself in any of them. He hoped it was not apparent and winced as he remembered his mother's lament that the fever had taken his two sisters instead of him. His mother was still alive, a smoky exhalation beside the fireplace in Cromarty, telling her ghost stories, still seething at Lydia's dislike of her. She had never come to Edinburgh. She had never been invited. Lydia's mother visited from Inverness, but then, as Lydia said, she knew how to behave in polite society, she was educated. Sometimes, when he thought of his mother and his stepfather with their two daughters, he had that feeling we all have sometimes in moments of childhood despair that we have been kidnapped, that we can't possibly belong to these people. However, he was no child and perhaps it was just the result of Lydia's endless carping about his silly, superstitious mother. 'A bad influence on you, Hugh,' she would say, and in front of visitors too!

He loved Lydia. She had been a good mother, he supposed, and had supported him and given him a push when he needed one. And sometimes when he did not. She had a sharp eye for money too, and this house had been a sound investment. She managed much of his negotiations with publishers behind the scenes and had a keen eye for what would sell. However, she was disappointed in him, he could tell that by the way she commented on the success of the Candlishes, or her laments at never being invited by Chambers and his circle. He had been disappointed in Chambers too. They had seemed to be getting on well in their meetings in Waterloo Place, but then he had just been dropped and kept away by the substitution of the publisher by Mr Serra. Chambers had seemed cold to the new book he was working on. Perhaps they were not as alike as Hugh had fondly supposed.

The door was pushed open and Harriet appeared.

'Papa, I have brought you some rosewater. I made it myself from petals from the garden.'

His instinct was to send her away, but he had done that too often already. And she was his special child, with her mother's neatness and a talent for writing that equalled Lydia's flowing prose and an acuteness of observation that he hoped she had inherited from him. She had a lovely long slender neck and dark oval eyes. She would make some man a good wife.

He loosened his shirt collar so she could pass the towel with the rosewater around his neck. It felt good. He closed his eyes and willed his lungs to clear while she put her hand in his. All of a sudden, she buried her head in his shoulder, as she used to as a young girl, and began to cry, telling him he had to rest, he had to get strong, that she needed her father, that she would always be at his side whenever he needed her. She said more, but he understood the words were not important, it was all a cry for help. But how could he help her if he could not help himself? He suggested they say a prayer and that seemed to work, for her at least. She left the room and said her mother would be up shortly. Lydia's back was causing her pain again, which is why she slept downstairs. She said that climbing up to see him gave her an hour's pain. So her coming up was an act of love, he supposed. You never can tell with a sore back though, unless there is a clear dislocation or inflammation. Lydia had neither.

He kept his eyes closed but was careful not to fall asleep so as not to let the monsters in. He pinched his arm every few minutes to keep himself alert. He was in a daze. Days were passing. Days. He played with the sound. And then he thought of his first days in Edinburgh and that painful time with the workers in Niddrie and his farewell to Willie. And he remembered the Panorama, the first he had seen. Now he saw creation as a Panorama, with each day in Genesis as a different prophetic scene. Yes, Genesis was not a simple account but a vision, with the curtain falling at the end of each day then rising to reveal the next. And a day was not a period, neither the twenty-four hours some saw it as nor the epoch he and others had previously defended: the biblical day is what Moses saw in a single vision. And visions cannot last long, they are granted only briefly. If we see the seven days of creation as seven visions, we remove them from the province of chronology and the accuracy of Revelation is preserved.

He sprang up and hurried over to his writing-desk. It took him two hours to forge these thoughts into words which did not melt at the first questioning. Nevertheless, he was elated. He stood up to stretch and then his eye caught that day's edition of *The Times*. How had it got into his room? Lydia normally gave it to him, and they would read and comment on the news together. However, he had not heard or seen her. What day was it? He picked up the newspaper and saw it was Tuesday. He must go to the office in case Fairly needed help for tomorrow's *Witness*. Fairly was a good fellow. He had got used to running the newspaper without Hugh ever since that time a few years ago when Hugh had gone on a tour of England to see if he could overcome the lowness of spirit that had assaulted him after the struggle with Candlish.

The door was ajar, and he hurried to press it shut. He would calm down, change his shirt, this one was soaked in sweat. He wanted to go down and see Lydia. He would tell her about his discovery and perhaps she would be impressed with him, though her admiration seemed to have subsided as the years passed. They would go for a walk on the beach together if the weather was fine enough. He stuck his head through the open window and at the bottom of the garden could see the two boys playing. They were building something out of odd pieces of wood, with William handing pieces to his brother. Then Bessie came running out holding one of his old shirts. They were building a scarecrow! He ducked his head back in, sure that they would want to surprise him with it later. He stood beside the curtain and peeked out again, laughing at himself for playing hide-and-seek like a bairn. What a strange head the creature had, with a long wolf-like nose. It reminded him of the Egyptian paintings and statues he had seen in the Museum in London. Their false gods assumed the form of brutes, only the true God took on man's form as the only one that could have united Him directly at once with the matter and the mind of the of the universe. Nature is matter, God is mind, man is matter and mind. He must write this down!

Lydia found him two hours later, asleep at his desk, his shirt tails flapping in the breeze from the window, his papers scattered on the floor. She picked them up and was startled at the crude rough sketches of wolfmen and snakes.

'Hugh,' she said. 'I have brought you your dinner. You must eat. You haven't touched your breakfast.'

He nodded weakly and smiled as if it were just another ordinary day, as if he had just come back from the office or from collecting specimens on the shore. He watched as she laid the tray on the table. It was covered with a teacloth, to keep the food warm, she said.

'What horrible drawings' she shivered. 'I hate snakes.'

He explained about the scarecrow and the Egyptians and about matter and mind. She did not seem to be following him.

'It is true the snake is a poisonous creature and as such it figures among the lowliest most degenerate creatures, just as the tribes who use venom are lower than the civilised races. That is why God created the snake just before the advent of man. The first in creation, like the angels, are always the most perfect.'

Lydia frowned. She felt like telling him she wanted a conversation and not another lecture. She felt like telling him she wanted her husband back and not this doddering rambling old man. She knew that to be passed over not once, but twice for the Edinburgh Chair left vacant again by Professor Forbes' death had wounded her husband's pride, his sense of self-worth, perhaps irrevocably. He was inconsolable. She, at least, felt she could not console him, or perhaps would not console him. Timbers cracked under less strain than she had suffered in the last years, her mother had said to her on her last visit. Her back started to throb again and she told him she had to go down to the children, Harriet was in one of her nervous moods today and the younger ones were too trying for her, poor dear. And hand on hip she left him.

Hugh sighed. He pulled off the cover and almost screamed. A flounder! He hated flounders and she knew it! It was a degenerate, ugly, misshapen fish yet one of the oldest found in the fossil record. It was scepticism on a plate!

One Definition of Hell

On the final day of his period of notice at the printing shop, Enric received a call to Waterloo Place. When he arrived he was met by an unusually abashed Mr Johnson, who told him that his master could not meet him personally but wanted to thank him for his labours. He handed Enric a letter of reference that he said he was free to use in any other country except the United Kingdom.

'Mr Chambers as a rule, does not meet with ex-employees.'

'I am still an employee, but no matter. Mr Chambers already gave me a letter, which I presumed was the reference.'

'Did you not open it?'

'I was not sure of leaving his employ just then, it is among my papers at home.'

He left Waterloo Place for the last time and walked towards the Mound, past the prematurely greying Scott Monument then up and over to Mathieson's to meet up with John Arthur.

'I mind the first time we met and you came to see Dr. Knox. A sad case that. He has now found it impossible to get a university post and he was turned down for medical service in Crimea because at sixty-three he was judged too old. The man has more energy than a platoon of Cossacks!'

'So how does he occupy himself?

'Well, he gives talks. I saw him at one last month in the Tanfield Hall. He has been working on a new edition of his book, *The Races of Men*. Each race is suited to its environment, he maintains. We Lowland Scots must be smoky creatures, I said to him, but he didna laugh. I think he is a bit put out that his most recent publication has sold more than any of his other works.'

'What does it deal with?'

'*Fish and fishing in the lone glens of Scotland.* It's aboot salmon!'

They had talked on until the tavern closed under the new licencing laws. John Arthur had offered his hand to bid his friend farewell and almost jumped off the pavement when Enric made to embrace him in a hug.

'It's no oor way. Folk willna ken ye are a foreigner and what will they think?'

It was like a key clicking the door shut. All these years, and still a foreigner. Perhaps I should go straight home to Catalonia, Enric thought as he walked down the Lothian Road. Back to the sun, to folk who looked like him, walked like him. But they didn't think like him. Not anymore.

• • •

When he pushed the heavy front door open, he spied the light from the kitchen. Two people were talking. He took off his jacket, put down his satchel and went into the room to find Alia and her brother sitting at the table around a pot of ale and some cheese and soused herrings laid out on a brown earthenware plate. Roddie beckoned him to join them and poured some ale into a mug.

'We were waiting for you,' Roddie said, and Alia nodded.

There was something strange in seeing Alia as part of something, of a group and not the pure individual she had always seemed to Enric. But it was a good strange; she looked happy in the way that someone who has found their place does.

'We are off to give the Reverend Hardie a fright tomorrow,' Roddie said.

Before Enric could respond Alia answered him.

'Elspeth and Roddie and I are all going.'

Enric felt wrong-footed again as he had with John Arthur; was this an invitation or an apology?

'Well, as you know, today was my last shift at work.'

Alia reached across to place her hand on his.

'You would be welcome to come, we have talked to Elspeth and she wasn't too happy at first, but that's not the problem. It's just that Maggie would be on her own. She refuses to go over to Fife to stay with Nell and Alec, told me it was a plot to get rid of her. We can't take her along as we do not know what awaits us. It would be of great help if you could stay with her here.'

Enric drank from the mug as if looking for an answer in the brown frothy liquid.

'Elspeth will settle, Enric. She is agitated by the thought of confronting Hardie and seeing her mother again.'

Enric finished his ale, replaced the mug on the table exactly on the damp ring he had lifted it from, nodded and went to his room.

The next morning, while Maggie was still asleep Alia and Roddie slipped out of the house, both giving Enric a farewell hug. For some reason that seemed to knock him off balance and he stood awkwardly on the doorstep waving goodbye to them. Elspeth had bought the tickets to Dunbar and was waiting for them at the station, impatient to catch the North British Line train already grunting and clinking at the platform.

The thirty-mile journey seemed to last an eternity. Roddie shouted out as they rolled past Inveresk and seemed to be studying the terrain, the brown fields and the sycamore trees. Alia supposed he was running over his boyhood flight down to Dunbar, but who knew? She had no idea what Elspeth was thinking either as she appeared to have taken a vow of silence. She had looked both relieved and disappointed at Enric's absence when she had met them. Alia occupied the trip in going over the plan they had elaborated. First, she would approach Elspeth's mother. If she could win her confidence, she would bring in her daughter and they would offer her protection if she helped them against Hardie. It had all sounded so easy in Edinburgh; now with every rock and rattle of the carriage, bits seemed to detach themselves from their design. What if the woman would not even talk to her?

At Dunbar, the two of them waited as Roddie went in search of a carriage, leaving them standing on the platform with the sea breeze nipping at their dresses like a nervous puppy. With every gust of air, Elspeth seemed to be shrinking; she had lost several inches since they had left the city, Alia thought to herself, then shook her head. I must concentrate. I must get her through this.

'This all seems so far from Edinburgh, from home.'

Elspeth shuddered at the word, 'home.' If a train had arrived at that moment, she would have got on it. However, Roddie pulled up in the coach and Alia helped her mount. She then went over the plan, to ensure everyone's agreement and to coordinate their actions.

'When we arrive at Innerwick, Roddie will stay with the coach while you, Elspeth, can visit your father's grave. I will knock on your mother's door and tell her I have an important message for her. If I am well received and can convince her that you have come in search of reconciliation, I will signal to Roddie to fetch you from the cemetery and we will talk to your mother together. If at any time you want to be alone with her, then just say.'

Elspeth only nodded and the silence grew in the carriage till it was like an extra passenger, making the rest shift in their seats and look out of the window as if interested in the scenery, even though it consisted of bland rolling fields and scrubby woodland. In the distance Elspeth could spy the ruined form of the Castle, laid waste by one of Cromwell's generals, the Duke of Somerset, in what was called the 'rough wooing.' She and Alia alighted without saying a word.

'Why did I say I wanted to visit my father's grave?' Elspeth wondered. Could love survive abuse, and if it could, was that a good thing or just a sign of the power of the abuser? She entered the graveyard behind the small kirk after pointing out the dirty black door of her mother's cottage.

Roddie perched on the edge of his seat, following Alia's every step as she walked slowly to the house. The village was deserted and so quiet that the sound of Alia's knocking on the door reverberated over to him in rhythm to his own heartbeats.

Alia held her breath till the door opened. In front of her stood a small, rather plump frumpy woman, with wisps of mousey brown hair escaping from under her cap. She had Elspeth's eyes but not her daughter's direct way of looking at you. While not welcoming her, the woman showed no hesitation in granting her entry.

'I have nothing better to do today, hen. And my foot is giving it laldy and I canna work. So come in and tell me this important message. I willna buy anything from ye, mind. You don't look like a commercial traveller, but then they turn up in all guises.'

Alia sensed the woman was a talkative person who had few people to chat to. And so it proved. As they sat down on two worn armchairs next to the front window, she could see the woman spent her days peeking out through the lace curtains. Had she spied Roddie and her daughter?

The woman talked without drawing breath. Her name was Annie, but folk called her Agnes. 'Don't ask me why, dear. They say I don't look like an Annie, though I dinna ken what that means. You look like a Susan. Am I on the right track? No? Alia, well that's an unusual name. Are you from a travelling family? No, from Inveresk? That's awfie like Innerwick. A bit too close to Edinburgh and all those Irish tinkers.'

Alia was at a loss how to proceed: it is difficult to establish confidence with someone who is so uninterested in the person she is talking to. After a few minutes more of mind-numbing chatter, Agnes/Annie solved the problem by saying,

'Why don't you call her over? I'm no feart of my daughter if she's no feart of me. But leave the laddie outside.'

'You were expecting us?'

'No' exactly, but there had to be a time when the bad penny would turn up here. The Reverend Hardie tell't me it would happen one day, though he called her the prodigal daughter, but that's just his highfalutin way of saying the same thing.'

Elspeth looked alarmed when Alia came to find her so quickly. 'She doesn't want to see me, and you couldn't convince her to change her mind.'

'No convincing was necessary; she turned the tables on me. You never told me your mother was such a determined woman, but then I might have known.' Alia bit her lip, she should not have said that, but now she felt frustrated, seeing their plans come tumbling down.

When they left Roddie again and passed through the half-open door to the cottage, the woman was still seated in the same chair.

'Well, you havenae got any bonnier. You always were a scrawny wee thing, a drip o' water. You took aifter your faither in that too.'

Elspeth's face reddened and she made no reply. Her mother went on, relentlessly.

'You will have seen the braw stane over your poor deserted faither's grave. Paid for not by you, but by the Reverend Hardie.'

She pronounced that name defiantly, as if flaunting knowledge of their joint disgrace and as if to turn the cannon around on them.

Elspeth almost staggered back. Alia gripped her by the arm and attempted to regain ground.

'We wanted to ask you to let bygones be bygones and to know that you and your daughter are not the only victims of this terrible man and that together we can strike back.'

'Victims! I was never a victim. He showed me kindness and understanding before my husband died and even more when I was left alone by that drink-sodden excuse for a man and after he was insulted by this ungrateful daughter of mine.'

'Insulted! He would have raped me!'

'Oh, you always did say the most ridiculous things. Not content with wild accusations against your faither, you had to say dirty, yes dirty things about a man of the cloth. The good man never laid a finger on you. Who would? Look at you, a pretty little sack of bones. Men like women with a bit of body on them, not scarecrows like you. It's all a pack of lies. Instead of thanking him for that lovely dress, for giving work to me and welcoming you to his home you went hysterical, as always. The proof is you ran off!'

Elspeth made to turn and go but was held back by Alia.

'If you do not believe your daughter, how do you explain that the same thing happened to me?'

'The Reverend Hardie never laid a hand on you. Oh yes, I ken all about it, the demon girl of Inveresk they called you. A home breaker, a wanton hussy like your mother. I ken the whole dirty story.'

Now it was Alia's turn to recoil against the blows. How could they have thought of this woman as a possible ally, because of her sex and her motherhood? When would women ever learn? How easy it had been to sit in Edinburgh and plot, like spiders spinning their silken webs unaware of the strength of the prey! She reached into her bag to take out the letters from Hardie but desisted when the old matron smacked her palms together as if shooing off a scabby dog.

'You said you had a message for me, Mrs High-and-Mighty! Well, I am the one with the message and it is to take this ungrateful bitch away with you and to never darken my door again. I am a decent woman and cannot be seen with the likes of you two! Think yourselves lucky the Reverend is in Inveresk and not here to have you driven out of town.'

And with that she spat at their feet and pointed to the door.

They ran across the street like two scared chickens. Roddie was amazed and at first made to go over to the house, imagining they had been victims of some physical attack. He saw the curtains twitch but had to turn back when Alia begged him to just get them away from there. 'It was horrible, horrible, Roddie. Take us away before I am physically sick.'

The two women huddled in the back of the coach while Roddie urged the horse on towards Dunbar. Not since the Scots troops had escaped from Cromwell's onslaught had there been such a dejected retreat from Innerwick.

'We will stay the night at a hostelry in Dunbar and you will tell me what happened and then I will go and see this man. I will give him a fright he has never dreamed of. I have nearly thirty years of grievance in my bones.'

Alia closed her eyes and grimaced. It seemed she and her brother had gone back to the beginning of their story. She could not have phrased it thus, but Enric told her later that this eternal return was one definition of hell.

A Beautiful Face

They sent a telegraph message to Enric to tell him they would be staying overnight in Dunbar then going on to Inveresk on the morrow to see Hardie. Roddie had had to insist on the meeting as his sister and Elspeth were at first adamant on abandoning the venture.

'And do what? Move out of the house and sell it for a pittance? This time I will lead the conversation. I won't be swept away so easily.'

They had argued after that, the first time the three of them had fallen out. As the two women retired early to their room, Roddie stepped out for a walk to calm his spirits. He went down to the harbour and saw himself all those years ago being transported out on the boat over to Fife. He felt sequestered once more as if he were still bobbing about on the schooner on his way to a destination determined by others.

Alia and Elspeth were sharing a bed as they had got the last room available. Alia had stripped to her undergarments with pretended carelessness then clambered up onto the high bed and turned her back to give Elspeth some privacy. Elspeth regarded Alia's soft white shoulders and spine as they lay next to each other in silence, each going over the day's events and wondering where exactly it had all gone wrong. The curtains were flimsy and the shadows from the red-stoned street painted the room in bloody whorls. Alia turned around and saw that Elspeth was still but that eyes were open.

'Tomorrow we will use the letters if we have to, Alia.'

'Yes, but we have to decide what we want from him, Elspeth, and not just how to force him to give it to us.' And on they talked late into the night.

The harbour hadn't changed much, Robbie thought, though there was no sign of McCranish the Chandlers. It was quieter now, no doubt because much of the merchandise these days was transported by road or rail. Business had moved west to Glasgow too. As the swollen sea licked the breakwater with its sullen waves, he was suddenly overwhelmed by a new sensation, a bitter deep pain in his chest. He was homesick for Canada! He felt like a man who has just realised his old lover and he are at an end, despite her beauty and their intimate knowledge of each other's ways. He felt released as he almost saw the ties cut free and blowing out over the waters. He thought of the wide Atlantic and determined to make his way back as soon as possible to his Ontario home. He let himself be sentimental, maudlin even, looking around him and saying goodbye to poor, abandoned Scotland, deserted by so many of its population. He would write to Hamish and tell him to expect him in a month. He hoped Alia would accompany him, but she was difficult to read; she had seemed so decided on their plan this morning and now was all for giving up the fight. Well, he would make Hardie see sense, force him to make amends for the harm done to his family.

He walked up past the red sandstone houses to the hostel and slipped into the dormitory he had to share with two fellow guests. One of them was already asleep but the other, a commercial traveller, he thought, had not returned. Roddie took his boots off and put his trousers under his pillow. He was quickly asleep, dreaming of sailing back to Canada and trying to make out whether Alia was with him. So many weel-kent faces appeared to him, some come to bid farewell, others to welcome, till their faces were blurred. Was she there? Would she come?

He was beckoning to her when he felt a hand shaking his shoulder.

'We have to go, brother, we must get to Inveresk early and catch Hardie before he has time to leave. I shouldn't be in here, but we have been waiting for half an hour.'

When he climbed into the carriage after hitching up the fresh horses, Elspeth and Alia had already mounted. They both looked tired and drawn. At least nobody was arguing, he thought as they started off, leaving the stirring town behind, and heading inland.

Alison Clerk, Reverend Hardie's housekeeper, had travelled with her master to Inveresk just a few days before. She hoped this would be the last time she visited the place, not just because of the need to bring the towels and bedsheets as well as fresh crockery, but because her master seemed to turn even more melancholy and bitter when he stepped into the old Manse. He had bought it from the Church and many local people gossiped about their tithes being used for speculation, at least so Janet Ramsay, the housecleaner, had told her while they made the bed.

'And folk laugh at him,' Janet whispered, as she gave a pillow a smack to plump it up. 'At first they had pitied him when his wife wouldna come back frae England. And then they started to feel sorry for the way they treated the Thompson family. Calum said that Roddie had aye been good to him, and Jessie was a hard worker. The lassie was a bit strange, it seems, a dreamer, but she was young; my ain Mary can be moody too! It was a long time ago and I hear Roddie came back to the village. Folk say he is a fine, prosperous man; Canada has been the making of him, so maybe it was all for the best.'

Now Alison was making the morning tea to take up to the study adjoining the main bedroom. There were so many stairs in this house and her knees were acting up. She deposited the tray with the tea, milk and bannocks on the polished table by the window along with the morning's post and withdrew. As she descended, she could hear the door to the sleeping-chamber creak open.

At the same time as Arthur Hardie was reading his mail and sipping his tea, and Roddie, Alia and Elspeth were riding towards Inveresk, Enric was clearing out his room. He had been up all night, a ritual he followed when he had decided to quit a place and move on, eradicating his traces, packing up, in the past to avoid pursuit, but now to make changing his mind more difficult. He had not quite decided where to go next, nor whether he would wait and say goodbye to Alia and her brother, and Elspeth. He could not bear to see the accusation in Elspeth's eyes and though he had already taken her reproach into his heart, he did not know if he could stand to be condemned by the sweep of her hand over her lovely face. If it hadn't been for Maggie, he would have been on the train south by now.

He had only stopped when Maggie had come into the room, bleary-eyed and searching for Alia. He had calmed her by saying they would be back; had shown her the telegram and said she could keep it as a present. He told her he was leaving but she could always come and visit him.

'And Elspeth?'

'I will make us both some breakfast, some eggs and wild mushrooms I picked in Dean Village.'

Maggie had accepted the bribe and not asked any more awkward questions. She kept reading from the telegram while she breakfasted. It was the first one she had seen, she said, and she seemed to regard its staccato print as a magic formula, hiding a spell within it.

'*No luck Innerwick. Staying overnight Dunbar. Last chance Inveresk Manse tomorrow. Home tomorrow night.*'

He left her with it and returned to his room. Only a few things remained to be packed or destroyed. It was then that he found the long yellow envelope lodged in the back of the writing desk drawer. He took a few seconds to identify it as the one Chambers had given him the last time they had met, and he remembered Johnson's remark. When he cut the sleeve open, he realised he would have to dash down to Inveresk and decided it was better to take Maggie than leave her alone. In less than an hour they were both on the train, with the girl laughing and drawing shapes on the steamy windows, and Enric's brow damp with sweat. He kept asking fellow passengers, to make sure they did not miss their stop and after about forty minutes the two clambered down at Musselburgh station. Now how were they to get to Inveresk and would they be able to find the others in time?

• • •

Arthur Hardie let the letter he was reading fall. A place in England, but could he adapt to London? He closed his eyes, not through weariness, or the sopor of old age, as others who saw him doing so increasingly commented. 'As you get older and nearer to passing, you start to spend more and more time visiting the other quarter,' some old fool had sighed to him. He was not dreaming of life after death, but of Susan. He had lost her in life but kept a hold on her through secret investigations of her doings, and in his reveries. For they had been happy, had they not? He had not realised it at the time, but he had been fulfilled not only by her beauty, her smile, but by her harshness, too. Even the deceits only really made sense when it was her he was duping. He still thought of her with every little conquest over the young hussies he took into his, his protection. He was too romantic, that had always been his failing. Look at him now, sitting in the seat she used to sit in, closing his eyes and imagining she was behind him in the bedroom. He had only held onto the house so he could come back and recapture moments like this.

He was ejected from his daydreams by a rapping at the door and then the entrance of Mrs Clerk. This was most unseemly but also unusual enough to warn him something was afoot. Had the Duke died? It was difficult to get her to make sense; it was like talking to a sparrow, her speech reduced to chirps and her head bobbing back and forward. When he succeeded in getting her to compose herself, he learned that three adults had barged their way into the house and were waiting in the dining room to see him. Two women and one fearsome-looking fellow who had told her that if Mr Hardie was not down in five minutes he would come up and fetch him himself. They had warned her not to run away or help her master to do so. 'They also said it was to your advantage to see them.'

This was not the first time he had had to face outraged parishioners or raging fathers. He could not think of any recent reason for such ire, but he determined to see it through, as he had many before. Calmness was all, it disarmed the beasts. 'I will be down in ten minutes, Mrs Clerk. I need to make myself decent. Serve them a cup of tea and see if it helps to civilise them.'

When he stepped into the room, he saw what he called later the triangle of infamy, with the Thompson woman over on the right near the window, a younger woman, whom he did not at first recognise but who revealed herself to be the daughter of his Inveresk trollop, in front of the other window, and then before the fireplace a dark-haired stocky fellow who was burning with a quiet anger that he understood would be difficult to quench.

'I trust Mrs Clerk has served you tea. Can we act like civilised people? Do sit down and tell me what has brought you to invade my home.'

'Serve us? You believe that's what people and especially women are for, I am sure, but...'

Alia interrupted Elspeth's ascent into a bad-tempered harangue, knowing it was just what would suit their opponent best.

'The last time we met it was in my house, sir. We are only returning the visit. We hope it will be a brief one and end better.'

Hardie sat down. It would be more difficult for the man to assault him if he did not confront him eye to eye.

Alia's voice was clear and firm as she told him they had been down to Innerwick, that she and Elspeth were both willing to publicly shame him and to detail the abuse they had suffered and of how he had abused Elspeth's mother.

'What is your evidence for this slander? It certainly cannot come either from the poor departed father nor Mrs Grieve, a woman who has expressed only gratitude for my kindness towards her. She enjoys her home at my favour. And you, madame, would be literally laughed out of court once your life of sin, not to mention your notorious enmity towards me and your treatment of my wife, were to be made public. It is your words against mine and forgive me for comforting myself which would bear the sway. Now run along, take the very generous offer of purchase of your house, and never let me hear from any of you again. I cannot be eternally patient, I warn you.'

'There are more than just our words, there are your own!'

Elspeth produced the letters, waving the two sheets before the clergyman and reading the dates and the signature out loud. Hardie closed his eyes and concentrated as she read it all. Perhaps he was repenting!

He opened his eyes and smiled.

'The text is ambiguous. That these servant girls would benefit more from my education than that of some rough workingman is something your own mother, Miss Thompson, obviously believed. I could go on, but I assure you I have no doubt that what these purloined letters signify is the opposite of your low insinuations. I am very clear what virtue and consent mean; I regularly preach on them both. And you two? One of you lives off vice and the other off the rotten fruits of that vice.'

'We would be very happy to put that to the court of public opinion.' Elspeth stood her ground, though her hand shook as she handed the letters back to Alia.

'Ah, the court of public opinion, that modern invention. First of all, what makes you think it has not been consulted? There have been several scurrilous rumours spread about me by low, dirty people. My reputation has remained intact. To impugn me is to impugn the Duke of Buccleuch and the sacred Church of Scotland. That may not mean much to you three, but it still holds sway among decent people. And, in any case, no reputable organ would dare publish such slander.'

'Aye, well, we will maybe have to test that.' Alia stepped forward, shoulder to shoulder with Elspeth.

'Go ahead. I should just warn you that all the correspondence between my unfortunate wife and myself was classed as non-disclosable under legal order as part of our separation settlement. Anyone wishing to break the seal would be subject to severe penalties. My lawyers would see to that. So do your worst, but do it far from here. I insist you be gone from my sight! This minute! I will suffer no more outrage!'

It was yesterday all over again, just in fancier language, both Alia and Elspeth realised. They looked over at each other as if to say, how do we retreat intact from this? How do we rescue ourselves?

'Should I just hit him and run off back to Canada?' Roddie thought, before he realised the irony. History often tragically repeats itself in the struggles between the powerful and the poor, but this would be just farce. He had hoped his presence would intimidate the man.

'Hold on a moment. You may think you can browbeat two women, but I will not bend so easily. You have persecuted my sister and I demand justice.'

Hardie turned his head towards Roddie and studied him from head to foot, like a piece of livestock.

'If it isn't the young criminal! My, my! Despite the prayers of the faithful it seems some people really are beyond redemption. I would caution you against violence, justice is harsh on repeat offenders.'

Roddie cursed and said he would be off to Canada where the police could not catch him, but he and Hardie could both sense the empty bluster of his threat.

Hardie stood up and waved his hand towards the door. 'Mrs Clerk has gone to request the presence of a member of the local constabulary. You are welcome to await their arrival and be charged with unlawful entry to my property and threats to my person. I suggest, however, you hotfoot it immediately back to your own abode.'

As he said this, the housekeeper did indeed enter the room, accompanied not by the police but by Enric and Maggie!

The girl ran over to embrace Alia, while everyone stood open-mouthed. The housekeeper whispered to Hardie that the foreign gentleman had told her he had come to take the intruders away and the wee girl had confirmed it.

'And he seemed a polite, douce sort of lad.'

'And what if they hold us hostage, you silly woman!'

Enric exchanged a few words first with Alia, then Roddie. He was elegantly dressed in a long-frocked jacket with loose sleeves, a white shirt and red cravat. He nodded to Elspeth who lowered her eyes. He now stood in the middle of the room and addressed Hardie directly. The minister still wore the mantle of victory and seemed relieved that the two men had not come to manhandle him.

'Mr Hardie. That you have been deaf to decency, that you have mistreated us all and refused to make amends does not surprise though it does sadden me.'

Enric ran a hand through his black hair and the air seemed filled with electricity. His eyes flashed and he commanded the room, a showman in front of his audience. Only the minister seemed unimpressed.

'May I suggest you save all of us time. I am the only one authorised to preach here. Please take your friends away, as you promised Mrs Clerk. I have no intention of listening to more defamatory accusations without one shred of evidence to support them.'

Enric laughed then walked over to where the housekeeper stood. He reached behind her and as if by magic produced two sheaves of yellow paper from her collar. He held them up so they all could see the frontispiece with an eye, and WE NEVER SLEEP on each.

'I have been a printer for more than a decade. I inform you of that fact to explain that it would be a simple matter for me to have printed more copies of this document in addition to the two here. Before going further, I would recommend that your housemaid withdraws and takes Maggie to the kitchen with her.'

They were mesmerised. Hardie gestured to Mrs Clerk to do as Enric said and once the door was clicked shut, muttered, 'Very well, I will grant you five minutes more.' Now it was his turn to feel the emptiness of bluster.

'This document details nine cases of abuse committed by you.

The investigators possess sworn testimonies they are willing to give to the authorities. I don't know if that will be necessary as we will print and distribute hundreds of copies in your parishes and in Edinburgh. And both Roddie and I will be out of the country, so any claims for defamation will be hard to pursue.'

Hardie studied the document and sank down into the chair. At length he hissed, 'How much?'

'We are not blackmailers. We demand restitution, that is all. You will give me three hundred pounds in compensation for the damage you have caused me. You will purchase Miss Thompson's house in Edinburgh at the market price and you will resign from your post. I understand Elspeth's mother may depend on you, so you will provide her with a pension. None of this will cause you undue expense and you can sell the Edinburgh house when you like.'

Hardie breathed in. He nodded. Sweat beaded his brow.

Alia stepped forward. 'And you will transfer the deeds of this house to Elspeth.'

The look of amazement on Elspeth's face almost matched Hardie's.

'This house? This house! The home of my wife, Susan, to be given to a common woman! She is not even from here. This is absurd!'

'The donation of the house is not only a matter of justice but your protection from further accusations. It will be in Elspeth's name and she and I will open a refuge for abused girls. I will use the money from the sale of my house. This all involves much moral compromise but you and I in our separate professions know all about that.'

Alia turned her back on him and left the floor to Enric. Roddie and Elspeth felt they were witnessing a performance, but one that had them in thrall.

Hardie twisted like a snared animal but Enric would not let him go and answered every objection with acuity and a swift intelligence which fixed the prey deeper in his press. He was magnificent, Alia said to herself. The only concession he made was to surrender the payment he had claimed for himself. This was what clinched the agreement, perhaps because it gave Hardie the feeling he had clawed something back, that he had not lost face entirely. Roddie understood this and it only increased his admiration for his friend. And Elspeth started to look like Elspeth again, perhaps because as she said later, Enric had freed from enslavement not just the girls they would help but released the love she felt towards him.

Enric fixed a date ten days hence. 'If the contracts are not drawn up, the deeds handed over by then, we will distribute the report. And before we leave you today you will write a letter to Alia outlining the agreement and signing it in front of us all.'

Though Hardie twisted and turned again, he felt like a salmon played by a master fisher. He read the document several times, searching in vain for a loophole, looking for flaws in the evidence. With downcast eyes he wrote and signed the letter. The room seemed to levitate as he did so.

Back in the coach, Maggie sat between Enric and Roddie and held onto the reins, feeling like the queen of the world. Behind, Alia and Elspeth laughed and dreamed and made plans.

'I will go with my brother to see my mother and then come back, if you can look after Maggie and start to organise the home. And I want it to be a home, Elspeth.'

They caught the last train back to Edinburgh and walked along Princes Street, an army of hope.

Elspeth and Enric let the others walk onwards while they stopped at the foot of the Mound, looking up to the Castle while the yellow moon pushed the clouds aside and shone down on them.

'Are you really going away? You don't have to leave on my account.'

'Yes, I am going. My time in Scotland was up a while ago. And you and I have had our time too. There is nothing to be sad about, though there may be if I stay and you are consumed by your new work. I have decided to go to the United States. It is a capitalist economy and a slave state. However, I think, as a printer, and perhaps even as a sailor, I may be able to help in the coming battle against slavery. I will go to say farewell to my parents then cross the ocean. If so many Scots can do it, it can't be so difficult!'

A wry smile crossed his face.

'Oh, my beautiful Enric,' she said.

The Mantrap

The sound of bone splitting. Shouts of pain and then a stretcher carried onto the pitch. The players all huddled round the supine figure while one of them, in white slacks and a brown cap, shook his head and made gestures to show the contact had been clean and innocent. Then the clapping as the injured fellow was carted off.

'I say, your Arthur shows no mercy,' Argyll said to Lord Kinnaird as they both observed the scene from the grandstand. It was 1868 and in deference to his new appointment in charge of the India Office, the Duke had resigned from his post as President of the *National Bible Society of Scotland* and had wanted to have a chat with the new President, the Tenth Lord Kinnaird, a Perthshire man, a successful banker in London and someone mindful of the gradations of social prestige that placed Argyll, a cabinet minister and one of Scotland's largest landowners, several rungs above him. 'He lives over the shop!' the Duke had joked to Lady Argyll, when he explained why it was not a good idea to visit Kinnaird at home. The 'shop' was Ransom & Bouverie's Bank and the property above had that clear, no-nonsense comfort and confident plushness of its owner.

Young 'Hacker' Arthur Kinnaird was already an accomplished tennis player and all-round athlete, but it was in this new sport of Association Football that he was to shine, eventually winning nine FA Cups and becoming the head of the Association. Despite his skill with the ball, he never shook off the 'Hacker' epithet, though some said it was a slander by less gifted rivals.

Argyll knew all about epithets and how they stuck to you. He was known as 'The Radical Duke,' though some would have said he was radical in the manner of Genghis Khan. His tenants did not always appreciate the daring nature of his racking up of rents even during the famines and depressions which hit Lewis, Mull and Tiree in the 1840s, but then again, what was to be expected of such a degenerate backward-looking race?

He was an aggressive debater in the House of Lords, almost comically bellicose, as *The Times* put it; a small figure crowned with a crest of waving hair like the comb of a fighting cock, which contributed to his other nickname of 'Cocculus Indicus.' Both he and Kinnaird were Whigs, though the latter walked in the shadow of Palmerston while Argyll attached himself to Gladstone, till he could no longer suppress his alarm at the party's land reform bills and resigned. That was later, however; for now, he was the coming man and tipped for the highest office. Arthur Kinnaird Senior's position in the party was less prominent but steadier and he preferred the strategy of beneficent charities to help the Highland poor emigrate and to keep them alive while they adjusted to their fate, over Argyll's trust in the harshness of the conditions as sufficient spur to force out all but the very best tenants.

Today both were happy to leave politics behind and Argyll was a polymath who wrote on geology, science, political economy, and even religious affairs. He was eager to talk about any of them, individually or all at once and conversation with him could be like preparation for the civil service exams, as one of his sons was rumoured to have said. Today he was content to let his companion lead the way, at least for a little.

'When did your laddie start playing football?'

'Well, it was mostly at Eton, I think, but the first time I ever saw him with a ball at his feet was on Portobello beach. We took a house there for the winter in 1856, when Arthur was nine. He joined in a game with some other lads playing on the sands. Mary Jane was worried they might be rough types but then we saw a couple approach who turned out to be none other than the late Hugh Miller and his wife, come to watch their son. We got chatting and met up several times over the next month. A sad loss.'

The sound of leather bouncing on the hard ground and the shouts of the players seemed to melt into the background as both men went back in their thoughts.

'Aye, he was a talented man, but a strange character,' Argyll replied. 'I felt we had so much in common, both Whigs but with strong conservative principles, a respect for history and of course a passion for geology. I had long wanted to have an extensive private conversation after Chalmers talked warmly about him to me. Yet he turned down each and every invitation to meet me at Inveraray or even in Edinburgh. We coincided once on a platform at a meeting I presided over of the *British Association for the Promotion of Science* in Glasgow. I was greeted with polite applause, but the crowd roared when Hugh Miller was presented, and he was lost among the multitude.'

Kinnaird understood how difficult it was for Argyll to conceive of someone not wanting to meet him. And it was true that Miller and the Duke seemed to have much in common: their combativeness, their ad hominem attacks on opponents, their distrust of electoral reform and inability to see why others might be wounded by their spleen, or by what they saw as just robust defences of fundamental truths. He foresaw a rough ride for Argyll in his new post where he would have to negotiate policies with subtle civil servants and Indian nabobs!

Argyll turned his head towards Kinnaird. There was a bitter smile on his face.

'I know what you are thinking. I, like him, can find it difficult to build bridges with people whose motives I distrust. I think it may be because we were both solitary schoolboys with a defective social education. He never went to University and recounted in his autobiography how he felt cut off from the other boys and was eventually expelled from school. I was educated at home and, unlike you, never learned the art of making chums, of weaving a web of amity with different people. I am not clubbable, and I believe that explains why I never made it into the Commons and have to fight so much more to promote my policies in the Lords.'

'Mrs Miller told me you had even persuaded the Marquess of Breadalbane to offer Miller the post of Distributor of Stamps and Collector of the Property Tax for Perthshire. She was most grateful and, though she tried to dissimulate, was obviously furious that her husband had declined such a generous offer. She felt herself made for higher society, at least that is the impression my wife got from her during their talks over tea at our place.'

'Aye, my kinsman and I were taken aback by his letter, all high words but with a low meaning, explaining how he could not possibly accept a post that, at his time of life, he was not sure of being able to execute properly. It requires taking up residence in Perth but with at least two months annual leave. He could have done it in his sleep! And he also refused to come to Inveraray. I think he never understood that in science, religion or politics, allies are necessary. He and I were scientific comrades in our views of development, seeing the will of the Creator behind everything and not just blind competition. We differed a little on timings and I believe that he underplayed the importance of beauty.'

'Of beauty?' Kinnaird started.

'Well, Hugh Miller argued that if aesthetically-pleasing plants, animals and even landscapes had been created before the advent of man, then it meant that God had an aesthetic sensibility. They could not have been created so for the pleasure of a non-existent humankind. God also gave man the capacity to enjoy loveliness, which is one proof of our godlike nature. So far so good and I more or less agree.'

Kinnaird felt the bench slipping from under him. He recalled something about beauty, but not in Miller's talk. He saw himself trying to decipher the different fossils in Miller's collection and felt the Duke was being more succinct than that poor unfortunate fellow, who had wandered in his arguments and seemed to be grasping at thoughts rather than laying them out.

'The point about beauty is, I feel, that it is not necessary. For a hummingbird, a crest of topaz is no better in the struggle for existence than a crest of sapphire. Of course, Darwin and his fellow devils had not published when Miller was alive, but there was *Vestiges,* and the argument was in the air. If beauty or decoration exist it is a slap in the face for the idea of the survival of the fittest.'

Kinnaird sighed, as if trying to suppress an idea, a worry, though Argyll took it for assent. 'Yes, that was it.' He was remembering what Mary Jane had said when she read the news of Miller's death in *The Times*. He had thought it fanciful, but he was younger and duller then.

'He died for want of beauty,' she had said. 'Do you remember how drab the house was? And though it sounds cruel to say it of a dead man, he was not handsome. He fitted ill with the world.'

He had poohpoohed her words and proposed a prayer for the departed soul. But that night in bed she had opened a book by Miller, *The Old Red Sandstone* and read a paragraph.

'You see, there is detail, there is precise description and logical argument. But there is no beauty. And we cannot live without that, especially one such as he.'

Kinnaird had wished her goodnight and sighed. As he was sighing now. He was brought back to himself by Argyll's next question.

'Did he ever talk to you about me, that winter?'

Kinnaird glanced towards the pitch, hoping for a goal or an act of savagery from young Arthur.

'Well, he talked about your discovery of the fossilised leaves on Mull and said he had enjoyed the letters you and he exchanged from time to time about geology. I am afraid he was put out by your opposition to *The National Association for the Vindication of Scottish Rights*, of which he was a member and keen supporter. But no, I don't remember anything more. O look, my son has scored a goal!'

After the celebratory hubbub had died down, Argyll surprised him by repeating his question.

'I know this may seem tiresome, old sport, but I have a reason for asking. I want to know if I was in his thoughts in the months before his death. It might mean I will be visited by him. I still think we can have that conversation. Yes, I know, I know, but I believe as Miller did, in the spirits. On the day after my brother's death, I observed a white dove perched on the tree nearest to his bedroom window. Pigeons normally rest on buildings or rocks, but I thought little of it until I saw it again in exactly the same position. I threw pebbles but it simply resettled upon the same branch after each attack and remained there for three days before disappearing. This was no coincidence, but a token for good and proof not only of the existence of God but of a spiritual world with which there may be ways of communicating. And I have found that I sometimes hear whispers from departed friends in the middle of the night, trying to tell me things they had left unsaid.'

Kinnaird had shifted in his seat and cited the usual quote from Hamlet, but this confession unsettled him, both because it was an unexpected intimacy from someone he barely knew and perhaps due to the public setting at a football match. If it had been after dinner, he would have passed the port and nodded. What could he do now? He said it was too long ago to remember, but if Miller had said something it would surely have been complimentary. They both knew he was lying. He hurriedly introduced the subject of the *Bible Society* which kept them occupied till the match ended.

Just before Argyll stepped into his coach, he turned to Kinnaird and in a soft voice said.

'The Scotland of Chalmers is lost now, lost and broken. I am working to repeal the patronage that caused the Disruption, but we will never be able to stick the parts together again. Our only hope is to strengthen the Union with the United Kingdom. My faith in that at least gives me some consolation, some hope. I fear Miller saw the damage he had caused and saw no mend to it. Gooday to you, Kinnaird.'

As his coach weaved through the busy streets, Arthur closed his eyes and tried to bring back that hazy Portobello winter. He was not put out by his dissimulation to the Duke; bankers live by it. However, he had a nagging sense of having missed something, of not having done more to avert the catastrophe. Miller had criticised Argyll one evening as the two men sat on the porch, complaining about the conflict over the *Association* but letting it be understood that though he agreed with the Duke on the degenerate races, though the Irish might be one of them, the Highlanders were not, at least not all of them. If they were living in such poverty, it was not through choice but often because of landowners like his Grace, he had said, then apologised for slandering a friend of Kinnaird's. Kinnaird had reassured him that Argyll could take any criticism offered, another dissimulation, and had changed the subject. Miller was then a distressed man, there was no point in increasing his agitation by opposing him. Kinnaird noticed that his wife and oldest daughter, Harriet, seemed to be constantly pacifying him, agreeing with whatever he said, fearful of what? Of a breakdown? Of some act of violence? Kinnaird had felt that there was violence in the man, and he had heard about the pistols. At the time, he had accepted Mrs Miller's explanation for her husband's nervous state as a result of his concerns about ticket-of-leave men, released convicts, who he assured them all, were rife in the area and active by night. Hugh feared for his collection in the building at the end of the garden. It was his best hope for an appointment to a University Chair, she said, though Kinnaird sensed she did not believe that. Bankers are good at sensing both insincerity and the desperate necessity for it.

Harriet later confessed to Mary Jane as they went on a walk to Joppa, that her father had become obsessed by the threat of burglars. A few weeks ago, her brother William had been playing in the garden after dark and had run into the house saying he had seen a lantern moving among the trees and had heard whispered voices. Her father had gone out to check but though nothing was found he awakened the whole household and night after night the children and the servants outdid each other with tales of mysterious sounds overheard and strange sights seen.

'This has much affected my father's imagination, I fear, and he has pistols and swords at the ready to repel attack.'

Mary Jane had tried to calm the girl, but had reported the incident to her husband, complaining at the children being frightened by the madness of the father. 'For madness it surely is, Arthur. The whole household is on edge. Something will break soon, and I hope the whole edifice does not come crashing down.'

Kinnaird winced as he thought of it now. He had considered his wife too easily affected by the fancies of an impressionable young girl. Miller was suffering from overwork, he said. It was the vice of the century. He was older now and realised that you cannot wish madness away.

A few nights after Harriet's confession, Mrs. Miller was startled by her husband bursting into her room at midnight with firearms in his hand and asking in a loud voice whether she had heard unusual noises in the house. Lydia answered composedly that she had heard nothing. Hugh circled the room, looking behind the curtains and even up the chimney then went into his eldest daughter's room, and made the same inquiry. Harriet soothed him enough to persuade him back to his own room. She remained awake for the rest of the night, listening to him pacing up and down and composing his book aloud and ready to jump out and bar him from her brothers' and sister's rooms.

Arthur found Lydia Miller on the verge of tears while taking tea with his wife the next day. She was, she said, at the end of her tether.

'The book is killing him. It sometimes seems that he is not writing it, it is writing him. I know that is an odd way of putting it, but it is as if it is an already existing thing, demanding to be transcribed. I sometimes ask myself if this is how the scribes of the Holy Scripture felt, but even God cannot be so unrelenting in his demands.'

Mary Jane reached out and held the poor woman by both hands. 'There, there,' she said. 'Arthur too gets swept away by his work at the bank sometimes. It is what men do. Have you no family or close friends you can turn to?'

'Oh no, we are estranged from his mother and her husband in Cromarty. In any case, she would only encourage his superstitions. And my widowed mother is in Inverness. The Free Church has no more use for him, the ardour of a soldier is out of place in these conciliatory times, it seems. My husband's beliefs and strong character have frightened the wise and banished the foolish. And many invitations to visit have evaporated like rime on the path. Would you like to welcome a man bearing pistols to your home?'

She stopped and bit her lip. 'I don't mean he has brought them here. And I have no right to trouble you with all this.'

'Of course not,' Mary Jane replied. 'I mean, you are not troubling us.'

'It's just he is so afraid.'

'Of what?'

'Of everything. Of the dark. Of the light. Of noise. Of silence. And this ticket-of-leave scare has him terrified for his Museum.'

Lady Kinnaird had looked over at her husband. He knew that look.

'I will go over and talk to him, see what I can do.'

And when he was let into the house, the maid explained that the Maister was in the Museum. He made his way down to the bottom of the garden and found Miller standing staring at the door, like a general assessing his battlements for weak flanks.

And now he remembered the strange mixture of characters that poured forth. Miller greeted him, then like Carlyle, mused sage-like on the spirit of the age and what recent developments in the news meant for society. Then he paused and pointed over to Bessie playing with her brother in the opposite reaches of the garden. 'Not a care in the world, that lassie!' he explained with a mix of astonishment and perhaps bitterness in his voice. Then the scientist took over and he started to describe some specimens he had come upon at Granton. He then quoted some lines from a prayer by John Knox before asking

Kinnaird his opinion of the poetry of Cowper. Yes, Arthur remembered that conversation like a concert of modern music, full of dissonance and jarring stops. No doubt his memories were coloured by subsequent events, but there in the carriage, that is what it felt like.

He had felt out of his depth in so many ways. He tried to talk about banking, recalling that like him, Miller had once been a banker. He changed tack when he sensed he was in danger of being seen as patronising the man, something he knew would mean the end of their relationship. That had been tempting, he could not have a scene in his sitting room every day! But when he saw the fellow shifting from foot to foot in front of him, his hair unkempt and those wild eyes, he repented.

'I have just the solution,' he said.

'Oh, that is wonderful.'

There had been a pause while Kinnaird had run through different ideas in his head. He could invite the Millers to stay with them, he could take him to a specialist in London. Now he reflected that perhaps it was the banker in him that settled for the concrete and the limited, the safest option.

'A mantrap.'

'A mantrap. Are you speaking philosophically?'

'No, no, Mr Miller. I am no philosopher. Last week I was at an agricultural show in Perth and purchased a new ingenious invention- a mantrap which has the engaging property of holding the robber fast without hurting him. That makes it both legal and humane. We can install it here in front of the door to your Museum.'

Miller had seemed delighted, reassured and suddenly calmer. That evening both men set up the trap on the porch of the museum.

Lydia reported to them the next day that her husband had slept soundly, if for only a few hours and that the whole household was relieved. Arthur allowed himself some self-congratulation. He was a practical man with practical solutions and both men had been intrigued by the engineering of the contraption.

No thief was ever snared by the trap. But now as he stepped down from his coach, Miller's face came to him, his whispered confidence a few days later that the sly rogues now flew through the sky. But I will pursue them, I will catch them, don't you worry.'

He knew then that Hugh was caught in a trap. One no-one could escape from, one that bruised and battered. Arthur had left for London shortly after, taking Mary Jane with him. He too had abandoned Miller, frightened, like others, of being taken down with him: that was what was nagging him. You could not talk to the dead, no matter what Argyll said. But they could talk to you.

The Stone Salvation

He sat in his museum, feeling safer now as he counted his defences: the mantrap, his rifle, his six-shot revolver and the broadsword. Oh, and the dagger he kept secreted under his bed. Let them come for him if they dared. He got to his feet and wandered round the room, looking fondly at the neatly ordered fossils. These were his writings; this was his testament of the rocks. Without them his books would mean little: words can be erased or just twisted, stones cannot. No doubt that was why the Creator had printed the fossil record on them. 'Printed,' no not 'printed.' He thought too much like a newspaper man. He was beginning to hate journalism and regret all the wasted years churning out texts which served only to console the unthinking and irritate the argumentative. He would do something else from now on. But what? He really was too old or at least too tired to start another profession. He had to do something though. No doubt Harriet might marry in a few years but that still left his other offspring who would have to depend on him for years.

He must go in; it was almost time for lunch and then perhaps he would lie down. A nap. He dreamed less during the day, or rather they did not invade his sleep as much during daylight hours. He noticed a drawer which had not been properly shut. For a moment he panicked at the thought that it was a sign of an intruder. 'Stop it man,' he told himself. It was probably only young Hugh poking around. He would ask him later. He had to pull the drawer out to steer it back in properly. As he did so he noticed a small round black stone. Basalt, perhaps, perfectly smooth and with no fossils. Where had it come from? The stones were like children to him, he remembered where and when they had sprung from and noted it down. He did not recall this one. He rolled it round the palm of his hand, waiting for it to speak to him. It remained silent. He put it in his pocket and headed for his study, checking the locks on the museum door twice to make sure all was secure.

At the foot of the stairway leading to his study he met Lydia. She had that look on her that so irritated him lately. She thinks I am going to be felled by apoplexy. I heard her whispering to Lady Kinnaird. 'I am in terror that one night he will be struck down on the street and be carried into the house,' had been her exact words. Well, he would not give her the satisfaction. The way she hung about his bedroom at night when he needed to be alone, smoothing down his bedspread, lingering on one pretence or another, telling him he needed to eat more, trying to find a way into him, to insist that he sleep. He could see her biting her tongue, afraid to speak and making him feel cruel. Yet *she* was the harsh one, refusing to believe him when he told her about his night walks and his visitors.

Once he was alone in his study he felt calmer than he had for days. Kinnaird had helped, not only by his provision of the mantrap but by the feeling of solidarity, of understanding, that he transmitted. Perhaps there was something about them both being bankers after all. He decided to read and desist from writing today. First Cowper, his companion since his Cromarty days. Then he opened Milton, whose style he hoped infused his *Testimony of the Rocks*. He needed to be august like him and sweep away cold materialism. He did not notice the maid bringing in his supper and only picked at it while he read the prayer by John Knox. Ah, you did not read Knox, you inhaled him, his passion, his authority, and acceptance that he was a sinner. That night he was unmolested by visitations. Perhaps it was too chilly outside.

The next day was the 19th, and he accompanied Lydia to Sunday service in the forenoon, keeping his head down and his gaze averted from people. For what if he had met them on his sojourns in the streets or above the rooftops? It would bring shame on the Free Kirk and that he would not do. He got through the service without undue difficulty, though the minister's sermon seemed mostly fit for tremulous old ladies and lacked any sense of the church in action, of the muscular Christianity as they had started to call it, that was needed to advance. People were nice to him in the way they are to an invalid. When Lydia proposed a walk along the shorefront, he told her that the wind was cold.

'I don't feel well, my dear. Can we not go home, and you may sit with me?'

Why had he said that? Not because he wanted her to stay by his side, nor because he wished to go home. He had been sure he saw a dark-haired man keeking round the corner at him; probably Chas, come to blackmail him. Better take cover.

Lydia assented, though only after scanning his face. 'I am feeling very tired myself, dear. And my arm aches, so let us go home. We should have taken the phaeton, as usual. I am afraid the walk has tired us both.'

Was she getting at him? He had refused to climb into their coach, its large round wheels reminding him of pennies placed on the eyes of a dead man, though of course he had not said that, had only insisted that the stroll would do them good. They had walked home in silence, with Hugh holding Lydia's arm tightly, lest she run away. Run away? He knew it was ridiculous: where would she go? About fifty yards from their home at Shrub Mount, a lane led down to the beach. Aggie Fledsome lived there, an old hag whom he suspected of putting the evil eye on him. She had scalded her leg, it seemed, when her potato pot had overturned. Hugh had seen spirits hanging round her door, but of course he could say nothing to Lydia about that. And now she proposed going to inquire how the poor old dear was doing! Was there no end to the Devil's work!

Lydia was startled by the expression of pain on her husband's face, as if even a small separation represented a chasm they would never cross again. But she could not give into this madness.

'I will be back soon, dear. Just get yourself warm and we shall sit together by the fire.'

Once he had taken off his plaid and asked the girl for tea, Hugh sank down in his armchair in front of the fireplace. He was sweating but still felt cold. He pulled out his handkerchief to mop his brow and heard a rattling on the floor, like a crab scuttling away. Ah, it was the round stone from his pocket! He examined it but could not identify its composition. It was certainly not typical of the local specimens. He fixed his eyes on it then carried it upstairs to check with his magnifying glass. It appeared perfectly smooth and of a uniform black, almost like parrot coal but much harder. Beads of sweat dripped from his brow as the panic closed him in its vicelike grip. What if there were elements that were unclassifiable? What if there were new species of stone? A voice told him this was absurd, worse than that, it was madness. But he did not understand this stone, which meant either that it was of unknown origin or that he was losing his powers. He could not, he would not countenance either one! He reached for his trusty hammer to crack it open. His hand was shaking. The stone resisted all his efforts and suffered not a scratch. It was mocking him! A small voice whispered that he was a failure as a mason, as a man, as well as a scientist. The stone had been sent to him to teach him these lessons. Who had given it to him? His mind went back to Cha and Enric and Alia. That had been their mission: one to observe him working on stone, the other to flatter his scientific pretensions, and she to, well he knew not what but felt sure he would find out eventually. They were three devils sent to him to lay waste to his hopes of lasting fame and geological renown. It had all been predestined and he had invited them into his life, had given them the opening to bring him down. He picked up the blasted stone again and felt his hand burning. He must be rid of it! But where could he put it where it could cause no harm to others? He paced about the room with a mounting feeling of helplessness. He heard the front door open, Lydia returning, no doubt.

He must hurry. He thrust his hand under his pillow and deposited the stone there. He would deliver himself from it later.

'I came back as fast as I could, the poor dear was incredibly grateful for my visit and reluctant to let me go....' Lydia halted, as she perceived her husband was not in the living room as she had supposed he would be. What was all his talk of being cold and of sitting with her for, then? She turned as she heard his steps on the staircase and almost fell back against the door jamb. It was not her husband but some wild, desperate vagabond such as you sometimes witnessed through your coach window wandering the heaths of the Highlands, shirt awry and hair like seaweed.

'Hugh, whatever is the matter?'

He staggered down the stairs and walked past her into the living room. She went to fetch a towel, hoping the maid would not appear nor the children come back from Sunday School with Harriet. It took her almost half an hour to calm him and make him respectable, as she put it.

'Hugh, the children cannot see you like this. Little Hugh is already afraid of you. Harriet is dreadfully afraid *for* you. What has happened? Have you a fever?'

He had mumbled something about an unclassifiable stone, a 'sport,' as he put it. She began to fear more for his mind than his body and as she looked in his eyes she saw the same terror there.

'It was sent to destroy me, Lydia, using the stones I have built my life on.'

'Oh Hugh, calm yourself. It is just overwork. Leave your studies alone for a while and come back to your family.'

He seized her hand and got down on one knee then theatrically kissed it. It felt like a farewell, though he uttered no words save for a few whispers about the consuming darkness in his brain. She gently pulled him up, she would not have her husband kneel before her, it was degrading to them both. His face had that strange and painful expression which had flitted across it as they came back from church.

All of a sudden, he became calm and reached out for a little book he had been reading on a religious subject and wrote a brief notice of it for the paper. Lydia herded the children into the dining room on their return and bid them keep quiet. Harriet observed how tense her mother was, how her attention was on what might be happening in the other room, but what could she say? Later Harriet would blame herself for her silence. Though the volcano may erupt whatever we say, the person who has not sounded the alarm can carry the guilt all their life.

About seven pm Hugh bade his children goodnight and told Lydia he would not require dinner. Harriet proposed to her mother that they read together, but only holy texts as this was Sunday. Her sister and brothers were got ready for bed and silence took over the house with the white haar from the sea, only broken by the creaking floorboards as her father paced the room above. It was like being captive below as the mad captain strode the deck. During the night Lydia came out of her room and listened at the bottom of the stairway. Sometimes she heard her husband's voice, as if he were arguing with someone, other times he seemed to be reciting poetry then pleading with others. She was about to go up when the noise ceased, and she returned to her bed. 'This cannot go on,' she told herself. But what could she do?

Hugh had felt tired but stronger after his reading and the short burst of work for the Paper. Lydia was no doubt right, he needed to rest and perhaps take a break from work. But how would he keep his brain occupied, how would he provide the fuel it needed to keep moving? He plumped down on the bed and glanced sideways at the pillow. It looked different. He scanned the room for other signs that someone had intruded. His magnifying glass seemed closer to the end of his desk than he remembered, and was the window slightly raised? He began to sweat again. He slipped his hand under the pillow to retrieve the stone. He collapsed in a heap when he found nothing there.

He was unsure how much time had passed between missing the stone and the first visitation. At first he thought it was only a wisp of ashy smoke whipped from the fireplace by the keen December wind. However, it spiralled up and took form in front of him till he recognised Willie Ross in an opaque figure where he could see the forearms but not make out the distinction between the upper arms and the torso when he stood sideways.

'I do not have your stone,' Willie said to him before he could ask. He was always like that, always knew what Hugh was thinking in a way no one else could. When he asked Willie why he was here, he replied that he had never been away, except for that time in Glasgow. Hugh's writings had kept him close, and he had shown his descriptions of him and his claims for his genius to the others.

'I am sorry, Willie, I did not see until Alia insisted.'

'You never understood, Hugh. You were blinded by your strength, but don't worry, nobody makes apologies here. Those only serve when you can amend your actions, something which neither you nor I can do now. So don't fret, my friend. We will walk arm in arm again in Joppa to the house of Simon the tanner by the sea.'

He finished speaking, breathless perhaps, then reached out a hand and touched Hugh on his forehead. A sharp keening blade pierced Hugh's cranium and Willie disappeared, sucked up into the chimney. Hugh collapsed again, his head lying awkwardly, so that when he woke once more, his neck was sore and stiff. Perhaps that was why he didn't notice the three men standing in a circle next to the window, as if they had just climbed in, the eldest dusting his trousers down, obviously zealous of his attire. As they were facing into the circle he could just make out the side of one of their faces. It was familiar to him, he thought, then laughed at the absurdity of it. As they all turned to face him, he realised he was looking at three versions of himself! There was young Hugh, an adolescent schoolboy carrying a large-leafed book. He smiled, or rather, bared his teeth. Had he really been so aggressive as a boy? The fellow opened the book and held it towards Hugh, slowly flicking through the pages to reveal a series of half-forgotten scenes: raiding the honey from the skull on the Suitor hill, the slaughter of the pigs in the building next to the school yard and how they all laughed, the fight with the knife-wielding mulatto, the knockout blow to the dominie. They were drawn so that the characters seemed to move as he flicked through. Hugh leaned in, staring intently.

The book and the boy seemed to gradually fade away, but the pictures stayed, though they depicted different scenes. Willie was back and the room become a big tent. It was the Panorama! Hugh recognised the small man and Christopher North. And now, for the first time he spied Alia in the back of the room, looking towards Willie and Hugh's double. So she had been following him all along! She was mouthing something at him, something which suddenly became audible. 'Have no regrets, Hugh Miller. Never bow down, even in death!' The ships' decks cracked as they let rip their cannon, he could smell the sulphur. His double turned to look him in the eyes. There were flames in his eyes. Hugh looked away before his brain burned up into ashes. All the people in the tented room turned to look at him as the men-of-war in the scenery sank, and the room became filled with wailings and lamentations. 'You!' they said, 'You! You have witnessed but have not understood. You have treated us like actors in your play when all the time **you** are the puppet. And your strings are cut.'

He heard the sound of coins spilling and sure enough, the floor was spangled with guineas. The banker was holding a cow by a rope. 'That is what the local economy is, not the high-falutin' transactions of your Edinburgh financial institutions. You get to learn all you need to know about human nature in a branch office of a bank. But Cromarty was not enough for you!' The man was speaking but the sound came from Hugh's lips. 'You had to desert your mother, John Swanson, and the people who had looked up to you, and for what? To please a woman's desire for genteel respectability. You married the daughter of a bankrupt and yet it was you who had to prove you were good enough. See where that has got you! At least you learned to defend yourself against miscreants with me, you learned the power of the gun.' At that the banker pulled out his pistol and shot the cow dead.

Hugh darted to his feet and found himself alone, alone except for the fellow in the mirror, who stared at him as if measuring him for a shroud. Hugh raised his hand quickly and the fellow did the same but at a slower pace. Hugh spent a few minutes toying with his reflection, seeing if he could outsmart him. He was reassured, until it occurred to him that the man was expecting all his movements, he was the one being made a fool of! He took some crayons from his desk and scrawled over the surface of the mirror, bad words, obscene words he had never uttered before, but which were demanding release. Only a small fragment of the glass was left uncovered, but there were his nemesis' eyes, burning with the light of a thousand suns. He picked up his book and focussed on the poem. He read it aloud, chanted it and seemed to be surfacing above the panic when the blade pierced his brain again and he collapsed.

He was awakened by the feeble morning light pushing its fingers through the half-opened curtains. He heard a voice whispering, close enough so it brushed his ear with its tongue but far enough so that it seemed to emanate from the ceiling.

'I told you it would come to this, Hugh. You were a man of ashes and not of stone, after all.'

It was that rabble-rouser, Chas. Well, he would show him. He reached under the pillow. The stone was still not there! He began to panic again then was comforted by its weight in his chest. He could feel the smooth round stone lodged in his heart. Perhaps this was what the *Pterichthyodes* had felt like as it gradually petrified through the aeons. He had breathed in dust all his life. Perhaps becoming a stone was his only salvation. He slept.

His Final Letter

Dearest Lydia, —My brain burns. I must have walked; and a fearful dream arises upon me. I cannot bear the horrible thought. God and Father of the Lord Jesus Christ have mercy upon me. Dearest Lydia, dear children, farewell. My brain burns as the recollection grows,

My dear dear, wife, farewell,

"Hugh Miller"

Christmas Eve, 1856

The Castaways

On Monday morning Lydia slowly climbed the stairs before breakfast and met Hugh coming out of his room. He said that he had passed a bad, restless night. He patted his chest and then his head like a man searching for his pocket watch and his spectacles. At breakfast, which only his wife and Harriet partook of with him, his conversation was animated and copious. He ate nothing, however, merely swallowing a cup of tea, and his mind was evidently occupied with his sensations in the night. He spoke of sleepwalking and told an anecdote of a student who had left his room, clambered on the roof, entered an adjoining house, divested himself, night after night of his shirt, and hidden the garments, to the number of half-a-dozen, in a cask of feathers.

Harriet stared past him out onto the wind-tossed garden. Try as she might, she could not look at this impostor, for this could not be her father.

Breakfast over, he returned to the subject which had never been far from his thoughts. He insisted on the sleepwalking and the vagrant student as if trying to convince himself as well as them.

'What real horrors must he be hiding?' Lydia asked herself.

'It was a strange night,' he said. 'There was something I didn't like. I shall just throw on my plaid and step out to see Dr. Balfour.'

Now it was Lydia's turn to feel she was in the presence of an impostor. Hugh had never before volunteered to visit a doctor and indeed would make himself scarce when Balfour, who lived locally, popped in to check on the family. Once Hugh had left the house, she took Harriet's hand.

'We have to save him. Balfour is a general practitioner, good for colds and fevers but this is beyond him. I want you to come with me to see Professor Miller. And, ...'

'And we must not tell father, or he will rebel.'

'We will take the 12 o'clock coach up to town.'

As they were getting ready to leave, Hugh came back. He told them he had to call into the office and would be taking the coach and enquired where they were off to. Lydia was lost for words.

'Mama is taking me to see a picture in the Waterloo Rooms. They say it is a masterpiece and my schoolmistress insists I really must study it.'

'They are lying,' Hugh thought to himself. 'Like I lied to them this morning. How have we come to this?'

There was only one other passenger in the coach, sufficient to impede questions from Hugh and the four sat in silence as the vehicle made its way over the cobbled streets. Hugh stuck his head out of the window from time to time, looking back down to Portobello, as if to check they were not being followed.

Professor Miller was at home in Queen Street and he agreed to visit the next day at three pm, the same time as Balfour had promised to drop by. Lydia confessed her ruse and Hugh grumbled at first but finally acceded. That night Lydia heard no noise from his room and the next morning he told her he had spent a peaceful time.

'She did not hear me because I was on a walk outside,' he thought. 'She cannot have heard the window click open.' Neither had she been disturbed by the rustling of the flowing robes nor the soft singing of the witch. He looked uneasily down at his trouser legs, anxious in case some mud still stuck to them, but no, he was in the clear. He was ticking boxes in his head; he found he needed to give simple order to his thoughts, he could no longer trust his memory. After her betrayal yesterday, he was determined not to confide more in Lydia. The witch had warned him against that in any case.

'Oh, I am becoming callous and to those who most love me!' He wiped away the thought as he mopped his brow with his kerchief and followed his wife down to the breakfast table. Harriet was not there. She must be avoiding him, like her brothers and sister.

Immediately after breakfast he began to correct the last proofs of the '*Testimony of the Rocks*.' About midday he became restless, and Lydia feared some manoeuvre to prevent the consultation. The day was bitterly cold, with drizzling rain. She made pretences to be near him, watchful lest he should slip away unnoticed. At last, he proclaimed his intention of going up to town to anticipate Professor Miller's visit.

'It is too much to ask such a busy man to make the journey all the way down here.'

'It is so cold outside, Hugh. You will catch your death.'

He gave a curious laugh at that but acquiesced, as if to say, how could I defy you? She passed by his chair just then and gave a slight tug at his shaggy hair, half a caress, half a rebuke for his stubborn resistance.

'Don't,' he said mildly; 'it hurts me.'

He was on his best behaviour when the two doctors came. He admired Professor Miller and acted with the courtesy he always bestowed on those he esteemed. They examined him, asked about his habits, about his work. He talked about his daytime attacks when he was subjected to intense pain, followed by confusion and giddiness and the sense of being very drunk, unable to stand or walk. Often this was followed by faintness, but he had never fallen. What disturbed him most was a kind of nightmare, which for some nights past, he confessed to the Professor, had rendered sleep most miserable. He could remember accurately nothing of what passed in these visions, but they left him with a sense of vague yet intense horror. The Professor nodded and urged him to go on. Hugh took a deep breath, as if searching for fresh air, and confessed to a conviction of being abroad in the night wind and dragged through places as if by some invisible power. 'Last night,' he whispered into the Professor's ear, 'I felt as if I had been ridden by a witch for fifty miles and rose far more wearied in mind and body than when I lay down.'

Lydia heard a noise at the door at that point. She slipped out and found Harriet there, softly weeping.

Back in the room Balfour was quietly rejoicing. To participate in a consultation as an equal with the great Professor James Miller!

'His pulse is quiet, but his tongue is foul. The head is not hot.'

Professor Miller drew him aside and they compared impressions, then turned to their strangely supine patient.

'You are suffering from an overworked mind, my friend. It is disordering your digestive organs, enervating your whole frame and threatening a serious head affection. You absolutely must rest, go to bed at eleven, no longer make your supper your principal meal but have a light repast. We recommend thinning the hair of the head, and a warm sponge-bath at bedtime.'

Hugh nodded ready acquiescence to all their commands. This comforted Balfour to the same extent it disquieted the Professor.

After their departure Hugh asked to be left alone for a while. Soon it was time for dinner. The servant timidly entered the dining-room to spread the table and found him alone. The expression which once or twice already had been observed on his features was again there. His face was so distorted with pain that she shrank back appalled. He lay down upon the sofa and pressed his head, as if in agony, upon the cushion. The paroxysm flitted by and when Lydia returned to the dining-room he was in apparent health.

He chatted amiably with the whole family over the meal. After dinner, the conversation turned upon poetry. Harriet had to give a lecture to her schoolmates on literature and Miller showed her some verses by Cowper, reading the playful '*To a Retired Cat*,' to young Hugh, William, Bessie and Harriet. It was the first time they had communed together for a good while and Harriet blushed with pride in bringing her father out of himself, out of the hole he had fallen into. 'Poetry can save us,' she thought.

Lydia withdrew to arrange some things with the servant girl, who had been strangely out of sorts all evening. She would have to find another. From the kitchen she could hear her husband reciting another poem by Cowper, *The Castaway*, one not at all suitable for such young, sensitive souls!

> Obscurest night involved the sky,
> The Atlantic billows rolled,
> When such a destined wretch as I,
> Washed headlong from on board,
> Of friends, of hope, of all bereft,
> His floating home forever left.
>
> Not long beneath the whelming brine,
> Expert to swim, he lay;
> Nor soon he felt his strength decline,
> Or courage die away;
> But waged with death a lasting strife,
> Supported by despair of life.
>
> He long survives who lives an hour
> In ocean, self-upheld;
> And so long he, with unspent power,
> His destiny repelled;
> And ever, as the minutes flew,
> Entreated help, or cried ' Adieu! '

The maid was setting out the teacups. Lydia waited. Should she run to the dining-room? No, she told herself, the only one who can understand these lines is Harriet and she is strong. The others will be glad just to see their father perform with something of his old vigour. She hesitated when she heard him go on,

No voice divine the storm allayed,
No light propitious shone,
When, snatched from all effectual aid,
We perished, each alone;
But I beneath a rougher sea,
And whelmed in deeper gulfs than he.

The room was filled with castaways when she returned. The boys were sitting sullen in the corner, Bessie was talking to her doll, and Harriet, oh Harriet was staring at her father like one lost to the waves. Hugh seemed oblivious to all this and quickly read a romantic ballad by the poet, glancing coyly at his wife as he did so. It was too much. Two nights till Christmas and here they were adrift!

The whole family was exhausted. Only Harriet attempted to keep their spirits up, but she soon gave way and began to read the volume of poetry to herself. The younger children retired to bed and her mother went to the kitchen to give orders for her husband's bath. Lydia beckoned to Harriet to accompany her and once in the corridor suggested she go to her room. Harriet 's face darkened.

'What about the weapons, mother? What are we going to do?'

'The doctors said nothing about them, and James Miller knows your father has always carried firearms. No, child, they shield him from his fear of burglars. He would not sleep easy without them believe me; I know.'

Harriet still did not seem convinced.

'Hush, child, this is your father we are talking about. A man of sometimes violent expression who would not hurt a fly. We are all extenuated. Sleep well, daughter.'

Hugh was sitting staring into empty space when Lydia joined him again. She had been determined to try to soothe him, to utter words of comfort and love, but only whispered,

'I am very, very tired, husband. I am sorry but I will have to leave you earlier than I had hoped.'

Silence.

After a moment he began to speak in an almost whining tone.

'Now that I am forbidden ale or porter, don't you think that in future I might have a cup of coffee before going to bed?'

With some hesitation she assented and promised that the coffee would be brought to him.

He smiled as if she had promised him a treasure.

She bent down to kiss him goodnight and he closed his eyes as if shutting her out from something. She retired to bed and fell into a deep dreamless sleep, worn out by the anxieties and stress of the preceding days. Hugh went upstairs to his study. At the appointed hour he took the bath. He left the dose of prescribed medicine untouched. A voice told him it was poison.

From his study he went into his sleeping-room and lay down upon his bed. He too was exhausted. He had felt such lassitude before but always after the physical and emotional triumphs of a winning campaign, a new book. Here there was no victory, and the *Testimony* was as yet untried in the world. Of course, several chapters had been taken from speeches he had made, but the written word was different. The written word: why had he tied his fate so to it?

He was awakened from his musings by a tapping at the window. When he climbed out he was surprised to find not the witch, nor Willie, but Mr Robert Chambers!

Chambers evidently remarked his surprise.

'Sorry for dropping in on you like this, Hugh, but I was just passing and saw your light was on. I miss our old talks.'

Hugh was struck dumb.

'Oh, you wonder at my night walks? Well, since young Dunglas Home came to Edinburgh, many of the best society have become noctambulants.'

Hugh stepped out further and they both took a stroll above the waters of the Forth. The sea tossed below them and they had to hold hands from time to time so as not to be blown over by the gusts of wind.

'Look at Edinburgh over there. How small it looks, how provincial! Do you remember when we both came here to seek our fame and our fortune? Now the practical man heads for Glasgow or Birmingham and the writer to London, leaving us only with lawyers. As the Empire has grown, Scotland has dwindled. And we two have shrunk with it.'

Hugh felt disappointed. He did not need to come out on a walk above the sea to know these things. He had written about them in *The Witness*. A hardening in Chambers' tone caught his attention, however.

'Enric told me you are obsessed with my *Vestiges of Creation*. I believe your latest book is yet another attack on it. Let it go, man, let it go, as I have. Fifty years from now, no one will know of it and if you set your compass towards it, you will founder in oblivion too.'

'My *Vestiges of Creation*!' Hugh almost tumbled into the sea. When he flew up again, Chambers had disappeared, though he thought he could spy him walking towards Granton. He peered towards home, towards Portobello. No, he didn't want to return now, he needed time to compose himself. He felt his heart bursting and when he looked down, he could see it pulsating below his skin.

The clouds over the city parted and Arthur's Seat was ringed in moonlight. He could make out what looked like a procession snaking up its side from Duddingston Loch. When he approached it seemed to him that souls were emerging from the water, taking human shape, then joining the convoy. Should he join them or stay hovering above? This was the first time he had walked on his own and he decided it was safer to maintain some distance from the throng. Where were they going? He walked up through the air as if standing on invisible steps. He was a little out of breath as he neared the head of the procession near the summit. What he saw almost robbed him of the power to breathe entirely! His heart stopped, then started, then stopped again as he took in the horror. His brain burned as it tried to deny the evidence of his eyes.

It was a crucifixion! A man pinned to a cross was being raised into an erect position, with his face pointing towards the East Neuk of Fife. Once set up, the crowd began to whoop and wail. Some shed their garments while others danced a demented jig. He knew they would attack him if they could, so he stepped further away. He could see the crucified man's face now. Tears streamed from his eyes as he recognised the countenance of his blessed Thomas Chalmers. They were making him look over to his birthplace, they were taunting him. There could be no greater horror than this, he told himself. A bolt of lightning illuminated the whole scene. And there it was, even though it couldn't be! One of the crowd whipped off the man's garment, revealing the naked body of an albino ape!

After that all was darkness and Hugh had no recollection of how he made it safely back to his bedroom. He opened his eyes as the grey dawn crept through the frosty window into the room. He opened his eyes, but who was HE? What is my name? he asked himself. What is my name?

He sat up, sweat pouring from his brow. 'Clothes maketh the man' they say. He put on some he found lying there, he seemed to remember the thick woven seaman's jacket: visions of a drowned man, was it his father, came to him. Oh, the horror! He rushed to the table and on a folio sheet of paper, in the centre of the page, he scrawled his final letter. '*Life is one long suicide note*,' the Devil whispered in his ear. He frowned and concentrated, searching for her name and at last it came to him. He was given some small comfort when at the end his own name appeared to him like a citation in a court case, in quotation marks. That grace would be temporary, he understood that. Soon he and the whole world would forget his name.

Dearest Lydia, —My brain burns. I <u>must</u> have <u>walked</u>; and a fearful dream arises upon me. I cannot bear the horrible thought. God and Father of the Lord Jesus Christ have mercy upon me. Dearest Lydia, dear children, farewell. My brain burns as the recollection grows,

My dear dear, wife, farewell,

"Hugh Miller"

He reached for his revolver as he faced the window and the bitter unforgiving morning sun. He raised the seaman's jacket over his chest, he must not damage it, perhaps it was not really his. He pressed the cold muzzle of the gun against his skin and aimed at the hard, black stone inside his heart. He fired. The ball perforated the left lung, grazed the heart, cut through the pulmonary artery at its root, and lodged in the rib on the right side. The pistol slipped from his hand into the bath, which stood close by, and he fell dead instantaneously. The body was found lying on the floor, the feet upon the study rug.

An Edinburgh Suicide

Hugh Miller's funeral took place on Monday, 29th December. *The Witness* reported that "The wintry aspect of the day and the heavy-laden sky like a pall, was spreading across the face of nature." Sixty individuals, including the Lord Provost of Edinburgh, two MPs, the leading lights of the Free Kirk, and Miller's family and friends gathered at his Portobello house at 12.45. *The Witness* reporter goes on to record that after a brief service officiated by the Rev Dr Thomas Guthrie, those attending climbed into thirteen mourning coaches and followed the ornately decked four-horse hearse to Edinburgh. At the east end of Princes Street the procession was met by a huge crowd, including the entire Kirk Session and most of the congregation of Miller's own church, St. John's, as well as a large delegation of scientists and science enthusiasts from the Royal Physical Society, Free Church mourners from all over Scotland and even from England, and clerks, salesmen and typographers from *The Witness*. Between twenty and thirty private coaches joined the procession. All the shops on the route up the North Bridge to the Grange Cemetery were closed and it was calculated that more than 4,000 people crowded the streets to watch the cortege pass, more even than had witnessed Chalmers' funeral.

The ceremony had not taken place earlier because Guthrie had demanded an autopsy. He had arrived with Fairly the day after Hugh's death and comforted the distraught family, who were in denial about Hugh's suicide. 'It must have been an accident,' William said. 'He lifted up his jersey, son, it was a deliberate act. May God forgive him,'

Guthrie replied as he turned to Harriet. She had not spoken a word since her father's body had been discovered by the servant. He took her into the dining room and sat opposite her. He talked of God's love and compassion. She confessed her feelings of guilt at not removing the weapons. She also complained of her father's betrayal of her, of them all, abandoning them like this. Were they not worthy of more?

The arrival of Hugh's half-brother interrupted them. Andrew Williamson had been notified by telegram and he came in representation of the Cromarty clan. 'We must bury him discreetly, dampen the shame that will hang over all the family,' he insisted.

'It was not suicide,' Fairly replied. 'Mrs Miller has explained the troubled state of his mind.'

'That will be seen as the false testimony of his widow, no-one will believe it, especially coming from her. And besides, there is no insanity in my family. Such a statement would only increase the stigma on us all. A quiet funeral, with only the family.'

The Witness on 27 December reported that Hugh had died in a tragic accident. He had been awakened from a ghastly nightmare, had heard noises, and suspected a burglary. Grabbing a loaded pistol he kept in his bedroom, he missed his step, fell, and accidentally shot himself in the chest.

'He lifted the jersey,' Guthrie insisted. 'Lydia, the truth will out and will do more harm if it has been seen to be concealed.'

'What do you want me to do? How are we to live? How am I to support my family if his books are regarded as the hypocritical writings of a man who so loved his Saviour that he killed himself? A father who abandoned his family? What will become of us? You ask too much!'

Guthrie had no answer. He asked if he might inspect Hugh's room. On the table, partially covered by some letters wafted down by the dying man's falling body, he found the note. He called Lydia and they read it together.

'It is in his hand, Lydia. There is no denying this.'

'But why did he sign it "Hugh Miller"? His last note, to me, his wife, signed like a newspaper article!'

'I learned throughout the years I knew him that your husband and "Hugh Miller" were two different people. Whenever "Hugh Miller" wrote, he was **Scotland**, in life and now in death. Since his first writings he spoke as a prophet. As they say, never be one in your own country, and I would add, in any country. We will demand an autopsy. Your husband was ill, Lydia. The doctors will confirm it.'

'The doctors cannot do that, as it means accepting the blame for not seeing it before.'

Nevertheless, the autopsy report by Professor James Miller, Drs Balfour, and Gairdner and Edwards affirmed,

'*From the diseased appearances found in the brain, taken in connection with the history of the case, we have no doubt that the act was suicidal, under the impulse of insanity.*'

To ensure there could be no doubts, it went on, '*It is a melancholy satisfaction to reflect, that in no case of suicide which ever took place, can the evidence of insanity have been more express or conclusive.*'

'The self-satisfied scoundrels,' Guthrie thought when he read it. Still, it would serve. They must all explain, nonetheless, that Miller was able to write, to meet and discuss with friends and colleagues with apparent normality all the while his brain was imploding. Guthrie promised Lydia to use his influence to disseminate this account and she accepted. From now on the tale would be told of a strong man alternating sanity with distress. Hugh had declared his love for her and the children in the note and above all, appealed to God and his Saviour. If there was any one to blame it would be the Cromarty family and their backward superstitions which had always shadowed Hugh.

Lydia later declared that Hugh's mother told her that, '*on the night of Hugh's death, suspecting no evil and anticipating no bad tidings, about midnight she saw a wonderfully bright light like a ball of electric fire flit about the room, and linger first on one object of furniture and then on another. She sat up in bed to watch its progress. At last it alighted, when, just as she wondered, with her eyes fixed on it, what it might portend, it was suddenly quenched, — did not die out, but, as it were, extinguished itself in a moment, leaving utter blackness behind, and on her frame the thrilling effect of a sudden and awful calamity.'* This featured near the beginning of Peter Bayne's two-volume biography of Hugh Miller, written under the supervision of his widow.

More immediate support was given to the responsibility of superstition in a report published in *The Witness* and later cited by Samuel Smiles in his book on Robert Dick, the Thurso geologist, where he says that Dick was: "not at all astonished at the way it ended. His mind was touched somehow by superstition. I mind, after an afternoon's work on the rocks together at Holborn Head, we sat down on the leeside of a dyke to look over our specimens, when suddenly up jumped Hugh, exclaiming, 'The fairies have got hold of my trousers!' *and then sitting down again, he kept rubbing his legs for a long time. It was of no use suggesting that an ant or some other well-known 'beastie' had got there. Hugh would have it that it was 'the fairies!'"*

No one objected that a belief in the fairies causing itching is a mighty distance from them making you shoot yourself with a pistol. If there was an occult influence, it must have come from deeper demons, Chambers reflected when he read the article.

Most people accepted the new version of the death story, and it was laid out in full in the second black-trimmed edition of *The Witness* on Wednesday 31 December. Only a few dissented. Hugh's half-brother declared he could not see how someone could be insane and not insane at the same time. 'I can be afflicted with scurvy, or I can be healthy. I cannot be both.'

Some uncharitable onlookers in the crowd gossiped about syphilis, with all the certainty of the medically ignorant. Others said the stone-dust had eaten into his brain, the stonemason's disease they called it.

The most uncomfortable reports were in *The Times*, where it was asked how it was possible for the wife of a man in evident distress to be sleeping in a separate room.

Just before Hugh's body was lowered into the grave by his sons, his half-brother, Williamson, Guthrie, Fairly and three men from the University, Thomas Leslie, 52, was buried. In order to ascertain exactly how many shots had been fired, Professor James Miller had taken the pistol to the firm of Alexander Thomson & Sons of 16 Union Place, who had sold it to Hugh. The man in charge that lunchtime on Friday 26 was Thomas Leslie, a foreman who had worked there for more than twenty-five years. Mr Leslie was a married man with eight children.

'Mind, it is loaded,' Professor Miller warned as he handed the man the rusty pistol.

Leslie fingered the safety catch, lifted the hammer of the revolver, turned the gun towards himself to count the bullets in the chamber, and the gun went off, shooting him through the right eye and blowing his brains out. He was buried in the same cemetery, on the same day, and almost at the same time as Hugh Miller.

But it wasn't just Leslie who died with Hugh Miller. Scotland, the pulse of the Enlightenment barely beating now, sank into a deathly sopor. Edinburgh became just another provincial town, the Capital of nowhere. The gradual extinguishing of reason and of scepticism took place under the stifling influence of the Kirks and the thrusting new respectability-loving middle class. Some wag has even claimed that in the next fifty years the only distinguished writing from Scotland was made up of children's stories, by Stevenson and Barrie. Professor Wilson would have approved. Forbes' and Goodsir's reputations sank thanks to the unfinished nature of their writings and the tides of Darwinism.

Vestiges outsold *On the Origin of Species* up until the early 20th century. Robert Chambers took the secret of his authorship to his grave. To a friend who suggested he write his autobiography, he replied: 'I couldn't. It would be too sad a story.' When he was questioned on his deathbed whether he was indeed the author, he replied, 'Some have said so.'

At first, thanks in part to the shrewd business eye of Lydia, Hugh's literary career and reputation flourished and dozens of editions of his writings were sold around the world in the following decades. *The Testimony of The Rocks* was published in 1857 and was the first book ever to appear with a photograph of its author.

Harriet continued to be haunted by her father's death. However, can we ever identify the moment one can halt a suicide? Would Hugh Miller have been saved if he had stayed in Cromarty or if Chalmers had lived longer? Would Scotland have flourished if it could have stemmed the clearances and the banishment of its own people? It is too late to know. It is always too late.

David Octavius Hill was present in Tanfield Hall at the Disruption and was commissioned to paint a portrait of the Assembly. It took him twenty-three years to complete and was only finished in 1866. He and his partner, Adamson, took calotype images of the more than 450 participants and then positioned them in their seats, with Hugh Miller taking notes, witnessing, at the forefront. It is the first painting to be drawn from photographs, a subjugation of the artistic to the mechanical which is perhaps typically Scottish.

They say Harriet cried when she saw the image of her father, not because the portrait of him at the peak of his powers and the pinnacle of his fame reminded her of her loss. No, it was the bouquet of flowers placed by Hill at Hugh's feet, already shedding its petals.

About the Author

Brian McLaughlin
Brian was born in Scotland and currently resides in Edinburgh, though he has lived and travelled all over the world, especially in the United States, India, France and Catalunya. He has an honours degree in English Language and Literature from Edinburgh University, a Ph.D. from Pennsylvania State University, a master's in Communication from the University of Barcelona. He was an English-Speaking Union scholar and was awarded the Gold Medal for European History while at Edinburgh. He is married to Rhona McLeod.

Acknowledgements

I would like to thank Emily Ramsay, and Ruth Paterson, Tony Connor and Sunny for letting me use their houses to write in. Also thanks to Doug, Charlie, Jim and Susan for their readings and helpful criticism and to Stuart for technical help. I am of course completely responsible for any errors that remain. And thanks above all to Rhona for her faith in me.

A full bibliography and notes on the historical characters referred to in this work can be found on the website *fabricatedfictions.com* as well as information on the images used. These are all from the Creative Commons (http://www.creativecommons.org/) or Wikimedia Commons (https://commons.wikimedia.org/) to whom I offer my gratitude.

Printed in Great Britain
by Amazon